HOLLY BLOOM

SLASHER Heart

LAPLAND UNDERGROUND
BOOK TWO

HOLLY BLOOM

Copyright © 2021 by Holly Fox writing as Holly Bloom.

All rights reserved. No part of this book may be reproduced in any form or by any electronic or mechanical means, including information storage and retrieval systems, without written permission from the author, except for the use of brief quotations in a book review.

This is a work of fiction. Names, characters, business, events and incidents are the products of the author's imagination. Any resemblance to actual persons, living or dead, or actual events is purely coincidental.

*Whenever you're doubting your abilities, stop and think.
How many book boyfriends are you hoarding in that beautiful head of yours?
Damn, if you can store THAT many sexy peens away, then you can do anything you set your mind to.*

PROLOGUE
ZANDER

"Why did you do that, Zander?"

How dare she question me?

I made the rules.

They all knew it.

"Zander? Are you fucking listening?" Vixen crossed her arms over her chest like a petulant child. "Have you lost your damn mind?"

"You were quick to defend her." I turned away to signal our conversation was over. "Aren't you pleased? This is what you wanted."

"I didn't want you to fire her ass," she hissed. "But I didn't mean for you to make her one of us, either. This is a big fucking deal."

"It's done," I replied dismissively with a wave of my hand. "I trust you'll make her feel welcome."

Vixen had always been fiercely protective of the Sevens. She found it hard to trust people after her upbringing. We all did. She saw a new member as a threat, but it gave her no authority to question my decisions. The Sevens answered to me. The last word was mine, and mine alone.

"You're fucking insane," she blasted, slamming my office door shut.

Good. Now, I could finally be alone with my thoughts at last. Vixen didn't know it yet, but her intervention saved me a job. Candy would have become a Seven eventually, but Vixen's agreement had never been guaranteed. I couldn't have planned it any better myself…

The pink-haired stripper, who knew her way around a knife better than a butcher, intrigued me like no other woman had. Women were there for me to fuck. There was no space in my life for emotional ties, but Candy? She was different. When I looked into her eyes, defiant darkness stared straight back. The same blackness that consumed me enveloped her perfect curves. She didn't run from the shadows. She lived and breathed them.

'Everyone else may be too afraid of you to say what they really think, but you don't scare me, Zander… you never have.'

No one had ever dared to speak to me like that. Ever.

Her blatant defiance made me want to wrap my hands around her neck and choke her as much as I wanted to throw her against the wall and take her from behind. Her tongue was vicious, her words poison, and her fuckable red lips enough to make me hard instantly.

At first, I'd thought she was just another girl who'd walked in off the streets of Port Valentine wanting to make a fast buck. But she wasn't like the others. She was so much more than that. After seeing the mincemeat she'd made of my father's finest men, I knew she was special.

Candy may not know everything about me or the Sevens, but she'd accepted my offer for a reason. When the briefcase of money didn't entice her, that's when I knew for sure. She was one of us. As expected, she passed my test and didn't run. Although, there was still time for her to wish she had…

Candy may be a Seven now, but I craved more than her loyalty. Under my rules, no one else would ever fucking touch her again.

Candy would be mine.

ONE
CANDY

THREE MONTHS LATER...

"Did you even read the dress code?" I arched an eyebrow at Vixen's skin-tight leather pants and the harness wrapped around her torso. How could her boobs even breathe in that thing? Taking it off and letting the twins hang loose at the end of the day would be the biggest relief. "You know you look like a dominatrix, right?"

"That's what I was going for," she replied smugly, applying her third coat of black lipstick. How were they not permanently stained? She hadn't worn another shade since I joined the Sevens. My presence put her in a constant state of mourning. "All I'm missing is chains and a whip."

"It wasn't supposed to be a compliment."

When I first started working at the club, I'd never have dared say something like that. Now, our relationship had changed. Sure, I still wanted to rip her piercings out of her face... but we could *almost* spend an entire evening together without wanting to kill each other. Who knew disposing of a body would be such a great bonding experience?

"I still don't see why I can't stay behind." As well as being the world's biggest perfectionist, Vixen complained like it was an Olympic fucking sport. "Do we really all have to go tonight?"

"It's my coming-out party, so yeah." I tied my hair into a high ponytail to ensure my new tattoo was visible. I'd opted to get the number seven inked behind my ear. "We all have to be there."

"No one gave me a coming-out party," Vixen muttered, adjusting her top so the matching tattoo on her collarbone peeked over the black lace. Every member of the Sevens had one. It was our mark and a way of showing we were in this for life. When I was younger, I'd grilled Rocky about joining a gang. Times had changed, and I'd done exactly what I'd sworn to never do. "For joining the Sevens, or when I came out as gay."

"Would you have wanted one?" I arched an eyebrow. "A coming-out party?"

"Maybe," Vixen said, then paused, "but I guess hooking up with my math teacher pretty much sealed the deal."

"No shit…"

"She was hot." Hot or not, she will have been the last woman Vixen slept with who had a brain. For someone who saw through people's bullshit, she was completely blind when it came to airheads with zero personality. "It sucked when we got caught by the principal."

"How did that go down in your fancy private

school?" I asked. Picturing Vixen in a posh uniform was even more ridiculous than imagining the Queen of England twerking around a pole in tassels. "Did they kick you out?"

"I may be a Briarly by blood, but I didn't grow up with all the same luxuries as Zander." She laughed bitterly. Our conversations about the Briarlys never went too deep. Vixen and Zander were cousins, but they'd grown up differently. Every time I tried to probe them about their backgrounds, I got nowhere. "Where I went to school, no one gave a shit what went down… but I lost my extra credit."

Before I could press her, the devil himself walked in. How many suits did Zander own? He had one for every occasion. This sleek black number and bow tie had to be one of my favorites — not that I'd ever tell him that. If his ego could be turned into electricity, it would generate enough to power the entire Eastern Seaboard.

"The car's waiting," Zander declared. From his grim expression, you'd have thought we were about to embark on a funeral march. It wouldn't kill him to crack a fucking smile. After all, the outing had been his idea.

I clipped in large silver hoop earrings. "It can wait a little longer."

"You have two minutes, Candy," Zander ordered. "Or, you can make your own way there."

I held my hand to my mouth and gasped. "You mean West will actually let us borrow a car?"

Vixen snickered. We'd got to a point where it was *almost* acceptable to laugh about the Range Rover inferno — not to West's face, though. None of us had a death wish. One mention of the ruined car would send him into all out destruction mode. I'd lost count of how many bottles he'd smashed in an enraged frenzy. Fuck knows how the club pulled any profit when The Hulk loved playing whack-a-mole with the liquor.

"I mean it, Candy." Zander shot me a sharp warning glare, turning to stalk away then stopping abruptly to add, "Don't fucking push me tonight."

We were heading to an exclusive charity auction in town. The event was a bullshit charade, orchestrated by Bryce Briarly, to show the world he was a decent community-serving human. He wasn't fooling anyone. Zander's father was no better than the global oil companies that donated money to help with climate change. He was the problem. In fact, Bryce would probably use the proceeds to enlist more impressionable kids to his ranks.

"Have you always been such a mouthy bitch?" Vixen asked.

I smirked. "Always."

"It wasn't supposed to be a compliment," she mimicked, lacing up her knee-high boots. They definitely wouldn't fit the black-tie dress code, but no one would dare criticize a Briarly. Not if they knew what was good for them. In Port Valentine, the Briarly family was royalty. They'd ruled the town for as long as it'd been on the map. Zander may have seemed to shun his father's fortune, but it didn't change his blood.

"Are you ready?" Rocky burst into Vixen's room. I'd been spending a lot of time in the Sevens penthouse above the club, but I still wasn't used to the guys barging in unannounced every two seconds. "If we don't leave, Zander is going to—"

Rocky stopped talking as soon as he saw me.

"What?" I looked down to see whether my period

had come. Thankfully, Aunt Flo hadn't waved her magic wand yet. It wouldn't take a lot to ruin my skin-tight white bandage dress. I'd used almost an entire roll of tit tape to keep the twins in check because of the plunging neckline. "What're you staring at?"

He cleared his throat. "N-n-nothing."

It was weird to see Rocky all dressed up. Out of all the guys, he avoided attending formal functions. They weren't his scene. Unlike Zander, he hadn't opted for a bow tie. The top buttons of his shirt were open and his shirt untucked, giving the impression he'd already gone out and the night was over.

"Tell Zander to quit getting his panties in a twist," I said. "Or, are you afraid he'll shoot the messenger?"

"Knowing Zander," Rocky murmured, "it wouldn't surprise me."

Becoming a Seven hadn't automatically given me an all-access pass to the secrets in Zander's arsenal. He still didn't trust me enough to tell me everything about his underground empire. The only thing I'd been 'permitted' to take over was running Lapland's poker ring, whilst Zander tasked West with other covert operations. I understood trust had to be earned, but my patience would only last so long. I'd already spent too much of my life in a cell in Blackthorne Towers, and Zander couldn't keep me locked in the basement forever.

So far, we'd stayed quiet about me joining the Sevens. Now, our silence was about to break. After the auction, everyone would know I'd joined their twisted family. News travels fast in Port Valentine. Stepping out of the shadows as the newest member would paint a target on my back visible from outer space. Zander and the guys had enemies waiting to stab them in the throat around every corner. Bryce's army didn't frighten me, though. The only thing I worried about was Hiram's reaction. My evil ex-master wouldn't be happy to discover I'd publicly sworn allegiance to someone else.

So far, only Rocky and Q knew my history. A new tattoo didn't mean I was gonna spill my guts. If Zander wanted to keep me in the dark about everything going on, why couldn't I do the same? Everyone was entitled to secrets. The only problem was, Zander didn't know the dangerous game he'd become part of by letting me join them. When Hiram came for me, all of us would have to be fucking ready.

Vixen looked out the window and groaned. "Do we really have to go in the fucking limo?"

"Can you even hear yourself?" I rolled my eyes. "It's a fucking limo."

She wrinkled her nose. "Do you really want to sit down on a seat that would flash up like a crime scene under UV?"

"I guess you have a point." I pushed the image of the guys getting hot and heavy out of my mind. They may be juicy eye candy, but they were also assholes. Besides, I couldn't think of them like that. We were business associates. Everyone knows you don't shit where you eat. "Let's get this over with, okay?"

"I can't wait to see my uncle's face when we crash his motherfucking party." She spat out the word 'uncle' like it was a nasty STI — the type that'd make a dick sprout green blisters. Who could blame her? I'd be the same if Bryce Briarly was a relative of mine. Being a foundling had some advantages, at least.

The last time I saw Bryce was at the poker game in Briarly Manor, his millionaire gothic mansion, which held more secrets than Gretchen Weiners' hair. We attended the game for business, but the auction was going to be a social call. I didn't intend on being civil. Bryce lost that privilege when one of the Razors bled to death in the middle of Lapland's dance floor. It'd shown me the true monster he really was.

The crisp night breeze was a refreshing change to the sticky heat of the club. Under Lapland's neon sign, West rested his arms against the limo like a star in a cologne commercial. His sleeves were rolled to his elbows, and his suspenders hugged his pecks. He looked like he'd thrown off a jacket and was ready to launch into a fight. That, and the sight of his tattoos against the whiteness of his shirt, made my stomach flip. I'd only seen him a handful of times since joining the gang and never for more than a few minutes at a time. Whatever task Zander had given him meant he rarely visited the club. Seeing him again reminded me of how *big* he was. Did he have to get clothes custom-made to fit his biceps?

West held the door open. "Ladies first."

"Since when do you have fucking manners?" I grumbled as I got into the limo to join the others, thinking back to Vixen's comment and how the guys had dissolved women's panties in the backseat a thousand times before.

"I see you carefully considered your outfit, Vixen." Zander, already sprawled across the seats, sighed and shook his head. "My father will not be pleased."

"He can go fuck himself." She uncorked a bottle of champagne and managed to close her mouth over its end before the flow of bubbles erupted. After taking a swig, she wiped her mouth. "Besides, no one is going to be looking at me tonight. I'm not the main attraction, remember? No one is going to miss *those*."

"Hey," I snapped at her pointed look at my cleavage. Maybe it'd been a little too much of a risqué choice. "My face is up here."

She winked, passing me the bottle. "And so is your tattoo."

"Is everyone clear about what's happening tonight? We are going to the auction to show my father we are a force to be reckoned with." Zander's gaze lingered on me as he spoke. "I don't want any nasty surprises."

It's not like I purposefully went out of my way to cause trouble. I couldn't help it if I got caught in the middle of shit when it went down. Zander still hadn't gotten over how I'd saved Vixen and Rocky's life without his help. It was lucky for them I was around, otherwise, the two fuckers wouldn't have survived.

"It's a charity auction," I reminded him. "Not a shoot-out!"

"Oh, there's one more thing." Zander pulled a small velvet box out of his pocket and pushed it into my hands. "I got you a gift."

"A gift?" I frowned, half-expecting it to explode. "What is it?"

"Open it," he encouraged. "You'll see."

Inside the box, a large blood-red stone sat nestled on a silver band. The intricate design looked like two snakes coiling together to hold the ruby in place. I slid it onto my wedding finger and it fit perfectly. A ring like this would have cost more than feeding a family of four for a year.

"Well?" He studied my reaction. "What do you think?"

"It's okay." I shrugged and tried to keep my expression neutral. 'Okay' didn't cover it. It was the most beautiful damn ring I'd ever seen. "How did you know my size?"

"Lucky guess." Zander smirked, then turned to West. "How do you feel about your upcoming nuptials?"

West scowled. "I don't see why we have to do it this way."

I glared at him. Having a reputation as his soon-to-be gang wife wasn't exactly the statement I wanted to make, either. "Believe it or not, being your cock block is not my dream come true."

"We've been over this. It's part of the plan," Zander hissed. Of course, the elusive 'plan' he still hadn't divulged to anyone else yet. "Everyone already thinks you're a couple."

"How are you getting on with this plan of yours?" I pressed.

He'd better have a good reason for branding me as West's woman. The element of surprise could have its advantages later down the line. After all, no one expected a stick of dynamite to be planted inside a fleshlight. If anyone played with me, I'd blow their dick clean off.

"That's none of your business," Zander growled. "You'll know when you need to."

"Enough. No fighting on family night," Vixen said. Who knew she could be a decent mediator? "We're already facing enough people who want us dead. We don't need to turn on each other."

The auction was taking place in the town hall, an old building in the center of Port Valentine usually reserved for special occasions. As soon as our limo pulled in, the sight of Giles Briarly almost made me ask our driver to turn around. Giles, Zander and Vixen's English cousin, stood like he had something mounted up his ass. A reporter wearing a press badge from the local newspaper fussed around him with a camera while he lapped up the attention.

"Calm down, Vix." Rocky stepped into damage-control mode as Vixen ground her teeth like she was chewing on a mouthful of rocks. It was the first time Vixen had seen Giles since I showed her the video of him screwing her ex. "She wasn't even worth it."

"That's not the point," Vixen snarled. "It's the fucking principle."

"Let's wait until he's away from the camera, at least," Rocky reasoned. Vixen's verbal lashing would not be something worthy of a front-page news story. "You think you can do that?"

She nodded, but the look of determination glinting in her eyes meant we'd all have to watch her closely. If Giles wasn't careful, his philandering hands would be sold as one of the exhibits.

"Remember why we're here," Zander said. "We've come to make a statement. We're the Sevens, and this town? It's going to be ours."

"Let's fucking do this," Rocky agreed.

Zander got out first, followed by West. The big man paused, turning back and extending his open hand.

"Take it, then." Vixen shoved me forward. "He won't bite!"

Reluctantly, I took it. It was the first time we'd

touched since West almost crashed his car on our way back from the junkyard. He'd pulled over to kiss me with a possessive hunger that I'd avoided thinking about since. It was a kiss that never should have happened. A kiss he wanted to erase from existence.

Even in five-inch strappy diamanté heels, West towered above me. As we stepped forward into the crowd waiting outside, widened eyes and frozen smiles gave us the reaction we'd hoped for. They hadn't been expecting us. Zander sauntered over to Giles, whose charm quickly turned bitter at being upstaged by our arrival.

"We were not expecting you tonight, cousin." Giles's lips curled into a snarl. "Or your posse of waifs and strays."

"I assume our invitation got lost," Zander replied coldly. "Nothing happens around here without us knowing about it."

"I almost forgot you were still around, Vixie." Giles turned to her with a sly grin. He knew how to push her buttons and enjoyed every second of it. "I'm sure we'll have the chance to catch up this evening."

"In your fucking dreams," Vixen hissed. Someone needed to get her to the bar before she scooped out his eyeballs and used them to garnish a Dirty Martini. "Stay the fuck away from me tonight, unless you want your balls to be auctioned off with the rest of the junk Bryce is selling."

"Let's go inside," Rocky said, tactfully steering her away. "Now."

West didn't utter a word as we climbed the stairs. I may as well have been holding hands with a walking robot. What the fuck was his problem? Inside the hall, several circular tables were set up in front of the stage where the auction would take place. Amongst the attendees, I recognized a few faces from the Maven and the poker game at Briarly Manor. No one spoke. Instead, hushed whispers followed us as we strode through the crowd. Nothing attracted attention more than uninvited guests.

Bryce Briarly caught sight of us from across the room and made a beeline like a vulture descending on a carcass. I smoothed down my hair to flash the newest addition to my tattoo collection and flaunt the massive rock weighing down my finger. Bryce didn't miss it.

"What a pleasant surprise," Bryce addressed Zander sarcastically, then his frosty glare rested on Vixen. Even a chainsaw couldn't carve the tension in the air. At Briarly Manor, Zander told me not to mention Vixen's name around his father. If she got this kind of reception, it was easy to see why. Bryce looked at her with utter hatred. "And you brought *her*."

"Happy to see me?" Vixen countered. If Bryce's hit succeeded, she would be rotting in the ground. "It's always good to see you too, Uncle."

"Why don't we get a drink?" Rocky took her arm gently. His thoughtfulness continued to take me off guard. I still didn't know how he and Vixen met in juvie, but he took care of her like a younger sister. "It's a free bar."

I may never be able to forgive Rocky for what he'd done in the past, but I understood his motives after hearing the full story. Hiram left him with no choice. As a Seven, I had to abandon my plan to kill him. Besides, he owed me. What good would a corpse be when Hiram came to collect? Rocky's promise to do anything to make amends were only words, but a day would come when I'd need to cash in my favor.

"West, Candy." Bryce acknowledged our interlocked fingers with a curt nod. "I see congratulations are in order."

I held up my hand to show off the jewel, which glinted under the light. "They are."

"Have you set a date?" Bryce asked.

"Not yet, we have so much to plan," I said. Yeah, like how we could take down the entire Briarly fucking empire."But we're working on it."

"I'm sure you are." A hint of a challenge lurked beneath Bryce's words. "We're glad to have you here this evening."

"Giving to charity isn't your usual type of endeavor, father," Zander said.

"What can I say? So many children in this town lack direction," Bryce said. To a bystander, it almost sounded like he gave a shit. "I'm in a fortunate position to give back to our special community."

"How generous of you," I hissed through gritted teeth. West squeezed my hand in warning. If more damaged kids fell into his clutches, the only thing Bryce would give back to the community were unmarked graves. He wanted to enlist every lost man in town into his criminal operations. "We all know how much you care about giving young people direction."

On Bryce's orders, his newest recruit accidentally blew his own brains out when he'd shown up at the club to kill Vixen. We'd gotten rid of the evidence, but Bryce was no fucking amateur. He knew we had something to do with the boy's sudden disappearance. Bryce's plan to avenge the loss of his men backfired, all too literally.

"I didn't plan the event alone," Bryce said, gesturing to his right. "In fact, I think you will all be pleased to see a friendly face back in town."

A man with his back turned and spun around to face us.

Motherfucker.

How hadn't we heard about this?

Zander's face turned to stone as he addressed the man. "Welcome back, Cheeks."

"Didn't you know he was released?" Bryce clapped Cheeks on the shoulder as he joined us. We hadn't been the only people keeping secrets over the last few months. "Cheeks is working for me full-time."

Even Bryce Briarly's influence couldn't get Cheeks out of jail. Only one person was powerful enough to overturn Cheeks's damning conviction. The same person who was responsible for putting him behind bars... *Hiram.*

"Missing evidence," Cheeks announced proudly. He grinned to reveal a newly gap-toothed smile. When we last spoke, Hiram threatened that favors could be undone. This was his doing. "They threw the case out at court."

Prison hadn't treated him kindly. Convicts were not likely to welcome a former cop with open arms — even someone as crooked as Cheeks, who was more of a criminal than most of them. He'd lost weight and a broken nose had ruined his facial symmetry. Being a shadow of his former self only made him more dangerous. Losing his career cost him everything. He was a man with nothing left to lose.

"I've been enjoying my freedom," Cheeks continued, nodding his head towards a trio of women who giggled like starving hyenas on command. They'd better be getting five times their usual rate to put up with his limp dick. "You'd know all about that, West."

"I'm taken," West said.

"For now." Cheeks smirked. "Didn't you hear that Penelope Cole is back in town? Does *she* know about your engagement?"

West didn't blink, but his jaw tensed. He wanted to keep his cool, but this came as a shock. Who the fuck was Penelope, and why did the mention of her name spook him?

"I told you," West growled, "I'm fucking taken."

"And we couldn't be happier," I added.

"We have some final preparations to take care of." Bryce shut the conversation down, as Cheeks cackled by his side. If they auctioned the opportunity to knock out his remaining teeth, I'd be the top bidder. "Enjoy your evening."

One glance at Zander's face signaled the night had gotten off to a rough start. We had aimed to surprise them, but Bryce was always one step ahead and ready to sucker punch at the final second.

Zander spun to face West in accusation. "Did you know she was back?"

West shook his head.

"Who is she?" I asked.

They both ignored me. As usual, my questions fell into the fucking abyss.

West clenched his fists. "I need a fucking drink."

He stormed over to the bar, where Vixen and Rocky already had a row of shots lined up, and downed them all in quick succession.

Zander grabbed my arm to stop me from following. "Keep an eye on West tonight."

"He's a big boy. I'm sure he can take care of himself," I said, pulling myself free and pretending to check a non-existent watch on my wrist. "Oh, look at that. It's time we hit the free bar before West empties it."

Zander scowled but trailed after me to join the others.

"I don't see why you wanted to come here, Zander," Vixen grumbled, sliding glasses to each of us like we were part of a production line. "Rubbing shoulders with your daddy's rich friends is not how we should be spending our Friday night."

"Oh, it gets better. Just wait until you see our favorite ex-convict." I pulled up a stool and took a drink. The gold flakes from Goldschläger cutting my insides were the least of my concerns. "Cheeks got out."

"When?" Rocky's expression darkened. "Where is he?"

"Don't even think about it," Zander warned. His calculating gray eyes scanned the crowd carefully. Did he have another reason for bringing us here, aside from presenting me as West's trophy wife? "We're not going anywhere. Not until after the auction."

"What're they going to be auctioning, anyway?" Vixen flicked through the catalog and yawned. The pages were filled with boring antiques you'd be able to pick up at a garage sale for fifty cents apiece. "These people have already got rooms filled with shit they don't use."

"I think they will appreciate the Sevens donation," Zander said.

"Our donation? Since when?" Vixen crossed her arms. "We're giving something away? You've got to be fucking kidding me."

"It'd be rude to show up empty-handed." Whatever Zander had planned suddenly made the evening a lot more interesting. "Wouldn't it?"

TWO

West's brooding presence loomed over me like a dark cloud. He'd been a pain in the ass from the moment we arrived. We were meant to be working together but all he wanted to do was sit at the bar pouting while the other Sevens circled the room to gather intelligence. Everyone knew Bryce's guests would lower their guard and inhibitions after they'd downed enough champagne to sink the Titanic.

"We're supposed to be a happy couple, remember?" I reminded him. The last time I checked, I'd done nothing wrong — unless you count burning his beloved car, but that happened months ago. He couldn't hold it over me forever. Besides, the Sevens had enough money to buy ten more of them in an instant. "Are you planning to ignore me all night?"

"If you'll let me."

West took hot and cold to another level. With Zander and Rocky, I could at least try to guess what they were thinking. Zander cared about revenge and satisfying his desires. He made his demands clear, even if I ignored them. On the other hand, Rocky laid out his emotions for the world to see and used humor to conceal his pain. But West? He was fucking impossible to read. One minute, he almost crashed a car to kiss me. The next, he'd barely spoken for weeks on end.

"What the fuck is wrong with you?" I lowered my voice, thinking back to Cheeks's earlier revelation and being unable to stop the words that came next. "Are you too busy thinking about *Penelope*?"

It was no secret the Sevens had an appetite for women. I mean, they owned a strip club, which was akin to living in a fucking sweet shop for any straight guy with a penis. West's little black book was probably thicker than the entire Harry Potter series.

"Don't go there." West's furious stare burned into mine. "You have no fucking idea what you're talking about."

"Why don't you enlighten me?" I challenged. He didn't intimidate me, and I wasn't about to back down. "You know, open your mouth and verbalize something?"

"You think you have us all worked out," West hissed. "You may have joined the Sevens, but that doesn't make you one of us. You know nothing."

"And whose fault is that?" Being kept in the dark was getting boring. The whole point of joining a gang was to get a slice of whatever pie they were sharing. I didn't sign up to be left outside like a tethered dog and watch as they tucked into a sweet blueberry slice. I'd become a Seven because I wanted to be all in, not be a fucking extra. "If you talked to me, then maybe I'd be able to help?"

I may not have as much personally invested in bringing down the Briarly empire, but Bryce fit my 'type' perfectly. Whenever I killed, I assessed men based on my special criteria. He fit into the rich exploitative asshole category snugger than Cinderella's slipper. Murdering innocent people wasn't my jam, but when someone deserves it? Well, who was I to deprive them of a taste of their fucking poison?

"Help?" West snorted in disbelief. "I don't think so."

"If you didn't want me to stick around, then why didn't you say so?" All he had to do was say no, and then I'd have disappeared from their lives forever. Each of the Sevens had to agree unanimously for a person to join. "I'm only here because you didn't object."

His hands curled into fists the size of small soccer balls. "I should have."

We glared at each other. Neither of us wanted to be the first to break the silence. Vixen strode over to cut the tension, "Are you having your first fight?"

"West is getting cold feet," I said. "Isn't that right, *honey*?"

"I'm fucking done here." He jumped up, causing his stool to skid across the floor and tip over from the force. Onlookers cast a nervous look in his direction. "I'll see you at home."

"I don't know what's got into that asshole lately." Vixen let out a low whistle and shook her head, as we watched the crowd part for him to pass. No one wanted to stand in his way. "Believe it or not, he's normally the sweet one."

Yeah, as sweet as a Toxic Waste candy…

West's departure didn't go unnoticed. As if on cue, Giles sidled over to us like a piece of roadkill resurrected from the dead. Thankfully, Vixen had the sense to excuse herself before we made any more of a scene.

"How nice to see you again, Candy." Giles dropped a kiss on both my cheeks. On British TV, it seemed charming. In reality, having someone's germ-filled mouth on your skin made you want to head straight for a chemical peel. "I see your fiancé doesn't know how to behave in public. If I were you, I'd be reconsidering my nuptials. Don't tell me that big ogre really knows how to satisfy you?"

"You're the last person who should give advice about pleasuring a woman," I said, reapplying my lip gloss. The last time we were at Briarly Manor, I ruined his plan to sabotage the game and exposed his secret relationship with Vixen's ex-girlfriend. If I hadn't seen him and Charlene screwing, who knows how many diseases Vixen would have caught from sharing a girl with a piece of shit like Giles?

"I was impressed to find out you're an avid photographer," Giles said with a snide look on his face. Charlene must have squealed about the video. It wouldn't have taken long for him to put the pieces together. Judging from his new date this evening, their romance had been short-lived when her time as a Lapland spy ended. "And a talented blackmailer too."

"I'm sorry." My eyes widened innocently. "I don't know what you're talking about. But I do enjoy wildlife photography in my spare time."

"Can I give you some friendly advice?" Giles leaned in closer. Another inch and he'd be waddling around with gigantic balls for the next week. "If I were you, I'd watch your back."

What was a posh overgrown schoolboy going to do? I don't know what subjects they taught at private schools in England, but I'm sure the curriculum didn't cover the same material as my lessons with Hiram in Blackthorne Towers. While he'd been slaving away over textbooks learning Einstein's theory of relativity, I'd got an education on how to circumcise a cock with a vegetable peeler. Which was the more valuable life skill?

I looked over Giles's shoulder to see Rocky sneak up behind him. "What's going on?"

"Nothing." Giles attempted a smile. He looked like a starving alligator baring its teeth. "We're just having a friendly catch-up."

Rocky saw right through Giles's bullshit. "Nothing is ever friendly with you."

"We never see you anymore, Red," Giles said, changing the subject. "Do you have permission to be outside? I heard my cousin keeps you locked away. Then again, you're used to being in a cage."

"If you don't step away from Candy in the next ten seconds." Rocky lowered his voice to a threatening rumble and closed the gap between them. "You'll find out why I got locked up in the first place."

"Have it your way." Giles laughed coldly, then turned to face me. "Remember what I said, Candy."

I rolled my eyes. How could anyone take a threat seriously when it was aimed at your tits? If he got distracted by my cleavage, it wouldn't take much to throw him off during a fight.

"Are you okay?" Rocky asked as soon as Giles was out of earshot. "What did he want?"

"I didn't need your intervention," I snapped. "I had the situation under control."

"It's not you I was worried about," Rocky muttered. "West should never have left you alone here. Not with all these assholes around."

"Surely, you're not worried about Cheeks?" I raised my eyebrow. "I kicked the bastard's ass once before, and I'll do it—"

"Would you stop running your mouth for a second?" Rocky's fingers closed around my arm to silence me. If it wasn't for his serious expression, I'd have made my voice even louder. "Act natural and follow me."

"Hey," I objected as he yanked me violently to the edge of the room with a surprising amount of strength. "I thought you wanted to act natural."

Rocky ignored me as we came to a stop and nudged his head toward the entrance. "When you were busy talking to Giles, someone else walked in…"

I followed his gaze to a skinny, wiry man in glasses. He looked like a banker and was deep in conversation with Cheeks. With his flashy suit and spectacled face, the stranger fit right in with Bryce's guests. But he wasn't here for the auction.

Holy motherfucking shit.

My mouth went dry. "How did you know?"

"Remember when I said I tried to find you after Hiram took you? I went to Blackthorne Towers," Rocky explained. "I recognized him from one of my trips. Who is he?"

"They call him the Blackbird."

The Blackbird worked for Hiram.

As much as he had a God complex, Hiram couldn't be in a thousand places at once. He liked to have eyes everywhere and had an army of minions to do his bidding. The Blackbird was one of Hiram's surveillance experts. We'd worked together many times before, and now? I was his mark.

"Should we leave?" Rocky asked as his eyes flickered to the nearest exit. "We can go right now."

"No," I insisted. "He's not a threat."

The Blackbird was in town to gather intelligence and report back to his master. In the old days, he used to do the same for me. He'd compile a file on my target and hand it over for me to finish the job. He may have his nose in every dark corner of people's business, but he'd never want to get caught up in any real action.

The Blackbird's eyes met mine from across the room.

Rocky's body vibrated in anger. "I'll fucking kill him."

"I'm not scared of him." I grinned at the Blackbird and wiggled my fingers to invite him to approach. "Let him come to us."

The Blackbird took the bait and headed in our direction. It was the first time anyone from my old life had dared show their face in Port Valentine, which meant Hiram was progressing.

"Good evening." There was no ounce of friendliness in the Blackbird's tone. "Can I steal a moment with this lady?"

"I'm not going anywhere." Rocky drew himself up to full height at my side. "Whatever you've got to say to her, you can say in front of me."

"As you wish." The Blackbird raised his eyebrows in mild bemusement. "I haven't seen you in the longest time, Kitten."

"What brings you out this way?" I countered. "A little far from home, don't you think?"

"I'm here on business." His beady eyes analyzed my expression to search for a sign of weakness. Too bad I already knew his tricks. He'd get nothing out of me. "I hear you've been settling into Port Valentine, *Candy*. You've built quite a reputation in a short space of time. I've been told you have a new tattoo and are getting married."

No doubt Cheeks had been running his mouth. It'd only take one mention of my name for him to spill his guts. After our night at the Maven, I'd abandoned him in the shipping yard licking his wounds. The next time I saw him, he'd been beaten to a pulp and the cops slapped handcuffs on his wrists. If Cheeks still couldn't remember what happened in the missing time, it was natural he'd hold me responsible — even if he'd never admit it to anyone else. Why would he want to confess to being roughed up by a stripper?

"It's none of your fucking business," Rocky growled.

"Is this the lucky man?" The Blackbird looked him up and down then frowned. "You look familiar."

"Actually, my fiancé just left," I replied hastily. "He had urgent business to take care of."

"Shame." He sniffed. "I'd have liked to make his acquaintance."

"Don't hold your breath for a wedding invitation," I snarled.

"Why don't you come home to share your news?" the Blackbird asked. "You've been away for too long. We're basically family after all these years."

"The people in Blackthorne Towers were never my fucking family. This is my home now," I said, narrowing my eyes but keeping my voice quiet enough to avoid unwanted attention. "What's wrong? Are you too scared to tell him the news yourself?"

Hiram would not be able to ignore news like this.

After years of having me as his prized possession, this would make him explode.

"He'll find out soon enough, Kitty," the Blackbird said. We both knew 'killing the messenger' took on a literal meaning when Hiram was involved. "He's planning a vacation."

"I hear Hawaii is nice this time of year," I snapped.

"Is that the time already?" The Blackbird checked his watch and tutted. "I have somewhere else to be this evening, but I'm sure we'll see each other again soon."

I didn't take my eyes off his cheap suit until I watched him leave the building. He'd got what he came here for. What would he do with the information? If Hiram found out I was engaged and a member of a gang, the Sevens would be in immediate danger. A revelation like this would force Hiram to act quicker.

"Do you want to get some air?" Rocky suggested. "We can have a look around the rest of the town hall."

"Sure, why the fuck not?" I sighed. "It's not like things can get any worse."

First, my new 'fiancé' had gone AWOL on the night we'd announced our engagement. Second, the Blackbird's appearance turned my new life into a ticking time bomb. I wasn't naïve enough to think I could run from my past forever, but I wasn't ready to share it with the Sevens yet. If West regretted his decision, how could I trust them with my darkest secrets?

We slipped out of the main function room and walked through the corridors steeped in local history. Rocky pulled a hip flask from his blazer pocket. "Drink?"

I took a large swig. The further we got from the auction, the colder it got. Thankfully, Rocky's whiskey provided a much-needed alcohol jacket. We opened a door to a long narrow room that looked to be a file storage area. Small windows along one side allowed slices of moonlight to creep in and highlight layers of undisturbed dust resting on the cabinets.

"Remember how we used to go exploring?" Rocky asked as he knocked cobwebs out of his face. His head almost skimmed the ceiling. "It's like old times."

"Hardly!" I snorted. As teenagers, we'd spent summers exploring abandoned buildings and warehouses around where we grew up. Part of the fun had been setting out on an expedition and not knowing what we were going to find. "We'd never have been able to get into a place like this without someone calling the cops."

"They'd have thought we'd clean the place out," Rocky said, then chuckled fondly at the memory. Evergreen kids had a bad reputation that followed us like a contagious disease. Whenever we entered a store, the cashier's eyes never left our hands until we were back outside. "Do you miss it? Evergreen?"

"I don't think about the past." Surviving meant looking forwards. You could learn from the past, but you couldn't live in it. Nothing could change it. "Not if I can help it."

Rocky changed the subject. "Why did West leave?"

"He's not used to someone asking him hard questions," I said. "Is he always used to getting his way?"

"West doesn't do emotions. He prefers to smash things." Rocky paused as his expression turned somber. "You and him... are you... you know?"

"Wait…" I stopped in my tracks. "What?"

"I don't know, I thought you might—"

"It's called acting," I hissed. The kiss we shared

didn't count. It was a mistake. I flicked my hair over my shoulder to avoid meeting his probing gaze. "It's strictly business."

"I'm glad you're here." A small smile crept over Rocky's lips. "I wanted you to stay."

"Aren't you the one who told me not to?" I raised an eyebrow. "You said it's too dangerous for me to be here, remember?"

"That didn't mean I didn't want you around," he said. "Besides, you seem to be able to take care of yourself these days."

"Maybe you should leave me to fight my own battles then? I could have handled Giles and the Blackbird myself."

"You've fought battles alone for too long." Rocky turned solemn. "I meant it when I said I'd do anything to make things right with you."

I refused to have this conversation. What good would listening to his groveling do? I turned my back on him to avoid seeing his puppy dog eyes and continued on. "I don't need your fucking pity."

"There is something I still don't understand," he called. I'd reached the end of the corridor. *Fuck.* A brick wall blocked my path, forcing me to turn around and face him. "Why didn't you kill me when you had the chance?"

"Most people would say thank you and move on."

"I want to know why." Rocky stepped closer. "All I need to hear you say is that you didn't want me to die."

I could handle a confrontation with Rocky, but facing my feelings? That was terrifying, especially when I couldn't make sense of my actions. Killing him was something I'd desperately wanted to do, but something stopped me. Why couldn't I do it?

"Why can't you just let it go?"

"I can't." He reached out to stroke my cheek. A few months ago, I'd have broken his fingers. Hell, I once wouldn't have hesitated to disembowel him on sight. But his touch scrambled my thoughts and made me light-headed. "Because I can't let you go, C. I never have. I never will."

"Rocky…" My voice faded into the distance as I looked into his eyes.

"I need to hear you say it," he repeated. "You wanted me to live, didn't you?"

"What difference does it make?"

"I want you to admit it." The heat radiating from his body sent tingles racing over my skin. "You didn't want to let me go either."

"Rocky, I can't—"

Before I could finish my sentence, his lips silenced me.

The last kiss we shared had been years before, but so much had changed. We were no longer the two kids who dreamed of a better future. Rocky had grown into a man, and I'd become someone the old me wouldn't recognize in a mirror. Both of us bore fresh scars, held dark secrets, and had done unspeakable acts, but... if we'd both changed so much since our first kiss, then why did it suddenly feel like everything was the same?

I *should* want to push him away.

I *should* want to rip out his tongue and make him choke on it.

I *should* want to leave this town and never look back.

But, like the night I held my knife to his throat, I was rendered powerless.

My body responded to his kiss like a flower, turning to the sun, desperate to catch the last rays before darkness closed in. Rocky cupped my face like he held the entire universe in his hands. His mouth explored mine like it was the last thing he'd ever taste, and his body anchored me to the present like we were the last people left on Earth.

"I've missed you, C," he murmured, tracing the length of my collarbone gently with the tip of his finger. "So fucking much."

In the movies, this would be where I'd collapse into his arms and we'd swear our undying love to each other. Everyone knows real life doesn't work that way. True love doesn't exist. Our relationship was complicated, our history messy and our colliding again? Another fucking disaster waiting to happen.

How could he have gone from the top of my hit list to someone I made out with?

Reality burst the surrounding air with a bang, and realization rained down on me faster than a flash flood. It didn't matter that being in his arms felt like returning home. I needed to remember that 'home' didn't exist. It was nothing but a pile of ash because he'd set any chance we had of a future in flames. He'd ruined it. He'd ruined everything.

I pushed Rocky back, knocking him off balance.

"What's wrong?" His eyes widened. "I thought—"

"You thought wrong."

"I may not want you dead." I stripped all the emotion from my tone. "But it doesn't mean I want you."

"You're lying, C!" He grabbed my arm to stop me. "How can you say that after—"

"Don't." I shut him down. "We're only here because we have a job to do. The auction is about to start."

Rocky had broken my heart once before. He'd never get the chance to do it again. No one would. After what happened, a gaping hole was left in my chest from where he'd blown it to smithereens.

Zander's glare of disapproval burned into us as we walked back into the main hall. "You're late."

"It's not even started yet," I said, hoping he didn't notice my breathlessness from moving as quickly as my heels could carry me. Zander's stare had a disconcerting way of seeing past any bullshit. "We're here now, aren't we?"

"Where have you two been, anyway?" Vixen asked, as Rocky and I took our seats in stony silence. I'd vowed not to look at him again all night. What happened between us could never happen again. "You missed me almost knock out Giles."

"Quiet!" Zander silenced her as the auctioneer took to the stage.

I struggled to pay attention through the bidding war. The usual items you'd expect to see were sold for ridiculous prices: vases, jewelry, spa days, personalized photoshoots, and indulgent picnic baskets. Who even went for a picnic in winter? The prizes were meaningless, anyway. They were nothing but an elaborate ruse to keep wives or mistresses happy. While they appeared to be bidding on luxurious goods, it was a facade to hide the real trading happening under the tables. They were leveraging drugs or the services of the Briarly goons under the guise of charity. It made me sick.

"Finally, we have a last-minute addition from an anonymous donor," the auctioneer's voice boomed, causing Bryce to straighten in his seat as an item concealed by a red curtain was wheeled onstage. Zander leaned forward. This was the moment he'd been waiting for. The auctioneer pulled back the curtain to reveal a large framed painting. "And here we are!"

That was it? I'd wanted something a little more dramatic: an active bomb, or a severed head on a podium, perhaps? However, judging from Bryce's reddening cheeks, his perfectly controlled exterior was crumbling. He hated surprises, and the last-minute auction prize had ruined his evening.

"No fucking way." Vixen's mouth fell open. "How? I thought he got rid of them all..."

"Not all of them," Zander replied smugly and raised a glass in his father's direction.

I looked at the portrait again. I'd seen it once before. It was the same picture West and I collected from the junkyard. The women's beauty was even more apparent blown up on a large canvas. Whoever she was, Bryce Briarly wanted her to be forgotten.

"Who is she?" I asked.

"My mother," Zander said. Most families had their fair share of problems, but the Briarlys took it to an extreme. No amount of therapy could heal the issues they had; analyzing their family dynamics would be enough to send a shrink crazy. "It's a story for another time."

The auctioneer signaled for bids to begin. Watching

Zander and his father felt like being in the middle of a ping-pong game. The rest of the room observed with bated breath, both mesmerized and horrified.

"It's too much," Vixen hissed. The war between them reached a boiling point. The bidding had racked up to an eye-watering one hundred thousand dollars. It blew my mind how people could play with huge amounts of money like pocket change. "You need to stop."

"I will." Zander raised the paddle once more. "Soon."

"Do we have two hundred thousand dollars?" the auctioneer called.

Zander didn't move.

The slam of the hammer confirmed Bryce's win. "Sold!"

"You were bidding him up, right?" I whispered.

"Perhaps." Zander shrugged, then winked. "He doesn't need to know I made copies."

"Now, that's over with, can we finally get out of here and get home?" Vixen asked. "I'm done with these people."

Rocky slammed his glass down. "A-fucking-men."

"Change of plan," Zander cut in to dash their hopes, "we're staying in a hotel."

"A hotel?" Vixen groaned. "You've gotta be fucking kidding."

"Quit it!" I nudged her in the ribs. Wherever we stayed would beat returning to my dump of an apartment. "What the boss says goes."

"If I'd known it'd only take a hotel room to get you to comply," Zander murmured under his breath, so only I could hear, "then I'd have booked one sooner."

"Before you leave, cousin." Giles arrived at our table like a foul smell. "I want to thank you for your generous donation on behalf of the whole Briarly family."

"You may be the new Briarly heir, Giles." Zander rose from his seat, spitting out the words like bullets. "But it doesn't mean you'll ever be part of this family."

The landscape had been set for an upcoming battle.

THREE

Holy hell, the bedsheets were Egyptian cotton. They were even softer than the white, fluffy robe wrapped up around me like a fucking cloud. I fully intended to take it when we checked out.

"Do you want more ice cream brought up?" I asked, flicking through the television channels.

With Zander and Rocky staying on another floor, I wouldn't miss the opportunity to take advantage of room service when Zander's would cover the bill. Sharing a room with Vixen was bearable when you had an unlimited stream of desserts, complimentary slippers, and mini soap bars in cute shapes.

"I still don't get why we have to stay in a hotel." Vixen tucked into a piece of decadent chocolate cake, topped with a gold leaf. "We could have taken a car back. Fuck knows, we have enough of them."

"Come on, I bet this beats your cell in juvie…"

"Don't pretend like you know my history," she snapped. "You have no idea."

I rolled over to face her. "Why don't you enlighten me?"

"It was no fucking sleepover." Vixen's face darkened. "You had to stick together if you wanted to make it through your years at Redlake. Not everyone was so lucky."

"Redlake?" I nearly fell out of the bed. "You mean *the* Redlake?"

The place was infamous. A few years back, Redlake Juvenile Corrections Center made national headlines when an undercover operation revealed horrifying details of what prisoners endured under the wardens' care. The entire place got shut down. Ex-detainees were paid to cover up the worst of what happened and were forced to sign NDAs. Maybe that's why I'd never heard either of them mention their time there before. Paying for silence hadn't stopped the rumors from spreading, though…

"I told you, not every member of the Briarly family grew up in the fucking manor," she said bitterly, then changed the subject. "Now, it's your turn. Are you going to tell me why lover boy did a runner at the auction?"

I admired the ring on my hand, which still felt alien, and shrugged. "I guess we had our first lover's tiff."

"He's been acting so weird recently." Vixen shook her head. "He needs to snap out of it before he screws shit up."

"I mean, it didn't help that Cheeks told him Penelope was back in town…"

She stabbed her sponge violently. "I bet the bastard loved delivering that news."

"So?" I probed. "What's the deal? Who is she?"

"It's not my story to tell," Vixen said, then pursed

her lips while wrestling with her urge to tell me more. She decided against it. "All you need to know is that she hurt him. She's no fucking good for him. If I get my hands on her again, I'll wring her scrawny neck."

"Are you always so protective?"

"Only when he could do better," she said pointedly. Although, I doubted anyone would match up to her high standards.

"How long have you known West?" I asked.

She and Zander were related, Rocky had joined the Sevens after their stint in juvie, but where did West fit into the picture?

"As long as I've known Zander," she replied. "He and Zander went to boarding school together. He used to stay in the manor during summer break."

"West?" I spluttered. "He went to boarding school?"

Unlike Zander, he didn't seem the type to have been born onto a golden throne. What else didn't I know about the gang I'd sworn my loyalty to forever? Each new scrap of information only raised a thousand more questions.

BAM!

Our hotel room door swung open. I jumped to my feet like an abominable snowman and flicked open my knife. It's a good thing I carried it at all times. I clasped its hilt and held it out, ready to slash whoever stepped inside.

Zander clicked the door shut behind him. "Easy, little one…"

"You could have fucking knocked." I reluctantly tucked the blade back into my pocket. "What do you want?"

Zander's lip curled in disapproval as he surveyed the

empty plates and glasses. Liking to snack wasn't a fucking crime. Zander was a possessive asshole who thought him making the rules made me his property. If he knew everything that happened at the auction, our midnight sugar boost would be the least of his worries.

He looked at the two of us. "Did you really think tonight was just an excuse to have a sleepover?"

"How were we supposed to know you had other plans?" I challenged. "You don't exactly like sharing your plans with the rest of us, do you?"

"You knew I made the rules when you agreed to join us," Zander snarled. "Don't question me."

"The rules?" I laughed coldly. "What I *expected* is for you to tell us what's going on. From what I've seen so far, the only thing you want to do is taunt daddy dearest."

"If I wanted your opinion," he said, the darkness behind his eyes stirred, "I'd have asked for it."

"Can't you guys keep it down?" Vixen yawned, cranking up the volume on the cartoon she was watching. "This is my favorite."

Zander snatched the remote and cut short the episode.

"Killjoy," she muttered.

"When I agreed to join the Sevens, I didn't think I'd be playing the role of the trophy wife," I continued. "When I say I'm in, it means I'm all in. I expected *more*."

"You want to be all in?" Zander reached into his pocket. If he made a move to hurt me, I wouldn't hesitate to shred his expensive suit into ribbons. Instead of drawing a gun, he retrieved a key card and held it out. "Now is your chance to prove it."

I snatched it from him. "Go on."

Nothing intrigued me more than a challenge.

"We're not the only ones staying in this hotel tonight," he said. "This is the key to the penthouse suite where my father is paying for Cheeks to stay."

"You want me to kill him, right?"

Zander threw back his head and laughed in what looked to be genuine amusement. "Patience, little one."

"Is that a no?" I sighed. Killing Cheeks wouldn't be the worst way to end an evening. After my encounter with Rocky, I could do with expelling the extra energy.

"I appreciate your enthusiasm," Zander said. "But don't you think you've racked up enough bodies in your time here already?"

I bit my tongue. Based on my previous record, I'd basically lived as a nun since arriving in Port Valentine, but Zander didn't need to know that. Up until this point, both of us had honored our agreement. He wouldn't probe into my past, as long as I followed his rules.

"If you don't want me to kill him, what do you want me to do?"

"Cheeks had a little *too* much fun with some girls." Zander pulled a USB stick from another pocket like a magician would pull a rabbit out of a hat. What else was he hiding behind the pinstripes? "One of them ended up in the hospital with a broken jaw."

Vixen threw her fork, sending chocolate sauce flying over the room. "What a piece of shit."

I recalled how handsy Cheeks was when we went to the Maven. He'd messed with the wrong girl. If I hadn't known how to defend myself, the night could have had a different outcome. You'd think the bastard would have learned his lesson. I'd already given him a warning. It's time he got a little refresher he'd never forget.

"How did you get the footage?" I asked. As I said it, I already worked out the answer, "Cupid."

One of my old connections, Q — known to everyone else as Cupid — worked closely with the Sevens. As well as being the best money launderer in the biz, he ran a safe house for women trying to get out of prostitution and to make it safer for those who had no other choice. Q despised nothing more than a man who laid a finger on a woman. He'd be happy to bring a bastard like Cheeks down.

"I'm sure our old friend wouldn't want this video falling into the wrong hands," Zander said, dangling the stick in front of me like a carrot. "What do you think?"

"Fine." I took it. "What do you want from him in return?"

"I want eyes and ears on my father," Zander said. Anything less than killing him seemed like a waste of my fucking time, but I had to follow his orders. "I trust you can be very persuasive?"

Knowing Cheeks, it wouldn't take much persuasion to get him to do what I wanted. The gutless bastard would be scared of returning to jail and ruining what was left of his pretty face. Unlike cats, roaches don't have nine fucking lives.

I pouted. "Are you sure you don't want me to bring you his head?"

A small ghost of a smile haunted Zander's lips. He understood the darkness. Like me, he lived and breathed it.

"When we've got what we want from him, I'll let you do the honors," he promised. "But we're doing this my way first."

I wouldn't trust Cheeks to butter a slice of toast —

let alone pass along sensitive information on Bryce. However, Zander must have logic behind his motives. If we wanted to take down the Briarly empire, we needed access to Bryce's inner circle. Cheeks had been at its center for years. He'd also made his dislike of the Sevens clear, so Bryce would never suspect him of working with us.

"Fine," I said. "We'll try it your way."

"You wanted to prove yourself," he said as he turned to leave, "so fucking prove it."

Challenge accepted.

"How do you do that?" Vixen stared at me open-mouthed as Zander slammed the door behind him. "He never compromises."

"I'd hardly call that a compromise," I said. "Maybe he likes the thought of Cheeks's head as a Christmas gift? It'd look good on top of the tree. "

She snorted. "You're seriously fucked up."

"So I've been told." My mind was already racing with the possibilities of how we were going to pull this off. "Now, go back to watching cartoons. I've got work to do."

"*We* have work to do," she corrected.

"I work better alone."

"You're part of the Sevens now. We're in this together, remember?" A slow smile spread over Vixen's face. "Besides, I wouldn't mind teaching the bastard a lesson."

"Have it your way," I said. "Just try not to throw up around blood this time."

"Finally!" Vixen sighed. For the past two hours, we'd questioned whether Cheeks would return to the hotel at all. "Where the fuck has he been?"

From our window, we watched Cheeks stagger drunkenly down the street with a woman on his arm. It's no coincidence Zander had chosen this room. It gave us the best vantage point of the entrance. Had the painting stunt been a warm-up to throw Bryce off the real reason we'd decided to gate crash?

"He's wasted," I said. He couldn't walk in a straight line. "He won't be getting it up tonight."

"Nothing kills a boner more than a gun pointed in your face."

"But we don't have a—"

"Actually," Vixen interrupted, pulling up her pant leg to reveal a Glock, "we do."

After being held at gunpoint, she'd spent a lot of hours at the shooting range over the last few months. Society teaches little girls to play with dolls and finger paint, whilst boys play with tanks and soldiers. In reality, every woman should know how to defend themselves. What's going to help save your life: learning how to get out of a chokehold or how to make a chicken pot pie?

"I've been practicing," she said proudly.

"I'm impressed." I grinned, then nodded twice. That was our signal. "Let's fucking do this."

We had a limited time frame to work with. It wouldn't be long before the maids started their morning rounds, so we had no margin for error. We had one chance and no room for mistakes. I also couldn't shake the feeling this was another of Zander's games. After cleaning up five bodies I'd left behind, he knew exactly what I was capable of. He wanted to test my self-control… and my loyalty.

After giving Cheeks enough time to stumble to the penthouse, we slipped out of our room and up the three flights of stairs to his floor. Thankfully, his taste for finer things had its advantages. We had no adjoining rooms to worry about.

"Shh." I pressed my finger to my lips, as Vixen didn't cushion the slamming of the stairwell door.

"Chill out." She rolled her eyes. "We've got this."

I pulled out the key card and held up three fingers to begin the countdown. We could use the element of surprise to our advantage.

3… Vixen raised her gun…

2… I swiped the card in the slot…

1… it flashed green.

Bingo. We were in.

I turned the handle.

"Who is it?" Cheeks slurred from the bed. "Another whore come to join us?"

We charged inside. The sight of Cheeks in his underpants groping a girl in skimpy underwear turned my stomach. Angry marks around her throat made me want to defy Zander's orders, but I took a deep breath. As much as it pained me to leave the fucker breathing, we had to stick to the plan.

"Get out of here," Vixen hissed at the girl, spotting Cheeks's wallet and throwing it at her. *Nice touch.* "Keep the change."

She ran without turning back, leaving the three of us alone. Hiram taught me a target's first move would always reveal their hiding place when taken by surprise. Cheeks lurched towards the bedside table. He knew better than to travel unarmed. Unlike him, I didn't need a weapon to feel comfortable. My most dangerous weapon was my bare fucking hands. As soon as his body twitched, I knew what he was gonna do and acted quicker than The Flash.

"Fuck!" Cheeks cried as I slammed the drawer shut on his fingers. As soon as his body twitched. *Nice fucking try*. Unfortunately for him, he couldn't move as quickly as a girl high on four bowls of ice cream. "What're you doing here?"

Vixen pointed her gun at him. "You're going to listen to what we have to say."

"C'mon, Vix. You're not going to shoot me." Cheeks laughed. "You're not like your cousin."

She cocked the weapon and aimed at his head. "Do you want to test your theory, Checkersford?"

"So you've not come here for a three-way?" he mocked.

Prison must have had an effect on him. Before, he'd never have dared speak out when staring down the barrel of a gun. Not killing him was really testing my self-restraint. *Do not kill him*, I repeated over and over like a mantra. *Do not kill him.* Instead, I slammed the wood shut on his fingers again to teach him a lesson. Would broken bones teach him to keep his grubby hands to himself, or would I have to cut them off next time?

"Do we have your attention now?" I asked. "There are worse things we could do to you, or don't you remember?"

"Okay, I'm listening," he yelped. "Let me go!"

I paused, looking at Vixen, who nodded. I released his hand and, while he massaged his broken joints like a whimpering baby, I retrieved his gun from the drawer and emptied it. What could he do with no bullets?

"Cover yourself up." I wrinkled my nose in disgust at his shrinking erection and threw him a robe. "We need to talk."

"Talk about what?" he sneered. "How you put me in jail? I'm under Bryce's protection now. He won't be happy when he finds out about this!"

"Bryce's protection only goes so far," I warned. Bryce may rule the town, but he was not invincible. "Will you do the honors, Vix?"

"Gladly," she replied, plugging the USB stick into the TV and pressing play.

The CCTV footage of Cheeks entering a bedroom with two girls flickered onto the screen.

"We'll leave it there, shall we?" I suggested, hitting pause at his first strike. None of us needed to watch the gory scene unfold. Everyone knew what happened next and, if he didn't agree to our proposal, the rest of the world would, too. Nothing would give me greater pleasure than exposing him as the monster he truly was. "Have you seen enough?"

Cheeks paled. Where was a camera when you needed one? It'd be good to capture the look of horror on his face. The threat of going back to jail was a surefire way to sober anyone up. "How did you get that?"

"Not so untouchable now, are you?" I grinned triumphantly. We had him by the fucking balls. "It doesn't matter where we got it. The only thing you need to worry about is what we're going to do with it now. You have a choice to make."

"What do you want?"

"Bryce Briarly trusts you, doesn't he?"

His face went as white as the crisp bed linen. "You want me to be a… spy?"

"You said yourself you're under his protection." I shrugged. "We need you to be the Sevens eyes and ears. That won't be too difficult, right? I mean, your head is already stuck so far up Bryce's ass."

"I can't be a mole. If he found out…" Cheeks's voice trailed away, thinking about what punishment Bryce might inflict. Forgiveness was not in his nature. "If I got caught, he would—"

"Well, you better not get caught then," I cut him off. He was out of his mind if he thought we'd pity him.

"How much do you want to get rid of the video?" Cheeks begged. "What's your price? Girls like you always have a price! Don't forget I know what you used to do and the circles you screwed around in."

"I don't want your money," I snarled, ignoring Vixen's curious stare watching me out of the corner of my eye. She didn't need to know Cheeks believed I'd fucked powerful men, like Raphael Jacobson, for money. The leaked video Hiram sent Bella when I first came to town had given me a reputation that was hard to shake. "I'm a fucking Seven now. And, if I were you, I'd start showing women a little respect."

"What if I won't do it?" His bottom lip trembled. "What happens then?"

"I'm sure your old friends will be happy to see you back in jail." I shot him a sparkling smile and ran my tongue over my canines. "I bet they've been missing you…"

"You w-w-wouldn't," he stuttered. "I know things about all of you. I can tell!"

"Who are you gonna tell? What evidence do you

have?" I cocked my head to the side. He had nothing on us and he fucking knew it. "Who would believe a coke-head ex-cop? You've got nothing left."

"If I do this, what's in it for me?"

"You're only breathing because we still have a use for you," I snapped. "If you help us, the video disappears and you get to live. Think of your heart still beating blood to your cock as a gift."

"Fine," he relented. "I'll do it, okay?"

"Don't even think about crossing us." I threw him a look of pure menace. "We'll be in touch."

"Fucking bitches," he murmured under his breath.

Unlucky for him, I heard every fucking word.

"I've forgotten one thing…" I slowly spun around and punched him square in the nose. His bones cracked underneath my fist, and blood sprayed over the luxurious Texas king. The biggest tragedy was wrecking the Egyptian cotton.

"Fuck," he groaned into a pillow. "What was that for?"

"Never lay a hand on a fucking woman again," I said, grabbing a fistful of his hair and forcing him to look at my wild smile. "Next time I won't be so gentle. Understood?"

"Okay, okay," Cheeks wailed, shuddering at my murderous expression. "I understand."

"I think we're done here." I stood back to admire the blood running down his face and dusted my hands. "For now."

Vixen nodded in agreement, following me out. Punching him was a personal bonus. It's a shame we couldn't finish the job…

"You broke his nose again. Zander won't be happy,"

Vixen said as we headed back to the comfort of the lower floors. "What was *that*?"

"What was *what*?" I replied coyly. "Zander never specified the level of force we could use, did he? All he wanted was for Cheeks to be on our side."

She grinned. "My mistake."

It'd be our little secret. What Zander didn't know wouldn't hurt him. He may be the boss of the Sevens, but he would never be the boss of me.

We returned to our room to find Zander lounging over my bed like a Roman god and Rocky stuffing his face with the last of the cake we ordered.

"Well?" Zander demanded.

Before we had a chance to answer, Rocky jumped up from his chair with so much force one of its tiny legs cracked. Why did hotels insist on putting decorative chairs in every room? How many people broke them? Apart from throwing down your clothes, they served no fucking purpose at all.

"Are you hurt?" Rocky asked. He eyed the blood seeping between my fingers. "Your hand—"

"It's not mine," I snapped. At this point, I'd had more blood on my hands than lotion. It's a good thing red is my color. "We're fine."

Zander met my gaze. "I trust the job is done?"

"Do you really need to ask?" I narrowed my eyes. "I said I'd do it, didn't I? I keep my word."

"Good." He cracked his knuckles and made Vixen cringe. "That's step one."

"So?" I sat down opposite him on the bed. "What's step two?"

"Patience," he purred. "You'll see."

"Before we move onto whatever step two is," Vixen interjected, scouring the room service menu again, "can we order more food?"

"Gold leaf cake?" I suggested, making Zander's lip curl in annoyance. What was his fucking problem? It's not like he didn't have the money.

"Let's go for breakfast," Rocky said. "We'll go to the diner on the way home. The one that does the waffles you like."

Vixen threw down the menu. "Deal."

"Candy?" Rocky looked over hopefully. When he pulled that face, he reminded me of a wounded puppy. Goddammit. How could his eyes still have that effect on me? Sleep deprivation must be influencing my reasoning ability. "What do you say? Waffles?"

"I need to shower first." I may not have had a decent night's sleep in our beautiful room, but hell no would I be missing out on a hot shower. Washing in my apartment was akin to an icy hose-down. "You guys go without me."

"We'll wait," Rocky insisted.

"Okay, I'll come," I agreed grudgingly. I wasn't getting out of this one. "But they better be great waffles."

Rocky smiled, reminding me of the teenager I used to know. "You won't be disappointed."

Suddenly, I felt light-headed. Thoughts of our earlier kiss flooded my mind. A few months ago, I could have taken his life. Getting my revenge had been one of the main reasons I'd stayed in Port Valentine. How could a flash of a smile and the invitation to eat waffles send me spiraling to a place I'd sworn never to return? I needed to get my shit together. Joining the Sevens and sparing his life didn't mean falling back into his arms. I couldn't allow my guard to slip around him… not again.

FOUR

I rolled my eyes at Zander's earlier text.
Car is waiting outside. Bring an overnight bag.

Did he get his kicks from being mysterious all the time? He only ever told us the bare minimum. After our night at the auction, I'd hoped he may become more forthcoming about his plans. His whole 'puppeteer' act was growing old real fast. One person couldn't run an entire fucking show. Wasn't the point of a gang to do things together?

"It's good of you to show up," I muttered, tapping my foot impatiently, as Zander stormed into his office with West in tow. They both had serious stony-faced expressions.

This was typical of Zander. After summoning me, he'd left me to twiddle my thumbs for half an hour. Didn't he know I had a bunch of Netflix shows waiting to be watched? If a series got spoiled, I'd hold him personally responsible. Likewise, if I got back pain after sitting in this uncomfortable as fuck chair, I'd sue.

Zander took a seat behind his desk opposite me. "I've got a job for both of you."

West stayed standing in the doorway like he couldn't wait to get away, and grunted like an overgrown gorilla. *How charming.* Couldn't he use words now? My PMS raged like a bitch, but West gave me a serious run for my money. The last time we saw each other, he bolted without explanation. Judging by the scowl on his face, his bad mood hadn't lifted. I didn't know who Penelope was, or what she meant to him, but West needed to get his head in the game if we were going to work together.

"Is this part of your big plan?" I asked, resting my elbows on the wood and leaning in closer. "What's our next move?"

"I told you to be patient, little one." Zander lounged back with an all-knowing smirk. "This job is related to something else. You and West are going to head to the Seven Sins casino in Hammerville."

Another road trip with West wasn't top of my list of things I wanted to do. At the junkyard, West almost killed a man. If I hadn't acted quickly, we would have had a dead body to deal with and no package. It was a dumb stroke of luck I found the painting amongst the trash in Eddie's trailer — not that Zander needed to know it'd been a disaster. If Zander found out about what really happened, he'd never send the two of us out again... especially if he learned about the kiss we shared on the ride home.

"What do you want us to do?" I questioned, keeping my back turned away from West. "Don't you have enough money?"

We'd won a quarter of a million dollars at the poker

game in Briarly Manor. How fast did he burn through cash? Apart from the new club floor, the Sevens hadn't made any major investments. He had to have other motives, besides topping up his piggy bank, to warrant us traveling four hours to a casino in the middle of nowhere.

"This isn't about money. I want you to pay a visit to the manager," Zander said. "West will know what to do next."

Leaving the job in the hands of a man who could only speak one syllable didn't seem like a fantastic idea, but Zander said no more. If I wanted clear instructions, I should have referred to my daily fucking horoscope.

I jutted out my hip. "Why can't Vixen go instead of me?"

I used sass to cover my apprehension. My last trip to a casino ended in watching my best friend bleed to death on the sidewalk. Crystal wanted to skip town and start over with Q, but Hiram's men gunned her down before she got the chance. I couldn't do anything to stop it. Her death had been one of the worst moments of my life, and it showed me who Hiram really was. Pure fucking evil. Would visiting Seven Sins bring it all back?

"Because you're a couple now, remember?" Zander hissed viciously. How could I forget when I had to wear a ruby ring on my finger to declare my ownership like a fucking collar? I couldn't take it off in case it shattered our ruse. "And because I asked you."

"Lucky me!" I rolled my eyes sarcastically. Now, I knew how Harry felt when he got singled out by Voldie for being the chosen one. Why couldn't I be a fucking Neville?

"It's one night," Zander said. "I'm sure you can play nice for an evening."

"I'm not the one you should be worried about," I said, throwing West a filthy look that bounced off his muscles like they were made from iron. His jaw clenched, but he didn't break his sulky silence.

"Remember my rules, Candy," Zander warned, then began tapping away on his keyboard to show we'd been dismissed.

"I guess we'll see you tomorrow then," I muttered, then turned to glower at my new partner in crime. "I'll wait outside."

After spending two hours of the drive in frosty silence, West's snarky attitude was pushing me over the fucking line. Adjusting the AC had been our only form of interaction. We'd launched a passive-aggressive war over stable temperature. Whenever he turned it up, I'd flip it down. He had no appreciation for my freshly blow-dried hair, and I wouldn't let him ruin my hard work.

"Would you fucking stop it?" I yelled, slapping his hand away as he reached for the switch again. Usually, I wouldn't be the first to break a silence. But we were on a business trip. Someone had to back down for the greater good. I'd be the bigger person if he was gonna keep acting like a fucking child.

"Stop what?"

The bastard.

"You know what," I hissed, narrowing my eyes at him. "I don't know what shit you have going on, but could you at least try not to ruin my hair in the process?"

West didn't respond. He kept his gaze fixed on the stretch ahead and pretended he hadn't heard me.

"Are you going to keep trying to ignore me this whole trip?"

"If I can," he replied, "but something tells me I'm not going to have a choice."

"Why don't we have it out, huh?" We needed to sort out his issues before he derailed our plans. He couldn't lose control. Not again. Next time, I might not be able to bring him back from the brink. "I won't let you fuck this job up because you're distracted."

"I'm not distracted."

"Look," I said, trying to reason with him, "I know hearing your old piece of skirt is in town must be like a kick to the balls but—"

He slammed his foot on the gas, his voice rising above the roar of the engine. "Be careful what you say next, Pinkie."

"Point proven!" I gripped the edge of my seat as we flew down the highway like part of a high-speed chase. "Real fucking mature, West."

"You need to stay out of my fucking business," he growled. "You don't know what you're talking about."

"I know if you don't slow the fuck down, we'll be splattered over the highway for the next two miles. And another one of your cars will be a fiery wreck."

He relented slightly, slowing to a speed that wasn't in the triple digits.

"Sorry," he murmured. At least he had the decency to look remorseful. Every time I rode in a car with West,

I put my life in his hands. "I used to race… and I forget sometimes."

"Clearly." Interrogating West about Penelope when he was behind the wheel was a massive no-no, so I focused my attention on our task ahead. "Are you going to tell me why we're going to see the casino manager?"

"Nico is an old friend," West said. "We have some business to take care of."

"So, we're going to have a reunion?"

"Something like that…"

"How enlightening." Hadn't he learned his lesson after keeping me in the dark last time?

I craned my neck to look out the window as we drove past the 'Welcome to Hammerville' sign. Someone had crossed out the town's name and scrawled 'hell' over it. What a great omen. We kept on going, passing buildings that had fallen to ruin, then pulled into the parking lot of an aged motel. If it wasn't for the lights inside, I'd have thought it was closed down.

"We're staying here?" I asked. The two-story building looked like it'd burnt to the ground and been rebuilt using mismatching materials. It wouldn't meet any building codes. "Really?"

"What's wrong? We need somewhere to stay after visiting the casino." West grinned, the first real smile that had crossed his lips in weeks. His silver-plated canine glinted maliciously in the sunlight. "Is it not up to your standards, princess?"

"You've been to my apartment, right? You're the one I'm worried about," I scoffed, wiping the smile straight off his smug face. "I bet this was nothing like your private school."

He looked at me in anger. "Who told you about that?"

"It's not a secret, is it?"

"Wait here," he spat. "Don't fucking go anywhere."

When he returned, I looked from him to the lone key chain swinging around his finger. "Just the one?"

He raised an eyebrow. "Don't you think it'd look suspicious for a newly engaged couple not to be sharing a room?"

"It doesn't look like the sort of place where people ask questions," I said, nudging my head toward someone scoring crystal meth at the opposite end of the lot. Couples staying in separate rooms was the least suspicious activity going on. "But, be warned, I may stab you in your sleep if you snore."

Our room was on the second floor. The place had a damp, stagnant odor of rat piss and cheap pine air freshener to mask it. It's the kind of motel you'd take someone to before driving out to the woods and shooting them in the head.

West scowled as he surveyed the set-up. "I asked for a twin room."

"We're a couple, remember?" I rolled my eyes. "Don't worry, I won't bite. Hey, we can make a pillow wall, if you like?"

He threw me a dirty look. Would we both fit in the bed? It looked like a double and, for West alone, it'd be a tight squeeze. My cheeks heated at the thought.

"I'm going to hit the shower," he said. "Then we'll head out."

"But it's not even six yet." I checked the grimy clock on the wall, which ticked at an annoyingly loud volume. "Aren't we going at night?"

"We're going to dinner first."

"Like a date?" I teased.

He slammed the bathroom door behind him. The sound of water hammering down drowned out my laughter. I guess a date with The Hulk may not be the worst thing in the world…

West took longer than any person I'd ever known to shower. What did he do in there? Knowing his obsessive cleanliness, he probably had to deep clean the entire bathroom before stripping down.

He returned in a cloud of heady cologne. He wore casual attire; his white T-shirt displayed his tattoo sleeves and accentuated his masterpiece of a body. How many hours did he spend working out to stay in shape? Even in a simple tee and jeans, he wouldn't look out of place in statue form at an art gallery.

I twirled around to show off my outfit. "What do you think?"

While he'd been using up all the motel's water, I'd salvaged my frizz with a blow dryer that almost electrocuted me. Thankfully, I'd packed the right clothes for the occasion. I'd stolen a tight leopard print dress from the costume closet at Lapland before any of the dancers had a chance to wear it. The stretchy fabric hugged my curves and the spaghetti straps showed off my rose tattoos.

West's voice came out in a low gravelly rumble, "It's okay."

After joining the Sevens, Zander gave explicit orders that he didn't want me to dance anymore. I may have followed his rules… so far. But it didn't mean I couldn't take advantage of the Seven perks, like raiding the closet whenever I liked. I pulled on my leather jacket to complete the look. "You sure know how to charm a girl, West."

West grunted. His opinion didn't matter, anyway. The dress made me feel like a wild cat who couldn't be tamed. No one would get past me. Whatever lay ahead, I was ready to kick fucking ass.

"Where are you taking me then, husband-to-be?"

"I know a place."

He always knew the best spots to go for food. I still hadn't gotten over the orgasmic donut breakfast he'd once brought me, so my expectations were high.

A man wolf-whistled in my direction as we headed to the car. I wiggled my fingers in greeting. Hey, at least someone noticed when I'd taken over an hour to get ready. Before the poor guy had time to speak, a single glare from West turned his face ashen. No one wanted to be mown down by a man who looked like a fucking Transformer. *What a cock block.*

I pouted as West held the door open. "Do you have to ruin all the fun?"

"Just get in the fucking car, Pinkie," West warned, slamming the door closed as soon as I swung my ankle inside. He got in after me, cursing under his breath.

"You seem to know where you're going," I commented as we drove through the back roads of Hammerville. Apart from motels, bars, fast food joints, and an array of strip bars, there were no other signs of life. It reminded me of downtown Port Valentine. Another perfect hedonist's escape.

"Of course, I do." West chuckled. "Don't tell me

you haven't worked it out yet? You don't think it's an accident the casino is called *Seven* Sins, do you?"

"I…" I faltered. I'd dismissed the name as a coincidence, but I should have known better. "You mean, we fucking own it?"

"Yeah, but the place pretty much runs itself now. All we do is check in now and again," West explained with a shrug. "We only lived here for a few years, but it was where the Sevens were born. It's how we got our name."

"Why didn't you tell me before?"

I'd thought they'd always lived in Port Valentine, close to the confines of Briarly Manor. What made them leave and start over, then want to return later? It's not like Zander and Bryce had a strong father-son bond. They hated each other.

"Don't you like surprises, Pinkie?" West asked, taking a sharp turn.

"No." I scowled, annoyed with myself for not figuring it out sooner. "Are there any more hidden businesses you're not telling me about in godforsaken towns in the middle of bumfuck nowhere?"

"No, that's it." West laughed. "Despite how it looks, Hammerville isn't all bad. It has Big Al's. Trust me, it's the best steakhouse you'll ever visit. The place is hidden away. Only the locals know about it. Look, it's up ahead…"

I raised my eyebrows. It may have the best steak but, from the outside, the building looked close to falling apart. A gust of wind threatened to blow the windows from their frames and the restaurant's faded sign was unreadable. "Are you sure things haven't changed since you were last in town?"

"Trust me," West said. "It's the best."

Sure, biting cocks off had made me less picky about what I put in my mouth, but I was still choosy about what I'd swallow. West better be right.

The bell above the door alerted the server to our presence. A plump older woman hobbled over. It was hard to tell whether she was seventy or ninety. Either way, she looked too old to be working. Upon seeing West, her cheeks reddened in delight. She hurried over and threw her arms around him.

"It's been too long," she cried, squeezing him tightly. "Why'd you not come to visit me anymore, huh?"

"Easy, Pattie. I've been busy, but I'm here now." He laughed. Was that a blush on The Hulk's face? "Still looking as good as ever."

"You're not getting off that easy!" She swatted away his compliment with her notepad and turned her attention to me. "And who is this young lady? Is this your girlfriend, West? She must be pretty special for you to have brought her to Big Al's."

"This is Candy," he introduced grudgingly.

"It's good to meet you, hon," Pattie said, then turned her head to West. She had a warm aura that made you feel at home instantly. "You never bring girls in here, do you?"

He scowled to hide a smile. They were obviously fond of each other.

"I'll take ya'll to your favorite booth," she said, leading the way to a corner booth in the back. "You two lovebirds take your time with the menu."

"We don't need a menu." West shook his head as we sat down. "We'll both take my usual."

"Coming right up," she chirped. If Pattie's smile

wasn't so damn contagious, I'd have snatched the menus straight out of her hands to decide for myself.

I folded my arms and pouted as she hurried away. "I don't like guys ordering for me."

West winked. "You'll enjoy *me* ordering for you."

With his track record of providing delicious food, I'd take the risk. Besides, seeing Pattie again had started to lift his energy-sucking mood. Maybe our trip wouldn't be unbearable after all...

"You used to come here a lot, huh?" I asked.

"All the time." He draped his hands over the side of the booth. "You'll see why."

I rolled my eyes. "Why did you and Zander pick here to open a casino? You could have gone anywhere."

"To get things up and running, then—" He cut himself off, realizing he'd revealed too much. "Let's just say, people don't ask many questions here."

"Now, I'm intrigued." I leaned forward and dropped my voice. They'd laid deep roots, which meant our visit was about more than reuniting with an old friend. "So, there's more to this place than the Seven Sins?"

"Forget it," he warned as his eyes darted around the restaurant. We'd have to have the conversation behind closed doors. Whatever business they'd started, West didn't want it to be broadcast around a small town where rumors spread like wildfire. Pattie returned to place two cool beers down and cut the lingering tension. "Thanks, Pattie."

She pinched his cheek like he was a child. "It is so good to see you again, Westie."

I raised an eyebrow. "Westie?"

"Don't," he growled.

"Okay, so you don't want to talk about your time

here…" I took a long swig, leaving behind a perfect red lipstick smudge on my glass. "Why don't you tell me about how you and Zander met instead?"

"Why do you care?"

"I'm curious," I said. "You keep saying I don't know you. How can I if you don't let me?"

"We met when we were kids," he said after a long pause. "My ma died before I started school. My pa worked for Bryce. I used to spend summers at the manor with Zander. We were the only kids around."

I found it hard to imagine either of the two men as young boys. Between them, I'd bet they got into their fair share of trouble. With Port Valentine's overlord and a henchmen for a father, neither of them stood a chance.

"When my pa died on a job, Bryce took pity on me," he said bitterly. "Paid for me to go to school. He said it's what my dad would have wanted."

"And was it? You know, what he wanted?"

"I wouldn't know." West drained half of his glass. "The only thing my pa cared about was screwing whores and sorting his next fucking fix. He didn't give a rat's ass about what happened to me. If he didn't give a shit when he was alive, why'd he care if he was dead? The Sevens are my real family."

Family was about more than the blood running through your veins and the Sevens? They'd chosen and formed their kin.

"What was school like?"

"I knew what they thought of me." West shrugged like he didn't give a shit, but I could tell he was trying to cover up his true feelings. Being an outcast had affected him more than he wanted to admit. "Why did a hillbilly with a dead meth addict dad have to share their corridors?"

I related to West's feeling of not belonging more than he knew. As a kid from the Evergreen group home, I'd never felt a sense of being part of something. In grade school, I'd sat down in the canteen, and others at the table got up to move. It scared them that my misfortune might tarnish their own charming, perfect lives. We were the kids you didn't want to get paired with on a group project. We didn't get invited to slumber parties. We got picked last for sports. In High School, Rocky had been the only exception because he made the football team.

"But everyone knew who paid for me to go," West continued. "Even as kids, they knew better than to mess with a Briarly."

"I don't know whether you were lucky or unlucky."

"It's a question I've asked myself. The jury's still out," West said. "Enough about me. It's your turn."

Thankfully, Pattie spared me from answering. She arrived balancing two massive plates of steaks with fried mushrooms on her arms. It looked out of this freaking world.

"Cooked just how you like 'em." She slapped the gigantic mounds of food in front of us. "Medium rare."

Thank fuck he hadn't burned them to a crisp.

"You've always had a great memory, Pattie," West said.

"I never forget an order." She beamed and slapped him playfully with a towel. "I'll be back with the rest of it."

My mouth fell open. "The rest of it?"

Poor Pattie had to make multiple trips. West's 'usual'

comprised pretty much everything on the menu. Enough to feed five people easily.

I lifted my fork to my mouth. "Well, here goes…"

My tastebuds launched into cartwheels. *Holy shit. What seasoning did they use?* I rarely ate mountain man-sized portions, but I refused to waste a mouthful of heaven. Thankfully, my dress was made from a stretchy fabric.

"I told you." West grinned from across the table. "Just wait until you try the mashed potatoes."

"Mmm!" They were whipped up, perfectly smooth, and deliciously buttery. A small moan escaped me, and West's eyes rested on my lips. "They're fucking good."

"Does that mean you'll let me order for you again?"

I licked my fork clean. "Maybe."

Who was I kidding? He could order for me anytime. Even if we didn't go anywhere else, our meal had made suffering through West's sulk worth it. If I was on death row ordering my final feast, this would be my go-to.

"Do you always scout out the best places to eat wherever you go?"

"It's a hobby," he said. "Not that I need to eat out since living with Zander. He makes a mean steak..."

"Zander is a good cook?"

The thought of our scary suited boss donning an apron made me almost choke as I fought back a giggle. There again, Zander's meticulous nature would be well-suited to following a complex recipe. He'd execute a meal with fine-tuned culinary precision.

"Don't tell him I told you," he said. "Can you cook?"

"You'll be lucky if I made you a slice of toast without burning it." I snorted. Give me a body to dissect over making a Thanksgiving meal any day. I'd never had access to a proper kitchen to hone my skills. In Blackthorne Towers, Hiram's chef cooked me a diet of rabbit food. Since then, packet mac and cheese has become my specialty.

"Maybe I can ask Zander to teach me?" I joked.

West gripped his fork tightly, making his knuckles go white and his eyes darken. "I'm sure Zander wants to teach you a lot of things."

His sudden change of mood cast a thunder cloud over our booth, and we ate in silence. After we finished, West left a stash of cash on the table and a generous tip for Pattie.

"Let's go," he ordered. "We've got business to do."

FIVE

It felt too soon after Crystal's death to step into a casino, but I did my damndest to make sure West didn't notice my shaking hands. I ran through my mental checklist: tits out, lip gloss on, head held high… *you've got this, Candy.*

"Mr. Parker." The security guard on the door bowed his head so low his beefy chin vanished into his neck. "Welcome back."

West took my arm. "Welcome to Seven Sins."

As soon as my heel hit the sticky carpet, a suited man in his forties strode over to greet us. His teeth almost glowed from too many whitening strips, and his slicked-back hair hinted he took longer than a Lapland dancer to get ready.

"West!" The stranger opened his arms wide. "I heard you were in town."

West grinned. "News travels fast, Nico."

"You brought company too?" Nico held out his hand. "Let me introduce myself. I'm Nico, the manager here. It's a pleasure."

"Candy," I said. Nico's handshake reminded me of a flaccid dick coated in lube. "It's always nice to meet one of West's old friends."

"Why don't we all go somewhere to talk over a drink?"

"We can't stay long," West warned.

Thankfully, the casino was smaller than those I was used to. It was a rundown joint, where people came to kill time on a stopover. We wove through the sea of whirring slot machines. Cameras followed our every move as if someone was watching behind the lens. If Nico worked for us, why were we being followed?

"West!" A high-pitched woman's voice screeched above the dinging sounds as we made our way across the floor. She swanned over with the air of someone who looked good and fucking knew it. I hated the bitch already. "Nico told me you were in town."

West froze momentarily. "I thought you were in Port Valentine."

"I fancied a change of scenery for the weekend." She shrugged and ran her tongue over her lips suggestively. "That's not a crime, is it?"

"I'm Candy." I stepped in to interrupt whatever moment they were sharing. We were away on business, not to get him laid. "We haven't met."

"It's Penelope," she said dismissively, keeping her gaze firmly set on The Hulk. "Have you missed me?"

Shit. This was his *Penny*. The girl who'd fucked him up. Her straight glossy hair sat around her waist, but it looked too thick and shiny to be real. She had perfectly tanned skin, a toned body, and legs that went on for days. Hell, she looked airbrushed. How was it even possible for a human being to be so freaking perfect? She'd hit the lottery gene pool jackpot.

"What are you doing here, Penny?" West asked while his eyes searched for the nearest exit.

"Why don't we have a drink for old time's sake?" Penelope sucked in her cheeks to emphasize her lips as she trailed a manicured finger up West's inner arm, making me want to yank the skinny twig straight out of its socket. After that, I'd take great pleasure in displaying her doe-like eyes in a pickle jar. "I know you've missed me."

Why had my blood turned to lava? I needed to pull myself together before I exploded and turned the casino into a crime scene. We were in town to speak to Nico. I couldn't screw this up if I ever wanted Zander to trust me with more than the club's underground poker ring.

West's face remained an unreadable mask. "I'm here on business."

"Maybe later?" Penelope winked; her hungry eyes searing into West like she wanted to devour him whole. "I'll see you soon."

Not in my fucking motel room.

She walked away, swaying her hips like she was trying to hypnotize West into following her.

West shot Nico a filthy look in accusation. "You told her I was here?"

"I told you, news travels fast." Nico threw his arms in the air. I didn't trust him. The way his forehead was glistening with sweat told me he was lying. "We'll go into the private bar. We won't be disturbed."

In other words, we were running away from West's stunning ex, who they were too scared to say no to. If the overwhelming urge to break her limbs hadn't overtaken me, I'd have gladly told her to fuck off. Not that it was any of my business. It's not like I should even *care* what West does. But I couldn't have him screwing someone else and ruining our bullshit couple charade, right?

Nico led us into a separate room, clicking his fingers to order a round of cocktails I couldn't pronounce the names of. He looked at me nervously. "Can we talk freely?"

"I'm not another one of West's whores," I snapped, sweeping my hair from behind my ear to flash Nico my tattoo. "See?"

"She's one of us now," West confirmed, causing Nico's tense shoulders to relax. "Anything you have to say, you can say in front of Candy."

Nico eyed the ring on my engagement finger. Something Penelope had missed when she was busy groping West's muscles. The guy didn't miss a trick. "Do we have something to celebrate?"

"That's irrelevant." West shut him down, wanting to keep the meeting on track. "How's our operation going?"

"You know how it is, West." Nico sighed, waving for a server to bring another round. "With Red gone, the production quality is not the same. The guys miss him."

"He couldn't stay here forever," West said. "You know he had to come back to Port Valentine. He only came here to get you started. Show me the books."

"Certainly," Nico obliged, calling over one of his minions to bring out the papers. He may be working for the Sevens, but the growing sweat patches under his arms indicated our visit made him nervous. "I think you'll be pleased."

The pair of them then poured over the pages for the next hour talking figures, while I gritted my teeth, downed mojitos, and pretended it wasn't the first time I'd heard the Sevens ran a motherfucking drugs operation from Hammerville.

"I've seen enough," West said eventually. "Cupid will be in touch soon."

"Perfect." Nico bared his teeth in what he intended to be a smile as his shoulders sagged in relief. "We'll speak again soon, I'm sure."

"Why didn't you tell me?" I demanded as soon as Nico sidled away and we stepped outside. "You're fucking drug suppliers."

"We don't *deal* drugs," West corrected me. "We *grow* them. It's not illegal in this state. Not anymore, anyway. Why do you think Zander took Red on? The guy's a natural."

Somewhere along the way, Rocky must have graduated from smoking pot to growing it. He'd always liked to smoke a joint when we were in school, but I bit my tongue. West didn't know about the past we shared. No one did. It'd only bring more complications when our lives were already consumed by chaos… and we had a growing list of people who wanted to see us brought down.

Logistically, I understood how Lapland and the casino worked as a storefront. Q came in to clean up the cash from the drugs and poker games to make the figures look legit, but something didn't make sense. "Why do you need to use the casino to clean the money, if it's legal to grow?"

"Look, we don't sell our product to everyone the State would consider legitimate, okay?" West shifted on his feet. "Some of our stock goes elsewhere. That's where the casino comes in."

"So, you're not directly dealing drugs," I summarized, "but you're helping other people to do it."

"Look," West lowered his voice, "kids need to make an income, okay? People need medicine and can't get it. We help where we can."

"And profit off of it," I added.

"We're not complete fucking monsters," West said. "We let them keep some of the profits."

"So, you're running an illegal charity? It doesn't seem like a very *Seven* thing to do."

Since when did a gang care about giving back to society? I thought I'd joined a gang of hardened criminals, but there was more to the Sevens than what they showed on the surface. Could they really be up to the challenge of taking someone like Hiram down?

"You know nothing about what it means to be a Seven," West snarled as his cheeks flushed in anger. He turned to storm away at triple speed. "Keep up if you want a ride, Pinkie."

We'd only been back at the motel for five minutes when the aggressive knocking started. If the guy from the parking lot was too wasted to get into his room, I'd make sure he slept well by throwing him off the fucking balcony. Instead, I swung the door open to find myself staring at a beautiful brunette.

Penny.

"Can I help you?" I demanded. How the fuck had

she found out we were here? Was the bitch stalking us? I'd check our car for trackers before leaving.

"You can't." She looked through me like my skin was made out of plastic wrap. "But he can."

Without waiting for an invitation, she barged inside.

West paled. "What are you doing here, Penny?"

"I knew you'd be pleased to see me." She unbuttoned her coat and let it fall away from her body to reveal a lacy red lingerie set like we were in a romantic movie. Who even did that in real life? I may as well have been a fly on the wall for all she cared. "Have you missed me, baby?"

"Cover yourself up," West said. He didn't look down. For a man who could lose control quickly, his ability to stand firm under the circumstances was an impressive feat. Most guys would have already dropped their pants and been balls-deep by now. "Tell me why you're really here."

"What's wrong?" Penelope pouted, trailing a finger over cleavage to draw him in. "You're not still mad at me, are you?"

"It's time for you to go," I intervened. If they wanted to have a raging domestic, they could have it elsewhere. "You can take your perky tits to someone who actually wants to see them."

"Sweetie, I don't know who you think you are." Penelope looked down her pointed nose with an air of smugness and entitlement that came from a lifetime of getting whatever she wanted because of her looks. I could see why Vixen wanted to wring her neck. "But I'm not going anywhere."

"I think you misunderstood me," I hissed back. "It wasn't a request; it was a motherfucking order."

Penelope was a beautiful woman, but more deadly than a siren. She could lure men from safety and send them crashing into the rocks with the snap of her bra strap.

"Who even are you?" she asked in irritation, finally starting to acknowledge I was a living human. "I'm sure he'll still pay you for the hour if you ask nicely."

"Don't speak to her like that." West stepped between us. "Don't even fucking look at her, Penny."

Penelope's jaw dropped. "You're defending her?"

Game on, bitch.

"I'll defend her every single time." West's voice came out in a low possessive rumble. "Because she's my fucking fiancée."

Well, shit… I couldn't help but like this protective streak. It may all be for a show, but I'd enjoy it while it lasted.

"You can't be serious!" Penelope gasped in horror. "This must be some kind of joke."

"Does this look like a joke to you?" I wiggled my finger at her in triumph. Even the International Space Station couldn't miss the massive red rock. "We're getting married. Get over it."

"This is your way of punishing me, isn't it baby? You don't really want to marry *that* trash." Penelope grabbed West's arm. The thought of him choosing to marry me for anything other than spite was too much for her small mind to comprehend. "I know you were angry with me, but I'm back now. We can start over, can't we? Isn't that what you want?"

Her whining voice and crumpled face made her look like she'd been sitting on the toilet for hours trying to take a shit and failing. She may be pretty on the outside, but she was rotten to the fucking core. Her short-lived relief at thinking she had figured everything out didn't last long.

"We're over, Penny," West said, his tone devoid of all emotion. "We've been over for years."

"But you love me." Her desperation filled the room like a gas chamber as her bottom lip quivered. "You've always loved me!"

"Not anymore," West said, looking at her with dead eyes. "I used to *think* I loved you, but I realized long ago you were nothing but an easy fuck and not even a good one."

"So, you're going to marry this whore?" she snarled, showing her underlying vicious streak. "When you could have me."

"I wouldn't want you if you were the last woman on earth," West spat, wrapping a strong arm around my waist. "Candy is everything you're not."

"You heard him, *sweetie*," I said, narrowing my eyes at her. "Get the fuck out of *our* room."

"You can't get rid of me that easily, West," Penelope threatened, grabbing her coat off the floor and pulling it tightly around herself. "I know everything, remember? *Everything.*"

"Psycho bitch ex, much?" I checked the door was triple-locked behind her. It wouldn't surprise me if she tried to sneak in when we were sleeping to steal a strand of West's hair to clone him. "Are you going to tell me about her now? What happened with you two?"

West paced. I'd seen him lose his temper before, but

this? It was different. Something was clawing at his insides and eating him up.

"We were on and off for years," West said, frowning like he couldn't believe it himself. "We met at boarding school. Her family had different ideas of who she should be dating. That's what happens with old money. They always want you to date their 'own kind', but we kept seeing each other in secret. Part of her liked the notoriety of screwing the guy from the other side of the tracks. After we graduated, she left for college. We'd planned to elope. One weekend I turned up at her dorm to surprise her and caught her fucking someone else. Someone from our fucking school…"

He trailed off, lost in his thoughts. Despite his tough facade, the anguish in his eyes gave me a glimpse of his vulnerable side. A side he didn't want anyone else to see. He'd opened up once and never wanted to feel the pain of betrayal again. A pain I knew all too well.

"It'd been going on for years. Her seeing him behind my back when they spent summers in the Hamptons," he continued, the words tumbling out before he could stop them. "Their families wanted them to get married. They had the whole thing set up. The next thing I knew, the pair were engaged. A few years after they got married, his family went broke, and Penny lost everything. Then she found me again. She told me she'd made a mistake and spun me a bullshit line about how she'd changed. I gave her a second chance. She needed cash, so I helped her, then she fucked up again. I caught her screwing a fucking ambassador. It was never about me at all. It was always about money."

"Couldn't her family have helped her out with cash?" I asked.

"Penny's family may come from old money, but they're going extinct," he explained. "Apart from a name and fancy house, they have nothing. All she cares about is staying at the top."

"Shit, West. I'm sorry." I meant it. He'd given her everything, and she'd fucking burned him. I knew the feeling. The feeling you'll never be able to trust anyone again. "What does she have on you? She said that she 'knows everything'?"

"She knew me and Zander in school." West looked away, avoiding my probing gaze. "Stuff happened."

I waited for him to elaborate, but he didn't. It wasn't a line he was willing to cross… yet.

"You may not be able to hit a girl," I said, breaking the silence. "But I have no objection the next time she comes around."

West laughed. "You're a crazy bitch, Pinkie."

"Sure am," I said, owning it proudly like a Girl Scout badge. They needed to add it to the handbook. They should teach little girls how to look after themselves. "I may be a crazy bitch, but you're a damn good actor. You didn't have to say all that stuff to Penny about us."

He ran his hands over his shaven head, drawing attention to the angel tattoo scene on his bicep. "You don't get it, do you?"

"Get, what?" I frowned, replaying back our conversation. Had I missed something? "Your ex is a gold-digger who cheated on you twice and appeared out of nowhere like a nasty bout of herpes. It's fucked up. I get why you left the auction after hearing about it. It's okay to admit that shit gets to you."

"You think she is the reason why I left the auction?"

West's blue eyes pierced mine. "It's not about her. None of it is. I don't give a shit about Penny coming back to town."

"Then why your man period?"

"This is about you."

"Me? What have I done wrong?" I'd been doing a damn good job of pretending to be a dutiful wife-to-be. "I've done what Zander told me to. Just like you and the other Sevens. Does my presence upset you so much you can't bear to stick around the club for longer than one fucking drink?"

"You don't understand."

West punched the wall without warning, adding another dent to the many imparted by other angry men. Where had his Shakespearean dramatics come from? Whenever he didn't know how to express himself, he went straight to smashing shit up.

"Hey, stop!" I caught his bleeding fist to stop him from pummeling it again. I was more worried about him bringing the crumbling building down than him hurting himself. The motel's structural integrity violated a thousand building regulations. Another outburst from West could leave us buried under a pile of rubble. "Help me understand, okay?"

"You want to understand?" His eyes burned with passion. "I made a mistake."

I dropped his fist, my heart beating faster. "What did you do?"

"Do you really want to know?"

I nodded.

"You're going to regret this," he warned.

I put my hands on my hips and looked up at his

imposing figure. If he wanted to intimidate me, it wouldn't work. "Try me."

My mouth went dry as he stepped closer. The pounding in my chest drowned out the sound of the highway and the rats scratching above.

West's body collided with mine at full force, as he brought his lips crashing against my own and stole my breath away. Like the first time we kissed in Briarly Manor, my body responded to his touch involuntarily.

"Do you understand now?" West pulled away gasping for breath. "You're the mistake I made. A mistake I can't stop thinking about making again."

"But you don't even want to be in the same room as me," I stammered, still reeling from our kiss. Ever since our junkyard trip, West had done everything in his power to stay out of my way. "I thought you didn't even want me here."

"Ever since our kiss, you're all I've thought about," West hissed. His words didn't come out as sweet or kind, they burst from his mouth in a bitter fury like something poisonous he wanted to expel. "Your snarky mouth, that sweet fucking ass of yours… it's like you enjoy taunting me. I can't get you outta my fucking head."

He kicked the bed frame causing the weakened wood to crack. How was I supposed to respond? West's kiss set my body alight… but it didn't mean it was the right thing to do. The Sevens were a gang. We couldn't mix business with pleasure, right?

"West!" I pulled him back before he snapped the damn thing in half. "Can you stop smashing shit for two seconds?"

"I want you, Candy." West stared at me with a burning intensity, like he wanted to burrow deep into my brain and discover my deepest secrets. "But I can't fucking have you. You know the rules."

"The rules?"

"No one can touch you," he said. "Zander's orders."

"Zander may be the boss of the Sevens, but he doesn't own me." A wave of hot prickling anger spread through my limbs. Fuck Zander. What right did he have to tell me, or anyone else, what to do with their bodies? If I wanted West, then I'd have him on my fucking terms. Nobody owned me. "I'm not a piece of fucking property."

"You're playing a dangerous game, Pinkie."

I stood on my tiptoes, slowly edging closer. My lips grazed against his teasingly. Had I decided to act to annoy Zander, or because I wanted West as much as he wanted me? I wasn't sure, but it was too late to back out now. "Fuck the rules."

West didn't need any further persuasion. When his lips responded to mine this time, we had no audience. No Zander watching in a chair, no room of ogling old men, no stream of oncoming cars or worries about prying eyes. It was just the two of us. Alone. That's why it was so dangerous. When no one else could intervene, how would I know when to stop when the urge to jump his bones consumed my entire body?

His hands slipped under my ass and hoisted me into the air like I was weightless. He pulled me closer, yanking my dress up to my hips. His giant monster hands gripped my cheeks so hard he'd leave marks, but I didn't mind. I wrapped my legs around his torso, my thighs gripping him tightly, to feel every hard muscle of his body pressed against mine.

"You have no fucking idea how much I've wanted

you," he whispered into my mouth as if scared the world would collapse if he spoke too loudly. Maybe it would. Maybe this would destroy everything.

I sunk my teeth into his lip in reply. I couldn't have said anything even if I'd wanted to. West groaned, slamming my back into the wall and causing a part of the ceiling to fall at our sides. The whole fucking building could come crashing around us and it wouldn't stop me from wanting to be devoured by his passionate fury.

His tongue probed my mouth with an urgency. A thirst we couldn't quench. The heat of his body made my skin burn with longing, but it wasn't enough. No, we weren't close enough. Not yet. My nails clawed his back and drew blood. I didn't care. Hell, I wanted to. I wanted to claw every inch of him to mark what was mine. What Penelope couldn't have. The cool metal of West's belt rubbing against the heat of my lace panties left neither of us questioning whether we wanted this.

When was the last time I'd been this close to a man and wanted him to take me? I couldn't remember. But I needed to feel West more than I needed oxygen. Suspended in mid-air, there was nowhere for me to escape, and I didn't want to. I pushed my hips against the rock-hard bulge in his pants. West was a big guy and, unsurprisingly, his cock was a monster of its own. I reached down to undo his belt… then…

The cold ring of his cell pierced through our ragged breathing, causing West to break away.

"Leave it," I murmured in his ear.

West's lips trailed down my neck as we let it ring out, then…

It started again.

"I should get that," West murmured, his voice low and husky. "It might be Zander."

Well, shit... way to kill the fucking mood with a sledgehammer.

He placed me down gently like a rare fragile artifact he was scared to break. What happened to the raging beast who'd slammed me against the wall minutes before? After talking hurriedly in grave hushed tones, West hung up.

"Well?" I demanded. "What is it?"

"We need to go back." His words were heavy and loaded. He was talking about more than being summoned to Lapland. "Zander needs us."

"Fine." I smoothed down my dress and grabbed my packed bag. "I didn't want to stay in this dive, anyway."

What would happen when we returned? Would West go back to pretending I was a pain in his ass? Between Zander's rules, my history with Rocky and the fire I'd ignited with West, joining the Sevens had become even more complicated. Being bound to three dangerous men would open up a whole new world of unexpected threats.

SIX

By the time we arrived at Lapland, my head pounded from the heavy metal West blasted for the entire journey. It suited me. Better to pop a few aspirins, if it meant avoiding conversation and drowning out thoughts about my recklessness.

The gravity of my mistake started to sink in the closer we got to Port Valentine. What the fuck had I done? Seeing West and Penelope together touched a territorial nerve which made me forget everything I knew about men. The fucker turned me into melted putty in his massive hands. After our junkyard trip, I should have known better.

I knew men like West. They said anything to get a piece of the action. Hell, I'd bet he was sexually frustrated after seeing his stunning ex and settled for the backup option. The only person with a vagina in a block radius he didn't have to pay to screw. I should never have stopped him from smashing up the motel room. All the words he'd said? They were textbook lines. I needed to remember he was a player, like the rest of the Seven men.

As soon as we were back at the club, I flew from the car like a starving lion released from a cage before he'd put on the parking brake.

"Candy," West called, but I didn't look back.

We needed to put distance between us, and I needed to get my shit together to stop freaking out over what *almost* happened. My young naivety got me into this fucked up world in the first place. Why would West be any different?

Men were manipulators. They would say anything to get what they wanted – especially if 'anything' had a pair of tits and a hole between their legs. Criminals like the Sevens never had honorable intentions. They treated girls like toys. West used to hook up with Scarlett, another dancer, when I first came to town. If Zander hadn't called, I'd have become another name in his little black book, which I'm sure was already the length of Paradise fucking Lost.

"Candy!" Mieko greeted me as I rushed into Lapland with her usual sunny smile. "Vixen told me you were out of town for the night."

"Change of plan."

She nudged me gently. "It can't have been that bad, right?"

"What do you mean?" I snapped.

She raised her eyebrows. "You look like you want to rip someone's head off."

"Sorry, it's been a long day…" It wasn't Mieko's fault I'd offered myself to West on a plate. I only had my cock-starved vajayjay with questionable judgment to thank for that. "Is there space for me on tonight's schedule?"

"I think so," she said. "Vixen wouldn't mind, but didn't Zander say he didn't want you dancing now you're a Seven?"

"I couldn't give a flying fuck what Zander says." Thoughts rattled around my head like wrestlers in a mosh pit. Without a vibrator in hand, dancing was the only way I'd be able to find a release and empty my worries away. "I'm taking the stage."

"I'm not going to stand in your way!" She held up her hands, then surveyed my outfit. "You better change though."

Mieko made a good point. A wiggle dress wouldn't accommodate the splits. Besides, the delicious scent of West's cologne had absorbed into the fabric and I didn't need a reminder of how fucking good it felt to be pressed against his perfect abs.

I stormed into the dressing room like a tsunami. "Get out!"

The dancers obeyed, dispersing like a herd of sheep running from a wolf. None of them dared to argue. Since getting my initiation tattoo, they knew my upgraded status in Port Valentine. They feared me, but it didn't stop the bitches from complaining whenever they thought I wasn't listening. I could fire any of them with a flick of my wrist, but why waste my time with childish games? My real worries were far bigger… like how I'd kissed Rocky at the auction and fallen into West's arms a few days later.

I chose a neon pink dress that crisscrossed over my stomach and left little to the imagination.

It's showtime!

As I stepped onto the dance floor, a figure stepped out from the shadows. He'd been waiting. The furious look on Zander's face catapulted my heart to the back of my throat. He couldn't have rigged a camera in the motel, could he? I wouldn't put it past him. The guy's obsessive control issues were off the charts.

"Vixen told me you wanted to dance," he spat. "It's not what we agreed on."

If this was Zander's reaction to me grinding on a pole, I wouldn't want to see how he'd respond if he found out about the other agreement I broke… and who else I'd been getting close to.

"It's not a crime to let your hair down," I replied. "Why did you call us back, anyway? It doesn't seem like you need *me* to do anything else."

"West had other pressing business to attend to," he said, proving my point, but refusing to let me off so easily. "You're a Seven now. We have a reputation in this town."

"I may be part of the Sevens, but you can't control every part of my life. It's called having fun. Maybe you should try it?" I suggested. "Enjoy the fucking show, Zander."

I marched past, fully aware he'd get a glimpse of my ass due to the swishing fabric. What better way to make an exit?

The night was well underway, and a large bachelor party filled the dance floor. Dancers flitted around them like flies around shit, picking the group apart by beckoning individuals away for private dances. Everyone knew they had deep wallets when a last night of freedom was at stake.

"I see you've dressed up." Vixen looked me over with a smirk. "If you wanna dance, you better get your ass up on the stage before Zander pulls the whole fucking show."

"That bastard is not canceling me," I said. "Clear the fucking way."

"I thought you'd say that." Vixen winked. Having her as an ally came with advantages. She didn't care about calling out her cousin when he deserved it. "Mieko chose the song."

I took to the stage as 'Erbody But Me' by Tech N9ne blasted from the speakers. *Nice choice.* Everyone's eyes turned to look up and watch my every move. Most people hated performing for a crowd. I used to be one of them until I realized being seen came with power. Captivating an audience gave you the power to portray whatever you wanted. You could become an entirely different person. Performing rendered the real me, and the parts I didn't want others to see, invisible.

The rest of the song passed in a blur. I allowed my body to move to the rhythm, pushing aside the memory of West's eyes trying to pierce past my bullshit. Shimmying for strangers was easier. It was safe. Getting added to their wank bank wouldn't hurt me — not like The Hulk and his monster dick, who had the potential to penetrate more than my pussy…

"You were freaking hot," Mieko complimented as I stepped off the stage, and she readied to take my place. Her leather catsuit would not disappoint the hecklers.

"Says you." I blew her a kiss. "Now go break some balls."

Dancing had been the right decision. Zander may be in a sulky mood, but what was new? He'd need to get botox soon, because of the constant frown etched on his face. Performing had been exactly what I needed to blow off steam and think more clearly.

"Hey!" A stranger approached. He was standing in the front row during my performance and belonged to the bachelor party. "Can I buy you a drink?"

He was handsome in a clean-cut kinda way. Someone with a cheeky grin and enough confidence to sink the Titanic — the type who worked as a banker in the city and drove a fancy car to show off his status.

I shrugged. "Why not?"

It could be good for me. Maybe hanging out with a guy who wasn't a badass criminal would help cleanse my palette? The more I hung out with the Sevens, the less control I seemed to have over my desires.

"You're not the groom, are you?" I asked, eying him suspiciously as he ordered us tequila shots. Once poured, I took them straight from Scarlett's hands. You could never be too careful accepting drinks. I should know, as I used to slip drugs into my target's cocktails when working for Hiram.

"Hell no!" He laughed. "I'm the best man. I enjoyed your show. You're a good dancer. How long have you been doing this?"

I licked the salt from my hand, took the shot, and sucked the lime in record speed. "How about we dance?"

If I wanted to make conversation, I'd see a fucking therapist. I took his hand and led him to the center of the dance floor. Mieko was killing it on stage, but the man never took his eyes off me.

"You're stunning," he shouted in my ear.

As the beat dropped, he placed his hands on my hips. I turned to grind against him. His hands pulled me closer, allowing my ass to feel the half-tent pitching in his pants. At his touch, I felt nothing. No fireworks, no excitement, nada, zilch... zero. I may as well have been doing sudoku.

What the hell was my problem? There was nothing wrong with the dude. I spun around and put my arms around his neck. The thought of kissing him was about as appealing as drinking a cold cup of English tea. Even dancing with him bored the living shit outta me. Why did my body only respond to no good criminals? There were more guys in the world than Zander, West, and Rocky! I had to try, at least…

One minute, we swayed to the music. The next, the poor guy was hit with the force of a truck and lay sprawled on the floor clutching his face. The crowd stopped dancing to watch, backing away to create a circle around them.

Zander towered over him, fists clenched. "Nobody touches my girl."

"Hey, man," he stuttered, wincing as he rubbed the spot where Zander delivered his blow. He'd be sporting an attractive black eye tomorrow. "I didn't know she was yours. I was only messing around."

Zander grabbed his collar and hauled the banker to his feet. Two security guards were already waiting. Zander threw him into their arms, ignoring the objections from the rest of the party. "Escort him from the premises."

"What the fuck, Zander?" I demanded. As Lapland's owner, he seriously needed to re-read a customer service manual. "You didn't have to throw him out."

"My office, Candy." Zander rolled up his sleeves. He locked his eyes on me, seething in anger. "Now."

Being led into his office felt like doing the walk of shame after a regrettable one-night stand. As soon as we were inside, Zander turned the lock behind him.

"Are you going to explain yourself?"

"I've done nothing wrong," I said. "We were only *dancing*."

"Don't fucking lie to me, Candy." Zander stepped forward menacingly and loomed over me. He was so close that he had to incline his head for me to see his eyebrows lower in fury. The light cast shadows over his face, highlighting his rose tattoo. The thorns inked into his cheeks looked sharp and ready to draw blood. "I'm not just talking about the man out there who placed his dirty hands on you. Do you think I'm too stupid to see how you've got West and Red wrapped around your little finger?"

"I don't know what you mean," I lied. I couldn't waver or show weakness. He'd see straight through it. When you said something with enough confidence, it almost became a reality – right?

"I told you, you're all fucking mine," he whispered; his breath sent chills racing down my spine. "You know my rules."

The hint of a threat should scare me, but it didn't. Why does being in the company of an ordinary man make me want to call it a night, but I get drawn in by a man who has the power to kill me? Zander's words didn't make me feel intimidated… they excited me.

"But I haven't broken them."

Well, I'd gotten close with West but what Zander didn't know wouldn't hurt him.

"Actions have consequences, Candy." Zander placed one finger to my mouth to silence any further objections. "You already know that, don't you?"

My breathing heightened. "What are you going to do?"

"Turn around," he ordered.

"Wait, what—"

"You agreed to follow my rules, remember?" He pressed his finger into my lips harder. "You're going to do as I say."

When Zander gave orders, he had a way of putting you under a spell. Instead of telling him to fuck off, I obeyed. I turned my back, feeling his presence looming behind me.

"Bend over," he instructed.

"Excuse me?" I tried to turn, but Zander caught my hips to stop me. "What the fuck, Zander?"

"You heard me," he purred, holding me firmly in place. "Bend over my fucking desk, Candy."

Resisting wouldn't end well for either of us.

"Fine," I agreed. If Zander thought he could humiliate me, I'd prove him wrong…

I made a show of stretching my arms out in front of me, slowly lowering myself forward. My tiny dress hitched up my thighs, riding up my ass to give him a good view.

His hands stroked the back of my thighs. "Very good."

Zander's fingers danced over my skin so gently that it made me question whether he was touching me at all. My encounter with West had been a primal fiery embrace, but with Zander? His moves were calculated. Deliberate. He enjoyed taking his time to plan every single stroke.

His fingers slipped into my inner thigh and caressed my delicate skin with unexpected tenderness. I should tell him to stop. I should want to put an end to it but, instead, I stayed silent. If this was his way of testing me, then I wouldn't back down.

While I was vulnerable, with my butt raised like a kitty wanting attention, this position meant I didn't have to think. Dancing helped to calm my thoughts, but Zander's touch? It calmed my body. My nerve endings were tingling, anticipating where his fingers would brush next. It's all I could focus on.

Zander's palms slid up the back of my thighs, applying a little more pressure, then… HOLY FUCK.

Thwack!

Zander spanked my ass so hard it made me yelp in surprise. If I looked in a mirror, his red handprint would be staring back.

"You have been a bad girl, little one…" Zander tutted. "Bad girls deserve to be punished."

He yanked up my dress to completely expose my sparkly G-string. The rattle of his belt buckle and leather sliding loose made my pussy clench. In Blackthorne Towers, I'd been inflicted with pain but never like this. I tried to stand, but Zander's grip held me down firmly.

"I won't hurt you," Zander promised, sensing my

shift. "But I am going to teach you a lesson. A lesson I want you to remember."

"Zander, I..."

I let out a small moan as his hand softly caressed my cheeks, running his fingers over the burning mark he'd left behind. Taking a moment to appreciate his work.

"What a fucking ass," he admired, delivering another sharp blow with his hand in the crease where my ass met my thighs. The sting made me gasp aloud. "This is what happens when you break my rules. You like that, don't you, little one?"

I did. *Fuck*. I did.

Zander ran his leather belt over the backs of my thighs, warming me up for what was to follow. My shoulders tensed, anticipating the pain. When he swung and struck my whole body jolted. Hard enough to make a satisfying crack, but gentle enough that it wouldn't bruise. I sensed he was holding back. He didn't want to hurt me.

Then, he struck again, two quick blows in quick succession, perfectly delivered to give the same pain. The thudding feeling coursing through my body wasn't pain, but pleasure and excitement from not knowing what was coming next… a release I desperately needed.

He dropped the belt to the floor with a clang. "Now, everyone will be able to see that you're mine."

But Zander wasn't done yet. He stroked the raised marks, then trailed his fingers downwards. He used his hands to gently part my legs further, allowing enough space for him to dip between my legs and stroke my heat through the silky fabric.

"Fuck," I moaned.

He could feel my wetness. I couldn't hide the effect

he had on me. His teasing was torturous. He expertly navigated his way to my clit and gently rubbed in slow circles to prolong my suffering.

Shit, I wanted more. If he felt this good through the fabric, I couldn't even imagine how amazing it'd feel to have his skin against mine. I bucked backward against his hand in encouragement.

Suddenly, he stopped. Zander withdrew his hand and stepped back. "I think you've learned your lesson now."

"You're a bastard." I stood up breathlessly and pulled down my dress, acutely aware my face was as red as my fucking ass. For punishment, I'd expected him to rip off a few toenails. What kind of twisted game was he playing? Getting a girl close to orgasm and then stopping took torture to a whole new level!

"Actions have consequences, remember?" Zander grinned wickedly and popped one of his fingers into his mouth to taste me. "Delicious."

"Let me out," I hissed through gritted teeth.

He unlocked the door. "It was my pleasure."

Leaving Zander's office felt like leaving an alien spaceship after being probed. I had to splash my face with ice water and change my panties pronto.

"I've been looking for you everywhere!" Vixen burst into the bathroom and found where I'd been hiding. Thankfully, my heart rate had almost returned to normal. "What are you doing in here?"

"Nothing," I replied defensively. "What do you want?"

"We've got a gift from Cheeks." She waved a brown envelope in front of her face like a fan. "Our little chat in the hotel room worked."

"I still don't trust him."

Cheeks was a slimy handsy prick who accepted bribes for personal gain and slid through life with zero morals. The Sevens may have damning evidence that could put him behind bars, but it only scratched the surface of the crimes he'd committed over the years. Breaking a prostitute's jaw wouldn't be the worst thing he kept hidden.

"Neither do I," Vixen admitted. "But I trust Zander."

She may trust Zander's motivations, but I couldn't figure out what went through his head. Every time I thought I'd worked him out, he threw another curveball. If he was as calculating with business as he was with his hands, we should have nothing to worry about.

"Have you opened it?" I asked. Whatever information Cheeks passed over better be good. If we were going to work with the scum of society, I wanted it to be worth our while.

"Not yet, it's addressed to Zander." Of course, because it's out of the question that anyone other than Zander could pull the strings around here. "How was he?"

"How was…" My voice trailed off, thinking I'd misheard her. Why did my brain instantly go there? Of course, she wasn't asking about how skilled Zander was at getting me to the brink of an orgasm. I recovered quickly. "Sorry, what?"

"How is Zander? He dragged you into the office like it was the fucking reckoning, remember?" She looked at me funny. "I've had to give out free drinks to the bachelor party to make up for him throwing out the best man. Is he still in a bad mood?"

"Yeah, well..." I mumbled. "I think he's over it now."

"Thank fuck Zander didn't break any bones. The groom threatened to press charges," Vixen went on. My ass hadn't been the only one to face punishment after I decided to dance with a stranger. "That is, until West made an appearance. The guy wanted to have all his teeth for the wedding photos."

"West is back?"

"He went straight upstairs," she said. "What happened in Hammerville? He looked like shit."

"Penny happened."

"What was she doing there?" Vixen's jaw dropped. "I thought she was in Port Valentine."

"She followed us," I replied. "You were right about her. The bitch has a neck I'd pay to strangle."

Vixen snorted. "You'll have to join the fucking queue."

Raised voices outside the club piqued our attention.

"Want help breaking it up?" I asked hopefully. Smashing a few heads together may release some of my frustration.

"Do I look in the mood to be mopping blood off the floor all night?" Damn, she knew me too well. "Call yourself a cab, and I'll see you tomorrow."

Heading home early wasn't a bad idea. I'd been on a complete head-fuck rollercoaster in the past twenty-four hours. From getting steamy in the motel room to being bent over a freaking desk. This was not what I'd signed up for when joining the Sevens.

The universe wasn't done kicking my ass yet, though. I checked my cell to see three unread messages flashing on the screen. All from the same person.

Having fun?
It's been too long, Kitten.
I'll be seeing you soon.

I couldn't afford any more distractions, especially not in the form of three perfectly sculpted Seven men. Hiram was coming, and I had to be ready… we all did.

SEVEN

It'd been two days since Zander carried out his 'punishment', and I could finally sit down without feeling a sting, which made me more excited about the evening ahead. There's only so long I could put with Zander's smug sideways glances at knowing his prints were burned into my ass...

"Are you sure you don't mind me coming along?" Mieko sat cross-legged in front of my dirty mirror. A plethora of cosmetics surrounded her like a spell-casting circle. "Won't they mind?"

"I told you already," I said, running the straightener through my hair to iron out the final kinks. "I want you there, so you're coming. I'm a Seven too, remember? What I say goes."

We were heading to the Smoker for what Zander called a 'Sevens night'. Despite the pretense of going to have a good time, he would have an ulterior motive for our attendance. Zander always did. Why else go through the effort of getting us on the VIP list? The Smoker is an exclusive club in Port Valentine that opens every full moon in an abandoned warehouse. It's renowned as a cool hang-out, where they sell drinks so expensive you'd think they contained unicorn tears and centaur jizz.

Conveniently, Lapland had to close its doors for the evening because Vixen decided to get the dance floor redone for the second time. After the urgent replacement job following the kid's death, Vixen hadn't stopped complaining. After hearing her bitching for weeks, Zander finally relented and agreed to get it done again. When Rocky called me earlier, he'd said she'd been whipping the workers to get it finished quicker.

Mieko fluttered her thick eyelashes. She'd drawn a perfect winged cat-eye, complete with shimmering purple shadow, which made her look like an otherworldly goddess. "Is this too much?"

"It's never too much," I said, then smiled coyly. Vixen will be blown away."

"I don't know what you mean," she replied with indignation. Although her sparkling eyes told another story.

I rolled my eyes. "Sure you don't…"

Mieko's secret crush on Vixen blew my mind. Even more baffling than Mieko liking her was Vixen's complete obliviousness. How hadn't she noticed Mieko hanging off her every word like a lovesick puppy? For someone quick to call out bullshit, Vixen couldn't see what was right under her septum piercing.

"Your hair looks great with that outfit," Mieko said. With her help, I'd freshly dyed my tresses to a vibrant shade of fiery pink, which complimented my red dress. It had a floaty layered skirt with a lace corseted bodice — the perfect balance of an angel on the bottom but a devil up top. "Is there anyone *you* are trying to impress tonight?"

"Nope," I said, popping the p. "Is there anything wrong with a woman looking good for herself?"

"Of course not, but I'm just saying." Mieko shrugged but wasn't about to let the topic go so easily. "One minute, I thought something was going on with you and Red. Next, you're in a fake engagement with West and Zander knocks out any guy who looks in your direction. All I'm saying is, you could have any of them if you wanted to. You'll have to pick eventually, right?"

"It's not like that," I insisted as my cheeks heated. Hopefully, my bronzer covered their rosy glow. "We *work* together."

Business first, I reminded myself, that's how it needed to stay. I never intended to get caught between three guys, especially when bound to stay in a freaking gang with them forever. Mieko was right. I couldn't have them all. I needed to think with my head and ignore whatever weird pull I felt towards them before it ended in fucking disaster.

"Whatever you say." Mieko applied deep plum lipstick with a smug smirk, seeing right through me. Goddammit, it was okay for me to wind her up about Vixen, but not the other way around. "When will they be picking us up?"

I checked my new phone. After Hiram's last messages, I changed my number. None of the Sevens had questioned my excuse of accidentally stepping on my last one in platform shoes. It wouldn't keep Hiram at bay for long, but it gave me a few days without worrying about his unexpected calls. He enjoyed playing games, so why make it easy for him?

"They're bringing the limo around in five."

Mieko's eyes lit up like a kid being told they could eat as much candy as they wanted before bed. "I've never been in a limo before."

"Don't get too excited. With all of us squeezed in, it won't be much better than a school bus…"

Well, one with fancy champagne and bulging male muscles instead of whining kids with runny noses and juice boxes.

Mieko peeked through the curtains and squealed in excitement. "They're here."

Incessant beeping from the street signaled Vixen's impatience. She had a habit of forcing the drivers to press the horn to hurry people along. They were too scared to question the crazy bitch who hated waiting.

"Let's do this." I linked Mieko's arm in mine and led her out of my apartment. "The Smoker, here we come!"

When I first arrived in town, I swore not to get close to people. With Mieko, it was different. After getting rid of a body together and learning about her troubled past, we'd grown closer over the past few months. I never thought I'd have another true friend after Crystal's death, but Mieko was slowly re-teaching me the value of female friendship. Sure, I also had the Sevens… but I wouldn't be making them friendship bracelets anytime soon.

"Are you okay, Mieko?" Vixen frowned as we slipped into the limo. "You look a little… off."

I held back a snicker. Mieko was completely unprepared to see Vixen's bustier, which hoisted her boobs up into two perfectly shaped mounds. The girl knew how to make an impact.

"Y-y-yes, I'm fine!" Mieko squeaked, averting her eyes to the first thing in sight. "Wow! This cupholder… it's amazing. It really can hold cups. It's the, um... perfect shape."

Vixen yawned. "Is it?"

"Where are the guys?" I raised an eyebrow at the empty seats. Hell, I'd canceled my boxset binging plans for this shit. "What's the point in calling a Sevens night if you're not even going to show up?"

"Something came up," Vixen replied, pouring three Russian vodka shots. "They'll join us there later."

I raised my drink in toast. "Who'd have thought we'd have another girl's night so soon?"

Vixen rolled her eyes and clinked her glass against mine. "Fuck the guys."

I almost choked. Of course, she didn't mean *literally* fuck them. Why was that the first conclusion I jumped to? Perhaps it'd be best if they didn't join us later. My vagina needed a break from their presence.

"I've never been able to get into the Smoker before," Mieko said. The guest list was exclusive and invitations were almost impossible to come by.

"The Briarly name has some perks." Vixen shrugged. The name also came with downsides, like having your relatives order a hit against you. "We know a guy. Let me know next time you want in. I'll sort it."

"Why don't we play a game?" I changed the subject. "Never have I ever."

"Why the hell not?" Vixen reclined, while Mieko

looked like she wanted to shit herself. "We've still got a whole bottle left."

"I'll start," I said. "Never have I ever disposed of a body."

"Hey!" Mieko objected but took a sip anyway. "You're supposed to say things you haven't done."

"Fine…" I sighed. It'd be a short list. "You go next."

"Never have I ever been to jail."

"Is that the best you got?" Vixen laughed, taking a drink. "Okay, never have I ever killed someone."

Mieko and I both drank. What would happen if I made this a little more interesting?

"Never have I ever had a crush on someone I've worked with," I said.

Mieko narrowed her eyes and took a sip, but Vixen didn't notice. Was she incapable of seeing anything that might be good for her? She indulged in airheads, cigarettes, and spirits… but someone like Mieko didn't even come across her radar.

"Never have I ever kissed my boss," Mieko rebutted. "Candy, you need to drink. You kissed West!"

"He's not my boss," I replied, hoping the next question wouldn't ask whether a Seven had left bruises on my ass. "We're all equals."

"Look!" Vixen pointed outside as the limo started to reduce its speed. "We're here. Welcome to the Smoker."

The Smoker looked like any other abandoned warehouse. A gigantic building made from steel and grimy glass windows. You wouldn't look twice at it in the daytime, but, at night, it was lit up like a Christmas tree. Flashing lights bounced off the walls, music pulsed from every corner and mini fire pits burned to keep revelers warm.

"This way," Vixen instructed, leading us out of the car like soldiers heading to battle. She stormed straight to the front of the long queue, where we were let in straight away. No one would be brave enough to accuse a Seven of jumping a line.

"Isn't this place insane?" Mieko whispered in my ear as we stepped into the party. The building was broken up into multiple rooms with DJs playing different genres of music. There were small bars in each area, but the main space-age bar spanned the entrance lobby. Its sleek and sophisticated appearance contrasted the rundown warehouse which gave it an effortlessly cool vibe, and it was surrounded by tall tables for people to rest drinks and chat.

"I've got Zander's card," Vixen declared proudly, waving a platinum before our eyes. "Let's have a good fucking time, huh?"

After doing too many shots in weird and wonderful flavors, we descended on the dance floor. Considering Vixen spent most of her time in Lapland ordering dancers around, she had surprisingly great moves. Maybe she'd consider taking to the pole one day?

"Shit." Mieko gasped, pointing through the throng of moving limbs. "Look!"

The crowd parted for two men to pass. West's lip was split open, and his face twisted into his signature scowl. At West's side, Rocky didn't seem to be hurt, but his furious glare made him look ready to disembowel anyone who looked at him.

"What happened?" Vixen asked them as they

joined us.

West grunted in response, and Rocky shoved her out of his way to head straight for a drink. What had gotten their panties in a twist?

I smirked up at West. "Nice lip."

"Don't fucking go there," he snarled.

Considering men didn't get periods, they experienced worse mood swings than any woman I'd ever known. How would they cope if they had to deal with cramps and bleed out their peens once a month?

"Is someone going to tell us what the fuck went down?" Vixen placed her hands on her hips, staring West down like they were in a quick draw contest. "Who did that to you?"

West nudged his head in Rocky's direction. "Ask *him*."

Vixen's jaw dropped, as Rocky returned. She spun around in accusation and jabbed a claw into his chest. "*You* did this to him?"

"We had a disagreement." Rocky shrugged like it was nothing, but his shoulders remained tense. Landing a punch on West was impressive. Had he taken The Hulk off guard? "So what?"

"It's no one else's fucking business," West spat.

"Where's Zander?" I asked, expecting they would have arrived together.

"He has somewhere else he needs to be," West replied flatly. Typical. Zander was holding onto more secrets the rest of us were not privy to. Why did he suggest coming to the Smoker in the first place, if he had other plans? "He's not coming."

"Let's go dance in the other room. I hear Ash and the Basilisks playing. They're my favorite band!" Vixen turned to me and Mieko without addressing the guys. There was no point when they were standing with their hands in their pockets like moody teenagers forced to attend a family function. "Are you both coming?"

"My feet hurt. I'm gonna find somewhere to sit down," I lied, then whispered in Mieko's ear, "you can thank me later."

I'd be her wing woman and stay with the guys if it gave her the chance to make her move. Alcohol had lowered Mieko's inhibitions, so who knows? She had to act on her crush soon or forget about it. She couldn't waste her life pining after Vixen.

"Suit yourself," Vixen called, grabbing Mieko's hand and pulling her away. Mieko looked back at me in wide-eyed surprise and beamed. Playing the role of Cupid was new to me, considering I usually acted as the Grim Reaper.

"Not in the mood to party?" Rocky cocked his head to the side. He only acted snarky when something was bothering him... or someone. "Are you too tired?"

I looked between the two of them. "Are you going to tell me what happened tonight or not?"

Neither of them said a word, letting the stony silence stretch out as they didn't look at me or each other. You'd need a sledgehammer to lighten their fucking moods.

"Fine!" I threw my hands in the air. I wouldn't be getting any answers until my pubes turned gray and my labia shriveled into prunes. "If we're not gonna talk, can we dance at least?"

"But you said your feet hurt," West said, looking down at my red open-toed heels with straps that tied around my ankles like they were the devil.

"Well, they're feeling better now. See?" I wriggled

my toes. "Let's go into the other room."

Rocky frowned in confusion. "Since when do you like hip-hop?"

Like Vixen, I was also a huge fan of Ash and The Basilisks. Who didn't love heavy metal bands fronted by a kick-ass female singer? Ash was a freaking rockstar. But, if Mieko was going to pluck up the courage to make her move, we needed to give them space.

"Since when do you know what I like?" I snapped, marching onwards while the two of them trailed after me.

I pushed through until we were in the middle of the dance floor and let my body move to the music. I tried to ignore the simmering unrest growing between my companions as they stood still, shooting daggers at each other. Were they out of their minds?

"Come on," I encouraged them. We were not playing a game of musical statues, you had to move in the middle of a fucking rave. "Dance!"

West brushed my hair away from my face to lean in close and whisper in my ear, "Your ring looks good in this light."

I held it up in front of me and the ruby glittered under the strobes. I couldn't go anywhere in public without it if we wanted everyone to believe our act. My ring *was* pretty. Considering the unlikelihood of me marrying for real, I was pretty damn happy if this was the closest I'd ever get.

"It's too flashy," Rocky sniped.

I pouted. "Don't tell me you're jealous we're getting married?"

Rocky's expression turned thunderous. He moved behind me, placing his hand on my waist and forcing our bodies to move together to the beat. Had it suddenly got very hot? Or, was I slowly being suffocated in the middle of a man meat sandwich?

"Your ring means nothing," Rocky said, so only I could hear, "I know the real you, remember?"

"We're here to dance." I stepped out of his grasp. "Not talk."

West took advantage of the opportunity by grabbing my hand. He drew me closer to him like a fish on a line. His leg slipped between mine, coaxing mine apart and rocking our hips in time. Because of his size, I'd expected West to have zero rhythm but, from the way he moved, he knew exactly what he was doing. *I bet dancing isn't the only thing he's good at*, my vagina taunted like a bad yo' momma joke. What the hell had gotten into her? She was like a fucking rose in desperate need of watering.

I spun away from West, then raised my arms in the air and brought them back down over my sides, trailing down my curves. West closed the gap between us, cradling my swaying hips with his giant hands. While my ass circled West's crotch, Rocky stood in front of me and pulled my arms around his neck. If Zander was around, he'd knock both of them the hell out. He'd made it clear he wanted to be the only one to touch me.

Grinding in a club wasn't against the rules. We were supposed to do this, right? It was all innocent. If dancing would get the two of them to play along nicely, it was in everyone's best interest. Zander wouldn't want them to make a scene and attract unwanted attention. The Sevens had to present a united front. What other choice did I have?

We were so wrapped up in the moment we didn't

notice a figure watching us from across the warehouse. A figure who crept up behind us to ruin our evening as soon as the song ended.

"Hello, Kitty." A chilling voice snapped the invisible thread tying me to West and Rocky. "Pleased to see me?"

Hiram.

The floor turned to water beneath my heels. I struggled to stand. Even the party seemed to go into slow motion as I turned around to face him. I knew he would come to find me. Hell, I'd been expecting it since I'd left Blackthorne Towers... but now it was finally here? It'd come too fucking soon.

Hiram flashed me his twisted smile, making me want to carve his eyeballs out with an ice cream scoop. He was in his forties but looked younger. Most women would find him attractive. You could mistake him for a handsome doctor if you didn't know any better. As he'd aged, Hiram had only grown a sharper and more menacing edge. He liked to take care of his appearance and wore an expensive navy suit, which he'd think nothing of ruining with the blood of his victims.

Rocky sprung into action, pushing me behind him to provide a blockade of muscle. He stared Hiram straight in the face and growled, "You need to leave."

West's hands held onto my waist to stop me from falling. In the ocean, fish could sense predators coming. West may not know who Hiram was but, judging from how hard his fingers dug into my sides, he knew a shark was in our midst.

"Where are your manners? You are forgetting who you're talking to." Hiram tutted at Rocky like a child who didn't know any better. "Don't you remember what happened last time we met?"

Rocky stepped forward, but I was quicker. I grabbed his arm to stop him before he did something stupid. "Don't!"

Hiram never traveled unprotected. If I hadn't been so fucking distracted, I'd have noticed eyes watching us from all angles. If Rocky made a move to kill Hiram, his men would be on top of us faster than a detonating bomb.

"I've missed your spirit." Hiram's bitter laugh made my stomach churn, as his evil glare didn't leave mine. "You look at home here, Kitty."

"Why are you in Port Valentine?" I spat through clenched teeth. Around us, partygoers danced to a new song, but we stayed rooted to the spot. "What do you want?"

"I wanted to see if it was true with my own eyes." His gaze strayed to my hand and locked on my ring. "The Blackbird was right. It looks like congratulations are in order."

"They are," West responded, placing his hands on my hips protectively. "Do you have a problem with that?"

"You can do better than a caveman, Kitten," Hiram said as his lips curled into a smile. He surveyed West with mild amusement, disregarding him like an annoying mosquito he could swat away. "He's not good enough for someone as special as you."

My stare burned into Hiram's unflinchingly. He had taken me by surprise, but I wouldn't give him any more satisfaction. He had ruined my fucking life. He was the monster who had allowed Raphael Jacobson to torture me mercilessly. He was the bastard who groomed me into submission. He'd transformed me from a shy kid to a woman who could slit throats on command.

During five years under his control, I went to hell and back. He showed me the darkest corners of the human psyche. He filled my head with images too graphic to be included in a horror movie. Hiram wanted me to be his protege. He gave me the skills to bring any man to their knees, but his training would be his undoing.

He believed he taught me everything I needed to know, but he was wrong. I learned the most valuable lesson on my own. Unlike him, I didn't *only* kill to further my agenda. Sure, it helped... but I killed because I wanted to take out fuckers who deserved to be wiped from existence. I killed people because it made the world a better place, and I did it with a fucking smile on my face. Hiram would never understand because he wasn't capable of feeling anything or caring about anyone other than himself. And, like the other beasts I'd put into the ground, I wanted my smile to be the last thing he ever saw.

"Quit the bullshit," I snapped. "Why are you here, Hiram?"

"You changed your number," Hiram replied with a shrug. "You know I don't like being ignored."

"Maybe you should take the fucking hint?" Rocky suggested, cracking his knuckles. "She doesn't want to speak to you. Not now. Not ever."

"You used to be so accommodating when you were younger." Hiram stifled a yawn, then narrowed his eyes.

"Maybe I should have killed you when I had the chance? I still could. All it'd take is the click of my fingers, but I won't… not yet. Where's the fun in that?"

"I don't know who the fuck you are," West said, talking in a calm, arrogant drawl, "but Candy is ours."

"Did you hear him, Kitty?" Hiram threw back his head and cackled like a Disney villain. "*They* think you belong to them. We all know the truth though, don't we?"

"The only person I belong to is myself," I said, stepping out of West's grasp and standing on my own. "I'm a Seven now. But I'm assuming you already know that otherwise, you wouldn't be here. You're a long way from home."

"You never used to respect gangs," Hiram said, unperturbed by the two guys at my side, who looked like they were ready to beat his face to a pulp. He looked pointedly at Rocky. "No loyalty, remember?"

"You know nothing about loyalty," I said, hoping the music would drown the slight waver of my voice. Hiram had a doctorate in manipulation. He thrived in misery. Fucking with people's minds was his number one pastime. "I'm done with your fucking games."

"All I wanted to do was stop by to say hello," Hiram said, adjusting his tie. All the bravado was foreplay, leading up to the main climax. I wanted to give him blue fucking balls and cut straight to the point. "I thought you'd be pleased to see me."

"Do us all a fucking favor and say what's really on your mind."

"I'm not the only one who is playing games, Kitten." Hiram's expression turned frosty as he stepped forward and ran a finger down my cheek. He lowered his voice to make sure no one else could overhear. "I'm here to remind you of where you belong. I came to ask you to come home. It'd be easier for everyone if you agreed and came quietly."

"Over my dead fucking body," I snarled, jerking my face out of his noxious reach.

West and Rocky straightened up, gearing for a fight. If I ordered them to kill him, they may have a chance of snapping his neck before Hiram's men swooped in. But, if they did, none of us would get out of the Smoker alive.

"Pity. Everything could have been so much simpler." Hiram smiled wryly and checked his golden wristwatch. "I'm sure we'll see each other again soon. Remember, Kitty, I have eyes everywhere."

Hiram turned his back on us and melted into the crowd as if he'd never been there at all. *Was that it? He was giving up so easily?* My heart hammered in my chest, looking around to see whether snipers were ready to shower us with bullets. Instead, the party continued. Everyone was oblivious to the devil who lurked in the shadows.

"Is anyone going to tell me who the fuck he is?" West asked. "Why was he calling you Kitten?"

I had no time to give him answers.

Not now.

Not here.

My adrenaline kicked into overdrive, and I took off at speed. I raced through the mess of limbs, shoving people out of my way as I passed. Our Sevens night was officially over.

Hiram came to Port Valentine to spook me. He wanted me to know he was close. He wanted to reassert his dominance and make it clear he'd never let me go. When would it end?

I burst out of the warehouse, gulping the cool night air and letting it fill my lungs. My body shook — not from fear, but from being consumed by a wave of venomous anger. Hiram wanted to force me into a corner. His bitter poison sought to pollute my new life.

"Candy!" Rocky barreled out the exit after me. He hurried over to try to wrap his arm around my shoulders, but, instinctively, I shoved him back and winded him instantly. "I didn't see him. I swear—"

"Don't fucking touch me," I hissed. How could Rocky make me feel better after Hiram's reminder of his betrayal? Why did he think he could step into the same role he played in Evergreen as my protector? We were adults, everything had changed. "Leave me alone, Rocky."

"Candy, please!" He staggered forwards, clutching his chest like a wounded soldier. "This is what he wants. You know that, don't you? He wants to tear us apart again."

Rocky's betrayal had cut my soul so deeply that it'd become a permanent open wound. Whenever it scabbed over, a fresh reminder was enough to rip it open and make the blood pour all over again.

The Sevens limo sped around the corner and came to a stop at our feet. West swung the door open. "Get in."

"Don't!" I stopped Rocky from following. "Not now."

"You heard her," West spat as I slid into the backseat next to him. "Call a fucking cab."

Rocky's face fell as I slammed the door shut behind

me. I may as well have stabbed him in the gut. If I didn't get away from him, maybe I would. When my anger boiled over, I didn't trust what I was capable of. Rocky had apologized and vowed to make up for his actions, but seeing Hiram brought it all back. Would I ever get past what he'd done?

The wheels screeched as we sped away, leaving Rocky alone in the dark… just as he had left me.

West's eyes watched me closely like he expected me to explode. "Do you want me to take you home?"

"Can we drive around for a bit?" I tipped my head back, finally breathing easier again, and stared up at the number seven on the roof. "I don't care where."

Driving around in the dark was better than being alone in my apartment and dwelling on what Hiram's next move may be. He didn't enjoy losing. It wouldn't be long before he returned to collect what he thought was rightfully his.

Neither of us spoke again for what seemed like an hour until West finally cleared his throat. He opened a secret compartment concealed in the back of a seat and pulled out an aged whiskey. He poured us both a generous serving. I'd bet Zander usually offered us the cheap shit, and this is where they kept their real supply.

He pressed the glass into my hand and asked surprisingly gently, "Are you going to tell me who he is?"

"No." I downed the amber smokey liquid and held it out for a refill. It was a drink to be savored, but I didn't give a shit. The fiery fuel burned my throat and distracted me from the thoughts rattling around in my mind. "I don't want to talk about it."

"Sharing goes two ways," West said, filling me up again. "You said yourself you're a Seven now."

I drained the glass and wiped my mouth with the back of my hand. "Not everything in my life is up for negotiation."

"I think you've had enough," West said. He pried the glass from my fingers. "If you won't tell me, how does Red know who he is?"

"Why don't you tell me why Red split your lip?" I asked, changing the subject. West kept his mouth sealed shut. "You're not so keen on sharing now, huh?"

Point fucking proven. I wouldn't be able to keep my secret from them forever. News of what happened would soon get back to Zander. When he heard, he wouldn't let it go until he discovered the truth. But it didn't stop me from wanting to hang onto my past a little longer.

West frowned, taking my hand in his and turning my palm up to face him. "You're bleeding."

I'd gouged small crescent moon indentations into my skin from balling my fingers into tight fists. Damn it, stiletto shaped acrylics had seemed like a good idea when Mieko persuaded me to let her fix my nails.

"I'm fine." I snatched my hand away and closed it. I didn't need his fucking concern.

"He didn't seem happy about your engagement…"

"Did you not hear me the first time, asshole?" I snapped, narrowing my eyes. "I said, I don't want to talk about it."

"He seemed possessive." Possessive wasn't strong enough of a word to cover Hiram's obsession. When he sunk his teeth into you, he'd never let you go. When you escaped his reach, he'd do anything to get you back. "I guess we both have crazy exes."

My eyes blazed in anger, digging my nails further into my skin and relishing the pain. "He's not a fucking ex."

Hiram manipulated me into doing his bidding. He enjoyed watching me kill other men, but he'd never touched me. Not like *that*. I wasn't an object of desire to him, but a pet. A loyal dog tethered to him by a fucking collar.

West reached out to take my hand again and uncurled my fingers.

"Want to know a secret?" he murmured under his breath, almost as if he was talking to himself. "I don't have self-control. I mean... when I start, I can't stop."

"What does it feel like?"

"I can't think. I can't feel. There's nothing stopping me. All I can think of is the next punch. The next strike." He traced over the backs of my fingers tenderly. His touch was so soft it almost tickled, like running a feather over your skin. "It started after my pa died. My anger. They put me on the school boxing team to help me channel it. During my first fight, this *thing* inside me... it took over."

A shadow dulled the twinkle in his eyes. I recognized the look. I saw it in the mirror whenever I remembered watching Crystal die.

"What happened during the fight?" I asked, not sure whether I wanted to hear the answer.

"The kid almost died." He dropped my hand and avoided my gaze. "He would have if Zander hadn't pulled me back. Bryce had to pull so many strings to stop the school from expelling me."

When you had a big enough cheque book, it was possible to brush anything under the plush carpet.

"He even paid some of the other kids to stay quiet, including Penny," West continued, hanging his head in shame. "That's what she was talking about in the motel room when we were in Hammerville. Bad things happen when I lose control."

Seeing West's guilt made me hate Penelope even more for her use of emotional manipulation, but I tried to keep my anger in check. I didn't want to spiral when he'd only just started to open up.

"But you stopped in the junkyard," I pointed out, remembering what happened when he released the beast inside of him. The man was a walking powerhouse. He'd be capable of tearing anyone apart limb by limb if he chose to. "You could have killed Eddie, but you didn't."

"Only because you stepped in." West took a swig of whiskey straight from the bottle. "Whoever the guy in the Smoker was, I know he's bad fucking news. Monsters recognize monsters."

"You didn't recognize me," I said, taking the bottle from him and slugging its contents. It has been barrel-aged in a Scottish cave for decades and cost hundreds of dollars, but it still tasted like engine coolant. "Remember?"

He smiled. "You're not a monster, Candy."

"Oops, my bad. What was it you called me the first time you saw me?" I muttered sarcastically, allowing words to spill from my mouth like vomit. "An airhead?"

"Are you always looking for a fight?" He scowled. "The universe isn't against you."

"Isn't it?" I don't know whether it was the alcohol or

West's words causing tears to spring to my eyes. "You may have no self-control, but at least you have somewhere you belong. You're getting better. Hell, you could have killed Eddie in the junkyard, but you didn't. Look at me. I'm fucking broken, West. There's no fixing someone like me."

"You belong here." His index finger stopped a rogue tear from sliding down my cheek. I blinked the rest away, refusing to let myself break down in front of him. "I don't know what he did to you, but I won't let him near you again. I won't let him hurt you. Ever."

Words meant nothing. West didn't know what Hiram was capable of or the influence he had. His empire and reach spanned the entire country. After Hiram absorbed part of the Romano empire, he'd become one of the most feared and powerful men in the criminal sphere. From drugs to human trafficking, Hiram got involved in it all. He ended lives in the blink of an eye. He was an unstoppable force. Was there even any point in trying to fight him? What chance did I have?

"You don't know him like I do." I sniffed. "He won't stop, West. Not until he gets what he wants."

"What does he want?"

"Me."

West put his muscular arm around my shoulder and pulled my shivering body close. I hadn't even realized I was shaking but didn't have the energy to object. Being cocooned in his warm muscles and scent made me feel safe… for now, at least.

"You are a Seven, Pinkie," West murmured into my hair. "He can't have you. You belong to us now."

Maybe I did, I thought, as tiredness took over…

EIGHT

Where the hell was I?
    I woke in a mild state of panic, grappling with the thick white freshly laundered sheets like a fish caught in a net. My eyes darted around the impeccably tidy room. It looked like the lair of a twisted OCD serial killer who covered his tracks.

"Morning." West emerged from the adjoining room in a cloud of steam, wearing nothing but a towel wrapped around his waist. I guess my prediction wasn't wrong…

If my heartbeat wasn't already erratic, it sure was now. Intricate grayscale tattoos adorned West's muscled torso. I could spend days looking at him and still find something new in his ink each time. "How did I—"

"You fell asleep on the drive," he explained, then raised his eyebrows as I peeked under the covers to find I was still wearing my dress from the night before. Across the room, my shoes and handbag were neatly stacked. "Don't worry, I slept on the sofa."

"Thanks for… you know," I mumbled.

"Sorry for waking you," he said, then wrinkled his nose. "I don't use other people's bathrooms."

Waking up to a half-naked man was not the worst sight to see in the morning, but I wouldn't tell him that. Instead, I rolled my eyes.

"Are you hungry?" he asked. "Zander's making food."

"I think I'll shower first," I replied cautiously, expecting him to kick up a fuss about me invading his sterile en suite.

"Be my guest," he said. "It's all yours."

I stumbled awkwardly out of his bed and onto my feet. I needed to get myself away from The Hulk when all that stood between me and his monster cock was a precariously tied towel.

I breathed a sigh of relief as soon as I slammed the bathroom door behind me. Inside, West had already laid out a folded fluffy towel and one of his clean shirts for me to wear, alongside two mini bottles of rose-smelling fancy shampoo. If he ever wanted to start over, maybe he could find success by opening a hotel? Although, he'd probably try to kill anyone who left a mess behind...

After showering, entering the Sevens penthouse kitchen felt like entering a parallel world. Had Hiram killed me last night, and the afterlife resembled a gang edition of the Real Housewives? Zander busied himself behind the counter, while Vixen, Rocky, and West sat waiting impatiently around the table.

"Take a seat," Zander ordered as he finished serving up pancakes and carried them over to the table where a selection of treats was already laid out. He handed me a plate with a serious expression on his face like I was a famous chef about to sample his food. "Enjoy."

"Finally!" Vixen threw me a look of disdain as I sat down next to her, and her stomach grumbled loudly. "Can we start now?"

"You didn't have to wait on my account," I said, diving straight in and stabbing the waffle on top of the enormous pile she had her eyes fixed upon.

Vixen stuck her tongue out. "Bitch."

It's funny how fast life could change. A few months ago, most of the people around the table couldn't bear to be around me. Now, our lives are intrinsically linked.

"Holy shit." I exhaled after taking my first bite. I'd loaded my waffle with maple syrup, bacon, and chocolate chips — was there really any other way? "These are so good."

West told me Zander was a good chef, but damn! His breakfast game was unreal. Why did we ever need to eat out when he knew his way around a waffle iron better than Bella, my old stripper nemesis, knew how to give a blow job?

"Did you sleep well, Candy?" Zander asked.

There was a sharp undertone to his voice, which put me on edge. I looked at West for help, but the giant was too busy filling his plate to notice. Opposite West, Rocky sipped a black coffee and didn't touch any of the food. The tension between the two of them hadn't lifted after last night.

Suddenly, the door to the living area creaked open and everyone spun around to watch Mieko sheepishly stumble in wearing last night's clothes.

"What are you doing here?" I asked.

Mieko's cheeks pinked. Judging by the rips in her tights and the lack of grazes on her knees, it looked like someone acted in a hurry.

Holy shit… finally!

My wing woman duties paid off. Hiram may have ruined my evening, but at least some of us had a good time. Although, if Vixen hurt her, I'd kick her ass… regardless of her Seven status.

A smug grin spread over my face and I turned to Vixen, "Is *your* guest joining us?"

"Of course she is." Vixen pulled out a chair for Mieko, like her sleeping with my best friend wasn't a big deal. "You need to try these pancakes, Mieko."

Mieko smiled shyly as she slipped into place at Vixen's side.

"We're expecting another visitor," Zander said.

The buzzer rang as if he'd planned it perfectly. Zander was either psychic or had cameras linked to his wristwatch. He disappeared to answer it and returned seconds later with Q.

The guys nodded at Q in greeting, Mieko squeaked a hello to introduce herself, and Vixen simply scowled. All the while, I kept my stare focused on Zander. What game was he playing?

"Take a seat, Cupid," Zander said. "Thanks for coming at short notice."

From the sheepish expression on Q's face, this wasn't one of his usual house calls. Zander had summoned him…

Shit. Zander wanted answers, and by inviting Q, it meant he'd already found them.

This wasn't *just a* nice breakfast.

It was a fucking ambush.

I threw Zander my filthiest look in accusation and dropped my fork. "How long have you known?"

He calmly met my gaze. "Long enough."

"Why didn't you say anything?" I demanded, crossing my arms. My life wasn't a fucking book anyone could read. I'm the only one who could tell my story. "We had a deal."

"Look," Q began, shuffling awkwardly in his seat, "after the night at the Maven—"

"I'm asking Zander," I snapped, shutting him down.

Q held his arms up to surrender, then slouched back to hide behind Mieko to avoid having to look at me. *Smart move.* He knew better than to get in my way. He'd never enjoyed confrontation and knew what happened when I lost my temper.

"I didn't break our deal," Zander said. "I didn't go looking for answers. Cupid came to me."

Finding out about Hiram coming to town must have been what it took for Zander to reveal his hand. If he hadn't, how much longer would he have kept the knowledge stored away?

"It wasn't your story to tell, *Cupid*," I snarled.

"I didn't want the same thing to happen to you as…" Q's voice trailed away as his thoughts strayed to Crystal. "I didn't tell Zander any details. All I told him was how we knew each other from… before."

Wanting to make sure Hiram didn't kill me may be an honorable reason for divulging my past, but it didn't make me any less furious. Why hadn't Zander said anything before?

"Is someone going to tell me what the fuck is going on?" West slammed his fists on the table, making it rattle, and looked at the three of us. "It's to do with him, isn't it? The guy who showed up last night."

"Mieko, you should leave," Zander said. "This is Seven business."

"No," I objected as Mieko rose to her feet. This was *my* business and Mieko was a friend amongst a table filled with assholes and hidden agendas. "She's not going anywhere."

Mieko shot a nervous glance at Zander and stammered, "I don't mind going…"

"I want you to stay," I insisted. "I don't wanna go over this story again, and I want you to hear it."

Mieko had already told me her biggest secret. It's only fair she heard mine. I may have to put my trust in the Sevens because of our business arrangement, but I didn't owe them the same level of loyalty I owed her. The night she helped Vixen and me dispose of a body showed me she was someone who I could trust.

"Fine." Zander relented with a sigh. "Mieko can stay."

She sat back down obediently, and Vixen squeezed her hand. She must be as skilled in the bedroom as she was on the pole to get the Ice Queen to show affection.

"Someone needs to talk," West growled. His cheeks reddened in anger and accentuated his scar. "Now."

I took a deep breath. Whether I liked it or not, my past was going to be laid bare for everyone to see.

"The guy who showed up at the Smoker is the biggest kingpin on the west coast," I began. "You name it, he's involved: drugs, women, weapons… the whole fucking deal. I used to work for him. For the last five years, I was his right hand."

"What kind of work did you do?" West pressed.

"Would you shut the fuck up and let her talk, West?" Vixen snapped, then turned back to watch me intently. "Go on, Candy…"

"I did bad things," I admitted. "Bad things to bad people. Extortion, arson, theft, murder… you name it, I've done it. Fuck, I don't even know how many people I've killed. I lost count at thirty. It wasn't just my job, it was my whole life. Whatever he said, I did without question. I was under his spell. Until—"

Q cleared his throat.

"Until I saw who he really was," I added hastily. He didn't need reminding of the day Crystal died. "All that matters is I got away. When I left, we made a deal. I did… something… in exchange for my freedom. We even had a contract written up. But a deal changes nothing in Hiram's mind."

"Hiram? You mean *the* Hiram?" Vixen gripped the table and looked at Q for confirmation. He nodded. She knew enough about Q's decision to forge a new life to connect the dots. "Fuck…"

"So, that's how you knew how to dispose of a body," Mieko murmured.

"Hiram trained me." I nodded. Something he would wish he hadn't one day. "He taught me everything he knew."

"Like, an assassin school?" she asked.

I couldn't help but laugh. Only Mieko could make my time with Hiram sound like a scene out of Harry Potter.

"Blackthorne Towers is more like a fucking prison," I explained. "Five years there is enough to send anyone insane. Hiram manipulates people. He has… his ways.

Ways of breaking people down until they're nothing more than his puppet."

"And he wants you back to work for him," West hissed through clenched teeth. "I won't let it happen."

"You don't know what Hiram is capable of or the power he has," I said. "This is all a game to him now, but he's never going to stop. Not until he gets what he wants."

"How did you get into it?" Vixen questioned. "How does a guy like Hiram even go about recruiting a kid? You must have been young when he took you to Blackthorne Towers."

"Sixteen," I confirmed, catching Rocky's eye. He hadn't told the Sevens about our shared past, because he was ashamed. Knowing what he'd done would change their perception of who he was. He wanted to make amends and, just because I'd never get over his betrayal, it didn't mean everyone else had to make him suffer for his mistakes. "I guess I fell in with the wrong crowd."

Or fell in love with the wrong person...

Rocky took a deep breath and cleared his throat. "You don't need to cover for me, C. Not anymore."

Zander's head whipped around to stare at his friend in surprise. "What's going on, Red?"

Q must have told the truth when he said he hadn't told Zander everything. It wouldn't please a control freak like Zander to know he didn't know the full story.

"You don't have to do this, Rocky," I said. I respected how he wanted to take accountability for his actions, but he hadn't thought this through. Didn't he know his admission could get him kicked out of the Sevens? Or worse…

"Everyone needs to know what I've done, Candy."

Rocky held his head high and met my gaze. "I've lied to you. All of you."

"Red?" Vixen's voice shook. "What're you talking about?"

"Candy and I knew each other when we were kids. We grew up together in Evergreen," he said. "When Candy says she fell in with the wrong crowd, she is talking about me. *I* was the wrong crowd. *I* made a deal with Hiram. *I* was the one who handed her over to that bastard. It's my fault she ended up in Blackthorne Towers and lived through those years of torture. It's all on me. All of it."

Rocky had apologized to me before, but talk is cheap. Actions spoke louder than words, and this? Him confessing his sins to the Sevens? It changed everything. Maybe... just maybe... this could help me on my journey to fully forgiving him.

A stunned silence descended over the table at Rocky's revelation. Vixen's mouth opened and closed like she couldn't decide what to say first. Zander looked between Rocky and me, trying to discern whether Rocky was telling the truth, then gritting his teeth when he realized he was. Mieko caught my eye; her only concern was checking whether I was okay, while Q continued to hide behind her to blend into the background. West was the first to act.

He jumped up like he'd taken an adrenaline shot straight to the heart. "You did, what?"

"Sit," Zander ordered.

West's nostrils flared as he considered charging at Rocky.

"Please, West," I pleaded. "Let him explain."

Reluctantly, West returned to his seat. Even though

he was looking at Rocky like he wanted to tear his balls off.

"Let me get this straight," Vixen said, trying to wrap her head around his story, "you two *both* grew up in Evergreen?"

"Yep," I confirmed. They already knew Rocky's history. Them knowing we were forged in the same screwed up system is all they needed to know.

"Why didn't you say anything, Red?" Vixen addressed Rocky with the ferocity of a hungry hyena. After forming a close bond together in juvie, she'd take not knowing his secret the hardest. She put him on a fucking pedestal. "Why didn't you fucking tell us? Why didn't you tell *me*?"

"It was, and still is, the biggest mistake of my life." Rocky's eyes sought solace at the bottom of his cup. "I was ashamed, okay? I was a stupid kid and thought I was doing the right thing. But I was wrong... so fucking wrong."

"I knew there was something between you," Vixen declared, putting the pieces together. "When you came back from seeing the Razors months ago, Candy held a fucking knife to your balls. I brushed it off, but shit! Why didn't you say anything then? You had a chance."

"How do you think it feels to be constantly reminded of the worst thing you ever did?" Rocky asked, hanging his head in shame. "Whenever I look at her, it's all I see. I did something terrible to the one person I cared about more than anyone else."

"You cared about her?" West growled, wanting to get to the bottom of our relationship. "So, what were you? Friends? A couple?"

"It doesn't matter what we *were*," I stepped in to stop

West's line of questioning. I'd already revealed enough. They didn't need to know every detail of my life, including how Rocky was the person I'd lost my virginity to. It was irrelevant, and nobody's fucking business. "It was a long time ago, okay? So much has happened since then. Now, we're just two members of the same gang. That's it."

"You should have told us, Rocky," Vixen snarled, turning on him without pity. "We're *supposed* to be a family."

"All families have secrets," I muttered.

The Sevens had more than most.

"Don't defend him." Zander's commanding voice made everyone sit up straighter. He sent Rocky a glare so chilling it could have stopped a volcano from erupting. He would not let this go lightly. I don't know what made him madder: how he didn't know about our connection or learning what Rocky did. "Get out of here, Red."

Rocky nodded solemnly, leaving without saying another word. Unanswered questions hung in the air.

"Pinkie, if I knew—"

"Don't." I held up my hand to interrupt West. "I don't want to talk about it again, okay? You all know now. There's no more fucking secrets, and I think it's time I go too."

After laying out my past like a road map, it zapped all of my energy. I may have just woken up, but all I wanted to do was crawl back under the covers and never come out.

"Wait up!" Vixen grabbed my arm as I stood to leave. "Do you even know what day it is?"

"Funnily enough, checking the calendar is not something I'd had time to do today," I snapped sarcastically.

"It's Christmas Eve." With everything going on, I'd completely spaced on the date, despite the dancers being dressed like elves in the club for weeks. Although, with a name like Lapland, it was like Santa's dirty grotto all year round. "You're staying with us for Christmas."

"I'd rather be on my own."

Vixen crossed her arms and put on her strongest boss bitch voice, "This is not up for negotiation."

"But I don't have my things—"

"I'll get a driver to take you home and bring you back," Vixen said, then turned to Mieko. "What are you doing for the holidays?"

"I mean, I didn't have any—"

"You're staying too," Vixen decided, with an air of finality. There was no point in arguing when she hadn't given either of us any choice in the matter. "You too, Cupid. We're a fucked up family, but we're all sticking together. No arguments."

"I'll sleep on the sofa," West volunteered gruffly. He was still recovering from his earlier outburst. It'd take him a few rounds with a punching bag to release his simmering anger. "You can take my bed, Pinkie."

"What do you say, Zander?" Vixen pushed.

"I'll order more turkey," Zander grumbled reluctantly.

Vixen clapped her hands together. "It's settled then."

This would certainly be a Christmas to remember.

Vixen bundled Mieko and me into a car, giving the driver very strict instructions to escort us to our apartments and bring us straight back.

"Where does she expect us to run to?" I scowled. "It's not like I have anywhere else to go."

"I think it's cute she's being protective."

I scoffed. "She only gives a shit about me now because she thinks she owes me something."

"I don't think that's true," Mieko said, thinking the best of everyone as usual. "What do you think is going to happen to Red?"

"That's up to Zander," I said, trying not to let my thoughts wander to what his judgment would be.

Zander wouldn't do anything to hurt him, right? Rocky made a mistake, but he didn't need to keep being punished. Once upon a time, revenge is all I thought about, but now? Things had changed.

"I'm sorry about what happened to you," Mieko whispered. "I know you don't want to talk about it. You don't have to. But, if you ever do, I'm right here."

"Thanks." I squeezed her hand, touched by her care. "And you know I'm here for you too."

"I know." She squeezed back, then frowned. "Do you think the Sevens are really okay with me staying for Christmas?"

"Vixen invited you," I pointed out, then winked. "You must be a pretty good lay."

"I don't want to mess things up with her." Mieko wrung her hands in her lap. "What if she thought last night was a mistake? Maybe she felt she had to invite me out of pity?"

"Trust me, Vixen wouldn't have invited you, if she didn't want you there," I said. Vixen had no shame and didn't give a shit about who she offended. "Last night must have been pretty special…"

"It was." Mieko blushed, then her face turned to horror as she yelped like someone had poked her in the eye. "What about presents? We don't have any presents!"

I rolled my eyes at her sudden hysteria. "You can't be serious right now…"

"We can't turn up with nothing," she wailed like Armageddon had descended. How come she wasn't bothered about sharing a ride with a serial killer but gift shopping tipped her over the edge? A giggle-snort escaped my lips. "What's so funny?"

The seriousness of her face only made me laugh more. I laughed so damn hard my shoulders shook, and I worried I'd pee on the seats. To anyone looking in, I must have resembled a demented clown on crack. Mieko soon joined me. Both of us laughed until fat tears rolled down our cheeks and our jaws ached.

"Pull over at the next gas station," I ordered the driver.

Between us, we had seven dollars and twenty-five cents. The Sevens may be used to lavish gifts, but this was our only option.

I'd never really celebrated Christmas before. In Evergreen, a cold slice of meat and lukewarm vegetables was the best you got. My only fond holiday memories were days spent with Rocky. Christmas in the Evergreen group home was usually quieter because the other kids spent time with distant family members. One year, Rocky smuggled a portable television upstairs into his room. We watched Home Alone four times and ate so much chocolate we almost threw up.

When the car came to a halt outside the gas station, we bundled inside.

"What can we get?" Mieko asked, roaming the aisles in despair and attracting strange looks from other shoppers because of her hysterical tone. "All we can get is candy."

"Well, we'll get candy then," I said decisively.

After dwelling over choices of candy and spending twenty minutes annoying the cashier, he eventually caved and said he'd cover the cost of the bars where we fell short. Who said the Christmas spirit was dead, huh?

As we piled back into the car, Mieko looked down nervously at the assortment of snacks. "Should we wrap them?"

"I've got foil back at my apartment."

Who wouldn't want a wrapped up Twinkie as a gift?

NINE

After a quick stop at our apartments to collect our belongings and ten calls from Vixen to track our whereabouts, we finally arrived back at Lapland. The club was closed for the next few days, so the street was unusually quiet without music blaring.

Mieko pushed the door open, and her eyes widened. "Wow."

A long banquet table decorated with garlands, flickering candles, and fake snow had taken over the dance floor. Christmas trees of varying sizes decorated the different podiums. Lights twinkled through the cage bars, where dancers usually performed, catching the sparkly surfaces of the baubles strung across the ceiling. I blinked twice to check I wasn't imagining things. Had we stepped into a motherfucking grotto?

West's head poked around the side of the largest tree on the main stage. He was the only person tall enough to reach the topmost branches. He gestured down at the red Christmas sweater he was wearing, with a giant reindeer in the center. "Vix really takes the holidays seriously."

"I can tell," I murmured. How many balls of wool would have been needed to knit a sweater so large? "Who knew she'd traded her piercings and leather pants for pointed ears?"

"Where's the music, West?" Vixen screeched from behind the bar. If she worked in the North Pole workshop, the elves would unionize against her leadership. "You said you were putting it on ten minutes ago."

West cursed under his breath and disappeared behind the boughs. A few seconds later, 'Santa Baby' started playing. I mean, we *were* still in a strip club.

Mieko admired the table decorations, running her hands over the crackers, as Vixen joined us to lay the final touches. "It all looks amazing."

"There's not enough room for everyone to sit in the penthouse," Vixen replied nonchalantly. Although, the slight twitch of her lips hinted at her appreciating Mieko's compliment and trying her darnedest to hide it. "Can you help me hang the rest of the lights upstairs?"

"Sure!" Mieko jumped at the chance. Vixen's vagina must have done some weird Christmas voodoo on her. "Do you want to help, Candy?"

"You two go ahead," I insisted, not wanting to be a third wheel. "I'll hang out here."

Not that I had any company. Q sat alone in a booth, typing furiously away on his laptop. When he was in the zone, he wouldn't want to be disturbed. Meanwhile, West's obsessive tendencies extended to dressing the tree. I watched as he held up a ruler to measure the exact distance between baubles. There was no sign of Rocky or Zander. Had Rocky returned, or would he spend Christmas Eve roaming the streets?

"Candy," Zander's voice called to me from an open door, extinguishing any ounce of my festive cheer like a snowfall. "I need to see you in my office."

After our dramatic breakfast, something told me this conversation wouldn't go down well.

In his office, Zander gestured for me to sit down opposite him.

"I'm sure you know what I want to talk to you about," Zander said, watching me closely from across his desk. He'd changed and was wearing a black Christmas sweater with 'ho, ho, ho' over the front, which made him appear a lot less threatening than he intended. Vixen must have forced him into wearing it.

"Where's Red?" I asked.

"Out," Zander replied abruptly. His smoky gray eyes pierced mine, searching for answers he wouldn't find. There was also something else lurking in his eyes. Anger, perhaps? Finding out about Rocky and I's past had irritated him. "Red won't be coming back. Not unless you want him to."

"You're leaving it down to me?" My mouth fell open. Zander never relinquished control to anyone. Did he expect me to believe he'd suddenly had a personality transplant? I arched an eyebrow. "What's the catch?"

"No catch," he said. "Loyalty is everything in the Sevens. We can't change what Red did, but we can change the future. If you don't want him around, all you need to do is say the word. I can make him disappear."

"You'd kick him out?" My words came out in a furious burst as I slammed my clenched fists down on the wood. "After everything he's done for you?"

Ending Rocky's life used to be my sole motivator, but everything was different now. Even though Zander was on my side, his ability to turf Rocky out like garbage made my blood boil. Rocky was no fucking angel, but he'd been part of their gang for years. After hearing Nico's praise during our visit to Hammerville, I learned how Rocky helped to set up their growing business. Where the fuck was Zander's loyalty?

"You're a Seven now. Red wronged you, so the decision lies in your hands," Zander said with zero emotion. "Whatever you choose, know it is final. The Sevens don't give second chances."

Wasn't this what I'd been waiting for? It was my last chance to erase Rocky from my life for good. I tried killing him myself but failed. Now, I had the opportunity to stay in the Sevens and never see him again.

"How long have I got to decide?" I asked.

Zander cocked his head to the side, watching me closely. "How long do you need?"

Rocky had caused me unthinkable pain, but he was also the only person who I'd truly loved. The joy we had shared only made his betrayal more pronounced. He played a part in sending my life down the wrong path but, until then, he'd given me a reason to live.

My mouth started moving before I even realized what I was saying.

"He can stay," I blurted out.

No punishment would compare to the mental torture Rocky inflicted on himself every day. I knew how he felt. Whenever I looked at Q, my chest ached from the raw anguish of knowing I was the reason Crystal ended up dead.

"Noted." Zander nodded curtly. His shoulders slackened slightly. Despite his icy demeanor, he cared more than he let on about Rocky's fate. "But know there will be consequences for his actions."

"What will you do?"

He paused. "I'll think of something fitting to his crime."

"Well, whatever it is, keep me out of it," I huffed, crossing my arms over my chest. "I'm over all of your macho drama. You guys are worse than the dancers. First, Rocky punched West. Now—"

"He did, what?" Zander cut in sharply.

"It was nothing," I muttered. *Great job, Candy. Way to stick your stiletto in your mouth again.* "Just the usual homoerotic tussle. You don't see me tackling Mieko to the floor and trying to punch her in the tit, do you?"

Zander didn't look convinced. After this morning, how had I not learned my lesson? Zander didn't know everything that went on inside Lapland walls.

"And what do you think of macho guys, Candy?" Zander asked, steering the conversation in a new and dangerous direction. "What type of men do you like?"

Men like him.

Men like West.

Men like Rocky.

Wicked men who set my skin alight, and a twisted part of me fucking embraced it. Men who I should want to run from...

I swallowed hard. "I need to get back to decorating."

Zander looked at me in bemusement. "I didn't think you were into holiday celebrations."

"Says who?" I bluffed defiantly. "I *love* the holidays."

"Yet you didn't know it was Christmas Eve?"

Well, he had me there. *The bastard.* He saw straight through my lies.

"If you hadn't noticed, I've had a lot going on." I flicked my hair to make myself look bored with his conversation. "What's your excuse?"

"There are better ways to spend my time than dressing a tree." He looked me up and down hungrily. My cheeks flushed at the memory of what happened the last time I'd been in his office. Sitting down had only become bearable again. "I prefer undressing my presents."

"Enjoy sitting here alone, Zander," I said, rising from my chair.

"Don't you want to stay and keep me company?" he purred.

"I'm not another one of your girls, Zander," I snapped. My pussy wasn't a hose he could turn on with a flick of his wrist. "I'm not like Bella or the others."

"Oh, I know you're not." A panty-dropping smile spread over his face. "But you can't deny you want me, little one."

"The only present you'll be getting from me this Christmas is blue fucking balls." I flipped him off and stormed out.

The worst thing is, Zander was right. The more time we spent together, the less control I had over my actions. Being in his company was fucking intoxicating. Losing control left me open to being hurt, and worse? Zander wasn't the only man I felt drawn to. He, Rocky, and West had burrowed underneath my skin. Being around them felt like balancing on a cliff edge, so close to plummeting into jagged rocks below.

"Is Scrooge coming to join us?" Vixen asked as I returned to the main area.

"I doubt it," I said, surveying the club again in appreciation. Even the candy stripper pole looked like a purposeful Christmas accessory rather than an X-rated prop. "Who knew you had such an eye for interior design?"

"I always wanted to go to art college." Vixen shrugged wistfully. "This isn't my usual style."

"What kind of art do you normally do?" Mieko asked.

"I paint," Vixen replied, which only made Mieko look at her with even greater admiration.

"She's great," West chipped in. "Not that she ever lets people see her work..."

"Since when are you a fucking art critic?" she sneered. "You wouldn't know a damn Frida Kahlo if it hit you in the face."

"Isn't she the chick with the unibrow?" West asked.

"Exactly my fucking point, West. You're so—"

"Maybe you can show me your paintings sometime?" Mieko stepped in before Vixen could finish her sentence. Damn, she was brave. Who would try to stroke a dog after it'd bit off a stranger's arm?

"Sure," Vixen said, then coughed, trying to cover her keenness. "I mean, only if you'd like to see..."

"I'm almost done with the playlist, Vix," Q called over from his nook.

"Hey," West objected with a moody pout. "You put me in charge of the music. Isn't mine good enough now?"

"Hook it up, Cupid," Vixen ordered, then grinned mischievously. "None of us want to be listening to West's Spotify all night."

The Hulk looked outraged. "What's wrong with my music?"

Vixen snorted. "We're not all into the Spice Girls…"

"I only played Wannabe one time!" West's pout deepened. "So much for you being a fucking feminist."

Lapland's door opening sent a cold gust whistling through the building. Silence descended as Rocky stepped inside. West dropped his box of baubles with a crash and hurtled off the stage with the grace of a raging bull.

"West," I shouted, causing him to reluctantly halt by my side like I'd yanked him on a leash. "Don't."

West turned to face me. I saw the fury and disappointment in his eyes. The Sevens prided themselves on their closeness. Learning his brother hadn't been the person he'd thought had hit him hard. "How can you defend him after what he did, Pinkie?"

I put a hand gently on his arm and whispered, "Don't you have things in your past that you wish you didn't do?"

None of us had the right to act like self-righteous assholes. We'd all done things that could have had us locked up for the rest of our lives. We were all haunted by regrets, but didn't those mistakes make us who we are?

"Candy wants Red to stay." Zander's commanding voice echoed towards us, as he stepped out of the shadows. "If she wants to move past it, we must respect her decision."

Rocky blinked back tears of disbelief. "You really want me to stay, C?"

"It doesn't mean there will be no consequences," Zander cut in. "You will pay for what you've done."

"I understand." Rocky hung his head in shame, then turned to address me. "You know I'll do anything to make things right again with you, don't you?"

I nodded curtly, but couldn't meet his gaze. When I first returned to Lapland, Rocky appeared to be confident and outgoing. The longer I stayed, the more he turned into a ghost of his former self. My presence forced him to confront his feelings about what he'd done. Seeing him like this made me wonder whether it would have been kinder to kill him. This is the second time I'd saved his life, but what had it achieved? It only caused him more suffering.

"All of us have a past," I said, aware everyone's eyes were on me. "But it doesn't mean we have to punish ourselves forever. I don't want anyone's pity. I don't want you seeing me as a fucking victim. The only thing I want is to get Hiram out of my life for good, and I can't do it alone."

"We'll deal with Hiram together," Zander vowed.

"He will never take you away again, C," Rocky promised. "We won't let that happen."

"I'll fucking kill him if he tries," West growled, redirecting his anger away from Rocky to a better target.

"From now on, we trust no one outside these walls," Zander continued. "My father and Giles aren't the only ones mobilizing against us. Now, we have Hiram too. We will take them down together. All of us."

I looked at the faces around the room. We had all done fucked up shit but, for the first time since joining the Sevens, I finally felt like one of them. Alone, I was vulnerable. But together, with Mieko and Q? We were all in. *I* was all in. Heads would roll if anyone stood in our way.

West nodded in agreement, then turned to Rocky and held out his hand. Rocky took it and West pulled him into a man hug to slap him on the back. "Welcome home, brother."

Vixen cleared her throat to get our attention. "Now, before we take down all the motherfuckers, can we try to have a *nice* Christmas? For once, I'd like to have a few days without planning revenge."

"We can do that, right?" I aimed my stare at the Seven guys, then poured myself a glass of eggnog and raised it in the air. "Merry fucking Christmas, Vix."

The rest of the day passed in a weirdly wonderful blur. Zander served up a delicious meal, and we played drunken rounds of charades. We were so used to living in a world filled with darkness; it felt amazing to let loose for a change. Maybe Vixen would convert me to becoming a Christmas lover, after all...

"I'm callin' it a night," Q slurred, getting up from the table. The poor guy was a lightweight and had been trying to keep up with the guys. He'd be nursing a banging headache when he woke up. "See y'tomorrow."

"I'm feeling pretty tired too." Vixen yawned melodramatically, not fooling anyone. "I might head upstairs too..."

"Yeah," Mieko agreed, biting her lip. "I'm feeling kinda sleepy…"

"Sleepy, my fucking ass." I rolled my eyes. If I wasn't so happy for them, I'd have made retching noises. "You could at least try to be subtle about it."

"I don't know what you mean," Mieko stammered.

"Sweet dreams." West smirked, then added, "if you get any sleep."

"Go to hell, West," Vixen shouted, as she and Mieko stood to follow Q out. They had to put their arms around Q's shoulders to help guide him upstairs to the penthouse.

"Vix seems happy," Rocky remarked, as we heard the pair of them giggling in the distance. "I've not seen her like that for… well, ever."

How had she and Mieko not hooked up before now? They'd instantly clicked and had bounced off each other all afternoon. Their conflicting personalities complimented each other. Mieko's sweetness would help temper Vixen's fieriness, whilst Vixen's ball-breaking attitude could push Mieko out of her comfort zone.

"Why don't the four of us play a little game?" Zander suggested. He placed an empty bottle in the middle of the table. "Truth or dare."

"Come on, Zander." I sighed and rolled my eyes. "We're not teenagers."

"What's wrong?" he asked. "Too scared?"

My eyes narrowed. He knew how to get to me. "Spin the fucking bottle."

With a flick of his wrist, it spun in circles and slowly came to a stop in front of West.

"Easy!" West lounged back in his chair casually. "Dare."

Rocky rubbed his chin in thought, then grinned. "How about we get the tattoo gun out?"

"You bastard," West groaned, cupping his head in his hands. "Not again."

"What happened last time?" I asked.

West grimaced and stood to roll down his waistband. *Fuck*. His V-lines were out of this world. I pulled my eyes away to look at where he was pointing and snorted. A wonky inked heart on his hip bone with 'Red' scratched inside.

"How about we add a candy cane next to it?" Zander said. "You don't want to make your *fiancée* jealous."

"Perfect," Rocky said, nodding in agreement.

"Fuck it," West declared. There was no way he could talk them out of it. "Bring the gun."

Rocky vanished upstairs and returned with the case a few moments later.

"Why do you even have one of those?" I asked as Rocky busied himself with setting up the supplies in a booth.

"Vix used to tattoo," Rocky explained. "She got really good in juvie."

"Maybe we should ask her to do it then?" I questioned, thinking about what diseases West could contract. I'd been to enough decent tattoo shops to know sanitation was important. After leaving Hiram, I'd spent time on the road. I'd traded jewelry for cash and got inked along the way. Sure, I could have spent money on more sensible things, but you can't put a price on feeling like you belong in your body again.

All of them laughed. Hepatitis was the last thing on

their minds when screwing over their friend was at stake.

"Come on, C," Rocky said, pouring black and red ink into tiny caps. "Where's the fun in that?"

All of us gathered around the machine as it buzzed to life like a bat outta hell. The sound instantly made my shoulders tense. For people who'd spent many hours in a tattooist's chair, the noise took you straight back there. Thank fuck Zander took me to an actual studio to get my new Seven tattoo last month. Anything was better than getting my skin permanently marked by a group of psychos. Thankfully, West's body was already covered in artwork and a tiny candy cane would blend into the background.

Rocky handed me the gun. "Here."

"You want me to do it?" I gasped as West rolled down his pants to reveal more of his deep muscle lines and a delicious snail trail, leading down to his… "I can't."

"Sure, you can," Rocky replied. "It's easy."

"Do we have any gloves?"

Rocky chuckled, while West lay down across the seats to get himself into prime position.

"Just get it over with, Pinkie," West growled.

I'd watched people tattoo me before. How hard could it be? I dipped the needle into the ink. The gun rattled the bones in my hand and sent vibrations up my arm. How could tattooists make such precise lines? West held his skin taut to expose a small spot of bare skin between other designs. I took a deep breath and pushed the needle into his skin. The first stroke made me jump.

Zander shook his head and tutted. "You can slit someone's throat but can't do a little tattoo?"

His taunting made me push the needle in harder.

"Not so deep," West complained.

My hand shook as I completed the outline, which was about the size of my little finger. I wasn't sure whether I was shaking because of marking West's skin or because I rested inches from The Hulk's massive cock. Eventually, I settled into a rhythm. After the black outline and striped lines, I enjoyed filling in the red. His body was my own freaking coloring book.

"There." I sat back triumphantly to admire my slightly wonky masterpiece with uneven color. "What do you think?"

In twenty minutes, I'd been marked on West's skin for life. He wasn't the first person to have a candy cane tattooed in my honor. When Crystal got her ink, it symbolized our friendship, but it sentenced her to death. Hopefully, this wouldn't seal West's fate, too.

"She's on you forever now, bro," Rocky teased, passing him a towel.

"Fucking great." West scowled in annoyance as he wiped up the stray ink. "Who's up next?"

We all returned to the banquet table, where Zander spun the bottle again.

Fuck... it landed on me.

"What'll it be?" Zander asked. "Truth or dare?"

"Truth."

With the tattoo gun lying around, there's no way I wanted to risk getting a penis in the middle of my forehead or a 'property of the Sevens' tramp stamp.

"I've got one for you." Zander's cool, no-bullshit tone sent a shiver down my spine. "Which one of us would you rather fuck?"

Oh, shit...

I faltered as his gray piercing eyes ran over my curves. I looked at West, whose expression remained as dark and unreadable as ever. Then Rocky, who balled his hands into fists on the table.

All three of them were criminals. They'd all done twisted and terrible things. Their damaged pasts had brought them together, and they formed a bond deeper than blood. They were a family. Brothers. They were also all devastatingly panty-meltingly gorgeous.

How could anyone choose between them?

First, there was Zander. The leader with no limits. If you went against him, you'd be dead. No questions asked. Zander had a ruthless efficiency and vicious streak that made the hairs on the back of my neck stand on end. He had the money, power, and connections to get whatever he wanted no matter the cost. While he got off on power, more depth hid beneath his angular jawline. Zander was a fierce protector and didn't trust easily. He'd gut anyone who crossed his family and if you were in, he'd never let you go...

Then there was West. The giant who could rip your legs off with his bare hands. When West saw red, violence was the only language he could understand. He was a powerhouse of brute force and would do whatever needed to be done for those he cared about. Underneath his thick biceps, West had a softer side too. As much as he liked to make out he was a monster, the big, scary beast protected an inner teddy bear. Even if he was too scared to show it or admit how he felt...

Finally, Rocky. The only person I'd ever truly loved who betrayed me in the worst way. Gang life and Redlake had changed him. Over the years, he'd seen and done things no one should ever have to do. This is not the life he'd have chosen for himself and he hated himself for it. His anger at the world made him an unpredictable loose cannon who could explode at any moment, but I still caught glimpses of the funny laid-back guy I fell for as a teenager. Would it be possible for him to find his way back, or was he too broken to fix?

"Tell us who you want to fuck, Candy," Zander repeated.

Why the fuck hadn't I chosen dare? Flashing my tits would have been easier.

"I can't choose," I said finally, refusing to look them in the eye. "All of you."

On their own, they were powerful, but together? They were unstoppable.

"At the same time?" A sly smile crept over Zander's face. "Maybe we could arrange that."

He looked pointedly down at my nipples poking through the thin fabric of my shirt. Goddammit. Why did my body have to betray me? I'm supposed to be a badass chick with no feelings; yet, the twins instantly perk up at the thought of having a... wait, what the fuck would it be called? A foursome? A gang bang? A four-way fuckathon?

I jumped up. "I'm going to bed."

Yep, an icy shower would stop my cock-hungry vagina from wanting to munch on a man meat sandwich. I ignored their laughter and raced upstairs. Alone.

"Merry fucking Christmas to you too," Zander called after me.

Now, I didn't *want* all of them... I fucking *needed* them.

TEN

"It's Christmassssss!" A voice roared through the door like Noddy Holder. "Wake up!"

After my confession during our game last night, it was a relief to wake up in West's bed alone. The big man's mattress was as comfortable as a freaking cloud.

The light flicked on above me, causing me to shield my eyes and squint at the shadow looming in the doorway. "Vixen? Is that you?"

"Get the fuck up, Candy," she ordered, then continued to march down the corridor to screech at everyone to gather on the sofas. Aren't holidays *supposed* to be a time for relaxing?

"Okay, okay!" Rocky's cries of objection were drowned out by splashing water. Was waterboarding a fucked up Seven tradition? "Goddammit! I'm up!"

I jumped out of bed before Vixen got the chance to return and dragged myself to join the others, who had the same idea. I usually slept naked, but I was glad I'd decided to pack a tank top and shorts set. Rocky, still cursing, arrived with wet hair stuck to his forehead and a towel draped over his shoulder. There was always a casualty in a war.

I took a seat next to Q, who groaned and clutched his head. "Why did I agree to this again?"

Vixen scowled as she sat down, finally content after rounding us up like fucking sheep. "It's ten-thirty, asshole."

"I don't know what you're complaining about, Cupid." West glowered at him from the other end of the enormous sofa where he'd slept. The sight of him sprawled over the cushions without a shirt and in gray sweats made my stomach somersault. "You kept me awake with your snoring."

Zander didn't sit down with the rest of us. He busied himself in the kitchen, already chopping vegetables with ruthless precision. He knew his way around a blade. I'd never seen Zander without a suit before, but he suited his casual black T-shirt and jeans.

"We've already been awake for hours," Vixen declared smugly, slinging a protective arm around Mieko's shoulder. Mieko, unlike the rest of us, looked positively glowing in Vixen's oversized band T-shirt.

"I bet you have," Rocky chirped, unable to resist a cheap shot, making the rest of the guys snicker.

"Nice tattoo." Vixen raised an eyebrow at West, spotting the candy cane poking out of his waistband. She missed nothing. "It looks fresh."

"Truth or dare," Rocky confirmed, as West pouted and pulled his pants up to cover it.

"Fucking idiots." Vixen rolled her eyes, then rubbed her hands together and called over to Zander. "Is breakfast ready, Zander?"

"Of course," Zander replied, pulling a tray of

mouthwatering pastries out of the oven and leaving them on the counter.

The prospect of food instantly perked up Q's mood, and he clambered over my legs to be the first to dive in.

"Aren't you joining us?" I called over to Zander, as we piled our plates.

"I'm not hungry," he said, without looking in my direction and staying focused on his preparation. It seemed criminal he'd got up early to make us an incredible feast, but not touch it himself.

"Save some space for later." Vixen glared at West, slapping his hand away as he reached for a fourth croissant. In response, he added another two to his mountain.

"Cut him some slack, Vix." Rocky elbowed her in the ribs. "It is Christmas..."

After we filled our plates, we returned to the living area where conversation broke out in smaller groups. I seized the opportunity to speak to Mieko, while Vixen and Rocky tried to steal food off West's plate. They'd be lucky to keep all of their fingers.

I lowered my voice. "So you had a good night, huh?"

"I keep thinking this whole thing is a dream," she whispered. I raised my brows, then she added hastily, "Not *that*. I mean, Christmas. It's never been a good time for me. Since my grandma died a few years ago, I've spent it alone. But, this? It almost feels like being with a proper family."

We watched as West almost stabbed Rocky in the hand for trying to steal a pain au chocolat he had his eyes on. Sure, this may not be a traditional family Christmas, but it's the closest I'd gotten to a normal holiday season. In the past, the day had only highlighted everything I didn't have.

"I'm glad you're here," I said. "Although, I still think you're mad for hooking up with the Ice Queen."

She smiled. "She's not as much of an Ice Queen as you think…"

I held up my hand to stop her. "Spare me the dirty details."

"Besides, what about you?" Mieko asked, wiggling her eyebrows suggestively. "What happened last night after we went to bed?"

"We played a stupid game," I mumbled.

Yeah, a stupid game where I admitted to wanting to fuck all three of the Seven guys. Hopefully, my admission would be brushed off as a result of drinking too much of Zander's amazing eggnog.

Mieko leaned in closer. "Don't think I haven't seen how they look at you."

"I don't know what you mean," I said unconvincingly.

"You'll have to face it eventually…"

Vixen plopped herself down next to Mieko. "What are you two whispering about over here?"

"Nothing," I interjected, shooting Mieko a glare to make sure she kept her mouth shut.

"This tastes amazing." She crammed a mouthful of food into her mouth, causing her cheeks to bulge like a cute squirrel. "Mmm!"

Thankfully, Vixen didn't notice. She was too busy waiting for everyone to finish their food, so she could move on to her next item on her Christmas morning agenda.

"Is everyone ready for presents now?" Vixen asked

as Rocky finished the final crumb on his plate. A chorus of groans followed her question. "Cheer up, you miserable fuckers. Zander, you need to get over here, too."

Zander opened his mouth to object, but changed his mind after seeing the look on her face. He could see she was one step away from her entering full-on boss bitch mode.

"Okay," he agreed reluctantly, slowly lowering the knife. "I'll give you five minutes."

Vixen dove under their perfectly decorated tree to gather presents, as the rest of us stayed rooted to our comfy spots. She pulled out the badly wrapped foiled candy bars and held them up in the air.

"Who brought these?" she demanded.

"Let's do ours first," I said, biting the bullet. Mieko and I did what we could to source the gifts in haste.

"But they don't have labels," Vixen said, tossing them to me to distribute and throw at their intended recipients.

"Sweet." Rocky unwrapped his Snickers and started to scoff it straight away. "You remembered my favorite."

"Oh, was it?" I shrugged nonchalantly, pretending it was a fluke. How could I forget his penchant for Snickers when it used to be 99% of his diet? Considering his childhood malnutrition, it's a miracle he'd grown to be so tall and lean.

West winked at the sight of his Twinkie. "I'll eat anything."

Mieko bit her lip and mumbled apologetically, "It was a little last minute..."

"Don't worry, Reeses are my favorite." Vixen kissed Mieko on the cheek, making her light up brighter than Lapland's neon sign.

Zander discarded his candy to the side in distaste. I'd bet he wouldn't eat anything not made by a Belgian chocolatier.

I crossed my arms. "If you want something more extravagant, you need to pay your dancers better, Zander."

Before Zander could respond in his usual snarky fashion, West thrust an impeccably wrapped box into my hands. "Here. It's from all of us."

A lump formed in my throat. "Oh."

I ripped off the paper to find a box with a beautiful pocket knife nestled inside a sheaf. A sparkling ruby embedded in the hilt perfectly matched my ring. At the base of the knife, the number seven had been expertly engraved into the silver. When I lived in Blackthorne Towers, Hiram used to give me gifts. They usually took the form of expensive dresses, perfume, and shoes, but the knife? It seemed so... thoughtful. Hiram taught me caring about others was a weakness, but maybe he was wrong.

"Do you not like it?" Vixen watched me closely, then turned on the guys. "I told you I should have got the Jimmy Choos."

"No, this is perfect," I murmured. The blade was well-balanced and almost weightless. I'd never go anywhere without it. "I love it."

Vixen beamed. Who knew she had a beautiful smile underneath her resting bitch face? She proceeded to throw the guys their gifts. Their unwrapping process was total carnage. Shreds of paper flew over the place like a detonating pipe bomb.

Finally, there was only one box left under the tree. Vixen held it out for me. "Someone sent this for you."

My mouth went dry. From the black paper and silky silver bow, I knew instantly who my Secret Santa was. I took a deep breath. "It's from Hiram."

Zander jumped to his feet, dropping his new Rolex with a crash.

"Don't worry," Vixen said quickly. "I already had security check it out. It won't hurt her."

Everyone watched as I carefully opened it. A single black rose rested inside the tissue paper with a neatly written note.

These were always your favorites, Kitty.

They *used* to be my favorites. I *used* to be proud of who Hiram had turned me into. I *used* to be grateful for him showing me another way to live. I *used* to see myself in the black rose. Now, all I could see was something natural polluted by evil. Instead of admiring it, I wanted to destroy it. Just like I wanted to destroy him.

I ripped off the delicate flower head and let the petals flutter down at my feet.

"Are you okay, Candy?" Mieko asked, gently placing her hand on my arm.

"Never better," I said, slamming the box shut along with my memories.

Hiram had already taken so much from me. I wouldn't let him ruin my Christmas, too.

"You can come through now," Zander said, opening the door. He had exiled everyone in the dressing room for the last hour while he completed the finishing touches. It was a great opportunity for me, Mieko, and Vixen to dress Q, West, and Rocky in strange elvish hats and ears we'd found lying around.

We followed Zander to the main club area and banquet table.

My mouth fell open. "Holy crap, this looks…"

"Amazing," Mieko said, finishing my sentence.

I couldn't even find the words to describe how delicious everything looked. How had Zander made all of this? He must have a secret stash of house elves hidden in the underground tunnels.

Zander shrugged as if it was only a takeout from Taco Bell. He grabbed a plate and cutlery. "I'm eating in my office."

"No way, it's Christmas day," Vixen argued, but West caught her arm to stop her. She looked like she wanted to say more, but West shook his head quickly to silence her. Whatever look passed between them was enough to make her sigh and let Zander leave without resistance. What the fuck was his deal?

We all sat down around the table to eat.

"This is the best meal I've eaten in years," Q murmured, spilling gravy down his shirt. He had always been a slim guy, but he was the thinnest he'd ever been. Grief affected the body as much as the mind.

"Enjoy." Vixen grinned, spooning out green bean casserole and creamed potatoes onto her plate. "Save space for dessert."

ELEVEN

Why was Zander still skulking around in his office?

After serving dinner, he'd avoided everyone for the rest of the day. He'd missed West's embarrassing attempts at miming out 'Finding Nemo' during charades, then Rocky's hilarious acting out of 'Legally Blonde'. With everyone else wallowing in a food coma watching 'It's A Wonderful Life' in the penthouse, I decided it was the perfect time to track the miserable fucker down.

"It's your funeral, Candy." Vixen wished me luck. "Zander is not a holiday person."

We'll see, I thought, as I stormed down the stairs to find him. I rapt hard on the door. What business couldn't wait a few hours to spend time with his fucking family? He didn't answer, so I burst through.

"I'm busy," he snarled as his eyes snapped up from a pile of papers.

"Are you always such a Grinch?" I clicked the door closed behind me. "You're missing all the fun."

"I'm not interested," he said flatly, then spun around on his chair slowly and opened a drawer in the cabinet behind him to rifle inside. "But while you're here, I have something for you..."

I frowned. "For me?"

He pulled out a thin leather box and slid it across the desk toward me. "Open it."

I did as he asked. A gorgeous silver necklace with a circular pendant nestled against crushed red velvet. I pulled it out gently to get a closer look. One side of the pendant was smooth, while someone had etched thin roman numerals into the other. I ran my fingers over them. 2... 3... 1... 1... It's a good thing I paid attention during history class.

"What do the numbers mean?" I asked.

Zander was a womanizer, but, even he, didn't have time to fuck that many women.

"They add up to Seven," he replied. "It's platinum."

"Yeah, I can do the math," I muttered. What I wanted to know is why he hadn't saved the cash by getting the numeral for seven engraved. But I didn't feel bratty enough to ask — I mean, it must have cost a bomb.

"Thanks." I snapped the lid shut. I could understand them giving me a knife as a present, but this? Something felt off. "But I can't accept this."

"Don't be rude, little one. It's a gift." Zander's voice turned frosty. "Aren't you even going to try it on? Let me help you."

"Fine," I huffed. Reluctantly, I pulled my hair back as Zander joined me on my side of the desk. "I'll try it."

"This necklace will bring you luck," he said, gently slipping the cool chain around my neck. He could choke the life out of me if he wanted to. "Think of it as a present for passing your initiation and getting Cheeks on board. Now it's on, you can't take it off. Whatever happens."

I touched the strange necklace, which, unlike most things Zander owned, didn't seem brand new.

"What if it doesn't go with my outfit?" I joked.

"I mean it," Zander hissed, "never take it off. Promise me, little one. Whatever happens."

"Okay, fine. I promise." I rolled my eyes. Every time we were alone, it became strangely intense. Zander had a way of making me feel completely naked. I changed the subject to lighten the mood. "So, are you going to tell me why you're hiding away now?"

"I'm not hiding," he said. "I have work to do."

"Today?"

"What's wrong?" A small ghost of a smile lingered on his lips. "Missing me?"

"I'm just curious about what you're up to," I said, picking up a paperweight and playing with it in my hands. "Vixen said you didn't like the holidays. How come?"

"There's nothing to say. It's never been an occasion I've enjoyed celebrating. You can imagine it used to be a big occasion in the Briarly household," he said wryly. "My father always felt Christmas had to have a special… impact. It's when he used to do his best work."

He didn't need to continue for me to know what he meant. Bryce waited until the happiest time of year to deploy his most twisted schemes and leave a young Zander alone to explore the dark corners of their creepy gothic home.

"I've never enjoyed Christmas either," I admitted.

The season always felt like a special club I wasn't part of... until now.

"Red told me about what it was like at Evergreen."

"They were some of the better Christmases I've had..."

Like Bryce, Hiram thought killing over the holidays had a theatrical flair. As well as ruining family dinners, he used to enjoy mailing body parts out to victims' children. Horrified relatives had to explain Santa's elves had suddenly turned into psychopathic little monsters who killed their daddy.

"You don't mind Cupid being here, do you? I thought he might bring memories back," he probed, resting on the edge of his desk. "How well do you know each other?"

"He used to work for Hiram," I said, keeping my answer short and avoiding his gaze. "Our paths crossed from time to time."

"Why do I get the sense you're lying to me?"

"There are some things I don't want to talk about," I snapped. Although I'd suffered at Hiram's hands, Q had been punished the most. Losing your soulmate was a wound that would never heal. "You may know about my past, but you don't need to know all my secrets."

"I'll find them out, eventually. It's inevitable."

I folded my arms. "Why do you always act like everything's a game?"

"Isn't it?" He cocked his head to the side, studying my reaction. "I'm not the only one playing games here, Candy."

My mouth turned dry, and I stammered, "I don't know what you mean."

"You think you can play us all." Zander trailed his

finger across my collarbone, then shot me a devastating smile. When Zander went on the charm offensive, I could see why girls dropped their panties for him. He knew all the right words to say, but I knew better. Underneath his smile lay a vicious predator. "Usually, I'd never let a girl come between me and my brothers, but you're not like the others."

Zander may have figured out that Rocky and I had a brief fling as teenagers from our reactions yesterday, but there's no way West had talked about what happened in Hammerville. He'd been the one who'd insisted we'd keep our mistake a secret.

"No, I'm not just *any* girl," I replied, staring back and mirroring his intensity. "I'm pretty fucking skilled with a knife."

"I've been thinking about it," Zander said. "How we're going to fix the problem."

"Oh?" The feel of my new knife tucked into my waistband gave me the extra reassurance I could get out alive if I needed to. "And what conclusions have you come to, Your Highness?"

Zander was the leader of the Sevens, but he was also a lone wolf. He didn't answer to anyone but himself. He should remember how he'd cleaned up the bodies of five men I killed before jumping to any conclusions I didn't like.

"You're a Seven right down to the blood running through your pretty veins, but you're poison." Zander stepped closer, leaving only inches between us. His breath tickled my neck as he whispered, "Until you, the brothers were united. But now? You'll destroy us from the inside if I don't act."

"What do you plan to do about it?" I spat, squaring

my shoulders. "Kill me and cut me out of your gang because none of you can keep your hands to yourselves?"

"Not kill you." Zander laughed as his eyes glinted mischievously. "*Share* you."

"I'm not a piece of meat you can pass around," I said, my voice wavered slightly.

"You didn't seem to mind the idea last night," Zander went on. Shit, he must have been more sober during the game than I'd thought. "You're the one who gave me the idea."

"I'm a Seven," I said, regaining my assertiveness. "Not one of your groupie whores."

"Oh, I know." Zander put his hands on my hips and yanked me towards him. "I wanted to have you all to myself, but I can see it's going to cause us problems. The Sevens can't have secrets, and you're the little secret we've all been keeping. I'll be willing to share you with my brothers. On one condition."

"What condition?" I shot back sarcastically.

"Before sharing you with them, I get to have you all to myself."

I went to shove him, but he caught my wrists before they hit his chest. The spark from his touch sent a shiver down my spine. "Have you ever thought that maybe I don't want *you*?"

"Your body tells me otherwise." Zander shot a knowing glance at my hardened nipples. I may as well have a flaming 'please enter' flashing sign above my fucking head. "Do you think I haven't noticed how you are around West? How he squirms around you? How he tried not to look at you for weeks? Or, how about Red?

How he looks like he's ready to throw himself in front of a bullet whenever you're around?"

My heart rate quickened, but I kept my legs and lips pressed shut. Zander always had a hidden agenda. How was I to know this wasn't another of his plans? He enjoyed asserting his dominance and, after seeing him in action in the tunnels of the Maven, I knew he enjoyed women. A lot. How did he expect me to believe anything he said was real?

"You're the only woman who hasn't been afraid to say to me what you think," Zander continued. "You want us to be done with keeping secrets, don't you? You wanted to be all in. Sharing you is the only way."

"Don't you think Red and West get a say in this?" I called his bluff.

West lost his shit over me drinking his coffee. He wasn't exactly the sharing type. Then, Rocky… with our history, I couldn't even imagine how he'd react.

"We all want you, little one." The heat radiating off Zander's body made my throat feel like it was closing, and I needed to gasp for air. "I know you want us, too. "

"I won't be another Bella," I hissed. "I'm not waiting at home while you go out and screw other people. I'm not your fucking toy, or anyone else's."

I knew what they were like. Unlike them, sex meant something to me. My body may melt like wax under Zander's touch, but I'd rather die than become a trademarked Seven personal Kleenex.

"You're not a toy to me, Candy." Zander stepped back and dropped his hands to his sides. "I would never hurt you. You may think I'm a monster, but I'd kill for you. I'm going to make sure we bury Hiram for what he put you through."

"Not if I get to him first," I muttered.

"Your problem is our problem," Zander said with fierce determination. "We'll finish him together, but I'll let you deliver the killer wound…"

I snorted. "Who knew chivalry wasn't dead?"

"It may surprise you to know I can be a gentleman when I want to be." Zander stroked my cheek with gentle tenderness. "You're a Seven girl, remember? *Our* Seven girl."

Our Seven girl. I liked how those words sounded on his lips. He took a step forward, his hands trailing up my thigh.

I slapped his hand away. "I thought you were supposed to be a gentleman."

"I can be." He grinned, making the rose on his cheek dance. He was the same as the flower. He looked fucking angelic on the outside but hid thorns that could tear you into pieces. "But I didn't say I was going to be."

"Admit it," Zander whispered. "You want me as much as I want you."

Zander was the most arrogant, head-fuckingly smart, calculated, and twisted… his lips crushed me, stealing all my oxygen and putting a stop to my traffic jam of thoughts. His tongue probed my mouth with an unquenchable hunger. It wasn't just a kiss. He was fucking stealing my soul every second his mouth was on mine.

He pulled away, giving me a chance to come up for air.

"Take off your dress, Candy," he growled. Something about his tone told me this wasn't a question.

I raised an eyebrow. "You think you can unwrap me like a present?"

Zander grinned wickedly. "Why don't you sit on my lap and see what happens?"

"What if I don't take it off?" I asked, swishing the hem of my dress.

He looked me up and down then said, "Then I'll bend you over my knee and spank you so hard you won't be able to sit down for a week."

My cheeks flushed as I undid the bow holding my dress together. It fastened at the waist like a kimono. Zander watched my every move. He looked at me like a bomb he wanted to dismantle. It wasn't a friendly look. It was the same look a lion gave a gazelle before it sunk its teeth into its neck and tore it apart.

I let the dress fall open to reveal my underwear and felt pleased I'd worn one of my only matching sets of lingerie. My black bra may have shrunk in the wash, but it made my tits look great. Who says you can't rock lingerie and black combat boots together?

"Lie back," Zander ordered.

"Wait, what...?"

Zander pushed everything off his desk with a crash. Papers fluttered to the floor, pens rolled away and a glass smashed. Even his fucking lamp cracked.

"On the desk," he said, walking me back until my ass perched on its edge.

His firm hand grabbed my hair and forced my lips to his in a kiss that made me forget my name. Zander's hands snaked their way up my back, and fingers expertly unhooked my strapless bra. I froze as he threw it at our feet.

Zander usually fucked supermodels. I was used to being paraded in front of a crowd in scantily clad clothes, but no one had seen me this exposed since I lost my virginity to Rocky.

"You're so fucking beautiful, little one," Zander breathed, sensing my hesitation as he caught one of my hard nipples between his fingers and a moan escaped me. "This is all about you."

His hands slipped down further, making my heart race. Once we crossed a line, there was no going back.

"Zander, I—"

"Shh." The corners of his mouth twitched upward in a devilish grin as he pressed a hand to my mouth. The fingers of his other hand brushed over the thin fabric of my panties. He could feel the slick wetness soaking through. There was no hiding how much my body craved him. His fingers slid over my panties and circled my clit in slow, torturous circles. "There's a good girl."

He slid my panties to the side to slip his fingers into my underwear. My wetness met his hands as two fingers slipped between my lips, teasing my entrance. I pushed my hips into his hand, but Zander only laughed and pulled out of my panties. He wanted to make me beg.

"You're a bastard, you know that?"

My whole body craved more. Needing to be touched more than I needed oxygen. My pussy pulsed and all the blood rushing to the heat between my legs could have set his fucking desk alight.

"I'll give you what you want." Zander licked my slick from his fingers. *Tasting me.* "But only if you agree to be ours. *Our* Seven girl."

Between my legs, his hard erection pressed against me in the promise of what was to come. All I had to say was a few words.

"I'm *a* Seven," I said, ignoring my vagina screaming in objection like the guy from the 'Save Britney' video. Why was my brain being so fucking selfish? "Isn't that enough for you?"

"Fucking you isn't about getting my cock wet." Zander stroked my inner thigh, making me struggle to stay standing. "As much as I want to fuck your sweet little pussy, this is about more. You're not like the others. I'm asking you to be *ours,* and only ours."

How is a girl to think straight while his magic fingers are playing a fucking symphony on their thighs?

"Your body already knows that you're mine," Zander purred. "But I can stop if—"

"No," I interrupted, more violently than I'd expected. "Don't stop."

"Then tell me what you want," Zander murmured into my neck, as he slipped his hand back into my panties and found my entrance.

My experiences made trusting someone impossible. But I was already a Seven and, as much as I tried to resist, I couldn't hide my attraction to Zander, West, and Rocky any longer.

"You," I whispered, finally relenting to his will. "*All* of you."

I gasped, my head rolling back, as Zander pushed two fingers deep inside me until I felt the cold edge of his gold ring digging against me. I gasped as he withdrew and twisted his fingers around, slipping inside to stroke my swollen G-spot.

I cried out. Being with him felt like a devastating inevitability. The moment my mind stopped resisting, my body took over. I wanted him. Every fucking inch of him. I reached to pull up his shirt, wanting to feel his skin, but Zander grabbed my wrist to stop me and tutted.

"Sit," he ordered.

He pushed me backward until my ass was firmly on his desk and forced my legs apart. He slid my panties off so fast I hadn't realized they were off until I saw them in his hands. I tried to close my legs, but Zander stood between them. He didn't give a fuck whether I felt exposed. He wanted me spread wide and open for him.

"Don't hide from me, little one." He looked down at my pussy like the big, bad wolf who wanted to devour me. "I love seeing how you're dripping for me."

My breathing quickened as Zander started to kiss down the length of my body. He took my nipples into his mouth, swirling his tongue over my tented peaks then caught them between his teeth and made me yelp. He grinned and continued to trace his tongue down my stomach.

"Your piercing is fucking hot," he murmured, pausing to admire my silver jewel belly bar. I bucked my hips in frustration, making him chuckle. I didn't want a fucking compliment. I wanted him to touch me. Zander sensed my impatience, but he didn't speed up. No, he was taking his sweet time and enjoying every fucking second. His tongue tickled my ribs, roughly kissing down my snake tattoo, which coiled to my hips.

Zander paused, looking up at me, and grinned. "I've been waiting to taste you from the moment I first saw you."

"Zander, please…" I begged. If he wasn't careful, I would drip all over his fucking desk.

He took to his knees, grabbed my hips with his hands, and pulled me towards him. Having a man like

Zander bow down at my pussy like he was worshipping at an altar gave me a whole new sense of power. His tongue darted out, licking the length of my slit and spreading me open wider to taste my juices.

"You taste fucking incredible," he murmured, licking his lips, then burying his head between my legs.

I moaned, as his tongue found my clit and he applied soft pressure with his tongue. I wanted more. Hell, I fucking needed it. I ground against his face, as his tongue explored me like he was eating the best tasting ice cream. If Zander was skilled with his hands, holy fuck, his mouth was on another level. When Rocky and I were younger, we'd messed around, but neither of us knew what we were doing. But Zander had years of experience. He knew exactly what he was doing. He knew how to make a woman feel fucking incredible.

My legs shook with anticipation as my orgasm built. I held myself back, resisting the urge to tip over the edge of no return when Zander rose from his position. He undid the buttons on his shirt, but didn't take it off. His muscles flexed, as he unsheathed his belt, springing his cock to life.

It'd been five years since I'd last had sex, but I was no stranger to playing with toys. But this was not the same as using my cute pink rabbit… where was West's fucking ruler when you needed it? Eight inches? Nine? Hell, it could even be ten.

I eagerly reached out to feel his silky head.

"Be patient, little one," he promised, stepping closer and catching my hand. His cock felt hot against me as he parted my lips and slid himself up and down to coat his shaft. "You're doing so fucking well. Now, lay back and show me what I've been waiting for."

I lay back on his desk, legs spread, bearing my whole soul ready for the taking. Zander stood between them, grabbing my ankles and wrapping them around his neck. My flexibility from dancing around the pole was paying off now.

"I want to watch you while I fuck you," he purred. "I want to see all of you."

I gasped as his cock teased my entrance, rubbing against my wetness. I liked the feeling of him against me. We shouldn't be doing this. We shouldn't be mixing business with pleasure, but I wanted him. Damn, I wanted him more than I'd wanted anything, and I couldn't think of anything beyond this moment.

"You're so wet for me," he praised, as the head of his cock pushed into me. A twinge of pain followed, making me wince. "What's wrong, little one? I know you can take me. I can feel how ready you are."

I bit my lip as his cock slid deeper. Zander didn't need to know he was the second man I'd ever had sex with. *Holy shit.* I felt like I was being impaled. Was 'death by the sword' another way of saying killed by cock? As another inch slid in, my pussy started to open up and become accustomed to his girth. The pain was quickly replaced by the overarching feeling of fullness. His cock seemed to pulsate as he pushed in, burying himself as far as he could go, with a smug smirk.

"You're mine now, Candy," he said, beginning to thrust harder. His eyes never left mine, watching my whole body jerk with each of his purposeful motions. "You're my fucking girl."

Screwing my boss had never been part of the plan, but I wanted him. So fucking badly. Zander bent forwards, arching his back. The position hits my clit and sweet spot at the perfect angle. My breathing grew more ragged. He'd kept me on the edge for so long that my body begged for release.

"I want you to come for me," Zander ordered, as he coaxed my orgasm to the point of no return. I didn't need him to ask me twice. I cried out as my pussy squeezed his cock, like it never wanted to let go, as pleasure erupted from my core. "Now, say my name. I want to hear you say it."

"Zander," I moaned, rolling my head back and bucking my hips against him. My orgasm rippled through my whole body like a fucking tsunami. "Fuck, Zander."

At that moment, the office door burst open.

Zander didn't stop. His hips slammed into me harder, like it was the last fuck of his life, and sent my moans into an uncontrollable fucking tailspin. It was like we were at the top of a rollercoaster and started hurtling to the ground with no chance of pulling the brakes.

"What the fuck?"

I heard the shock in Rocky's voice as I turned my head to see him and West standing in the doorway. Finding Zander balls-deep in me was not the sight they'd expected to be met with.

My body shuddered as I gasped in surprise. I was already coming hard and couldn't stop, even though we had an audience. Instead of wanting to push Zander off, my pussy clung to his cock. The adrenaline burst and the shock of knowing West and Rocky were watching only intensified the sensation. The rational part of my brain had shut down, and I couldn't restrain my moans because of how freaking amazing it felt. Zander continued to thrust, riding the wave of my climax, then bucked into me for a final time, shooting a burst of heat between my legs. He had no fucking performance anxiety.

"We'll come back later," West growled, looking at us in disgust.

I was trembling and tried to say something, but it was too late. He slammed the door closed behind them with such force it made the wall shake.

Holy fucking shit.

Zander grinned, as he pulled out of me and zipped up his pants. "I told you I'd make you mine."

From the look of satisfaction on his face, he knew exactly what he was doing and who was watching. I wouldn't be surprised if he'd somehow paged the two of them to arrive at the perfect time. He wanted to mark his fucking territory.

I sat upright and pulled the sides of my dress closed around me. "Did you plan this?"

My pleasure was turning into a raging fury. How could he be fucking casual about this? Didn't he care about the consequences? Or, about what West or Rocky would say? Shit, I didn't know whether I'd be able to look them in the face again…

"They all have to know who's boss," Zander replied with a shrug. "Besides, they'll get their turn with you, eventually."

"Fuck you," I spat, jumping up and shoving past him.

"Candy?" Zander called after me. He twirled my wet panties around his finger. "You're forgetting these."

I snatched them from him, feeling my cheeks heat and his cum drip down the inside of my leg. "Go to fucking hell, Zander."

TWELVE

After cleaning up in the bathroom, I couldn't put off seeing them forever — even though I'd rather flash my tits to a coach full of freaking nuns than face West and Rocky. *You can do this*, I psyched myself up. *You've killed people, remember? This is nothing.* Ripping off a bandaid quickly is always the best way, right?

As soon as I walked back into the club, Vixen rolled her eyes and Mieko shot me the same smirk I'd given her this morning. It was a lot less satisfying to be on the receiving end of it. Karma is a bitch.

"Where is everyone?" I asked, looking around nervously to check for obvious signs of damage after a West rage attack. So far, everything looked intact.

"Q had to leave and the others went for a drive," Vixen said with a devilish smile. "They weren't happy to find out Zander got the first slice of dessert."

My cheeks burned, but the twinkling lights disguised it. "They told you."

"Sure did, but I'm kinda disappointed…" Vixen

sighed and slapped ten dollars into Mieko's outstretched hand. "My bet was on West."

"You two bet on it?"

"We all knew it was going to happen, eventually. I just didn't know which one you'd screw first." Vixen shrugged innocently. Why was I the only one who *hadn't* thought it was inevitable? "Hopefully it'll kill the sexual tension around here."

Mieko tucked her winnings into her bra and mimed 'I told you so'. I scowled back. They were fucking unbelievable.

"Do you want some pie?" Vixen asked, cutting out a large wedge of pecan goodness and sliding a bowl across the table to a vacant spot. "Do you want more cream, or are you good?"

"Real fucking mature, Vixen," I huffed but took a seat anyway. Dessert looked too delicious to resist and a girl needed a sugar boost to replenish after a mind-blowing orgasm. "At least we can get some before West devours it all."

Outside, the screech of tires caused Vixen to curse under her breath. "It's like he's psychic or something. How did he know I cut into the fucking pie? I've told West a thousand times not to slam on the brakes like that. He's not in a fucking race car."

Zander emerged from his office, bringing with him the festive cheer of a funeral march. The narrowing of his brows hinted whoever was outside was not a welcome visitor.

"We have company," Zander declared as someone started pounding on Lapland's door. "None of you move."

I ignored Zander and rose to my feet, ready to face

our new arrival. He scowled in my direction. "What part of my orders didn't you understand?"

Zander may have given me my daily cost of vitamin D, but it didn't mean I would submit to his demands every time. I widened my eyes and fluttered my eyelashes innocently. "You didn't say please."

Vixen snickered. "It looks like you've finally met your match, Zander."

Zander glowered at her, pursing his lips, but didn't argue with me again. He opened the door to greet the gatecrasher. "To what do we owe this pleasure, *cousin*?"

"It's Christmas!" Giles's English drawl grated my eardrums like the sound of toenails being sanded to the bone. A visit from him was akin to expecting Father Christmas and being met by Darth fucking Vader. "I'm here to return something that belongs to you."

"Come in," Zander hissed. From his glacial tone, it's not the type of invitation you'd accept unless you wanted your pubes plucked out one hair at a time.

Vixen's chair screeched across the floor, and she stood protectively in front of Mieko to shield her from view. "What the fuck are you doing letting *him* in?"

I was about to agree with her when I noticed Giles wasn't alone. Cheeks trawled behind him with shackles around his ankles. His freshly bruised left eye was so swollen he couldn't open it, while the other had a spaced out appearance. How was he able to stand? He looked like a zombie.

"It's a shame none of you received an invitation to lunch at the manor. You missed out," Giles said dryly as I scowled at him. "It was quite the occasion."

"I'm sure it was," Zander replied unflinchingly,

surveying Cheeks's disheveled appearance with distaste. "Father always enjoys playing with his food."

Blood congealing on Cheeks's chin and neck had left him with an unsightly crusty beard. His mouth slackened to reveal where the blood was coming from... a fleshy stump where his tongue used to be.

Mieko gasped, covering her mouth with her hands, at the sight of Cheeks's injuries. Although Vixen was squeamish, she didn't show it. She squeezed Mieko's shoulder to comfort her and gritted her teeth, waiting for Giles's next move. The girl was doing me proud.

"It looks like I arrived in time for pudding," Giles chirped. He cracked a smile and pulled out a chair at the table to make himself at home. "You don't mind, do you?"

"Of course not," Zander sneered, sitting across from him. Vixen and I followed his lead. We'd humor him... for now. "Candy, why don't you serve dessert?"

I scooped out a slither of pie and spat on it.

"Here." I slammed the bowl down in front of Giles. The glob of my spittle rested atop the cream like a garnish. *Eat shit, motherfucker.* "Enjoy."

"You're not as sweet as your name after all, are you?" Giles hissed, shoving it away. The bowl flew off the table, smashing on the floor and causing Mieko to flinch. What a waste of pie…

"Why don't you get to the fucking point already?" I snapped. "Say what you've come here to say, then get out of *our* fucking club."

"Can you imagine how surprised I was to find out what deal you made with Cheeks?" Giles laughed, tipping back and forth in his chair like a gleeful schoolboy. "All I had to do was offer money to get him to talk."

The double-crossing weasel rat bastard. I knew we couldn't trust him. At least Bryce had saved us the effort of keeping his mouth permanently shut. Cheeks would never be able to say another word again. The information he delivered to Zander before he blew his cover better have been worth the trouble…

"So?" Zander stretched out and yawned. "Do you expect me to be impressed?"

"Your father wanted me to deliver the Sevens a message," Giles said, his cheeks reddening in annoyance at Zander's attitude. Damn, what I wouldn't give to leave an imprint of my boots across those plump rosy apples. "He wants you to stop looking."

Stop looking? What did he mean?

"Couldn't you have written your message in a fucking Christmas card?" Vixen asked, balling her hands into fists in front of her.

"Only *family* makes the list," Giles rebutted, making Zander's jaw clench. "Besides, I also brought you a present. One I needed to deliver in person."

Giles stood and pulled a gun out of his jacket pocket, waving it around like a magic wand. Vixen acted fast. She grabbed Mieko and pulled her to the floor as Zander and I got to our feet, ready for whatever came next.

"Merry Christmas, cousin," Giles said in a sing-song voice, then pointed his gun at Cheeks and squeezed the trigger.

Mieko screamed as the bullet ripped through Cheeks's head, shattering his skull and obliterating his brain. His lifeless body landed on the floor with a thump.

Cheeks should have known better than to reveal he

was working for us. Even if he'd offered to feed us false information on their behalf, the Briarlys would never have taken kindly to learning how he'd been a spy. They were happy to send him to the grave like an old dog they no longer had a use for. Delivering a fresh corpse was Bryce Briarly's idea of a perfect gift. How many similar performances had Zander witnessed as a child?

"Is that everything, Giles?" Zander asked, tapping his foot.

Giles's face fell. He didn't like discovering his message hadn't gotten the effect he'd hoped for. *Poor diddums.* What toys would he throw out of his pram next?

Before I could stop it, a manic laugh escaped my lips.

Giles turned on me. "What's so funny?"

"I was just wondering why Bryce didn't send one of his henchmen to deliver his *present?*" I lifted my chin in defiance. I knew exactly how to get a rise outta him. "Are you doing all the dirty work now? I thought you were higher up in the ranks?"

Sure, it's never a smart idea to goad someone with a loaded gun... but, how could I resist? The uppity motherfucker needed a reality check. Think of it as payback for ruining our Christmas. Giles had extinguished any festive spirit along with Cheeks's life.

"I could shoot someone else if you'd prefer. Who's next?" Giles leveled his gun, his hands shaking and less confident than before. He aimed it at Mieko, who yelped and looked close to vomiting. "How about her? You can always replace a whore."

"In your fucking dreams," I snarled, staring him down.

Giles pointed the gun at my head. "Are you volunteering?"

"I'd think carefully about what you do next, cousin," Zander warned. His menacing tone slashed through Giles's courage like a dagger, causing him to lower his weapon and the color to drain from his face.

"We were only playing," Giles dismissed, stashing the gun away. Where was his backbone? He could kill a defenseless man but knew he stood no chance if forced to face his cousin's wrath. "Weren't we, Candy?"

"The only game I can see being played around here is chicken—"

"Candy," Zander interrupted. "Enough."

"What?" I asked, twirling a strand of hair around my finger. "I'm only *playing* — right, Giles?"

"Where is your fiancé, anyway?" Giles asked, flaring his nostrils like a raging bull. "Isn't *he* the one who should be protecting you?"

"We're already cleaning up one body tonight," I hissed. "I don't mind adding another."

Giles's corpse wrapped up in a pretty bow and left on the manor steps would be a perfect way to end the day.

"Have we missed dessert?" West's voice from the other end of the club cut short our confrontation as he and Rocky crept in. For big guys, they sure knew how to move stealthily. West's eyes skimmed over Cheeks's corpse, but his expression darkened at the sight of the ruined pecan pie. "What happened?"

"Giles decided brains would be a perfect addition to dessert," I replied as West joined us and draped his arm over my shoulder. Now, spilling Giles's blood was the only thing I was hungry for.

"It's time for you to leave, Giles," Rocky said. Unlike the other guys, who could remain calm, Rocky's expression was murderous. He was a loose cannon ready to explode, and Giles could sense it. "I'll show you the fucking door."

"No need. I'll show myself out," Giles said. He kicked Cheeks's dead body as he passed. He didn't care whether the blood would stain his tan leather shoes. Everything, and everyone, was expendable to a Briarly. Vixen would be furious she'd have to replace the new floor... again. Giles paused as he reached the exit, then turned to wink at me over his shoulder. "I'll see you around soon, *Kitty*."

Adrenaline surged through my veins with a reawakened bloodthirsty clarity. I felt *her* rise to the surface. The Kitten was ready to fight. If Giles wanted to meet Kitty, then he wouldn't leave Lapland alive. It wouldn't take long to pounce and break his neck in a swift jerk. This pussy had sharp claws and wasn't afraid to bite.

I dove to attack, but West was faster. His arms wrapped around me like an Iron Maiden. I wrestled against him and tried to kick out, but he pinned my back against him to hold me still. There was nowhere I could go.

"Let me fucking go, West," I demanded, thrashing against him.

Giles laughed as Zander slammed the door on him. The others were talking, but I couldn't hear what they were saying. Their voices became a hum like background noise. All I could think about was how we were wasting precious time. Giles was getting away.

Through the rage induced fog, I could hear West's voice in my ear.

"Stop struggling," West whispered, which only fanned the rage burning inside me more. It spread faster than a forest fire at the peak of summer. "You're only making it worse."

West didn't understand what he was doing.

Giles knew about *me*.

About Hiram.

Why were we letting him go?

Cheeks may have been too stupid to see me for who I really was, but Giles had worked it out. Knowledge in the wrong hands would put all of us in greater danger. How long could my secrets stay buried if Bryce Briarly wanted to unearth them? Letting Giles walk away was like signing a death wish for the Sevens.

"Fine," I said, pretending to play his game. "I'll stop, okay?"

West laughed, holding onto me even tighter. "Nice try, Pinkie."

The fucker. As soon as the roar of Giles's car engine faded into the distance, West's grip loosened and I turned on him.

"You fucking idiot!" I pummeled my fists into his chest to take out some of my building frustration. "We should have killed him!"

"You're not thinking straight," Zander said.

"I'm the only one thinking straight," I exploded. "He knows. It makes us as good as dead, don't you get that?"

Zander shrugged and checked his watch. "He's known for a while."

"He's, what?" I blasted in outrage.

Rocky's eyes darted to West nervously. "You might want to hold her back again, bro."

"Don't you fucking dare," I hissed, dodging West's lunge, and pointing at Zander. "You'd better start talking."

"I think we're going to get out of your way," Vixen said, grabbing Mieko's hand. Smart fucking move. "Can we go to your place?"

Mieko nodded shakily. Anywhere would be better than staying at the club with a dead body or around me when I was about to lose my shit. Before the two of them left, Vixen called back, "Please don't kill anyone else, Candy. Remember, the clean-up crew charges triple over the holidays."

"I can't make any promises," I snapped. As soon as they left, I zeroed in on Zander again. "Well? Tell me everything you know. Real fucking fast."

I wanted to rip his head off his perfectly tattooed neck. Why did everyone I had sex with make me want to kill them afterward? Was my vagina cursed?

"The envelope Cheeks delivered contained information about you," Zander explained. "My father has been busy investigating our newest Seven member."

We'd been overly optimistic to believe Bryce wouldn't question West falling for a stripper. The only thing more infuriating than my identity being uncovered was how Zander had kept it a secret. Keeping it from me wasn't his call to make. It was *my* fucking life.

"Why didn't you say anything before?" I demanded, crossing my arms.

"Because I was handling it," he replied smoothly.

"Yeah, it sure looks like it," I said, gesturing at Cheeks's bloody remains. "What information was in the envelope?"

"Pictures were taken at a party on the night

Giovanni Romano was murdered," Zander said. His calm, detached tone put me on edge. "Can you imagine how surprised my father was to see you serving drinks? Especially after hearing what Cheeks told him about the Raphael Jacobson video that mysteriously disappeared. It's a little too much of a coincidence, don't you think?"

He may have forced me to confront my past about how I used to work with Hiram, but I hadn't shared any details. All the Sevens needed to know was that I'd done bad things. Knowing any more would be too dangerous. For all of them. But Bryce's digging had left me with no choice. They were all going to find out what I'd done…

My mouth went dry. "How long have you known?"

"About how you had something to do with Raphael Jacobson's disappearance? Since the first time I saw the video," Zander replied. "Who do you think organized for all the copies to be wiped from Cheeks's hard drive before his arrest? Red got the dancers to erase their copies, and we made sure everything disappeared."

Hiram had been the one who'd arranged for Cheeks to be beaten to a pulp and arrested. I hadn't realized the Sevens were also working in the background to help cover my tracks. Back then, Zander barely acknowledged my existence. Why did he go out of his way to protect me?

"Why go through the effort to get rid of the video?" I asked. "You didn't even know me."

"I didn't want the Jacobsons sniffing around. It'd be bad for business," Zander said matter-of-factly. All he cared about was self-preservation. "It wasn't until later that I realized who killed him. After seeing what you did to my father's men, everything made sense. Then, seeing pictures of you at the Romano mansion—"

"Wait, hold up," Rocky interrupted, holding up his hand. "Let me get this straight. You killed Raphael Jacobson *and* Giovanni Romano?"

West stayed silent but studied my reaction closely. Judging by his tensed jaw and Rocky's incredulous expression, it seemed I wasn't the only person Zander had kept in the dark after learning this information.

"I told you I could take care of myself," I said flippantly. "Would you like a catalog of all the other people I've killed, too? If so, you better sit down because we'll be here a while."

"Holy shit, C…" Rocky ran a hand through his hair and looked at me with fresh eyes. I didn't know whether to be offended or flattered by his shock. "I mean, this is bad. Real fucking bad. I knew Hiram made you do things, but Romano's murder? That's—"

"A big fucking deal? Yes, I know." I snapped. "You remember I said I made a deal with Hiram? He let me go free in exchange for killing Romano."

"Why didn't you tell us?" Rocky asked.

"Why do you think?" I looked down and played with the ruby ring on my finger. My clammy hands made it slip around easily. "I didn't want to relive that part of my life, and I didn't want to put you at risk. Knowing who killed them implicates you all. It's dangerous."

"The Sevens don't run from danger," West said fiercely. "It doesn't matter who you killed before."

"It does, if Bryce is going to use it against us," I reminded him.

"What other evidence does Bryce have?" Rocky asked.

"That's everything," Zander said. "So far."

"A photo at a party proves nothing," West growled.

"And the video with Jacobson? It's gone. Bryce has nothing."

"You might have gotten rid of the video with Raphael, but Hiram will still have copies," I pointed out. "He can expose me anytime he wants."

"But he won't do that, right?" Rocky said, biting his lip. "Not if he wants you back working for him. And… those pictures… you may have been at the party, but it doesn't mean you killed him."

"The Romanos aren't the kind of family who listens to reason," I said. "They shoot first, then ask questions later."

Whispers still circulated about Giovanni Romano's mysterious murder. While his son had taken over and started to work with Hiram, it hadn't stopped the Romano family from yearning for revenge. They wouldn't stop until they got it.

When I struck a deal for my freedom, Hiram never thought I'd be able to kill Giovanni Romano. Hell, men had tried and none of them lived to tell the tale. Hiram had underestimated the will of someone with nothing left to lose. With Crystal gone, death would have been more favorable than staying in Blackthorne Towers forever.

"We need to find out how Bryce got those photos," Rocky said. "Then we can—"

"This isn't your problem," I interrupted. No one else needed to be dragged into my past. I'd made those choices. It was down to me to deal with the consequences. "*We* don't have to do anything. This is my fucking mess."

"You don't get it, do you?" Rocky said. His gaze softened. "You're a fucking Seven, C. We're in this for life."

"A problem for you is a problem for all of us," West agreed. "We're in this together, so we'll deal with it. What's our next move, Zander?"

"We do nothing," Zander said like this was a test. "For now."

"What?" Rocky gasped. "You expect us to sit around and wait for the Romanos to come along and kill her?"

"They could try." I scoffed. If I could take down the ex-head of the Romano empire, henchmen shouldn't cause me any trouble.

"I know my father. If he was going to tip the Romanos off and send them the photographs, he'd have done it already," Zander said. "He is holding onto the information until he wants something. We don't know what that is yet. We need to play the long game."

"I don't like it." Rocky shook his head. "Can't we get back the evidence?"

"Stealing from them will start a war," West said, nipping in the bud any elaborate fantasies about storming the manor. "Zander's right."

Rocky's fists clenched. "But we can't do nothing."

"That's exactly what we'll do, Red," Zander ordered sharply. "If you want her to stay alive."

"If they find out and want me dead," I said, "they'll find me."

"No one is going to touch you," Zander replied. "You're *our* Seven girl, remember?"

The three men exchanged glances between themselves and nodded. I appreciated the sentiment, but the Sevens didn't know who they were up against. They may run a casino, strip club, and weed-dealing operation, but they were no match for the people who could come looking for me... *or Hiram.*

"I have other matters to attend to." Zander pulled out his cell to signal our conversation was over. "I'll be back later. West, I trust you have this under control?"

"Seriously?" I asked in disbelief. We were used to Zander disappearing with no explanation, but vanishing on Christmas day with a dead body in the middle of your club didn't seem like ideal timing. "You really have to go now?"

Zander ignored me to prompt West. "You know what to do."

"I'll call clean-up," West grunted. It wouldn't surprise me if he had them on speed dial…

"Can we talk, C?" Rocky asked. "It'd be better if we're out of the way."

"Sure." I shrugged. I'd never got my kicks from cleaning up the mess after a kill — well, not unless I could get creative with body disposal.

Before I could follow Rocky, Zander caught my arm.

"Remember what I said, little one," Zander said, then lowered his voice so only I could hear, "you are *our* girl now."

His dark, possessive stare pierced into my soul to let me know exactly who *he* thought I belonged to. I turned my back on him before he could see the blush spreading over my cheeks. Even a bullet through Cheeks's head and discovering the Briarlys were closing in on my secrets wouldn't let me forget the ache Zander left between my legs.

THIRTEEN

"Where are we going?"

I followed Rocky through the club, figuring we were heading for Zander's office or the dressing room. Instead, he led me to another door, which I'd always assumed was a storage closet.

"I want to show you something," he said, pulling out a key and twisting it in the lock. He pushed the door open to reveal another stairwell. Lapland was like a Russian nesting doll, filled with hidden openings, secret floors, and an underground bunker.

I raised my eyebrows. "Don't tell me this is your torture chamber?"

I was only half-joking. I knew better than most how such rooms existed in the homes of twisted psychopaths. Hiram's favorite place was his workshop deep in the underbelly of Blackthorne Towers. I didn't want to think about how many people lost their lives there. Hundreds? Thousands? Anyone who messed with Hiram ended up dead, and those who were innocent? Sometimes he enjoyed killing simply for the fun of it.

"This is where I come to get away from it all," Rocky explained, leading the way up the narrow steps. Eventually, we came to another door which opened onto what looked like Lapland's roof. In the middle of it, he had set up two deck chairs. "It's nicer in the summer. Do you wanna sit down?"

"Sure," I agreed, plopping my ass down. My nipples felt like they were about to fall off, but it'd be preferable to sticking around while Cheeks's corpse got dragged out. "It's quiet up here."

Well, apart from the vans pulling up in the street below and hushed voices wrestling with a body bag.

"Doesn't it remind you of the old times?" Rocky asked, then added hastily, "The good times, I mean."

I eyed him suspiciously. "I guess so..."

After watching me moan over Zander's cock and learning I'd murdered the leader of an infamous crime family who could come after us, his laid-back casualness was the last thing I expected. Throwing me off of the roof would be a more natural reaction. Why wasn't he angry? Or maybe he was only pretending?

"What do you say?" Rocky pulled two freshly rolled joints out of his pocket and cocked his head to the side. "Just like the old days?"

I took one from him. "Thanks."

I hesitated, waiting until he lit up first.

"It's not laced with anything," he insisted, and I detected the hurt in his voice.

"I didn't say it was," I replied, balancing the joint between my lips.

"Here." Rocky held out his lighter, and I leaned forward to catch the end.

I inhaled deeply.

Holy shit.

It was better than anything we'd ever smoked in Evergreen. I let the smoke fill my lungs, holding it until my chest felt like it would burst, before releasing it slowly back into the December air. The slightly fruity aftertaste lingered on my tongue. What better way to unwind after witnessing a murder?

"It's good shit, right?" He grinned, watching my reaction, and flicked ash to the side. "I grew it myself. It's our most popular strain. They call it 'Candy's Breath' on the streets. It tastes sweet but pulls a hell of a punch."

I spluttered. Who needs to be a celebrity with a make-up line when your ex names his homegrown bud after you?

"How did it get to this?" I asked, not sure whether I was talking about him growing weed, Cheeks's death, or how our lives had turned out so differently from what we'd envisioned.

"We never got out, did we?" Rocky said forlornly. We may be out of Evergreen, but being a Seven was no less complicated. Kids trying to steal a CD Walkman had been replaced by the Briarlys and Hiram, who cast an uncertain shadow over our futures. "We were set up to fail from the start."

"Do you remember how we used to talk about how things could be?" I asked as I watched the sunset in the distance. The weed had taken effect and relaxed my muscles and mind, allowing me to peel away a layer of armor I kept up constantly. "You wanting to go to college… me coming out to join you later…"

As teenagers, we fantasized about going away to

study, taking road trips — hell, even traveling around the world hadn't seemed out of reach. We were stupid kids who dared to dream and should have known better. Why did we ever think our lives could have been ordinary?

"Sitting on the roof of a strip club and being members of the same gang was never part of the plan," Rocky said, shaking his head. "But we're together again now, right? Us against the world, like we always wanted."

The lights of Port Valentine sprawled ahead of us like a roadmap, and smoke swirled above our heads with unsaid words.

"Why aren't you mad?" I blurted out.

We both knew what I was talking about.

"It's funny." Rocky laughed, leaning back in his chair. "I always thought it was West who I had to worry about."

I spun to face him. "Wait, what?"

"We were fighting over you the night we went to the Smoker." Rocky took his final drag and crushed the roach underfoot. "And all along, it was Zander. Why him, C? West, I can understand, but Zander? You know he's a monster."

Zander *was* a monster. He hid his real feelings under the surface and had a twisted way of showing he cared about people. But if he did care, didn't that make him human?

"Why him?" Rocky pressed, pulling out his papers and tin to roll another joint between his fingers. His brows furrowed in confusion. "Zander is barely even a fucking human."

"It wasn't planned," I stammered, inwardly cringing

at the memory of him and West walking in on me mid-orgasm. "It just happened, okay?"

"Do you want it to happen again?"

Good question. It's something I was still figuring out. I finished my joint before answering. When stoned, I could be more honest — not just with Rocky but with myself, too.

"I don't know," I replied eventually. Zander was the second man I'd had sex with. The thought of fucking him again terrified me, but not doing it seemed even worse. When I lost my virginity to Rocky, he'd been slow and gentle. He didn't want to hurt me and kept making sure I was okay. With Zander, it was different. He fucked me to make me his. The experience had been both amazing and soul-destroying. He wanted me to come undone, and I fucking had. "I'm sorry you had to see... what you did."

"I have one more question for you..." Rocky's voice trailed off as he changed the subject. He paused to light up and blow three perfect smoke rings into the breeze. "When we kissed, at the town hall, did it mean anything to you?"

If it wasn't for the incredibly potent pot, I'd have told him to fuck off. Instead, a small voice in the back of my head urged me to stay.

"It confused me," I answered.

He held his joint to my mouth for me to take a drag.

"Why?"

"For so long, I thought I hated you," I said. "And I did. I mean, I really fucking did... then, suddenly, I realized I didn't. At least not in the way I thought. Kissing you showed me that."

"For what it's worth, I'm glad you didn't kill me when you had the chance," he joked.

I laughed, then his expression turned serious. Was this when he revealed his plan to hurl me to my death?

"What happened with Zander doesn't change anything," Rocky said, staring into my eyes with a deep intensity. "It made me mad, but I'll never make the same mistake again. I let you go once, C. I'm never going to do it again."

"We don't need to talk about this now," I said wistfully as Candy's Breath worked her magic. I pulled my chair closer to him and rested my head on his shoulder. "Let's just sit here for a while, like the old times…"

The two of us looked over the skyline. Sitting on top of the world used to fill us with thoughts of possibility. Neither of us had the same feelings of hope now, but it didn't matter. Somehow, through everything, we'd found our way back to each other. It had to mean something, didn't it?

"Did you two have fun?" West asked coldly when Rocky and I returned to the penthouse. The dropping temperature and high wearing off made it impossible to stay on the roof any longer.

West's gigantic frame took up most of the sofa, as he flicked aggressively through the TV channels. It's a miracle he hadn't punched holes straight through the remote from the force he was using to push the tiny buttons.

Rocky cleared his throat. "I've got to water the plants."

He hurried out of the room, leaving West and me alone. No doubt he had a secret stash of marijuana growing somewhere in the building.

"Did you get cleaned up?" I asked. Goddammit, I should have smoked another joint before attempting to speak to The Hulk.

"Obviously." West's stormy blue eyes studied me closely, looking me up and down to undress me with his stare, then scowled. "I know how to cover *my* tracks."

"You're mad," I said. *Talk about stating the fucking obvious, Candy.* "Look, I didn't know the pictures from Romano's mansion would get out, okay?"

After Zander, West cared about how the Sevens were perceived more than anyone. He'd be furious about the Briarlys holding information over our necks like an axe.

"You think I'm mad about that? I don't give a shit about the Romano party or what you did there." West turned up the volume on the TV so our conversation wouldn't be overheard, then he rose to his feet and approached me. He lowered his voice and snarled, "I didn't think you joined the Sevens to be another one of Zander's whores."

His words hit me like blunt force trauma to the head. When I started working as a dancer in Lapland, insults were a regular part of my day. But I was a Seven now. West had no right to judge or put me in the same category as Zander's old groupies. He knew me better than that… or, at least, I thought he had.

"So, it's not okay for Zander to fuck me? But it's fine if you want to?" I snapped. Unlike my weed namesake, West was about to face a Candy fire-breathing dragon. I'd roast the bastard over my fucking flames like a slab of hunky meat. "You didn't seem to mind breaking any rules when we were in your car or at the motel. You were pretty happy then."

"That was different." West slammed me backward into the wall with his body. He was a hypocrite. Zander was possessive, but at least he owned it. "You screwed *him*, Candy!"

"You're jealous," I hissed.

I knew the damage that West could do, but I didn't want to diffuse the situation. I wanted to draw out the fucking beast and let it loose.

"You don't know what you're talking about."

"Oh, I think I do," I replied, narrowing my eyes and looking up at him through thick lashes. "I'm not one of your airhead playthings. I'm a fucking Seven, and it's about time you started treating me like it. You're only mad because Zander got to fuck me, and you didn't."

West's nostrils flared in fury, and a vein protruded in his forehead. His trembling arms rose into the air and punched a hole into the wall to the right of my face like a passing train.

"If I was going to fuck you," West spat, "I'd do it somewhere better than over a fucking desk."

He stalked away, slamming the penthouse door behind him. It didn't matter what bullshit Zander said about them wanting to share me. How could I get involved with all three Seven men and expect it not to end up in a fucking disaster when being in the same room with them felt like riding a testosterone-powered rollercoaster?

Joining the Sevens had caused nothing but trouble. If I hadn't moved to Port Valentine, Cheeks would still be alive, and Bryce Briarly wouldn't be using my past to trap the Sevens under his thumb. As soon as I got involved, everything seemed to fall apart.

"He'll calm down," Rocky said, appearing conveniently as West's footsteps faded away. I had a sneaking suspicion he'd waited for The Hulk to leave. "Give him time."

Rocky may feel indebted to forgive me for anything, but West didn't have the same obligation. Although, the thought of losing whatever connection I shared with West stung more than I cared to admit.

"Who says I give a shit about West?" I lied, flopping down on the sofa and hugging a bowl of chips. I stuffed a handful into my mouth. The munchies were setting in, and I knew the barbecue ones were West's favorite. I didn't like the flavor much, but I'd polish off the whole bowl before he returned out of spite. "He can do what the hell he likes."

We were supposed to be professionals. West should be able to keep his dick from poking into Seven business relationships. Then again, I recalled my searing rage when Penelope tried to smother him with her perky rack. My stomach churned at the thought of West finding solace in her bed. If West was a hypocrite, so was I...

"I know you, C," Rocky said, sitting down next to me. "You care about him."

"Since when did you turn into my fucking therapist? I'm done talking," I snapped. "We're gonna watch a movie."

Rocky held up his hands in surrender. "Suits me."

I'd already seen Die Hard a thousand times, but it provided a momentary distraction from my thoughts. As we reached the one hour mark, Zander and West's voices alerted us to their return.

Fuck.

I didn't look up from the screen when they entered.

"Space for two more?" Zander asked with a cheeky half-smile.

I kept my legs stretched out while Rocky shifted around to make extra room. Zander may have wanted to assert his dominance earlier, but I was not giving up my sofa territory for his arrogant ass. And, for all I cared, West could freeze his balls off on the fucking roof.

West settled on the furthest seat away from me and scowled at the barbecue chip crumbs. A sly grin spread over my face. It didn't go unnoticed. West clenched his fist and shot me a venomous look, like he wanted to ram it down my throat until I choked.

Nobody spoke for the rest of the movie, but I felt their eyes watching me. Why the hell had Vixen, Mieko, and Q left? Was sticking around while a crew cleaned up a body really *that* bad? They'd have helped to break up the awkward atmosphere.

As the credits rolled, Rocky dared to speak. "Are we going to talk about what happened earlier?"

"That depends," I said, glaring at West in accusation. "Can West have a conversation without punching another hole in the wall?"

West looked down at his lap like a naughty schoolboy. He needed to learn it wasn't cool to destroy property every time someone touched a nerve. "Take it out of my salary, Zander."

"Where have you been, anyway?" I turned to Zander, not expecting him to answer.

"I reached out to some of my associates to find out more about what Giles is up to and what my father is planning," Zander said. As he talked, I sat up straighter to listen. It was rare for him to share his thoughts, so I wanted to pay fucking attention. "Killing Cheeks for betraying my father's trust was logical, but revealing they know Candy's identity? It makes no sense."

"It's not Bryce's style." West nodded in agreement. "The fucker doesn't reveal what he knows until the final second."

"So, you think Giles screwed up?" I asked.

I'd been winding him up, so it's possible he'd given away more than he should have in retaliation. He was hot-headed and would defend his pride to the end, even if it meant showing his hand. Bryce had a lot of work to do if he expected Giles's pompous ass to become his successor.

"If my father doesn't know, it gives us an advantage," Zander said. A plan was forming in his dark, twisted mind. "Giles isn't stupid enough to let him know that he made a mistake."

"So? We still know they have the power to bring me down whenever they feel like it," I muttered.

"Bring *us* down," Rocky corrected, looking pointedly at me.

"The plan remains unchanged. We do nothing," Zander decided with an air of finality, "until I say otherwise."

"C'mon, Zander," Rocky objected, his voice rising. "There must be something else we can do?"

"You're already walking on thin fucking ice, Red," Zander warned, shooting him a frosty glare to silence him. Rocky had crossed a line by keeping secrets from him about our past, which Zander wouldn't let him forget easily. "Don't fucking question me. I make the rules. You all need to trust me."

Trust had nothing to do with it. Doing nothing may be Zander's plan, but being a sitting duck wasn't my style. Didn't he understand the Romanos would be out for my blood if they discovered I murdered Giovanni? They'd kill me, and everyone I'm associated with. I was a puppet dangling on a string until Bryce decided it was time to cut ties and drop me into the Romano wolf den.

If Zander wouldn't act, I'd have to figure it out on my own. I needed to get the damaging evidence from the Briarly Manor before Bryce could share or use the information as leverage. From the look on Rocky's face, I may have an accomplice...

"I'm gonna have an early night," I said, then narrowed my eyes at West. "Enjoy sleeping on the sofa."

My eyes snapped open. Another vivid horror scene filled with blood and entrails. What did normal people dream about? Whenever I was lucky enough to fall asleep, the nightmares were never far behind. During the day, my brain compartmentalized the trauma, but at night? My head turned into a fucking Halloween fun house.

A gentle knock and the bedroom door opening startled me. I sat upright, switching the bedside lamp on, and scowled at the gigantic figure loitering in the shadows. "Do you make a habit of sneaking up on girls when they're sleeping?"

"Hey, Pinkie." West ignored my snarky response and

stepped inside, clicking the door shut behind him. "I couldn't sleep. I heard you—"

"What are you? The dream police?" I snapped, pulling the comforter up to my chin. I didn't want to talk about my sleep quality with a psychopath who pounded bricks like feather pillows. "I'm fine, okay?"

"About earlier..." West exhaled like it was causing him physical pain to speak. "I shouldn't have got up in your face or said what I did."

"Is this supposed to be an apology?" I snarled. "Because, if so, it's pretty fucking lame."

He grinned, and the orange glow of the light illuminated the scar on the side of his face. "I'm not good at apologies."

"Clearly."

"You were right, okay?" He sighed, shuffling from one foot to the other. "I was jealous. Seeing you with Zander made me want to kill him. My own brother. I acted out like a fucking idiot."

"Wait!" I called after him as he turned to leave. West paused as he reached to turn the handle. "You're not an idiot. Well, maybe a bit... but I get it, okay?"

"Go on," he urged, taking a step closer. If West could be honest with me, then maybe I could be open with him. "I'm listening."

"When I saw Penelope all over you, I wanted to rearrange her perfect fucking face," I admitted. The mattress dipped as he sat on the edge of the bed next to me.

"That's not the same," West said, staring into my eyes with a deep intensity. The big guy was hurting. "You *fucked* him while I watched."

"Look, it's complicated..."

"What's complicated?" he asked. "You picked *him*."

"I've not picked anyone," I said, too quickly, then took a deep breath to regain my cool. "I don't even know what's going on here, or how I feel. I know it's greedy and unfair. I don't want to play you off against each other, but things just happened."

"I thought we had something…" West's voice drifted off as he looked away. "When I want a girl, I want her to be all mine."

Zander was right about how one person could alter the dynamics of an entire group. For the Sevens to work together and bring down our enemies, we had to be on the same page. We couldn't let anything get between us… least of all, me.

"I understand." I nodded, gulping down the lump forming in my throat. "Whatever happened between us, we'll forget about it, okay?"

As I said the words, I knew I didn't want them to be true. West was the main reason I stepped into Lapland. Watching him release his monster drew me in. As I watched him, I saw someone who was like me. He made me want to learn more about the people who ran the joint. West's rejection stung like a bitch, but I had no right to feel sad. No one had forced me to spread my legs for Zander. I'd wanted his cock as much as he'd been willing to give it.

"But I realized something else today." West slid closer, narrowing the gap between us. "My brothers are my life. No one can get between us."

"I never wanted to—"

He reached out and pressed a finger to my lips. What was he going to do? Smother me to death? Choke me until I turned purple? No one would hear me gasping for air through the thick penthouse walls.

"You'll only get between us if I let you," he whispered. His rough touch gently skimmed over my cupid's bow. "There's no point in fighting it, Pinkie. We all want you, even if it means I might have to share you."

My mouth fell open, not comprehending what he was saying at first. "I thought you said—"

"The thought of not feeling your sweet lips on mine made me feel worse than watching Zander make you come," he said, his eyes lingering on my mouth as he grinned. "You look fucking beautiful when you come, by the way. Only next time, I want you to be saying *my* name."

"We should sleep." I cleared my throat and tried to ignore the heat between my legs, wanting to do anything *but* sleep. What else was I supposed to say? My sassy ass mouth had no response. Was I still dreaming? "It's late."

West tenderly kissed my forehead. Who'd have guessed he was the same man who had me pinned against a wall a few hours before? He was a gentle giant beneath his skull smasher facade.

"Do you want me to stay?" he asked.

"It's your room," I said, not sure what response he was hoping for. "You make the rules."

He pulled the blankets back and flicked the lamp off to plummet us into darkness. I moved to make room for him to slip into the warmth. It was a squeeze, even in a Californian King. I turned my back on him, thinking he would give me space. Instead, his body moved closer, curving around mine.

"Are you still tired?" West murmured into my hair as I froze in place.

"Uh-huh," I mumbled unconvincingly, as his hand slipped around my waist and stroked my stomach.

"There's always something that helps me sleep," he said, drawing swirls over my skin. "Wanna try it?"

"West, I—"

"Don't worry, Pinkie," he whispered. "I'm not going to touch you. Not yet."

He rolled me gently onto my back and placed his hand over mine. Unlike Zander, West's hands were lined with scars and rough skin. He was no stranger to hard work. He pushed my hand down, forcing my fingers to glide over my front until they reached the waistband of my pajama shorts. In the blackness, the sound of our shallow breathing was amplified.

"I told you, I'm not gonna touch you," West murmured.

He guided my fingers down further, slipping underneath the soft fabric. My heart hammered at the heat of West's skin against mine, but I didn't object. I stopped at the point of no return. I couldn't touch myself in front of him, could I?

West paused, sensing my reluctance. If I moved a little further, the tips of his giant fingers would rest between my legs as his hands dwarfed my own. He pulled back, sliding upwards, to stroke the back of my hand and wrist. For someone with the strength of a grizzly, he had a softer and more considerate side. He wanted to make sure I was comfortable.

"Make yourself feel good for me, Pinkie."

It didn't count if it was dark, right? My clit begged to be touched and welcomed my soft caress like an old friend. I teased her, gently circling to make my body beg for more. West could feel the rhythm of my motions, and I sunk my teeth into my lip to stop myself from sighing. The feel of his heavy, muscled arm resting on mine only added to the excitement building in my hot core.

"Does that feel good, Pinkie?" West purred.

"Yes." I breathed, squeezing my eyes shut and daring to explore myself more.

"Keep going," he urged. His cock pressed into my side as his fingers stroked the back of my hand in encouragement. "This is all about you."

I moaned as my fingers slipped between my lips and welcomed the wetness. I teased my entrance to mirror West's strokes and imagined it was him touching me. I slipped a finger inside, wondering how many it would take to fill me as much as his cock would.

"West..." I panted, slowly withdrawing my fingers from my pussy and hoping he would take their place.

Instead of taking my hint, he retreated and stroked my inner arm. "What is it, Pinkie?" he asked.

"I want you to touch me."

"I told you I'm not gonna touch you. Not yet." His voice came out in a low, gravelly rumble which sent tingles shooting up my thighs. "I want you to come all over your fingers for me."

West took my wrist in his grasp and pushed it back down between my legs. I explored my pussy with urgency this time, unable to hold back a moan as I stroked my clit.

"After my actions earlier, I'm not worthy of you," West said. His hardness left me under no illusion he wanted me, but his self-control was impressive. "When I have you for the first time, I'll claim you as my own. I'll worship every fucking inch of your body and bury my cock deep in your wet pussy. But tonight? It's all about you."

My breathing grew more ragged as I slid two fingers down my slit and into my wetness. West's grip guided my hands deeper, forcing me to fuck myself again and again. Each push rubbed against my clit and made my thighs tremble with longing.

This was not how I'd expected the night to end, but I couldn't stop now. I relished the hotness of his body against mine and fantasized about how good it would feel for him to roll on top of me. As well as West, I thought about how Zander pounded into me like a speeding truck and how kissing Rocky ignited a flickering inside me that I thought was lost forever. The Seven men would be the fucking death of me. How was a girl supposed to function surrounded by smoking hot men all the time?

"West," I cried out as my orgasm rolled in.

My legs tensed as an explosive burst rippled through my body. I rolled my hips onto my hand, wanting it to never end. I prolonged the sensation, teasing out my pleasure by applying and releasing pressure on my clit to enjoy the pulsing. I'd mastered the art of making orgasms last three times the length. When you used to spend a lot of time locked in a bedroom, it was one way to pass the time… but this was different.

The lights were off, but West had *seen* me as he'd made me come undone. The blackness allowed us to focus on the other sensations. The heat of our bodies. The swell of his cock against my ass. The sound of our breathing blurring into one. West may not have used his own hands to give me pleasure, but his guiding touch felt even more intimate. If I'd fallen apart in his arms now, what would happen when he touched me himself? I'd unravel and never be able to be put back together again.

"I knew you'd be moaning my name," West murmured triumphantly as I slid my hands out of my shorts. "Next time you come, it'll be all over my face."

Self-consciousness replaced my wild abandon as I snatched my hand away. In the throes of passion, I didn't think about anything other than chasing a release. My cheeks burned at the thought of what I'd just done. What did this mean for us? For the Sevens?

"I need a minute," I stammered, slipping out of his bed on wobbly legs and stumbling to his en suite.

I purposefully took my time and, when I returned, West's snoring greeted me. As I got in, he slung his arm around my shoulders and pulled me close, so I could hear the thud of his heart through his muscles.

"Sweet dreams, Pinkie," he whispered sleepily into my hair.

"Night, West," I replied as tiredness swept over me.

FOURTEEN

"Sleep well?" Zander raised an eyebrow as West and I emerged from his room simultaneously. Rocky didn't look up from his cereal. He was busy dunking fruit loops violently into the milk like he wanted to drown them... or someone else.

"He didn't touch me, okay?" I said defensively, grabbing a piece of toast from the rack on the counter. I mean, it was *technically* true. West may have lain next to me while I touched myself, but there wasn't even a freaking base for that. It was basically PG-13.

"Not all of us are like you, Zander," West said, making me choke on my mouthful.

After West's blow-up yesterday and our conversation last night, the atmosphere felt lighter in the penthouse. Sitting in a room together without one guy trying to assassinate another with dagger-like side glances was a sign of progress.

Zander poured himself a black coffee and cleared his throat like we were in a business meeting. "It's time we addressed the Candy situation."

"I'm not a fucking *situation*," I objected, crumbs flying everywhere. "And FYI, I'm also not a morning person. I'd think carefully about what you say next, asshole."

The three of them snickered.

"Rocky, West," Zander continued, addressing them like I wasn't even in the freaking room, "are we all in understanding?"

They nodded curtly.

"Hello! What understanding?" I pointed my toast at Zander like a weapon. "Why do I feel like I'm missing something here?"

"We've finalized our arrangement," Zander said, then caught West's eye. "Haven't we?"

"Yes," West growled.

"That's settled," Zander said, placing his cup down like a judge slamming a hammer in a courtroom.

My brows furrowed in confusion. "What arrangement?"

"We have all agreed to make you our Seven girl officially," Zander said. "We'll share you, little one. You're all fucking ours."

"Don't you think this should have been a conversation we all had together?" I asked, heat rising to my cheeks in anger. What the fuck had I signed myself up for? "Maybe I don't want any of you anymore."

Zander chuckled. Who was I kidding? What woman alive wouldn't start gushing at the thought of screwing one of the Sevens? Let alone having all three!

Rocky smiled slyly. "You've never been a good liar, C."

"Fuck off." I scowled at him, then glared at the

others. "What else did you talk about when I wasn't around? Did you draw up a fucking schedule?"

"Would you like that, little one?" The mischievous glint in Zander's eyes returned. "One-on-one time with each of us? Or, how about a group session?"

As I looked at the three of them, West's neck tensed, and he sat up straighter in his chair. For a guy who didn't like sharing, he'd kept his cool… so far. He may be happy with Zander's proposal, but it would take him time to adjust.

"You said you couldn't choose between us," Zander continued, "now you don't have to."

"I'm not a hole in the fucking wall you can bone whenever you feel like it." I threw down my toast. "Is this how it's going to be, huh? Leaving me out of important conversations? I'm not being a Seven groupie."

"You would never be, C," Rocky said, the corners of his mouth quirked upwards in a smile. "We agreed you're the only girl we want and the only girl we'll have. There's no pressure on you, okay? And you don't have to do anything you don't want to. If you don't want any of us, that's fine, but we're not gonna be screwing anyone else."

There may be no pressure, but my head felt like it had been jammed inside a crock-pot. Would they really be happy leaving behind their bachelor lifestyle? It felt as ridiculous as the Pope deciding to become a rapper. Could I be enough for them?

"I need some time to process whatever 'this' is," I said. Suddenly, I felt very aware of how much of my skin was on display, and I pulled down the hem of my pajama shorts. I'd opted not to change before breakfast and now regretted it. "Is this really what you all want?"

I half-expected them to burst out laughing and claim it was their idea of a prank, but they didn't. They all nodded solemnly. Zander's eyes scanned my body possessively, visually marking me as his territory. Rocky remained straight-faced and serious. His inner determination to win me back meant he would do anything to get a second chance. West looked more apprehensive. Sharing a woman would be an adjustment for him, but he nodded with more ferocity than the other two. He wanted me to know that he would make it work.

"Being a Seven is a lifetime deal, remember? So is this," Zander said. "Take the time you need, but why keep fighting the inevitable when we all know you want it? We can all see how much your body wants us."

"You're such an ass, Zander," I hissed. His gaze lingered on my nipples pebbling beneath my top. I folded my arms across my chest to hide the twins from any further visual violation. "If I had a schedule, then you wouldn't be fucking on it right now."

West snorted, then added possessively, "This is why you're our Seven girl."

"Well, can your *Seven girl* have some pancakes?" I asked.

I couldn't decide whether I found the 'Seven girl' label a douchebag misogynistic move, or whether I liked how these men wanted me to be theirs and weren't afraid to own it.

Zander grabbed his spatula and headed to the kitchen like a knight going into battle. "Of course."

I blinked twice to make sure I wasn't imagining it. Nope, it was definitely happening. Who knew he could be so obliging? Maybe I was seeing another side to him… one he liked to keep hidden under layers of sexy ink.

"And that doesn't mean I'm agreeing to your arrangement either," I said hastily. I may have got myself caught in the middle of a tangled muscled mess, but I had to take advantage of the perks. "I want pancakes with no strings attached."

West and Rocky chuckled as Zander shot back, "Oh, little one... you're still acting like you have a choice."

"Ignore him," Rocky said, then lowered his voice and winked. "Zander's used to getting his way."

"Well, things are gonna change around here," I muttered, making West and Rocky laugh.

If they wanted me in their lives and beds, they needed to understand I wasn't the type of girl who'd worship their every move. I'd call their sexy asses out if they were acting like jerks every damn time. Could they handle a hot stab-happy mess with serious trust issues? Or, better question, could I handle them?

"What's so funny?" Zander called from behind the kitchen counter as he violently whipped up a fresh batch of batter.

I widened my eyes innocently and smiled. "Oh, nothing..."

After eating breakfast with the guys, I needed time alone to get my head around their proposal. There was no rule book to read about being the girl who three criminals share. How would our arrangement work? Managing one relationship was complicated enough, but juggling three simultaneously? I had years of experience in seducing men for extortion but fell short in the romance department.

When Rocky broke my heart, I vowed to never let it happen again. I built armor to protect myself. Why let anyone in and give them the power to hurt me? The Sevens changed that. Those fuckers were pulling my guard down, piece by piece.

Despite my resistance, I was coming to the realization that Zander was right. I had no choice. Rocky, West, and Zander had gotten under my skin. No matter how hard I tried, it was impossible to fight my instincts. I didn't need an arrangement or a fucking label to tell me what my gut already knew. I was theirs, and they were all fucking mine.

"I can come with you?" Rocky offered as I gathered my belongings.

"I told you already, I'll be fine," I said, slinging my bag over my shoulder and heading out of the penthouse.

"Are you sure?" Rocky pressed.

He followed me out onto the street, where Zander and West were already waiting to say goodbye. I didn't need a fucking farewell party; I was only going home until my shift later that night. Like Rocky, West and Zander didn't look pleased about my departure, either. West donned his signature sulky pout, and Zander's arms were crossed.

After an eventful Christmas in Lapland, returning to my grotty apartment would be a jolt back to reality and provide a break from the growing sexual tension. The only appointment I had this evening was with my pink vibrating pet rabbit.

I raised an eyebrow at West as a bullet-proof Lexus pulled up at my feet. "I thought you'd called a cab?"

"We're not letting you get into a car with a stranger," West said with the seriousness of a bodyguard being tasked to protect the President. "Our best driver will take you wherever you wanna go. He'll be permanently stationed with you from now on."

"I don't need a fucking escort." I jabbed my finger into his chest, then remembered how Giles and Bryce were digging into my past. I could take care of myself, but it *would* be nice not to worry about having to fight my way out of a cab. I sighed and added reluctantly, "I guess it beats waiting in the cold for an Uber..."

West shot me an 'I told you so' look.

"We'll see you tonight," Zander said, opening the car door and undressing me with hungry eyes. We hadn't been alone together since we'd fucked in his office, but the thought of it happening again kept slipping into my consciousness when I least expected it. When he served my pancakes, I couldn't even look at him without thinking of how good he'd looked with his head between my legs. As soon as my mind strayed to what happened between us, Zander sensed it. Was he psychic? A dark grin spread over his face like a promise of what was to come the next time he got me alone. "Our girl can take care of herself."

"Damn right I can," I said, slamming the door shut and leaving them behind as the car takes off.

As soon as I arrived back at my apartment and turned the key in the lock, I knew something was wrong. I got the same feeling whenever a creep who'd been checking me out all night slid a drink across the bar. My skin crawled, and every instinct told me to run.

I reached for my new knife and tried to push the door open, but the wood is met with resistance. I forced it open with my shoulder until I created a big enough gap to slip inside.

Well, shit... this was the complete opposite of a home makeover.

"Hello?" I called out, brandishing my blade.

There was no response. Whoever had broken in had either already left or had hidden somewhere. Where could a person conceal themselves amongst the mess?

It looked like a small tornado had ripped through my apartment and destroyed everything in its path. The sofa was upturned, and cushions slashed open, spilling out their stuffing like entrails. My tiny adjoining kitchen was no better. The blocked sink was overflowing and flooding onto the floor while the cabinet doors had been torn off.

"Anyone here?" I asked, fairly confident the culprits had made themselves scarce.

I picked my way over the rubbish to enter my bedroom and survey the damage. The entire contents of my wardrobe had been shredded into piles. Hell, they'd even transformed the freaking curtains into strings. I wrinkled my nose at a suspicious-looking stain and smell coming from the mattress. Casual vandalism was small fry and didn't bother me... but something else did.

Above my bed, a gigantic pink graffiti outline of a cat had been sprayed over the wall. You couldn't miss it. Someone wanted to send me a message.

It was too messy to be Hiram's style. If Hiram wanted to trash your place, he'd set fire to the whole fucking block — not make a shit sandwich outta your sheets. No, this was an amateur scare job. The last words a British asshole said to me sprung to my mind instantly.

'See you soon, Kitty.'

Behind me, something stirred.

"Giles." West's deep growl over my shoulder confirmed my suspicions as he reached out to place his hand on my arm. I grabbed his wrist and twisted it, making him yelp. Hey, at least it confirmed I hadn't started hearing voices in my head.

"You should know better than to sneak up on me."

"Noted," he muttered as I dropped my hold on him. He pouted, massaging his wrist. The big guy could dish it out but didn't know how to take it.

"How the fuck did you get here so fast, anyway?" I asked, peering around him to check whether the others had arrived, but it looked like West had come alone. Surely, it couldn't be a coincidence? He'd appeared out of fucking nowhere like a superhero.

West held up his hands and started backing away slowly. "I may, or may not, have installed a hidden camera in your apartment."

"You did, what?" I spluttered. It's a good thing he was out of stomping range. Otherwise, I'd have crushed his toes under my heel. "Where? When?!"

He strolled casually through to my main living area and pointed to a spot above the TV, where a crack ran down the side of the wall. "I installed it the last time I was here."

I racked my brain to remember. He'd only ever been over once, before our trip to the junkyard, months ago. How many hours had he spent spying on me while I'd been curled up with a tub of ice cream? We were not in nineteen-fucking-eighty-four.

"You've been watching me all this time. Why? I wasn't even a Seven then!" I balled my fists and shoved his muscled chest as a fresh swell of rage rose inside me. For a guy the size of a house, he could be sneaky. "What am I to you, huh? Your personal reality TV show? Did you get bored with watching the Real Housewives?"

I wasn't only mad with him, but with myself. How hadn't I noticed before? If this had gotten past me, I'd let myself get too comfortable. Being comfortable meant making mistakes and getting sloppy. It couldn't happen again.

"It's not like that," West said, catching my wrists before I could push him again. "You attract trouble, Candy. When Cheeks got locked up, I wanted to make sure you'd be safe."

I couldn't decide whether to be horrified or flattered The Hulk cared about what happened to me enough to set up a live stream to my fucking sofa.

"Why go through the effort of installing a covert surveillance system when you didn't use it when it mattered?" I said, gesturing wildly at the ruins around us. "Couldn't you have stopped all of this?"

"I didn't realize someone had cut the feed until after you left Lapland. I didn't check it over the holidays," West mumbled, looking at his feet and finally having the decency to look ashamed of himself. He'd fucked up, and he knew it. "The last thing the footage showed was three guys wearing balaclavas. The fuckers cut the power, which messed with our signal. Zander's looking into it. We're working on the theory that Giles paid a group of local kids to do it."

At least something good had come from the break-in. West's private cable channel had got taken off-air.

"Figures," I said, rolling my eyes. Giles, like his uncle, wasn't above using easily influenced kids to do his bidding. "Now, you've seen I'm alive. Are you here to help me clean up, or what? It's the least you could do."

West laughed in disbelief. "Did you think we'd let you stay here after this? I'm here to bring you and, what's left of your things, home."

"Home?" My mouth fell open in shock. "You want me to move into the penthouse?"

Spending the festive period in Lapland with the Sevens was one thing, but moving in with them permanently? It was a big step…

"You're a Seven, so it makes sense that you live with us," West said, with a casual shrug. From the way he was acting, you'd have thought he'd asked me to go out bowling. "It would have happened, eventually. I want you somewhere I can keep my eye on you."

"But where will I sleep?" I stammered as my mind worked quickly to count the number of bedrooms in the penthouse. There was nowhere for me to go. A twinge between my legs reminded me that there was one obvious solution… no, Candy! We may have made an arrangement, but a girl needed her space — especially if she had to juggle three Seven men. "There's not enough room."

"It's taken care of," West answered. "Vixen is giving up her walk-in closet."

"I bet she'll fucking love that…" I muttered sarcastically, imagining her reaction to giving up storage would be akin to an earthquake. I'd never seen inside her closet but knew she had a vast collection of leathers she liked to store correctly.

"It's small," West said, "but it's nicer than—"

"Than this place?" I finished his sentence and placed my hands on my hips in defiance. "I could sleep in my car."

"That piece of junk? I've already sent it to scrap." West laughed as I sent him a scathing look, then his expression turned deadpan, and he took a step forward. He leaned in closer, running his knuckle over my cheek. "Look, Pinkie. We can either do this the easy way or the hard way. If you don't come with me, I'll carry you out. It's your choice."

"I can walk myself," I hissed, turning my back on him and marching out empty-handed.

I may be stubborn and not want to bend to West's will, but what choice did I have? Getting Zander to make me pancakes every morning was better than dealing with my headache of an apartment. There was no point in trying to salvage any of my belongings either. Giles's stooges had done a thorough job of trashing everything I owned.

My nuisance neighbor poked her head out of her apartment across the hall. "What's all this noise about?"

"Mind your own fucking business," I spat, flipping her off as I passed. "I'm moving out."

Starting over with nothing didn't scare me. I'd done it before. But moving in with three monsters who I either wanted to strangle or jump their bones? That was fucking terrifying.

I refused to speak to West on the journey to Lapland. I may have gone with him willingly, but it didn't mean I was happy about being coerced under the threat of violence.

Vixen was waiting for us to return. She stood outside the sparkly entrance with a pile of cigarette butts at her feet. She'd been chain-smoking, something she only did when she got stressed.

"After you," West said, holding the car door open for me. I scowled as I got out without thanking him. Who was he kidding? He was no gentleman.

As my heel hit the sidewalk, Vixen hurtled forward like a cannonball. I clenched my fists to gear up for a fight. Instead, she threw her arms around me in a tight hug.

"I came home as soon as I heard," Vixen said, squeezing me harder than a boa constrictor. "I'm sorry about your place."

"It's fine." I patted her awkwardly on the back. What had Mieko's magic vagina done to her? The old Vixen would have electrocuted anyone who got within an inch of touching her. "It's not like anyone died."

Vixen flinched and pulled away. I guess it was too soon to be making jokes after Cheeks's murder…

"Where's the rest of Candy's stuff?" Vixen snapped at West like a concierge addressing a porter. "You can carry them upstairs."

"There was nothing worth saving," I answered.

"When we found out what happened, we figured you might need new clothes, and it's a good thing we did. Zander's gone shopping with Mieko to get you some," Vixen said, then scowled bitterly. "He didn't trust me with his platinum."

I bit my tongue to stop myself from saying it may

not have been a bad thing. I didn't want a full closet of fetish club gear.

"Or, maybe Zander didn't want you going on a spending spree of your own, because you had to give up your walk-in?" West teased. "Didn't you say you wanted compensation?"

"You try finding storage solutions at the last minute." Vixen shot him a venomous glare. "Do I look like Marie-fucking-Kondo?"

"If you don't want me to stay," I said, "I can find somewhere else."

Now, I was on the receiving end of Vixen's 'shut the hell up, if you don't want me to rip off your nipples' look.

"This is your home now. I'll show you to your new room," Vixen insisted fiercely. She grabbed my arm and pulled me inside before I could say any more, or try to talk her out of it. I followed her up to the penthouse as she chatted about her conditions for sharing. "I'm happy for you to have the walk-in, but I draw the line at sharing a bathroom. My nails are too expensive to be picking your long pink hairs outta the drain."

"Sure," I agreed, as West snorted behind me. It blew my mind that not sharing a bathroom was an option some people had. Growing up in Evergreen meant you were lucky to shower with hot water.

"Good luck, Pinkie," West chirped, disappearing into his room, which only made me more anxious. For all I knew, Vixen could be luring me away to be sacrificed.

"We rarely have guests, so the main bathroom can be yours," Vixen said, pointing at a sign on the door with my name on it. Her refusing to share a bathroom was no fucking joke. "Through here…"

I followed her into her bedroom. Instead of resembling a gothic playboy mansion, it looked more like an art studio. She'd decorated tastefully; abstract paintings hung on the walls, candles burned on every spare surface, and the lingering smell of incense gave the air a mystical quality. Off of her main suite was a door to her bathroom and another which, I presumed, led to my new box room.

"Go on." She gave me a push in encouragement. "There are no monsters in there."

My jaw dropped as I stepped inside.

Holy shit.

My new room was only slightly smaller than hers. An enormous bed with powder pink bedding and a sweeping overhead canopy sat in the middle. Around it, shelving and a beautiful Hollywood-style dressing table lined the walls. How had they had the time to pull this together?

I turned to Vixen in disbelief. "This used to be your closet?"

"Well, duh!" Vixen rolled her eyes. "I haven't had time to clear all of my stuff out yet."

"You can keep it here," I said. "I wouldn't be able to fill half this room, even if I went shopping every day for the rest of the year."

Vixen flopped down on my new bed and kicked off her New Rock boots. "Are you ready for the rest of the rules?"

"There's more?" I groaned, collapsing next to her.

"Rule one, no smoking in the room," she counted the points off on her tombstone painted talons, "rule two, you can borrow whatever you like as long as you put it back where you found it."

"Anything else?" I asked sarcastically.

"I'd rather you didn't fuck the guys when I'm in the next room," she said, then a sly smile crept over her face. How the hell did she find out about our conversation this morning? On second thoughts, I didn't even want to know. "Although, I don't think that's gonna be a problem when everyone else is down the hall."

Rocky's head poked around the door to interrupt our conversation. "How are you settling in?"

"Hey!" My voice came out three octaves higher than usual. He'd spared me from having to talk to Vixen about whatever was going on between me and the guys. I ignored her growing smirk, which told me this wasn't the end of our conversation. "Yep, all good here."

"Candy's settling in fine, no thanks to you," Vixen said. "Where the fuck were you when I needed help with moving my latex?"

"What can I say?" he replied. "Business called."

She threw a pillow, *my* new pillow, at him. "Smoking pot does not count as business."

"I need to sample the goods to check the quality." His lopsided grin made my stomach flip. "Do you need any help with unpacking, C?"

"Sure, now, he turns into the knight in shining armor," Vixen grumbled under her breath.

"I have nothing to unpack," I said. "Nothing was worth keeping."

My ruby ring, pendant necklace from Zander, and the knife in my back pocket were the only items I owned of any value. I wasn't dumb enough to let them out of my sight for a second.

Rocky's expression turned stony. "Giles is a fucker."

Strangely enough, Giles may have done me a favor. I'd be glad not to have to deal with my neighbor nagging about noise or worrying about getting fried by dodgy electrics whenever I wanted to curl my hair.

"You should be grateful you're not related to the asshole," Vixen said.

"Oh, I am," Rocky said, then pulled a clumsily wrapped package from behind his back. "I got you a moving gift. I've been saving it for a special occasion."

I took it from him, turning it over suspiciously in my hands, then ripped it open. I gasped at the CD Walkman. *It couldn't be, could it?* I ran my fingers over the familiar smooth plastic. The stickers had faded after all these years, but it was the same one. *My one.*

"Did you travel back to the nineties or lose your fucking mind?" Vixen asked, making it clear what she thought of his gift. "How much green did you smoke, Red?"

Rocky ignored her, giving me his undivided attention. "Now you have something else worth keeping."

"You kept it all this time?" I murmured, feeling the grooves where I'd etched my initials into it with a compass during math class.

Music brought me salvation when I lived in the Evergreen group home. As a teenager, I spent hours listening to CDs when everyone had already moved onto iPods. The Walkman had been my gateway to another world. A way for me to dance, dream and wish for better things.

"Of course I did," Rocky said, burying his hands in his pockets and looking bashful. "I wouldn't let them take it off me — even in Redlake, the guards let me have it. I hoped I'd be able to give it back to you one day."

"Thanks." I sniffed and looked away, hoping he wouldn't see the tears forming in my eyes. The Walkman wasn't only a way to play CDs. It was a symbol. A symbol of Rocky showing he remembered. A symbol of his words being true. After all the shit he'd gone through, he could have given up and tossed it into the trash with our memories. Instead, he dared to hope we'd find each other again. "It's perfect."

Rocky's eyes sought mine and held my gaze for a few seconds. We shared a look of understanding and promise. We couldn't change what happened in the past, but he'd proved himself. Together, we'd find a way to move past our mistakes.

"Welcome home, C," he said.

Being 'home' was a strange concept when you'd grown up in a world where you felt like you'd never truly belonged. Coming to live with the Sevens scared me, but it didn't make me want to run. Who knows? Maybe it meant I'd finally found what I was looking for...

"You two are so fucking weird." Vixen frowned and shook her head, breaking our moment. Her face lit up at the sound of approaching footsteps. "They're back."

A second later, Mieko stumbled into my room with bags stacked up her arms. She wouldn't need to hit the gym anytime soon. Carrying them looked like a fucking workout. Zander followed close behind her, holding even more boxes.

"Did you buy the whole freaking store?" I asked, surveying the mountain of goods they laid on the floor.

"Mieko seemed to feel bad about spending money,

so I helped," Zander replied. "I only want the best for our Seven girl."

Hiram always had an ulterior motive when he used to buy me clothes. He wanted me to look the part for whatever twisted job was coming up next, but it was different with Zander. His thoughtfulness and desire to look after me made me feel warm and fuzzy. As an independent, kick-ass woman, it was something I had no fucking idea how to deal with…

I pushed my emotions aside and picked out a dress from the closest bag, which looked like it'd be fit for a red carpet event. "When will I get a chance to wear *this* in Port Valentine?"

When I didn't know how to react, resorting to my usual snarky self was the only way.

"I'm sure you'll find the occasion," Zander said, then turned to the others. "Why don't we leave Candy to unpack? We'll need to get ready for tonight."

"Tonight?" My head jerked upright. "What's happening?"

"We're going to the Golden Gloves," Rocky said. The Golden Gloves is Port Valentine's underground cage fighting ring, most famous for the number of men who died in it. "I've been drafted in at the last minute."

"You fight?" I spluttered, thinking I'd misheard him. "At the Golden Gloves?"

When we were younger, Rocky never used his fists unless he had to. Being locked in Redlake and joining the Sevens must have changed him more than I knew…

"You didn't know?" Vixen let out a low whistle. "Red's a fucking legend. You should have seen him in juvie."

"I want you all to be there," Rocky said. "I need cheerleaders."

I scowled. "If you want me to be peppy with pompoms, you have another thing coming…"

"You're coming too, Mimi," Vixen said.

Mimi? If the two of them weren't so damn cute and happy, I'd have barfed over my new shoes.

"What's the dress code?" Mieko asked nervously.

"Whatever it is, I'm sure I have something you could borrow," I said. There was no way she was getting out of it.

"It's boiling in there, so wear something short," Vixen said, then considered it further, "but with a crotch."

Why couldn't a woman go into a crowded place without worrying about sweaty hands trying to slip under their skirt? If any asshole dared to touch me, or the girls, I'd rip off their fingers with my canines.

"Don't worry, little one," Zander said, turning to me with a playful grin. "No one will touch you when I'm around."

I rolled my eyes. He never missed an opportunity to step into his role as the alpha. "Save it, Zander."

"It'll be a fun night," Rocky said, cracking his knuckles and shooting me a mischievous smile. "You'll see."

FIFTEEN

Our limo pulled into the Golden Gloves parking lot. The boxing gym looked like it'd been around since the dawn of time. People queued around the building, raising bottles of beer, throwing smack talk and betting on who would bleed out when the bell rang. I recognized many of Lapland's regular customers and members of the Sevens security team waiting in line. A real charming crowd.

Rocky was somewhere inside, preparing for his fight. Could he handle himself around thugs who fought for a living? He usually made use of his green fingers, not fists in boxing gloves.

"Have you ever seen Fight Club?" Vixen asked, holding the door open for me and Mieko to get out of the car. "This is the real fucking deal."

Zander, already waiting outside, beckoned us forward. "This way."

He greeted a pair of beautiful women, who hung on his every word. While they competed for his attention, he watched me out of the corner of his eye, searching for a reaction. Being treated like royalty would do nothing for his ego, and the bastard wanted to make me jealous. A woman took his arm, and I stepped forward. I wanted to bash the bitch's head against the ground for touching my man.

"I won't be needing an escort tonight," Zander said, carefully removing her hand. He held out his arm for me to take. Her face fell like she'd been diagnosed with gonorrhea as I linked my arm through his. *Good fucking riddance.* I'd rather have made a show of running my fingers through his hair, but we had to be careful. Everyone in Port Valentine believed I was engaged to West, and it was easier to keep it that way… for now.

"It's like we're celebrities," Mieko murmured as we sauntered to the front of the queue.

Vixen snorted. "You expect the star treatment when you hire half the staff as dealers or clean-up crew."

A few daring men wolf-whistled as we passed, which Zander silenced with one deadly glare. Vixen and Mieko looked incredible; their outfits reflected their contrasting personalities. Vixen wore leather pants with a fishnet halter top, while Mieko had borrowed a gorgeous sparkly playsuit, which looked way better on her than it ever would on me. I'd ignored Vixen's advice and opted to wear a skintight black Bardot dress. Why should I have to cover up because of assholes who couldn't keep their hands to themselves? Besides, my sharp stiletto heels could easily pierce a scrotum.

Zander approached the beefy guy guarding the entrance, who nodded to let us pass. As we did, the guard bent down to whisper in Zander's ear.

"What did he say?" I asked as Zander turned to look

at me wearing his 'I want to rip someone apart limb by limb' expression.

"Giles is here."

That only meant one thing... trouble.

Inside, the Golden Gloves smelled like stale sweat, iron and alcohol. Uncomfortable folding seats had been crammed around the ring, and groups congregated in the back. The crowds parted for us to make our way through. Even though the chairs were ass-numbing, they were reserved for a privileged minority.

People came here looking to settle scores. They wouldn't fight clean. It'd be hard, fast, and dirty. I understood why West had elected to stay behind and look after the club. If West lost self-control at a place like this, someone would end up dead by the end of the night... and it wouldn't be him.

Zander led us to the ringside, where our seats were waiting. Mieko was right. It felt like we'd got a front-row ticket to the most anticipated premiere of the year. We were close enough to smell the sweat of the fighters, but far enough away to be out of blood splatter range.

I turned to Mieko on my left. "Is this your first proper date?"

"I guess it is," she said, shooting Vixen an adoring stare on her other side.

The referee climbed into the ring. Beside him, a half-naked girl paced with a sign to declare the night was starting and winked at the hecklers.

"Are you ready for the fun to begin?" Zander purred in my ear as his hand rested casually on my knee. We were sandwiched so close together, no one would be able to see. His touch on my bare skin sent hot tingles up my thighs, but I kept my legs pressed firmly together. I knew how skilled his fingers were, but right now? I was playing the role of West's fiancée, and we needed to keep it that way.

I grinned back at him. "I was born ready."

Adrenaline fizzed in the air, ramping up the crowd's energy and engaging their 'fight or fuck' response. Humans liked to think we were more civilized than our ancestors, but we couldn't hide from our innate drives: sex and violence. Places like the Golden Gloves drew out our most primal, raw and deadly urges.

Two opponents staggered into the ring. From the chanting and symbols on their chests, I guessed they were from two opposing gangs. I'd seen how this situation went down before. Whoever won would gain a slice of turf and the respect of their group, but the losers would become hungry for vengeance. Whatever the outcome, lives would be lost.

The shorter of the men wasted no time. He charged at his opponent and landed a punch with a thwack. The crowd jumped to their feet and cheered as his head spun. His opponent staggered from the blow, but only for a second. He recovered and advanced for revenge by smashing his fist into the jaw of his enemy. Teeth flew out of his mouth and landed at our feet with a ping. It was weird not to be the person knocking them out for a change.

"Want a souvenir, Candy?" Zander asked.

"I don't keep trophies," I said, talking about more than what was happening in front of us. Some serial killers got their kicks by collecting mementos, but I was smarter than that. Why take anything that could lead back to you?

Zander leaned in to whisper, "Do you think you could do better?"

"Well, duh." I flicked my hair over my shoulder. "Of course, I fucking could, and you know it."

The fight didn't last long. It only took three minutes for the loser to collapse in a bloody heap. This wasn't just any ring. Here, nothing was off the table. There was only one rule: fight until your opponent can't fight anymore.

Zander caught the eye of a man, who brought us beers in glass bottles. They didn't serve drinks in plastic by principle. Why would they? Any extra bloodshed in the crowd was seen as a bonus between rounds.

I saw Vixen nudge her head out of the corner of my eye. "Spawn of the devil incoming at four o'clock."

Zander gripped my leg tighter. "It was only a matter of time."

"Front row, I see?" I ground my teeth at the sound of Giles's irritating drawl. He swanned in front of us, flanked by two cronies. Why did he think wearing a white suit to a fight was a good idea? Clearly, he wasn't worried about anyone hurting him. The spineless bastard was too afraid to come to the Golden Gloves without reinforcements. We may not be able to touch him without causing an outright war with the Briarlys, but some of the locals may not be afraid to throw a punch his way. I'd like to see his suit with a new red splattered accent. "I hear there is a last-minute change to the schedule."

"Don't tell me you're going in the ring?" I feigned surprise, knowing he wouldn't last ten seconds. I'd be able to take the motherfucker down quicker than he could say 'God save the Queen'.

"It looks like Kitty has claws. I hope Red has your enthusiasm," Giles taunted. "He's up against the Rhino."

The Rhino? I didn't think we were in a zoo.

"The Rhino?" Vixen blanched, the color draining from her face. "Since when? That wasn't the fucking plan."

"Things can change quickly, Vixie," Giles said, with a wicked glint in his piggy eyes. A change of plan was easy to orchestrate when you were being bankrolled by the deep pockets of Uncle Bryce. "Enjoy the show."

"Oh, we will," I spat as he walked away.

Zander rose from his seat. His jaw set in furious determination. "There's someone I need to speak to," he growled, then stormed into the crowd while Vixen shifted around in her seat like she'd caught crabs.

"Someone's gonna lose their job over this," Vixen muttered, shaking her head. "Anyone with loyalty to the Sevens would know better than taking a bribe from Giles, especially one like this."

"What's so bad about the Rhino?" I asked.

"You'll know when you see him," she said, squeezing Mieko's hand so hard her knuckles turned white. "Red's a good fighter, but the Rhino? He's a fucking animal."

A few seconds later, Zander returned with a thunderous expression. He was not a person who took kindly to being double-crossed. Who needs enemies when your family is obsessed with trying to screw you over? Before I could ask him whether he'd sourced who had accepted a dirty bribe, Mieko squeaked at the sight of a man entering the ring.

"He's the Rhino?" she asked shakily, her lip trembling.

"See what I mean now?" Vixen said.

The Rhino looked like he weighed as much as a small transportation truck. His skin was thick and leathery, covered in scars from stab wounds and bullet holes from head to toe. I don't know how many steroids he'd pumped through his veins, but it looked like he could crush two cars between his hands. He might be the only person who could rival The Hulk…

"You've got to be fucking kidding!" I looked at Zander incredulously. "You're going to let him fight *that*?"

"Red's made his choice. He wants to fight," Zander replied nonchalantly with a dismissive wave of his hand. He'd been more bothered about finding out someone accepted Giles's bribe. Didn't he care that Rocky was going up against a guy who looked like a scary creature from a fairytale? "I have money riding on this now."

Was he out of his fucking mind? I appreciated his confidence but, being a gambler myself, I didn't favor Rocky's odds.

Vixen echoed my concerns aloud. "You'll be spending more on a hospital bed when the Rhino's through with him."

Suddenly, a night to unwind had turned into something darker. There was a lot more at stake than dignity or wiping the smirk off of Giles's face. Rocky had to fight to stay alive.

"It's starting," Zander said, sitting up straighter.

A hush fell over the crowd as Rocky entered the ring shirtless. His torso revealed scars I'd never seen before. Unlike West and Zander, who were covered in ink, Rocky's only visible tattoo was the number seven in the center of his chest. He was built like a surfer, tall and toned. Someone like West wouldn't look out of place in the Golden Gloves, but Rocky? The Rhino could snap his spine like a twig.

"I don't know if I can watch," Mieko mumbled, covering her eyes and peeking out through her fingers.

Seeing Rocky stand next to the Rhino was like looking at a bus and a kid's bicycle. Everyone knows it only takes a second for a bike to become mangled under bigger wheels.

"It'll be fine," I reassured her, trying my best to keep my voice steady.

If anything happened to Rocky, Giles would pay. I'd make sure of it. Hadn't the Briarlys learned their lesson after what happened when their henchmen and Razor groupies tried to take us down? How many more men could they afford to lose?

The bell hadn't rung to start the fight, but the Rhino was ready to go. He stomped towards Rocky, each step making the ring vibrate. The blank stare in his eyes would be enough to make anyone run, but Rocky didn't move. His eyes found mine in the crowd, and he grinned. What the fuck was going through his head? I was already planning on avenging his death and the crazy bastard was smiling?

Dinging signaled the start of the fight, and the Rhino lunged. Rocky was quick on his feet. He effortlessly dodged the punch, ducking under the Rhino's muscled bicep. After a few more thwarted attempts, the Rhino was panting and his cheeks were reddening in fury. The Rhino ran at Rocky, who managed to spin out of his reach and trip him over in the process.

"Are you going to fight or dance, Twinkle Toes?" the Rhino grunted as he heaved himself to his feet.

"Catch me, if you can," Rocky replied unflinchingly, which only angered the Rhino more.

Rocky moved in the ring like he was part of a strange ballet. He didn't fight with force but with skill like a trained athlete. The Rhino's aimless slings were no match for Rocky's slick motions. I was impressed. With each of Rocky's misses, the crowd grew restless. The Rhino was a big name and, so far, they were not getting the bloodbath they'd been promised.

Rocky approached us ringside, as the Rhino struggled to get up off his ass for the third time in a row.

"I'm glad you came, C," Rocky said, leaning against the ropes and making me smile. He wasn't even out of breath. Where the fuck had he got his moves and nerves of steel?

Before I had time to respond, the Rhino was up quicker than we'd expected. Rocky's momentary lapse in attention meant he was *just* a second too slow to avoid a right hook delivered to his shoulder.

The audience clapped and cheered. *This* is what they'd paid money for. I expected Rocky's confidence to get knocked by the blow, but he shrugged it off and bounced back on his feet. His level of casual confidence had sent lesser men to the hospital with brain injuries. Did he have a fucking suicide wish? As the Rhino tried to swing again, Rocky tripped him over, and he dropped with a bang.

"Do you think you can concentrate on not getting your ass beat?" I asked as Rocky approached us again.

"Keep your eyes on the fucking game," Vixen shrieked.

The Rhino staggered backward to prepare to make another dive to the delight of hollering fans.

"If I finish him," Rocky said, his soft brown eyes met mine, "I'll do it for you, C."

"Do it," I urged, sensing he was holding back. I wanted to see what he could do and end the fucker. "Give me a fucking show."

"Don't encourage him," Vixen wailed. "He'll be lucky to get out of the ring alive."

Or, maybe I'd given him the best chance he had. I knew he wouldn't want to let me down.

The Rhino charged with a vengeance. Rocky narrowly avoided another punch but got caught by the Rhino's knee cracking into his middle. Rocky fell to the floor, clutching his stomach, and curled into a ball. It must have hurt like a motherfucker.

The Rhino grinned triumphantly, wanting to take advantage of the opportunity. He kicked Rocky in the back, but Rocky didn't move. The Rhino didn't relent. I edged closer in my seat to get a better view.

"Sit back," Zander urged, but I couldn't.

Vomit rose in my throat. I asked him to give me a show, but not like this. *This wasn't supposed to happen.* How could I have thought Rocky could take on someone like the Rhino and get away unscathed?

"Can't we do something?" I asked, wincing as another kick drove into Rocky's side.

"Red knows what he's doing," Zander replied coolly, seemingly unperturbed by his friend getting beaten to death.

From where I was sitting, the only thing it looked like Rocky knew how to do was to take a beating without passing out.

"Be patient," Zander murmured.

The Rhino took a few steps back, gearing up for a

body slam. The weight of the beast would turn Rocky into nothing but a bloody pancake. I couldn't let him get crushed by a steamroller and do nothing.

I stood to my feet. "No!"

As the Rhino leaped into the air, Rocky rolled away at the last second. The Rhino slammed into the ground, and Rocky jumped on top of him. How had he sustained such an ass-kicking and recovered so fast? Rocky raised his fist and slammed it into the Rhino's head, causing his nose to explode. Rocky didn't stop, though. He kept going, like a crazed animal, pummeling the Rhino's face until his eyelids fluttered shut.

"We have a winner," the referee called, racing over to check the Rhino's pulse. The audience waited with bated breath, followed by a disappointed sigh at finding out he was still breathing. I didn't care whether the Rhino had a pulse. The only thing that mattered was Rocky being okay.

"Now do you believe me when I said he could handle it?" Zander said smugly.

The crowd cheered and stamped as Rocky punched the air in victory. Vixen and Mieko jumped up and down clapping, but I struggled to join their celebrations. Not after thinking I was about to lose him...

Rocky stepped out of the ring, slightly unsteady on his feet, but I wouldn't let him off so easily. He stretched his arms out, expecting me to walk into them. Instead, I punched him square in the chest. I may not have as much power as the Rhino, but my fist hit an already blossoming bruise.

"Ouch." He rubbed the painful spot. "What did you do that for? I won, didn't I?"

I wanted to scream at him for putting everyone

through that. For what could have happened. For what we could have lost. But I didn't say anything. I simply glowered at him and debated whether he could take another punch.

"Were you worried about me, C?" Rocky teased. "I had him all along."

Zander slapped him on the back. "Good job, Red."

"Well done," Mieko stammered, still looking a little queasy despite his victory.

"Congratulations, Red," Giles said, creeping up behind us. Zander grabbed my wrist before I could spin around and twist his tiny balls off like screwcaps. I gritted my teeth, hoping we wouldn't have to suffer through his presence for long. Giles pulled an envelope addressed to Zander out of his pocket and thrust it forward begrudgingly. "Here's an invitation from your father to the Briarly New Year Ball. All of your waifs and strays are welcome."

"How generous," Zander replied coldly, snatching it from him. "We'll see you there."

Giles nodded curtly and turned on his heel. If he didn't have Rocky's loss to gloat over, what was the point in him sticking around?

"We aren't seriously going, are we?" Vixen groaned.

"And miss a chance to find out why my father is summoning us?" Zander furrowed his brow. "This is the first invitation we've had in years. It's no accident."

"I think Zander's right, Vix," I said, already formulating a plan for how I could use the visit to my advantage. If we were going to Briarly Manor, I could slip away to try and find the evidence they were holding over us.

"Why don't we get out of here?" Rocky suggested,

draping his sweaty arm around my shoulder and casting a worried glance at the jostling spectators. Fights were breaking out, and it'd only be a matter of time before we got caught up in the brawl. "It can get ugly fast."

"Fine," I agreed, shrugging him off, "but if you touch me again before you shower, I'll give you a black eye."

"But I thought you were my cheerleader, C?"

I narrowed my eyes. "I wouldn't be seen dead waving pompoms."

He smirked. "You'd look pretty cute in a cheerleader outfit, though…"

"Gross. Can you keep your dick in your pants until we leave?" Vixen interrupted, shutting Rocky down. "Let's get the hell outta here before I heave."

We shoved our way through the crowds and into the parking lot, where a driver was waiting.

"I know a place we can go for drinks," Zander said, getting into the limo. "We have a win to celebrate."

"Count us in," Vixen said, clambering after him with Mieko.

I held back. Mixing alcohol with the lingering adrenaline in my system would only lead to more trouble we didn't need.

"Why don't you drive me back, C?" Rocky asked, sensing my reluctance. "I can't leave my car here overnight."

It was a bad neighborhood, and the only reason his car hadn't been stolen yet was because people knew the Sevens were nearby. If we abandoned it until morning, it'd be free fucking game.

"Fine, but only because it'll annoy West," I said. West hadn't let me behind the wheel of any of the

Seven cars since we'd burned one of his babies. How was it fair that a small incident got me blacklisted from the entire garage? "But I'm not your fucking chauffeur, okay?"

"We'll see you back at Lapland then," Vixen called through the lowered window, then winked. "Don't wait up."

The three of them sped away into the night as Rocky threw me the keys to his red shiny beauty. "You think you can handle my Mercedes?"

"Hell yeah," I said, or at least I thought so...

"I can see why West doesn't let you drive anymore," Rocky said as I narrowly avoided taking out the wing mirror of a parked car. It's not my fault it's a narrow street, and I was sat next to an asshole who'd just evaded death.

"It beats letting someone behind the wheel with a concussion," I pointed out, slamming my foot on the gas to make us jolt forward.

He flinched. "You're still mad about it, huh?"

"Where did you learn to fight?"

"They didn't print all the reasons why Redlake got shut down in the papers," Rocky said, keeping his eyes fixed on the road ahead. "I may not have got any qualifications when I was there, but I got a different type of schooling. The safety of inmates wasn't exactly high on the list of their priorities. They were more interested in cashing in on boxing."

"They made you fight?"

"Trust me, being a fighter made you one of the

lucky ones," Rocky said. "Winning gave you privileges. I was coached by one of the best."

"Those fuckers got someone to coach you?"

"Hell no!" Rocky laughed bitterly. "They'd rather we were untrained. It was more fun for them to bet on which of us would die, but I made a friend in Redlake. Do you remember reading about Oliver Filey?"

The name sounded familiar, then it came flooding back. Oliver's face had appeared in the news. He was a promising boxing star who was killed in his cell by other inmates. They blamed it on gang violence and no one questioned it. His death acted as the catalyst for the riots which broke out and eventually led to Redlake being shut down for good. It wasn't until it closed that stories of abuse circulated and the state paid to silence survivors.

"You knew him well?" I asked gently.

We pulled into the Seven garage down the road from the club, but neither of us made any effort to move as I turned off the engine.

"Ollie was my bunkmate," Rocky said, his voice thick with emotion. "What those reporters said about his death was all bullshit. He died in the warden's fucked up games. No one in there was stupid enough to jump Filey. Hell, he was one of the good guys."

"I'm sorry about what happened to your friend," I said, reaching out to take his hand, "and I'm sorry about what happened to you there."

"I don't like talking about it." Rocky took a deep breath to regain his composure as he blinked angry tears away. "It brings it all back, y'know?"

I got that. When Hiram kidnapped me, I'd spent my first weeks in Blackthorne Towers locked in a dungeon cell without natural light. Therapists talked about how looking back at your past helps you to move forward, but I've never found solace in revisiting the dark times. Why would I ever want to relive my personal hell?

"You don't have to talk about it," I said. "All that matters is you got out."

"At least I got something good out of my time there," he said wryly. "I know how to fight now."

"You scared me tonight," I admitted. Seeing him helpless at the Rhino's mercy was terrifying and left me wondering whether he'd ever get up again.

Rocky nudged me in the ribs playfully. His cheeky grin reminded me of the playful side he used to have but didn't come out as often anymore. "Maybe you won't underestimate me next time?"

"You can't blame me," I said scornfully. "The last time you got in a fight, I had to step in and kill five guys to save your sorry ass."

"You'll never let me live it down, will you? I got ambushed in the dark." His defense argument fell on deaf ears. "You're not the only one who can fight their own battles. Remember, you don't have to fight everything on your own. I said, I'd be here for you, and I meant it."

"Even if it means going against orders?" I whispered. If Zander ever found out about this conversation, we'd both have to face the consequences.

"I'm listening…"

"What if I wanted to get the photographs back from the Briarlys at the ball?" I asked. "Would you help me?"

This was a test of Rocky's loyalty — not to the Sevens, but to me. Actions spoke louder than words, and I was giving him a chance to prove he meant what he'd promised. I didn't know what our plan was going to be, or what our actions could set in motion, but it would be dangerous. If we got it wrong, we'd be putting the Sevens at stake.

His face set in serious determination as he answered with zero hesitation, "For you, I'd do anything."

"How do I know I can trust you?" I asked, studying his face for any sign that he was lying.

"Let me prove it," he said, keeping his eyes locked on mine.

"Okay." I nodded. A look of agreement passed between us. "I'll let you try."

It transported me back to a simpler time, when it was the two of us against the world. We may be part of the Sevens now, but we were also C and Rocky. Once upon a time, we'd been the only person the other could depend upon. The only constant in our fucked up world.

I may be a fool for trusting him, but he knew how it felt to be powerless. I refused to leave our destiny in the hands of Port Valentine's rich overlords. Zander and West grew up with connections. They focused on what was good for the gang, but neither had to claw their way up the ranks from nothing. Rocky had to earn his position. He knew it was important to take matters into his own hands. When he hadn't, he lost me.

"I won't let you down again, C," he said.

His burning stare and set jaw told me he was telling the truth. I believed him. Suddenly, I realized how close we were... and how he was a half-naked, sweaty, delicious mess. Letting Rocky into my life and heart again was a risk. One I didn't know whether I could come

HOLLY BLOOM

back from for a second time but after tonight? I couldn't fight it any longer.

Rocky opened his mouth to speak again but, before he could, I leaned in to crush my lips against his own.

His hands immediately cradled my face like he held the entire world in his palms. Sure, we'd kissed before... but never like this. When his lips explored mine, he cracked open a small part of me I thought I'd never get back.

He pulled away breathlessly. "I need to shower, or you'll give me a black eye. Remember?"

"I like you like this," I murmured as my eyes trailed down to see the outline of his hard cock through his silky red shorts.

"I don't think you understood me, C," he said. His fingers slid over my thigh, feeling the raised skin of my scar underneath my dagger tattoo. He continued upwards, dipping into my soft inner thigh and stroking my delicate skin. "It was an invitation. West is working all night, and the others won't be back for a few hours..."

My heart hammered. Who could refuse an offer like that? Plus, I wouldn't want to see West's face if he found cum stains on the car seats.

We only made it out of the garage when Rocky pushed me against the brick wall outside. His hand ran through my hair then grabbed it in a hold, pulling my face towards him and coaxing my mouth open with his tongue. Neither of us cared about someone walking past to find West's fiancée kissing the hell outta his friend. We were like horny teenagers again, not able to get enough of each other, and stopping was out of the question.

"If we don't go inside, I'm gonna have to fuck you out here," he murmured.

I caught his lip between my teeth, making him groan, then pulled away.

"It'd be just like our first time," I said breathlessly, tracing my fingers down over his chest and stroking his Seven tattoo. I'd lost my virginity to Rocky on the roof of an abandoned warehouse. It'd been the only place we could go to have privacy.

The sounds of footsteps and giggling growing louder made him grab my hand.

"Come on," he urged, tugging me down the alley towards Lapland's side entrance and into the empty kitchen.

As soon as the door closed behind us, Rocky's mouth was on mine again with a desperate eagerness. He cupped my ass, guiding my hips towards him until we were pressed together. I didn't stop for air. I kissed him back with ferocity and enjoyed the salty taste of his skin.

"Fuck, C," he moaned as I trailed my fingers gently over his back. His muscles were pronounced and defined, but they'd be sore after taking a beating. "I want you so bad."

I squealed as I caught a glass with my elbow and sent it smashing to the floor. Way to ruin the fucking moment...

"You've left me with no choice," Rocky growled. In a slick motion, he threw me over his shoulder.

"You're hurt," I objected as he threw open the door to the club. "Come on, Rocky. What if people see?"

He grinned, already two steps ahead. "I'll say you twisted your ankle in those ridiculous heels."

As Rocky carried me across the dance floor, I caught

sight of West behind the bar. His eyes met mine with burning fury, then he turned away to serve a customer. Was he going to be okay with this? The Hulk was green with fucking jealousy.

"You can put me down now," I insisted as we reached the staircase to the penthouse.

"No way," Rocky said, continuing onwards to his room. "I'm a gentleman."

He took me into his room, which boasted a massive sound system and TV. The lingering smell of weed hung in the air, but not in an unpleasant way. He placed me down gently on his bed.

"So, this is your room..." I said, looking around.

My burning passion had been replaced by something else. Nerves. It took me back to the last time I'd been intimate with Rocky. I was sixteen and had no idea what I was doing.

He sat down by my side, taking my hand in his. "If we're going too fast for you, we can slow things down?"

"No," I said quickly, then tried to play it cool. "I mean, no..."

"It's just me, C," he said, softly stroking my cheek. "Can I kiss you?"

I nodded. Rocky leaned forward, allowing his soft lips to graze mine, and pulled me close. I clung to him, remembering my fear of thinking he was about to die. I parted my lips to greet his tongue. The years that had passed without each other melted away as I climbed onto his lap, craving closeness. He was smeared in blood and sweat, but none of it mattered. This was our reality. Relationships weren't neat and simple; they were raw and imperfect. They challenged and pushed us until we broke, then had the power to fix us again.

Rocky's fingers found the zip at the back of my dress and undid it slowly, running his hand over my back as the fabric came undone. I took a deep breath and pulled my dress over my head, leaving myself vulnerable and open.

"You're so fucking beautiful," he murmured, his voice low and husky with desire. His finger slipped under my bra strap to stroke my shoulder, then I pushed him backward.

I liked the feeling of his body being trapped between my thighs. When we were younger, I let Rocky take the lead, but I wanted to feel in control this time around. His body felt familiar but new, like the same landscape but in a different season. There was so much we had to learn about each other and he stretched beneath me like a new territory to explore. I took the time to run my fingers over the scars covering his chest and arms like a roadmap.

I slipped my hand down further, stroking his hard cock over his shorts. Instead of being even, it felt...

"You're pierced?" I gulped as I slid over the smooth metal balls adorning his shaft.

"Do you wanna see?" he asked.

I nodded and shuffled to allow him to slip his cock out of his shorts. A six-rung Jacob's ladder glittered against his thick brown cock. The two balls nearest his head were bigger than the others, presumably to maximize pleasure and sensation. The ladder ran up to an impressive silver ring at the top of his shaft.

Shit, would *fucking* it hurt? Or worse, get hooked inside and rip me apart? Everyone has read horror stories online about something like that happening after not being able to sleep and falling into an internet black hole. I stripped for strangers on a pole and didn't get nervous, but this was different.

"Don't worry," Rocky said in a soothing voice. "I'll be gentle."

While his cock looked like something from a futuristic movie that would set off metal detectors in an airport, it was fucking *hot*.

"You're forgetting I'm in control here," I said.

Before we did anything else, I needed a closer inspection of robocock. I slid down his body, admiring the tense muscles hiding underneath his hazel skin. He moaned as I traced the tip of my tongue along his V-lines, salty with a hint of iron. He kept his hair trim and short, and it tickled my face as I moved down to face his reverse Prince Albert. Who knew royalty would be so pleased to see me?

I locked my fingers around his base, having to use two hands, and licked up his silky shaft, feeling the cool raised metal against the flat of my tongue. His cock twitched underneath me, craving more. I paused at his swollen head, gently playing with the ring and flicking it back and forth with the tip of my tongue.

"Candy, you feel so fucking good," he moaned as I bent forward to seal my mouth around his dick. I took his cock deeper, enjoying the feel of his piercings and imagining how they'd feel inside me. They'd bring a whole host of new sensations.

Giving head wasn't something I thought I'd enjoy doing, with the memories I had of tearing cocks off whenever one stared me in the face. But I loved giving him pleasure and feeling his body writhe underneath me. He grabbed a fistful of my hair as I sucked on him gently, pushing him to the back of my throat until he was panting. His thighs tightened as his balls clenched, but I wasn't giving him a release... not yet. I paused, then slowly withdrew my mouth with a pop and slid my tongue over his tip to lick a drop of his pre-cum.

"I want to taste you," he demanded, pulling me up and into a kiss. At the same time, he expertly unhooked my bra and threw it to the side. His hands found my nipples and gently squeezed them between his thumb and forefinger, sending tingles shooting down my body.

I pulled away, propping myself up on my elbows. The last time he saw me naked, I'd been an A-cup. "You don't think they're too... big?"

"I think you're perfect. All of you. You were then, and you are now," he said in a gravelly voice. "Now, are you going to keep torturing me, or are you going to sit on my face and let me worship you like the fucking queen you are?"

I'd never been interested in becoming a monarch before, but damn. Now, I could see why having a throne would have some perks.

I slipped off my panties, and his eyes trailed down to my wet slit, groaning appreciatively. Any self-consciousness or hesitation I had evaporated as a primal groan erupted from the back of his throat. "You're driving me fucking crazy, C."

I used the headboard to balance my weight, as his palms grabbed my ass to lower my pussy onto his face. His soft stubble gently tickled my thighs, and his tongue slipped in between my lips to taste my wetness. He moaned, sending vibrations up my legs, and devoured me like I was the first meal he'd eaten in weeks. He licked upwards and I tipped my hips, allowing his tongue to probe my clit and making me gasp. It's a good thing the music was loud downstairs…

Rocky's hand snaked up to my breasts to tease my nipples as his wet tongue rediscovered my entrance. It darted in and out of me in hot hard strokes. My thighs clenched around his head. He looked right at home there, like he could lick me all night long.

"Fuck," I moaned, closing my eyes and rocking my hips to allow the flat of his tongue to knead my clit. Warm arousal dripped out of me, coating his face as he hungrily lapped it up.

My heart rate quickened as he drew me closer to climax. But I wanted more… I wanted to feel his pierced cock tease me and tip me over the edge of no return. Taking his Robocock was not something I would shy away from.

"Hey," Rocky objected in a growl as I rose to my knees to get my pussy out of his grasp. "I wasn't finished."

"Neither was I," I said, meeting his gaze and sliding down his body.

"I want to make sure I don't hurt you," he said, reaching over to grab a bottle of lube from his bedside table. He smeared his cock until it was glistening like a freshly polished statue.

I rolled my eyes. "As if I'm not wet enough…"

"Are you sure you—"

His sentence turned into a moan as I slid my wet heat over his dick. I lowered myself onto him gently. I expected his piercings to feel like being impaled on a bumpy tree stump, instead, it was smoother than I expected. The nubs provided extra sensation, like a ribbed dildo, but nothing I couldn't handle. If anything, it turned me on more.

I sunk my pussy down, taking him as deep as he could go, then rolled my hips. The angle and how we fit together meant one of the metal balls rubbed against my G-Spot, bringing me closer to release. Meanwhile, Rocky's thumb found my clit as we locked eyes. Neither of us looked away. His pupils seared into my soul, and everything else around us fell away. I wasn't the virgin he'd fucked all those years ago. Our bodies had changed, *we* had changed, but it still felt just as good to be together again.

Intense pleasure built from the tip of my toes to my flushing cheeks, causing my whole body to tense like we'd reached the peak point of a rollercoaster and were about to plummet fifty feet below.

"You feel so fucking good," Rocky groaned.

I cried out as my pussy clamped down on his dick like it never wanted to let go. An orgasm shook through me and drowned him in a gush of wetness. Rocky didn't stop though, his fingers continued to work their magic until a second ripple descended over the first, like waves crashing over the beach. I collapsed onto him, breathless, as his hands held me in place and fucked me from beneath, grinding into me.

"Fuck, C," he gasped as his hips bucked into me for a final time and came hard. I rolled off him, trembling and panting, completely incapable of moving.

"I never thought I'd get to do that again," Rocky murmured, propping his head on his elbow and tucking a rogue hair behind my ear while looking down at me.

"No one is more surprised than me," I breathed.

"Are you glad you didn't kill me now?"

I laughed. "I guess not killing you has had its upsides…"

"I've missed you so damn much," he said. "And we will get the evidence back from the Briarlys whatever it takes."

"Shh." I pressed a finger to his lips to silence him. "Not here."

"If you want to shut me up, there are other ways to do it," he said with a wink.

I'd never had a proper home before, but being in Rocky's arms felt like I was returning to a place where I'd always felt safe. The problem was, I couldn't decide whether the feeling of comfort trumped my deep-rooted fear of worrying it would be snatched away…

SIXTEEN

The day of the Briarly New Year Ball had finally arrived. Rocky and I had stolen a few conversations on the roof about our plan, but it'd been hard to find time when we had to focus on running the club, a poker game, and him dealing with a moldy plant outbreak. We would have to wing it.

Thankfully, Rocky knew his way around Briarly Manor and had a few ideas about where Bryce may be keeping evidence of my involvement in Giovanni Romano's death hidden. It would be his job to find it while I created a diversion. All we had to do was get through the dinner first. It couldn't be too difficult, right?

"You've been quiet today." Vixen poked her head into my bedroom as I finished getting ready. "Everything okay, or do I need to be worried about finding body parts under your bed?"

"PMS," I lied, to avoid answering any more questions. "Mood swings."

She snorted. "I don't think you can blame those on PMS."

I shot her an 'I'm not in the mood to be fucked with' look. "Do you want something, or are you just being a pain in my ass?"

"I wanted your opinion." She stepped inside and did a twirl. It was a black-tie occasion, but Vixen was wearing jeans so ripped they showed more skin than denim and a leather crop top. "What do you think?"

"Bryce will love it," I said, rolling my eyes sarcastically and adding, "like a severe case of genital warts."

"Perfect." She smiled in satisfaction and made herself comfortable on my bed. "Did you know this is the first time they've invited me? Bryce puts on his bullshit ball every fucking year. Maybe he's going senile in his old age…"

Somehow, I doubted it. Bryce would have a motivation for wanting all of us there. Whatever it was, it better not interfere with Rocky and I's plans. Finding the photographs of me in the Romano mansion was our number one priority.

"What's his deal with you, anyway?" I asked. Bryce hated Zander, but still acknowledged his existence. Hell, he even pretended to be pleasant to West. Vixen was his flesh and blood, but he treated her like a deadly contagious disease. "Did you burn down his summer house as a kid or something?"

"If only." She scoffed, her eyes blazing. Whatever grudge Bryce held against her ran deep, and the feeling was mutual. "Although, I'd happily strike a match under the manor and watch it burn if Zander would let me."

"The car's waiting," Rocky called through to us from the corridor. "Zander and West are meeting us there."

Vixen pulled a hip flask out of her back pocket and drained it. "It's motherfucking showtime."

After spending the night with Rocky, I hadn't seen a lot of Zander or West. They'd both gone to Hammerville three days ago to sort out a crisis at Seven Sins. Even though we'd all come to an arrangement, the three of them reuniting made my palms sweat — especially after seeing West's reaction to Rocky carrying me through the club when we returned from the Golden Gloves. Sharing didn't come naturally to him.

"Rocky, can you help me reach something?" I called, pretending to be helpless, then turned to Vixen. "We'll see you outside."

"Suit yourself," she said, swaying slightly as she swaggered out. Keeping a drunk Vixen under control at the manor would be like trying to pin a firework to the ground and telling it not to explode in your face.

"How can I be of assistance?" Rocky asked, in an awful attempt at a British accent, and made a goofy bow. He wore a black tux and had even fastened his top buttons. Fitting in would be important if he didn't want to draw any extra attention to himself when sneaking around the manor.

I pointed at the patent red leather clutch on the top shelf and asked loudly, "Can you get it down for me?"

The bag would go perfectly with my black satin dress, which made me feel like a million dollars. It had thin spaghetti straps and a cowl neck which showed off the pendant necklace Zander gave me for Christmas, which I hadn't taken off since.

Rocky retrieved my purse with ease, then grinned mischievously as he blatantly checked me out. "Is this just an excuse to get me alone? We can be late to the party, if you want..."

"You wish," I said as my cheeks heated under his scrutiny. *Don't get distracted, Candy.* I waited until I heard the penthouse door click behind Vixen, then lowered my voice. "Are you ready?"

His teasing demeanor vanished. He knew instantly what I meant and nodded. "We're getting the fucking evidence."

If our plan didn't go smoothly, monitoring Vixen wouldn't be the only mess we had to control...

Despite Rocky's attempt to wrestle bottles of champagne from Vixen in the limo, she was wasted by the time we reached Briarly Manor.

"Should we send her back with the car?" Rocky asked. "Zander is going to flip..."

"I can hear you," Vixen replied indignantly. "I'll be fine."

"It's your funeral," I muttered as the limo came to a stop by West and Zander, who were awaiting our arrival.

They both looked ridiculously handsome in their black pressed suits. I couldn't help feeling a smug swell of pride at knowing those men were all fucking *mine*.

The manor itself was as imposing as I remembered. If Vixen ever lit the place up, the whole skyline would be ablaze for miles. I'd enjoy watching it burn to the ground almost as much as seeing the Briarly empire turn to ash.

West opened the limo door and extended his hand for me to take. His fingers eclipsing mine sent a sizzling spark of desire racing through me. Goddamn you, body. I needed to concentrate on my real reason for being here, not my vagina's uncontrollable urge to pounce on the Seven men.

"You look… incredible," West admired. His Adam's apple bobbed as his gaze lingered on the slice of skin peeking through my dress. My gown was floor-length but had a slit down the right side, opening the fabric to expose my upper thigh with every step.

"Thanks," I said, smiling coyly. "You don't look too bad yourself."

"What are you wearing?" Zander hissed at Vixen, who practically fell out of the limo after me and Rocky. He turned to Rocky in accusation. "Why did you let her come like this?"

"I'm not a fucking child, Zander," she said, getting up in his face. "Last time I checked, we live in a free fucking country."

Zander beckoned over a server standing nearby, who carried a tray of champagne flutes. "She drinks water all evening. Nothing else."

"Killjoy." Vixen pouted and slung her arm around the server's shoulder. He looked like he wanted to run or cry… or both. She squeezed the poor guy's cheek between her fingers. "You'll give me a drink, won't you? Don't listen to nasty Zander."

"She drinks water," Zander spat through gritted teeth. "Or, you'll have me to deal with."

"Shall we go in?" I asked West, nudging my head in the opposite direction and leading him away. I wasn't going to be Vixen's babysitter. She was Zander's problem. "How was the Seven Sins?"

"As expected," he replied, staying as tight-lipped as

ever. Even if he wanted to talk, he'd give no details now. "Are you ready to mix with Bryce's nearest and dearest?"

"You mean the lowest of the low," I corrected in hushed tones as we mounted the sweeping steps to the manor.

"What does that make us?" West asked.

"The bottom of the fucking barrel."

West chuckled. I lost my footing and almost stumbled, but his strong arms were there to steady me. I'd need him to lean on if I didn't want to break my ankles.

"Don't worry," he said. Seven-inch heels were ridiculous, even for me, but they looked gorgeous. They were red and shiny, with a golden snake wrapped around the pointed heel. "I'll catch you if you fall."

"You better," I said, then added under my breath, "because I'm sure the hyenas will be ready to close in and destroy my carcass."

As soon as we strolled into the grand foyer, Bryce hurried over to greet us with a fake ass smile. He had fewer wrinkles than the last time I'd seen him, so he must have invested in Botox or a face-lift for the occasion. New year, new him.

"I see you all made it," Bryce commented as his eyes rested disapprovingly on Vixen's brawling figure in the distance. "And you've all dressed for the occasion."

"Your messenger didn't mention a dress code," I said defensively, noticing Giles standing a few feet away and smirking out of the corner of my eye.

"No matter," Bryce said, waving his hand dismissively, and greeting me with a kiss on both cheeks. His attitude would only antagonize Vixen more. She needed to sober up before facing him, otherwise she could get us all kicked out. "How are your wedding plans coming along?"

"We're in no rush," West replied gruffly.

"Pity," Bryce said with a dramatic sigh. "One never knows what is around the corner."

I bit my tongue to stop myself from adding how it was hard to plan for a day when he and Giles kept trying to get a Seven killed every few months. If Zander's father had his way, there would be no wedding or guests left alive to attend.

"Great things take time to plan," Zander said, appearing out of nowhere. "You taught me that, father."

Bryce's eyes were cold as he regarded his son with indifference.

"What a shame none of the valuable lessons stuck," Bryce replied dryly as Giles strode over to join us. He wore a ridiculous pale blue suit and a pink shirt, which made him look like a candy wrapper. "Giles has always been a better learner."

Giles puffed out his chest like a peacock at the compliment. Bryce may have the business acumen and ruthlessness to have built an empire, but it wouldn't last if he trusted a moron to stand at the helm when he was gone. Bryce should know better.

"I'm going to take our newest Seven member on a tour of the manor," Zander said. "She didn't get a look at the family art collection on her last visit — did you, Candy?"

"Sadly not," I said quickly, masking my surprise and going along with Zander's suggestion. Who knows what he had up his sleeve? "It was *such* a disappointment."

Bryce eyed me suspiciously. "I didn't realize you were a fan of art?"

"Oh, very much," I gushed. Well, if you counted graffiti and tattoos. "Zander has been telling me about the pieces you have here."

"We have quite a collection," Bryce said proudly, not missing an opportunity to inflate his ego. "They have been passed down through the generations. Some from the town's original founder, can you believe?"

I'd never understand why people paid immense sums of money for crusty old relics that didn't even look great. Bryce lapped up the prestige that came from owning such a collection. He wanted what others couldn't have.

"I'll show you now," Zander insisted, taking my arm.

"I can't wait to see." I feigned a smile, then made a show of kissing West on the cheek and whispered, "Look after Vixen, okay?"

With Zander throwing in a curveball tour, someone had to take care of her to free up Rocky's time. How could he search for evidence when he was busy trying to stop Vixen from turning an expensive vase into a hat?

West glowered, unimpressed by his new responsibility. "I'll try."

Eyes followed us as Zander and I ascended the staircase. Whatever Zander wanted to show me must be important. Otherwise, he wouldn't leave the others unattended with Bryce, Giles, and a circle of their closest friends.

The Briarly family had resided in the manor for decades, but it didn't seem like a home anyone lived in. Everything was staged from the obscure marble statues to the furniture positioned with an interior designer's eye. The manor was nothing more than a mausoleum to the Briarly wealth.

"Are you going to tell me what the deal is?" I asked as Zander escorted me down a winding corridor.

"Maybe I wanted to get you alone?" he said in a husky tone.

"Puh-lease." I scoffed. His sexy voice wouldn't work on me. "I know you, Zander. You always have a reason for everything you do."

"Perhaps I wanted to show you the place where I was brought up?" he suggested. I wasn't buying it. Since when was he the sentimental type? He took us through large wooden double doors into a square room that resembled a museum exhibit. Canvases hung on the walls showing sullen faces from times gone by. "This is the Briarly family personal collection. The rest are downstairs in the library."

"Don't you feel you're being watched in here?" I asked. My heels hitting the floor left an eery echo as I examined the art. "There are so many eyes everywhere…"

"On the contrary, it's one of the few places I don't feel like my father is standing over my shoulder," Zander said, looking around at the paintings of his ancestors. Many of them had the same piercing gray stare. "When I was a kid, I used to make up stories about them. About how they would be better than the father I knew."

Zander talking about his past was a big fucking deal. I didn't want to push him too hard as soon as he'd started to open up, but I wanted to be someone who he could confide in. I wanted to get to know the *real* Zander.

"What do you know about them?" I questioned, seeing his brow furrow, deep in thought. "Were they better than Bryce?"

"Fuck no." Zander shook his head, his lips pressed into a thin line. "The Briarly family has always been the same, but I didn't know that then."

I came to a painting of a young boy who must have been around three or four. He looked like a cherub with his blonde, perfect ringlets and rosy cheeks, but the serious expression on his face made me uneasy. Behind him, two figures rested a hand ominously on each of his shoulders.

I pointed at the youngster. "Is that you?"

"Yes," Zander said, tucking his hands in his pockets and coming over to join me.

I recognized Bryce from the painting. He looked younger, similar to how Zander looked now, but with a sharper nose and more menacing stare. The face of the woman on Zander's other side was painted over. My heart sank at the blur of colors obscuring where she used to be like someone had reached into the image and blended the oils together. A few strokes of a brush had erased her from the painting, but it couldn't erase her from existence.

"What happened to your mom?" I whispered, fearing I already knew the answer, but unsure whether Zander would be willing to tell me more.

"My father doesn't want to be reminded of the woman who wronged him," Zander said, running his fingers over the ruined image. He swallowed hard as if he was fighting inner demons. "She's dead, not that I have any proof. They never found her body. My father knows how to make people disappear."

"Zander... I'm... I'm so sorry," I said, placing my hand gently on his arm. Sorry didn't seem enough, but it's all I had. We stood in silence, lost in our minds. I'd never known who my parents were after being dumped on the doorstep of Evergreen as a baby. I used to think it was a curse, but after meeting the Briarly family, it made me realize that it may have been a blessing. "What was she like?"

"She was kind," Zander said, donning a rare smile. "She taught me to cook and filled this place with laughter. She was beautiful, too. You've seen her, remember? The painting you tracked down at the junkyard that we put for auction was the last trace of her after he erased her from existence. He destroyed everything else after she disappeared."

I exhaled slowly, looking at the painting of a younger Zander and thinking about how he didn't know then what his life would grow to become.

"How did you find out about the painting?" I asked.

"My mom had a lover," Zander explained matter-of-factly. "I didn't blame her. My father was a violent man and was never around, so she fell in love with someone else. He was an artist. I have no proof, but I believe my father killed them both when he found out about their affair. When I was older and conducted my own investigations, I found out they had declared his death a suicide. But my father didn't know my mother's lover had kept some of his earlier art in a storage facility. It took me months, but I tracked down his old paintings."

Suicide my ass. Bryce got to him. If he killed his wife, then he would want to destroy everything and anyone associated with her.

"How old were you when she... disappeared?"

"Fifteen," he said, averting his eyes from the painting. I could see behind his neutral expression to the hurt he was holding onto inside. A pain you pushed to the back of your consciousness because it was too hard to process. "When I was away at school, she used to call me every week. The calls suddenly stopped. I'd hoped she'd come to her senses and left him, but I knew something bad happened when I came back home for the summer. She was gone, and so was everything she'd ever touched. I knew then... what he'd done."

Getting kidnapped by Hiram as a teenager showed me the darkest side of human nature, but how would it have felt to have been shown that by your own father? How did a teenager ever come to terms with the fact their dad had killed their mom? I can't even imagine how someone, especially at a young age, could deal with that…

"He's a monster," I spat as my shoulders trembled with anger. "How can you even stand to be here? In this house? In this town? Knowing what he's done."

"He's still my father," Zander said bitterly, his eyes darkened, "and, as long as I play along, he won't break our deal."

I gasped in shock. "Your deal?"

What deal could they have possibly made to stop Zander from cutting his father's throat? He loved his mom. What was more important than giving her the vengeance she deserved?

"Do you want to know why he hates Vixen so much?" Zander paced back and forth. He was speaking words, but only for my benefit, as he allowed his mind to stray to a dark place. "Why he can't stand for her to be around? He couldn't erase her from existence. He would have if I hadn't found out about his plans."

"I'm not sure I'm following," I said, frowning. "What does this have to do with your mom?"

"Keep up, Candy," Zander snapped in annoyance. Under normal circumstances, I'd have retaliated with a snarky response, but I knew his anger wasn't directed at me. Reliving a horrific event brought raw emotions to the surface. "An affair wasn't all my mother was hiding. When my father found out she had birthed a child with another man and kept it hidden from him for years, how do you think he took the news? He didn't want his reputation being muddied by a bastard child."

"Vixen's your half-sister?" My jaw dropped as realization set in, then my heart twisted with dread. "What deal did you make?"

"He allowed Vixen to live in exchange for my silence on her birth and signing over my inheritance and any stake I had in the Briarly empire," Zander said, turning away so I couldn't see his face. "He didn't think I'd take the deal, but he was wrong."

I'd always assumed Zander had been another spoiled rich boy growing up, but I was wrong. So fucking wrong. Zander's revelations fueled my hatred for Bryce even more. He'd been willing to kill an innocent child because he didn't want her tainting the Briarly fucking bloodline.

"To explain why a teenager fell under my care, we decided it was easier to say she was my cousin," Zander went on. "When I first tracked down Vixen, she was already in juvie. It turned out she'd known about me all her life. My mom used to see her when she could, but not enough, and her dad struggled to make ends meet with his art. She had to fend for herself, whilst I was away at school and on holidays to fucking ski resorts. She had nothing, and I had everything."

Zander's shoulders slumped as soon as he'd finished

talking as if retelling the story had drained all of his energy.

I didn't know a lot about Zander and Vixen's mom, but I knew what kind of man Bryce was. She must have been incredibly brave to conceal a pregnancy and hide a child without him finding out for so many years. When he killed her, had Bryce even considered how it would leave two children without a mother? Worse, he'd left Zander to pick up the broken pieces.

"You can't blame yourself," I said, reaching out to take Zander's hand to bring him some kind of comfort. I wasn't good at this kinda thing. I'd rather run from emotions than face them, but I wanted to be there for him. I needed to be. Zander's eyes met mine, and my gaze softened as I saw the guilt written all over his face. I could understand now why he was so protective of Vixen and how he seemed older than his years. "There's nothing you could have done for her. You were only a kid."

Zander shrugged and dropped my hand like youth was no excuse.

"Why did you come back to Port Valentine?" I asked gently. "Why not stay in Hammerville after you started over? You and West had Seven Sins. You could have stayed there."

"I'm here because I want to make my father pay for what he did." Zander's voice was as hard and cutting as a razor's edge. His words were a fucking promise, and he'd do anything to make Bryce suffer. "I had a hundred dollars when my father cut me off, but I still have my name. I may not have an inheritance, but being a Briarly still means something here. I play along with his games knowing, one day, he'll slip up.

And, when he does, I'll be there. Ready to take him down."

Zander took the phrase 'keep your friends close, but your enemies closer' to the next level. I don't know how he could breathe the same air as Bryce without wanting to rip his heart out. Zander was playing the long game, which explained his obsessive control freak tendencies. It was easier to take down an institution when you were on the inside. When he made his move, I'd fucking be there alongside the rest of the Sevens. We'd do whatever it took for him and Vixen to get justice for their mom, and all the other lives Bryce had mercilessly ruined over the years.

"I'll help you," I said fiercely, realizing I would do whatever it takes for him and the other Sevens. They were all I had, and I'd protect them with my fucking life.

"I know you will, little one," Zander said with affection, tucking a stray hair behind my ear. "You're already helping more than you know."

"Why didn't you tell me all this sooner?" I probed. "Why now?"

"I needed to be sure you were one of us," he replied. Like me, Zander didn't trust easily. Him sharing his past showed I'd finally earned his confidence. He was breaking down his barriers and letting me get to know the real him. "Now, I know you are. You were made to be a Seven, little one."

"I'm all fucking in," I confirmed, flashing him my number seven tattoo and reminding him of the lifelong commitment I'd made to them.

"There's something else I need from you too," Zander said, closing the gap between us to ensnare me in his delicious scent. Fresh citrus bergamot with musky undertones brought back memories of him pressed against me. "I need you to give me your word you won't speak about this to anyone outside of the Sevens. Not ever."

My body tingled with the anticipation I get before a kill, but I reluctantly suppressed my urge to serve Bryce's head on a silver platter. If Zander and Vixen could restrain themselves, then I could too. I made a zipping motion with my hands. "My lips are sealed."

Zander ran a finger over my lips, leaving a blazing hot trail behind. His eyes looked at me like he wanted to draw me into his darkness, consume me and never let me go. His gaze flickered to my mouth like he was contemplating what he was going to do next, then dropped his hand abruptly, like I'd scorched him.

"There's something else I want to show you," Zander said, turning on his heel.

I had to race to keep up with him. His head swiveled around as he scanned the area for any sign of movement. Why did I get the sense we were doing something wrong? During my time with Hiram, I developed a knack for remembering building floor plans. As we pressed into the depths of the manor, its layout was becoming clearer in my mind. Who knows? Maybe it'd come in handy...

"This used to be my room." Zander paused outside a door. I thought we'd go inside, but he continued on. "I only stayed here in the summer when my father couldn't enroll me on an overseas summer program. Austria, England, Germany, France... I traveled all over."

After what I'd learned about his childhood, spending vacations in Europe would beat staying at home with his father.

"Come through," Zander said, hurrying forward and looking over his shoulder before opening a door that led into a room lined with books. It was too small to be a library but too big for an office, and there was no desk. "In here."

I looked around as he closed the door behind us. "What is this place?"

Zander grabbed my arms, pushing me backwards and pinning them to my sides against the door, meaning no one else could walk in. He showered gentle kisses up my neck until he reached my ear, then whispered, "I want you to listen very carefully. To the left of this room is a door which is always locked. It's an old servants' entrance. It leads downstairs into their old quarters and onto the manor grounds."

"Why are you—"

Zander cut my question off with a kiss. He took my breath away as his lips pressed against mine, consuming me in a frenzied heat like he wanted to seal away secrets in our embrace. Secrets that I didn't understand.

"No more questions," he murmured, catching my lip in his teeth and nipping it gently. "Just remember what I've told you, okay? You never know when you might need it."

I nodded breathlessly, unsure what relevance this had to anything, but unable to shake the feeling that what he'd told me was important. If his kiss hadn't rendered me incapable of any logical thought, I'd have pressed him more.

"We need to get back to the others," he said, straightening his tie, and looked down at my necklace with a smile. "It suits you."

I stroked the pendant, warm against my skin, and cleared my throat. "I keep my word."

"I know you do." He held out his arm for me to take. "That's only one reason why we're lucky to call you our girl."

I cleared my throat and fluffed up my hair, hoping my flushed cheeks wouldn't rouse any attention when we went back to the party.

Zander and I returned to the foyer, where West stood at the side of the crowd eating a tray of canapés. He towered over everyone else and growled at someone who looked like they wanted to take a snack from him. I couldn't see the others anywhere.

"I thought you were looking after Vixen?" I asked, rejoining West. "Where are the others?"

"I've been busy," West said, wiping crumbs off his jacket and gesturing at the stack of empty trays. "Rocky has everything under control."

Zander looked on edge. After finding out how much Bryce had once wanted Vixen dead, I'm shocked he hadn't put her on a fucking leash and installed a tracker in her arm.

Before we could find them, Bryce made his way toward me. I flashed him a smile like a shark baring its teeth before it ripped its prey in two.

"What did you think of the art, Candy?" Bryce asked.

"You have quite the collection," I said, trying to keep my tone level and control my urge to snap his neck.

Over his shoulder, people parted for a drunken

figure to stagger through. How the fuck had Vixen gotten into such a mess? Rocky was supposed to be sobering her up. Zander's jaw clenched as she stumbled over to join us. It was the first invitation to the Briarly New Year Ball she'd received, but it would be her last. Maybe that had been her intention all along?

"What a great party," Vixen slurred, attempting to poke Bryce in the chest, but missing. "All paid for with blood money. Isn't that right, Uncle Bryce?"

Bryce's nostrils flared in fury as other guests tutted and looked down their pretentious noses in disgust at her. I wanted to force their heads into Lapland's urinals until they licked them clean. Vixen was twice the person they'd ever be.

"I'm going to take Vix for some air." Rocky appeared at her side to steer her away before she said something else to anger Bryce further. "We'll be back by dinner."

"We won't wait," Bryce spat through gritted teeth.

As Rocky passed, he caught my eye and winked. Enabling Vixen to get so drunk had been no accident. Looking after her was the perfect excuse. What better time to slip away to steal the photographs? All I needed to do was keep Bryce occupied until he returned.

Before we had time to recover from Vixen's outburst, Bryce beckoned Giles and his female companion over.

"Have you met Giles's new girlfriend?" Bryce asked. "I think you may have gone to school together, Zander."

A fresh swell of anger grew in my chest, and West slipped his arm around my waist to hold me tight. I'm not sure whether it was for my benefit, or his. The giggling bitch on Giles's arm would make staying in this room of fuckwits even more unbearable.

Zander regarded the woman coldly, with no emotion. "It's been too long, Penelope."

"Not long enough," I muttered under my breath.

I'd last seen Penelope Cole in a motel room where she tried to fuck my *fiancé* in front of me. Her history with the Sevens went way back. She knew what West had done in school as a teenager, and even though she'd been paid to keep quiet about him almost killing a kid in a fight, I didn't like the thought of her knowing our business.

"I met Giles through work," Penelope simpered, stroking Giles's arm, but allowing her gaze to rest on West for a few seconds too long.

I wanted to rip off her ridiculous false eyelashes and skin her eyelids with a peeler, so she couldn't look at him ever again.

"Easy," West whispered soothingly into my hair.

He was fucking delusional if he thought it would calm me down. He wasn't the one having to watch a gold-digger undress him with her eyes like he was a slab of delicious meat. The Hulk was *mine*, and the bitch needed to keep her dirty paws off.

"I'm the new property manager for Giles's development," Penelope announced with a sense of self-importance as if she'd secured a presidency. "Have you heard about it?"

"I didn't know you were interested in property, Giles," I hissed, unable to stop myself, "considering your habit of trashing it."

As much as I hated my dingy apartment, I hadn't forgotten how he'd carelessly ruined everything I owned.

"Some places are beyond saving," Giles said,

flashing me a snide smile. "There is nothing to do but start from the ground up."

"The work starts next month," Penelope gushed. "At Bayside Heights. The entire estate is going to be ripped down and turned into luxury apartments. You're familiar with Bayside Heights — aren't you, West?"

The name meant nothing to me, but West tensed. Penelope was goading him. She was only doing this to make him pay for rejecting her. From her smug expression, her revelation was getting the reaction she'd hoped for.

"It's going to be real estate gold," Giles declared, rubbing his hands together gleefully. "A whole new generation for Port Valentine."

"What about the people who live in the Heights?" West cut in. His irritation crackled through the air like thunder. "What's going to happen to them?"

"What about them?" Giles laughed, clinking his glass with Penelope's. "They'll get their eviction notice two weeks before."

"But those are people's fucking homes," West snarled, lowering his voice to a threatening rumble. "You know there's nowhere else for them to go."

Giles waved his hand nonchalantly. "They're not the type of people I'd want in *my* neighborhood."

Unsurprisingly, the unfeeling bastard knew nothing about what it was like to have a place you feel safe snatched from you.

"I can give you a discount on a new apartment if you'd like?" Penelope purred, running her tongue over her lips and not looking away from West. "I'm sure you'd be *very* comfortable there."

"See? That's my girl. She never stops working." Giles

slapped her ass in encouragement, oblivious to how she was offering herself as part of the fixtures and fittings.

"Thanks for the offer," I snapped, narrowing my eyes at Penelope like a lion locking in on its prey. "But I think we'd need something bigger than an apartment. We wouldn't want to keep the neighbors awake at night — would we, West?"

Penelope winced. If she thought her dating Giles would make West crawl back, she was wrong. Flaunting our relationship in front of her was a better form of torture than tearing off her fake nails and extensions.

"Oh, look…" Penelope mock-whispered in Giles's ear, loud enough for everyone to hear, and pointed at the entrance. "It looks like the trash is back."

Vixen and Rocky had returned. I studied Rocky's face, as he inclined his chin in a nod so subtle only I noticed. I don't know how he'd done it, but our mission had been accomplished. His guess for where Bryce might have kept the evidence must have been correct.

"What is *she* doing here?" Vixen demanded, putting her hands on her hips. Her lip curled as she looked at Giles and Penelope's linked hands.

"Be nice," Rocky encouraged.

"What's wrong, Giles?" Vixen taunted, undeterred by Rocky's polite request. "Can't find a girlfriend of your own? You're going through all of the Seven's sloppy seconds."

I disguised my laughter in a cough as Giles's cheeks reddened in anger. The ring of the dinner bell conveniently diffused any confrontation. If this is how things were before the entrees were served, I'm not sure we'd make it until the main course.

"Let's take our seats, shall we?" Bryce said, leading the way to the dining hall.

All we had to do was get through the rest of the evening without someone finding out Rocky had taken the photographs.

The giant dining hall boasted a long banquet table, which could seat forty people. Candelabras cast the plum walls and guests in a flickering orange glow. Embossed name cards in front of the place settings indicated where we should sit. Whoever was in charge of the seating chart needed firing.

The Sevens were sandwiched between a group of men who looked like ancient mummies resurrected for the occasion, and Bryce, Giles, and Penelope. Bryce's older associates said very little. He seemed to prefer to surround himself with people who had no opinions of their own and mindlessly did his bidding.

When everyone was seated, servers brought out the first course and laid the plates down like a perfectly timed synchronized dive. I couldn't pronounce the name of the dish, but it contained figs and something floral which made my tongue taste like bad perfume. Whatever it was, I finished it in two bites. Why was it that the more zeros on the price tag, the less you got to eat?

"What was it that attracted you to Giles?" Vixen asked, ignoring her food and focusing her attention on Penelope. If looks could kill, West's ex would already be six feet under. "His lack of charm or his bank balance?"

"I told you we shouldn't have invited everyone, Uncle," Giles said, cutting his food into tiny pieces. "Not everyone was brought up to act civilized. It's all about the blood."

"Now, now. Let's all get along nicely!" Bryce raised a hand to silence the bickering, then grinned. "At least until after dessert."

The atmosphere was fraught. Zander's glare burned into his father like he was afraid something bad would happen if he looked away. Rocky tried to talk to Vixen about music, but she ignored him and glared at Penelope, who was trying to eat Giles's face while making eyes at West. West didn't look in her direction; he was too busy finishing Vixen and Zander's plates. Neither of them had touched their food.

"When do you think we can leave?" I murmured in West's ear, making a show of walking my fingers seductively up his arm.

"Whenever Bryce tells us why we're really here," he muttered as the plates were taken away.

I laughed loudly like he'd told a funny joke, causing Penelope to scowl. She wasn't the only bitch who knew how to play games.

Shortly after, the servers reappeared with the main course. An expensive cut of steak which was smaller than my palm. It had nothing on Big Al's in Hammerville.

"I'm a vegetarian," Vixen declared.

"Since when?" Rocky asked in disbelief.

She pushed her plate away. "Since now."

"I'll find out whether the chef can bring you an alternative?" the server offered. From the furious look on Bryce's face, he wouldn't be hired for a Briarly function again.

"Don't bother," Vixen said, folding her napkin and fanning herself with it. "I've lost my appetite."

Next to her, Rocky devoured his meal like an alien who'd never experienced human food before and couldn't get enough of it.

Penelope shot him a look of disdain as some of his food flew off his fork in her direction. "We're surrounded by savages, Giles."

I fought the urge to giggle. If Rocky heard her, he didn't give a shit. It spurred him on more. He ran his tongue down the side of his knife to lick up every drop. After growing up not knowing when you were next going to eat, it was a hard habit to break.

Aside from the classical music playing in the background, the room ate in silence. I struggled to enjoy the taste of the food when I was imagining tearing through Penelope's tongue with each chew.

"Are you going to keep us waiting all night, father?" Zander asked, dropping his cutlery and causing everyone to stare. "When are you planning to tell us why you summoned the Sevens here?"

"Did you forget one of my rules?" Bryce tutted, dabbing his mouth and clicking his fingers for the servers to clear the empty plates. "We never talk business at the table."

"I'm growing impatient," Zander snarled.

"We all are," West growled in agreement. His hand tightened around his fork, making me wonder whether he'd morph the metal out of shape.

"You don't have to stay," Giles said, turning to West and speaking slowly like he was talking to a child. "You're here as the muscle, not the brains. Why don't you leave the business talk to the real men at the table?"

"Are you counting yourself as a real man?" I spluttered, then laughed maniacally before turning deadpan. "If you were a real man, your new girlfriend wouldn't be panting over every cock in sight."

"That's rich coming from the Seven's personal whore," Giles hissed.

"Say another word to her and I'll break your jaw," West warned. His body shook like he was ready to dive over the table and carve Giles up. There would be something satisfying about seeing him strung up with an apple in his mouth like a pig.

"See?" Giles smirked. "What did I say? All muscle and no brains. You're nothing but a monkey doing my cousin's bidding."

I stood up, slamming my hands on the table and making everything rattle. "Say that again and *I* will break your fucking jaw."

"Does every dinner have to devolve into a brawl?" Bryce asked, leaning back in his chair and sipping a glass of wine. The bastard wasn't fooling anyone. This was the type of shit he lived for. "Can't we enjoy a peaceful meal?"

"Why don't we skip the bullshit and you get to the fucking point?" I snarled, unable to hold back my anger.

"I see they did not teach you manners at Blackthorne Towers," Bryce said without losing his cool.

How dare he bring that up?

"They taught me a lot more than manners," I sneered.

West was on his feet. He grabbed my arm to hold me back as rage seared through my veins. I wanted to rip off the tablecloth, smother Bryce with it, then set fire to his corpse along with the whole freaking manor.

Rocky clenched his fists under the table. Vixen was too drunk to realize what was happening, and Zander? His expression remained emotionless. Why wasn't he bothered? Surely, throwing my past in my face was a sign of Bryce escalating the threat against us.

"West, Candy. Why don't you go back to the club and check everything is in order?" Zander addressed us coldly. "The three of us can handle it from here."

I glared at him. Why did I suddenly feel like we were the ones who had done something wrong? He was treating us like naughty children who couldn't behave. It wasn't our fault *his* family was filled with the world's biggest assholes. He may be content to sit back and play the long game, but I wouldn't let the gruesome twosome speak to us like that. How could he even bear to sit in the same room as them, knowing what they'd done?

"If I'm staying, I need more fucking wine," Vixen slurred, gesturing for the server to top her up. Luckily for her, Zander was too busy staring me down to notice. It wouldn't be long before she passed out at the table.

"It's probably for the best you two leave," Bryce agreed.

"Fine," I said, knocking over my chair. If Zander was going to treat me like a moody teenager, I'd fucking act like it. "We didn't want to stay at your shitty ball, anyway."

"See you around, West," Penelope said, wiggling her fingers in farewell.

"You'd better hope you don't," I snarled, then grabbed what was left of my glass of wine and drained it. Zander may want me to go, but he didn't say I couldn't take my sweet fucking time. I licked my lips, staining them red. "You may be a psycho bitch, *Penny*.

But you have nothing on me. If you come near him again, you'll have me to deal with."

Penelope gulped. Maybe she'd finally get the message this time?

"Out," Zander ordered, pointing at the door. "Now."

"Thank you for dinner, Bryce," I said in my most sarcastic tone and slammed my glass down. "The pleasure was all mine."

I took West's hand and swung my hips as we left. My ass looked killer in this dress, and Zander needed to remember who he'd sent away. Making an impression when you entered any room was important, but everyone knew a good exit made a lasting impact. *Always leave them wanting more.*

SEVENTEEN

West and I were like high schoolers who'd got kicked out of prom for sneaking vodka into the punch bowl or smoking pot under the bleachers.

"How do you feel about having a little fun?" I asked as we burst out of the manor. Just because our evening got cut short, it didn't mean our night had to end yet.

West looked at me like I was crazy. Hell, maybe I was... but I knew he'd bite. He was every bit as crazy as me, and I already had a plan. A smile danced over my red lips. "You know how to hot-wire a car, right?"

I nudged my head towards Giles's classic Cadillac. There was no question it was his from the personalized plate. Who else would leave it in the most prominent spot to show off their success to the other guests? The piece of metal on wheels costs more than a normal person's freaking house. Giles may have money in his bank account, but dollars couldn't buy class. He was practically begging for someone to take it away. It's about time someone taught the asshole a lesson.

"Obviously," West said. It was a stupid question. Of

course, he knew how to hot-wire a car. He was a guy who treated waxing cars with the same attention to detail as a Korean skincare regime. "You want to go for a joyride?"

"Maybe." I sauntered over to Giles's car and ran my hand over the shiny hood. "But we're not just gonna steal it, we're gonna destroy it."

West smirked. He needed no more persuasion. "It's a good thing Giles is into vintage motors, and I know where the Briarly tool shed is..."

With all of Bryce's staff inside assisting with the elaborate dinner service, it was easy for us to scale around the side of the building and for West to force his way into a small outbuilding, where the manor's gardener stored his supplies. Next, all West needed was five minutes with a screwdriver and a hammer...

"You sure know your way around an engine," I said, slipping into the passenger seat as Giles's car whirred to life.

"Are you ready?" he asked, raising his eyebrows in anticipation.

"You said you used to be a racer," I said, then winked. "Let's relive your glory days."

West slammed his foot on the gas and we sped down the drive, leaving a trail of dust and destruction in our wake. I stuck my hand out of the window and gave the manor a middle finger as we zoomed past the CCTV cameras monitoring the entrance.

Fuck you, Giles.

We wouldn't make it far before he realized his precious toy was missing, but that made it even more fun. If Giles couldn't play nice, then he shouldn't play at all. I laughed, keeping the window open and letting the wind whip my hair into a frenzy.

"You're a bad influence," West said, but he couldn't hide the wide grin spreading over his face as our speed climbed and we weaved through the empty roads like we were competing in the Grand Prix.

My purse vibrated in my lap. I glanced at my cell, then switched it off. Zander could wait. He was the one who had wanted us to leave, remember? We didn't need a lecture. If he thought we'd come rushing back at his beck and call, he was wrong.

"I thought you couldn't destroy cars?" I asked.

"I can make some exceptions," West replied. "Giles is one of them."

"You know everything he says is bullshit, right?"

Giles may think West had nothing more to offer than muscle, but I knew better. West was smart. One of the best poker players I'd ever seen. He was also the glue that held the Sevens together. A fierce protector who would do anything for those he loved.

"He can say what the fuck he wants about me," West said. His jaw clenched as he gripped the wheel tighter. "But no one speaks to you like that."

"How chivalrous…"

"I mean it, Candy." West sped up. "I'll fucking kill him if he talks to you like that again."

The car screamed in objection as we hit three figures. It was a beautiful vehicle, but no one had pushed it this hard before. I couldn't hear anything but the roar in my ears, which sounded like a train about to derail. I wanted to wreck the car, but not while we were inside it.

"Pull over," I shouted. West didn't listen. He was too

busy chasing the adrenaline rush, no matter the consequences. "I said, pull the fuck over."

West swerved suddenly, and we hurtled off the concrete down a bank. Our seat belts held us in place, but my teeth rattled as we flew down the uneven terrain. As we neared the bottom of the incline, he slammed the brakes, jolting us to a halt. After taking a second to check we were both alive, my hand was on the door handle, and I jumped out before West took us on another death-defying ride.

"What's wrong, Pinkie?" West asked, following me out. The wild look in his eyes told me the beast was coming out to play. "Too extreme for you? You're the one who asked me to race the car."

"And now, I'm asking you to destroy it," I said. My voice shook, but I refused to admit he'd scared me shitless. "Any ideas?"

West roared like a wild beast and smashed his foot into the side of the car, kicking a huge dent in the door. The metal crunching told me it wouldn't be long until the car wasn't the only thing damaged.

"C'mon, West," I said, standing in front of him before he could take out his repressed anger again. "You'll break your leg."

"Get out of my way," he snarled.

He'd already tipped past the point of no return.

"Make me," I challenged. I didn't move an inch. "I know you won't hurt me."

"You don't know a thing about me," he said, advancing towards me and pinning my body against the cool metal. He leaned down, his hot breath tickling my cheeks. "We're all alone in the middle of nowhere. This is where I bring men to die. This is a place where people disappear and never come back."

"You know, West," I said, raising my eyebrows in amusement, "I don't think you're as scary as you think you are."

"And you're not the bitch you pretend to be," he whispered in my ear, making the hairs on my arms stand on end. "You pretend not to give a shit about anyone or anything, but I see the real you. The parts you want to stay buried. The pain you want to pretend doesn't exist. You care about people, Pinkie, even if you won't admit it."

"What about the parts of yourself you keep buried, West?" I fired back, ignoring his assessment and how scarily accurate he was. "How does it feel to have to hold back every urge inside your body to stop you from losing control?"

"I'm a fucking monster," he warned, "and the sooner you see that the better."

"Show me," I said, raising my chin in defiance. I knew how to deal with the dark side of West. I could channel darkness, and right now? I wanted it to consume me. I didn't want to think about Giles's reaction when he found out we took his car, how Zander would be furious, or what Bryce would do when he realized we stole from him. I needed West to take my worries away in a way only he could. "I want to see your monster."

I couldn't decide what I wanted to see more: the depraved animal who had the power to slay anyone on sight or the growing bulge in his pants that looked like it'd tear me in two.

"You don't know what you're asking..."

"What's wrong, West? Not man enough?" I taunted, cocking my head to the side, knowing this would rile him. "You said you're a monster, so fucking prove it."

Bingo. A low rumble erupted from the back of his throat as the beast's attention turned to me. His hands closed around my throat, squeezing until I was gasping for air. His vicious streak was coming out, and all of his previous concerns for my safety vanished. He pulled my face close to his but didn't kiss me. He enjoyed feeling my pulse constrict under his grasp.

"This is what you want, huh?" West murmured menacingly. His pupils dilated — big black saucers eclipsed his blue irises.

My eyes watered, and my breathing quickened as I nodded. This is what I'd asked for, and there was nowhere to run.

West loosened his hold, making me go dizzy as the blood rushed back to my head, and fuzzy dots eclipsed my vision. Meanwhile, he grabbed my hips and forced me to turn around. The spear in his pants jabbed into my back like an enticing promise of what was to come as he threw me forward over the hood, still warm from the overworked engine, and held me down.

He tore the back of my dress open to reveal my legs and ass in an explosion of passion, spiking my excitement. Before I knew what was happening, he ripped my panties off, allowing the cool night breeze to tickle my pussy. Above us, the headlights of cars from the highway rushed past. All anyone had to do was look over the edge of the grassy verge to see us, but I didn't care. His urgent desperation to have me only heightened my desire. We were too far gone. We couldn't stop now.

West spat roughly onto his hand and forced my legs

apart, exposing me in the most vulnerable way for the best access. His wet fingers found my heat, but he wasn't gentle. He forced his way inside me, and I cried out. No one could hear my cries here.

"I'll fucking destroy you, Pinkie," West growled.

His fingers fucked my pussy in hard, brutal strokes. The beast wanted to take everything he could from me by using my body for his gain. He was raw, real, and unrestrained. This was a version of West he never let loose, and I was the only person he could share it with. It's what I'd been waiting for since the first time I saw him.

"Do it," I begged.

His fingers withdrew, and he unbuckled his belt. A few seconds later, he unsheathed his cock. His head found my entrance, rubbing against it, then plunged in as far as he could go. I gasped, rooted to the spot as my insides stretched to accommodate him. My hips slammed into the hood with each of his deep thrusts. I tried to shift to adjust my position, but West held me down, using me like a rag doll and continuing to pound into me mercilessly. The beast took what it needed and gave me what I desperately craved.

"Is this what you wanted?" West grabbed a fistful of my hair and jerked my head back as his balls slapped violently against me. My ass throbbed, and I'd be bruised in the morning, but he wasn't done… far from it, and I was loving every second. "Have you seen enough?"

"More," I pleaded as he released his grip on my hair. His inhibitions were shedding, which only made me desire him more. I'd lusted after him for so fucking long but never wanted to admit it, but now that it was happening? I didn't want it to end. "Show me more."

He grunted, slamming me forwards until my cheek was pressed against the car. Looking to the left, all I could see was darkness. It consumed me, just like West.

"You're gonna regret asking that," he murmured, then cleared his throat.

His spit dripped down my ass as his fingers explored me in places where no one had ever touched me before. Ass play was new to me. I tensed, trying to shuffle away, but West was too strong. His wet thumb circled my asshole, and a giggle escaped my lips. No one said it tickled.

My laughter only infuriated him. He pushed his thumb into my ass and continued to pound into me from above. Initially, it burned, but as his thumb pushed deeper, I got used to the weird but arousing sensation. He built up speed, fucking both holes with the same aggressive vigor.

"You like being our Seven girl, huh?" he growled. "You like being fucked by all of us?"

"Harder, West," I begged as the car shuddered from the force. It felt like I was being taken from behind by a fucking truck, but my pussy welcomed it. I needed it. I've needed *him* for so long. "Fuck!"

West roared like a wild animal, then slammed into me one final time. He grunted as his hot cum spilled into me, flooding my insides with warmth. He pulled out and murmured, "Shit…"

No one could tame West's monster, but I'd happily volunteer to take it out of the cage again. I knew how to handle his darkness. He'd given me everything he had and, now I'd seen the side of him he tried to repress, I never wanted to let him go.

I turned to face him, slightly unsteady on my feet and aching all over in the best possible way. A sheen of sweat covered West's skin from the exertion, but the beast was gone. He had fucked it out of himself. Instead, West's eyes were wide with horror, like he'd seen a ghost.

"Are you... are you okay?" he asked. His eyes searched me for damage and lingered on the tattered bottom half of my dress, swallowing hard. "Did I... did I hurt you?"

My hips would be bruised tomorrow, but it'd be a welcome reminder of how his body had ripped through mine like a hurricane. I traced a finger up my thigh to collect his cum dripping between my legs, then popped it into my mouth to suck it clean. "I told you I could handle it."

Did that answer his question?

West's eyes widened, then a half-smile spread over his face.

"Get in the car, Pinkie," he ordered, his voice deep and husky.

"Why?" I asked as he opened the door to the backseats. "Are you gonna try to kill us again?"

"Maybe later." He grinned, pulling me to the open door. His hand cradled my head as I ducked down, then he pushed me backward. "But, first, I always clean up my mess."

Well, duh. He was a clean freak... but this time, it took on a whole new meaning. West climbed in after me as I backed up, enjoying the chase and teasing him. His gaze trailed down my body, but I kept my legs pressed shut and slid out of his reach, pressing my back against the car window opposite him. I felt behind me for the handle. It was locked.

"You can't escape me," The Hulk said, his patience wearing thin. He grabbed my legs, pulling my knees over his shoulders and pushing my crotch into his face like he was bobbing for a freaking apple. "This cunt is mine."

Most guys were afraid of their cum, but West didn't flinch. His mouth eagerly dove between my legs. He parted my lips, then fucked my pussy with his tongue, savoring the taste and making me writhe uncontrollably beneath him.

"I could eat your pussy all night long," he murmured, his hot breath tickling my inner thighs.

"Then fucking eat it," I demanded, pushing his head back down and grinding onto him. He'd taken what he wanted from me, and now it was his turn to oblige.

West didn't disappoint. Damn, he approached the task like his life depended on it. The sound of him murmuring in appreciation between lapping up my wetness turned me on even more. His tongue glided over my clit. He took it into his mouth, sucking softly, and sending vibrations shooting through my whole body.

Suddenly, he caught my clit gently between his teeth. My back arched with the change of sensation, and I cried out as an unexpected toe-curling orgasm rattled through me. I dug my nails into his shoulder, clinging on, as West latched onto my clit, teasing out every drop of pleasure.

"It's too much." I shuddered as the rising peak left me a shaking puddle of mess.

"You're not done yet, baby," West said, sliding his tongue down to lick up my juices and his cum seeping out. He spat on his fingers before pushing one inside me. Then two. His hands were so gigantic that two of his inked fingers were wider than an average man's cock. They made a squelching noise as they slid in and out. "You're so wet, Pinkie."

He stroked my G-spot, massaging it gently, then returning to kiss my inner lips before returning to pay my clit more attention. My legs clamped down around him to lock him in place, as the pleasure built inside my pussy and begged to explode. I thought I'd already got off the pleasure train, but boy was I wrong. West didn't stop. His determination to get me off only turned me on more. He kept licking and probing my insides with a hungry enthusiasm until I couldn't take it anymore…

"Fuck," I screamed.

My pussy squeezed around him, and hot liquid gushed down his hands onto the seat. My head rolled back, and I closed my eyes as I embraced the orgasm enveloping my body in blissful pleasure. I forgot where we were. How we'd got here. Nothing else mattered other than this fucking feeling. If you asked me my name, I wouldn't be able to tell you.

As soon as I returned to my body, I realized I was soaked. What the fuck was that? I'd never been so wet before. Is this what squirting was? West groaned into my pussy, licking it up. Whatever it was, he seemed to love it.

"Now you're officially *our* Seven girl," West said, sitting up to wipe his chin with the back of his hand. He had to slouch to stop his head from hitting the roof.

"Damn, you have no idea how long I wanted to do that."

"How long?" I asked breathlessly, unable to move from my position for fear I'd pass out. My thighs shook uncontrollably like the aftershocks of an earthquake.

"Since the moment your smart mouth whipped my ass in poker and didn't give a damn about what anyone else thought of her," West said. "I was so used to getting my own way, but you? You came in and fucked everything up."

"What did you call me again? A gutter trash whore?" I asked, raising an eyebrow. "Maybe you have a better poker face than I thought..."

"Just because I had to have you, it didn't mean I had to like you," West snapped, then leaned back, deep in thought. "When I watched you dance in blood on the stage, it made me realize you were as fucked up as the rest of us. When we kissed that night after the Maven, I broke Zander's orders for the first time, and I didn't care. You were like a fucking poison. It didn't matter how many girls I tried to screw to get you out of my head. You were the only one I could think of. Yours is the only face I could cum to, and I fucking hated you for it."

Knowing that The Hulk had felt as drawn to me as I had to him only deepened our connection. Our lust had been forbidden, but we'd fought our desire for too long.

"And now?" I slid closer, running my hand over his chest to feel the tense muscles underneath his shirt. "Do you still hate me?"

"Now, you're still driving me insane." West cupped my chin in his hands and forced me to look up at him. His pupils dilated as he maintained eye contact and drew me into his world, where I could get lost forever. "You've seen the monster that lives in me first-hand. You didn't run from it. You trusted me not to hurt you when I could rip you apart."

"I knew you wouldn't."

"How could you know that when I didn't even know myself?" he said, dropping his hold on me and looking away. The car windows were steamed up, so there were no other distractions. He couldn't avoid this. "Tonight... I lost control... I could have really hurt you."

"But you didn't," I reminded him. "You may have darkness living inside you, but so do I. Instead of keeping it chained up, maybe you should let it out sometimes?"

His eyes trailed down to my pebbled nipples and swallowed hard. "Are you volunteering?"

"Maybe," I whispered, then kissed him, tasting myself on his tongue. Whenever we kissed, it made me ravenous. A hunger that could never be satiated when he was around. My pussy ached, but I still wanted more. Where the Sevens were concerned, there were no limits. Is this how normal people felt when they cared about someone? Like they were an addiction, and nothing ever seemed to be enough? I sunk my teeth into his lip to draw blood, then sucked it off. "Your monster and mine can be friends."

"You're crazy." West shook his head. He ran a finger over his lip to collect the blood, then held it out. I licked it off slowly, mesmerizing him like a hypnotist's pendulum. "You're all fucking ours. We're never letting you go."

"Don't make promises you can't keep, West."

"I'm not planning on breaking it," he growled. My

eyes flickered to his lap, where his cock was as hard as a rock. He chuckled, following my gaze, then sighed. "What I wouldn't give to make your tight pussy gush for me again."

"I've never done that before," I confessed, a blush creeping over my cheeks. His fingers had been in my ass, and he'd made me squirt all over his chin, but now I was embarrassed?

"It was fucking hot," West said. "I like knowing you were so wet for me that you couldn't control yourself. Wait until I tell Zander and Rocky..."

"Hey." I nudged him in the ribs. "Just because we have an arrangement doesn't mean we have to share everything."

"So, I can't even tell them how fucking good you taste?"

I cleared my throat. If we kept talking like this, Giles would find us before we destroyed his car. In the distance, fireworks showered the night sky in pretty colors and sparkles. I'd forgotten changing a calendar was an occasion people celebrated. A new year had never made a difference to me before but, with the Sevens by my side, maybe this one would be different...

My heart and soul had been crushed under Hiram's regime, but slowly, the Seven men were helping to put me back together and rediscover who I really am.

"Happy New Year, Pinkie," West said, grinning wickedly. "Way to start it with a bang."

"We may be in another year, but there's no excuse for dad jokes." I rolled my eyes. He looked way too pleased with himself for that comment. "Now, are we gonna ditch this ride or not?"

Before we could be the dazzling 'new year, new me'

versions of ourselves, we had to get rid of last year's problems.

"I have a plan," he said, getting out and hopping into the driver's seat. "Belt up."

I wasn't convinced the engine would start after West pushed the car to its limit earlier, but it didn't object. Just like me, the car couldn't resist his magic touch. My heart hammered in my chest, and I hoped we wouldn't have to get out anytime soon. I needed longer for my legs to recover and not feel like they were made from Jell-O.

We took quiet roads, snaking around the edges of Port Valentine until we arrived in an area I was unfamiliar with. There were three high-rise apartment blocks, a worn basketball court, and other tired surrounding buildings. It was a place where society put people they wanted to forget about — just like Evergreen, where I'd grown up.

"Where are we?" I asked as we parked. So far, no one had followed us, but the sun would come up soon. A Cadillac was hardly inconspicuous in this neighborhood.

"This is Bayside Heights," West said. "The place Giles wants to knock down. Here, put this on."

He handed me his suit jacket to wear. It dwarfed me, but at least it covered up my ass and ripped dress. He got out, and I followed. A group of teens played basketball nearby and listened to rap music. Overhead, pot plants lined the modest balconies. It may not be a wealthy neighborhood, but it was a place where people were trying to make themselves a home and a decent living. A place where parents wanted their children to do well and had to work damn hard to provide for them.

"What are we doing here?" I questioned. While seeing what buildings Giles intended to turn to rubble was interesting, it wasn't the time for a tour. Driving around in a hot vehicle wouldn't do us, or the residents, any favors.

"Fixing our problem," West replied.

Before he could explain, a young kid from the court sprinted over. He must have been around twelve years old, wore an oversized cap, and almost tripped over his laces to get to us.

"West," the kid panted. "Have you brought anything today?"

"Not today, kiddo." West ruffled his hair fondly. "Next time, though. Is your brother around?"

"He's over there." The kid pointed, racing off at a hundred miles per hour again, and his voice trailed after him. "I'll get him."

A few minutes later, an older kid swaggered over. He was in his late teens, but looked older and had the attitude to match.

"Is this your new girl I've been hearing about?" The kid looked at me suspiciously. He may be young, but I could tell he had a shrewd eye. He knew better than to trust outsiders. I liked him straight away.

"Sure is. Candy, this is Jacob. He and his family do odd jobs for me," West said. I smiled, and Jacob grunted back in acknowledgment. It's the best I'd get. West turned back to Jacob and asked, "Is your uncle still around?"

"It's a sweet ride." Jacob walked around the car and

let out a low whistle. His eyes narrowed. "How much for the job?"

"As long as it's off my hands, you'd be helping me out," West said.

"I'm no charity," Jacob said, crossing his arms. This is what happens when you grow up hustling. You learn quickly that nothing good ever comes for free. It's better not to owe anyone anything.

"Fine, we'll split three ways. You, your uncle, and me," West grumbled. He didn't need the money, but it was worth compromising for Jacob's pride. "We got a deal?"

Jacob nodded curtly. "Done."

"It needs moving fast," West said. "People are looking for it."

Jacob asked no more questions. A second later, he jumped behind the wheel. We watched as he drove to a row of garages down the block. A few moments later, the car vanished from view.

I stared after him and frowned. "Is he even old enough to have a license?"

"The kid is a better driver than you," West said, making me scowl. "Jacob and his uncle can flip the car. It'll look completely different when they're done with it. Jacob's parents died a few years back. Their uncle does what he can, but it's tough. For them, and most of the other kids around here."

"You seem to know them well," I said.

"This is where I grew up." West looked around wistfully, then threaded my fingers through his. "Come inside. I want to show you something."

He led us into the nearest block. The hallway was cramped and the air stale, but it pleasantly surprised me to see the lift still worked. We stepped inside and took the squeaky ride up to the fifth floor, while I wondered whether we were about to plunge to our death.

"This is where my father lived," West explained, as we climbed upwards. "When he died, his lease got passed to me."

The lift pinged at our stop and West took me through a dimly lit corridor. It was narrow and the ceilings were low, making him look like a giant. At its end, West ducked down to feel around underneath a doormat for a key.

"Home sweet home," he said, unlocking the nearest door and letting us into an apartment. "After you."

Inside, it was basic but spotlessly clean. Apart from cans of beer, a TV, a sofa, and a side table, there was no other furniture or signs of life. It was the opposite of the flashy penthouse in Lapland, where the Sevens lived.

"Do you come here often?" I asked.

"Here and there." He shrugged. "It's another place to come to when I want space. The club can get... intense."

While there are many benefits to living above Lapland, I understood the appeal of having a place to escape when things got too much. This was his refuge amongst the chaos, and I felt special he'd chosen to share it with me.

"I help around the Heights, where I can too," he said. I followed him over to the window, where we made sure Jacob had hidden Giles's car from sight. The kid was good. "I try to get the kids here to make better choices. It's too easy to fall into the wrong crowd. This is one of the places where the Razors and other gangs come to recruit. "

"I get it. They're easy pickings for those fuckers," I muttered. "What will happen to them if this place gets bulldozed?"

"The only other places they'll be able to afford are outside town. If you think it's bad here, it's fucking anarchy on the fringe. The Razors—"

"Run riot?" I finished his sentence.

After watching a new member of the Razors bleed out on Lapland's floor, I didn't want to see any other kids suffer the same fate.

"Exactly," West said, strolling over to the fridge and grabbing a bottle of beer. He held one out for me, but I shook my head. He cracked open his and drained it.

When Rocky and I lived in Evergreen, he joined a local gang. He wanted money, and selling drugs was the only way for him to make enough to go to college. It was supposed to be a way of financing our future. Instead, his decision had devastating consequences for both of us. If he hadn't joined the gang, would Hiram have seen me that night? Would things have been different?

"Is there anything we can do to help?" I asked. I couldn't change the past, but I could help make the future a little less bleak for others. I knew what happened to vulnerable kids. How easy they were to exploit.

"Stopping the development would help." West laughed hollowly. His eyes narrowed. "But that'll never happen. The Briarlys have allies everywhere — even tying ourselves to the building before they blast it down wouldn't be enough to stop their plans."

They'd probably see crushing us in the process as a massive bonus.

"But there must be something," I said, surprising

myself with the passion of my conviction. Hell, it'd been a while since I'd felt strongly about something that didn't involve spilling blood or revenge. The passion to make a difference got stamped out of you after you realized bad things happened to good people, no matter what you tried to do. Had West's tongue fucked with my brain chemistry?

"This isn't a battle we can win." West sighed in defeat, then checked his cell and frowned. "Zander has called a meeting. We have to go back."

"Do we really have to go so soon?" I asked, running my hand down his chest and lingering on his waistband. "Doesn't this place have a shower?"

"You'll be lucky to get hot water," he said, then winked. "Besides, I want you to walk back into the club smelling of me."

"I'm not a piece of territory, you know." I scowled. "My leg is not a fucking tree you can piss all over."

He roared with laughter. "I can't say anyone has ever said that to me before."

When he smiled, small crinkles appeared around his eyes which I hadn't noticed before. I concentrated hard to keep my sulky pout firmly in place. There's no way the bastard was ever going to find out his smile was contagious and gave me butterflies.

"Do you enjoy showing off all of your conquests?" I said, then paused after seeing the mischievous twinkle in his eyes that matched his silver canine. "Don't answer that."

"Is the girl with no feelings getting jealous?"

"You wish," I lied.

"You know, I've never given a girl a ring before..."

"Am I supposed to be flattered that I'm your first fake engagement?"

He grabbed me by the waist and pulled me close. My heart sped up, remembering how his hands held me down as his cock pounded into me.

"Fake or not," West said, sweeping a loose hair off my cheek, "you're the only girl I'd want to wear that ring."

I turned away before he could catch my smile. "Let's go before Zander sends his minions out looking for us."

West may think he was a monster but, beneath it all, he was a teddy bear.

EIGHTEEN

We hitched a ride back to Lapland with a kid from Bayside Heights. West tipped him a hundred bucks for his trouble, making the kid's face light up brighter than a neon sign.

"Zander is going to be furious about the car," I muttered as we made our way through the empty club.

New Year was usually a busy time for Lapland, but we'd made a lucrative deal with the manager of the Smoker. He had hired all of our dancers for the evening for their burlesque-themed celebrations. We had tasked Mieko with making sure they behaved. It worked out perfectly with the rest of us attending the Briarly event.

"Maybe," West said, grinning. "But it was worth it."

The ache between my legs agreed, but I shushed him. We were like naughty teenagers sneaking home after curfew…

The first thing I saw upon entering the penthouse was Vixen sprawled over the sofa like a limp piece of lettuce. A bucket rested on the floor in front of her and a large glass of water perched precariously on the arm, close to toppling over.

"Are you okay, Vix?" I asked. "You look like death."

"I *feel* like fucking death, too," she croaked like a zombie coming back to life after being killed one too many times. "Do you have to talk so loud? I blame Red. It's his fault for giving me all those shots."

"Let's not pretend you didn't force them down yourself," I said, catching Rocky's eye from across the room. He sat on the floor next to Vixen's bucket, presumably on hand to throw it under her face if she retched. We were getting into dangerous territory. The last thing we wanted was for anyone to wonder how she'd gotten so drunk after Zander cut off her supply.

"Where's Zander?" West asked, looking around. "I thought we were having a meeting?"

"He's coming soon," Vixen said, then clutched her head and groaned, sinking back into the cushions.

"What did we miss?" I asked Rocky.

"Vixen throwing up over Bryce's new Bengali rug was the highlight of the evening," Rocky said with a smirk. "Well, until Giles noticed his car was missing."

"Oh, really?" I feigned shock. "What a shame."

Vixen raised a sharp eyebrow in our direction. Even when recovering from alcohol poisoning, she had the radar of a bat. "What do you two know about that?"

"Nothing," West declared. He sat down on the opposite end of the corner sofa to Vixen and pulled me onto his lap. "Nothing at all."

Rocky laughed. If West wrapping his arms around me bothered him, he didn't show it. I didn't know how this whole sharing thing would go down, but I couldn't help feeling guilty. I didn't want to rub it in his face. I'd be furious if another girl came within an inch of him.

Rocky shook his head and said, "I haven't seen Giles so mad since—"

"What's that smell?" Vixen interrupted, wrinkling up her nose and staring pointedly at me like I was a walking cum rag. "You smell like a fucking—"

"I'm going to shower," I said, jumping up before she could finish her sentence. West chuckled. The big man loved claiming his territory.

By the time I cleaned the smell of steamy car sex off me and re-joined the others, Zander had returned. I expected him to launch into a lecture. Instead, his expression remained impassive as he sipped his drink.

"You shouldn't have taken his car," Zander said, keeping his tone light as I sat down next to West.

West slung his arm over my shoulder and pulled me close. He didn't seem to mind that I'd chosen to wear his T-shirt. I had a whole wardrobe filled with new skimpy clothes, but I opted for comfort. There was something nice about wearing the guy's clothes.

"Karma is a bitch. Maybe *he* shouldn't have been such an asshole?" I retorted huffily, then decided changing the subject was the smartest course of action. "What did Bryce want to talk to the Sevens about, anyway?"

Before they sent us away from the table, Bryce was building up to the climax of the evening. He invited the Sevens to his ball for a reason, and I wanted to know what it was.

"That's why I've called this meeting," Zander said. "He made us an offer."

"And?" I flicked my wet hair over my shoulder impatiently, showering West in water. "What was his offer?"

"He wants us to join forces," Zander continued. "He thinks it'd be best to combine all of our assets. He feels having two Briarlys in the same town is giving mixed messages. He wants us to be partners."

"He's gotta be joking," West growled.

"Okay, I'm done." Vixen threw her arms in the air and rose to her feet. "I'm going to bed, where none of you fuckers can disturb me."

"Why would he do that?" I hissed, dropping my voice until I heard Vixen's door slam. "What did you say?"

"I didn't give him an answer," Zander said with a shrug. "Not yet."

"Joining forces doesn't make sense," I said. Bryce had more wealth, power, and influence in Port Valentine than the Sevens. *Why would they want to team up with us*? Sure, we had the Seven Sins casino, a decent weed-growing operation, and a strip club, as well as doing extra jobs on the side, but it was small fry compared to the Briarly empire. "There must be a reason."

The way I saw it, there were only two possible reasons why Bryce would want to merge. Either the Briarlys were burning through cash quicker than they were making it or, the more likely option, they were looking for a fall guy for something else they were planning.

"In case you haven't noticed, my father isn't exactly transparent," Zander said, rubbing his chin. "He gave us a few days to think about it."

"You're not seriously considering it though, are

you?" I asked. "I know it'd be easier to take him down from the inside, but—"

"Of course I'm not considering it," Zander snarled, cutting me off. "I'd rather die than work with my father, but I am going to find out why he put forward the proposal. One way or another."

"What can we do?" West pressed.

Zander tapped his foot impatiently. "I'm working on some leads."

"Care to share, or are we always the last to know?" I snapped.

West squeezed my knee in warning. Fuck his warning. Zander may be our boss but, if he wanted me to be *their* girl, he had to get used to me saying what was on my mind.

Zander's stare burned through me as his eyes narrowed. "Maybe I'm working out who I can trust."

"What's that supposed to mean?" I hissed, trying my hardest not to raise my voice. After opening up to me about his mom, I thought we'd got past the point of keeping secrets from each other. "If you have a problem, why don't you just come out and fucking say it?"

"Why should I trust you if you go against my orders?" Zander said, holding up a USB stick and dangling it from his fingers. From the way Rocky squirmed in his chair, I knew exactly what it was. *Shit.* "I have my sources within the manor, and Red's disappearance didn't go unnoticed. Neither did his attempts to cover it up or lie about it."

Well, I suppose Zander finding out on his own was better than Rocky throwing me under a bus. I wasn't going to apologize for doing what was right. The Briarlys owned a lot of shit, but I wouldn't let them own *me*. We'd taken back what was rightfully ours. Didn't he understand why we had to do it?

West frowned, completely oblivious. "What's going on?"

I ignored West's question, not taking my eyes off Zander. "We wouldn't have had to steal the photographs if you agreed to help."

"I told you I was working on it." Zander slammed his glass down on the table, all of his prior calmness gone. "You realize you have made things worse, don't you? When he notices it's missing, he'll know who to blame. The only good thing to come from your covert operation is access to my father's computer, which gives us a few days to find out what he's working on."

I looked at Rocky, who'd sunk back into the sofa and tried to make himself invisible. "What's he talking about?"

"I may have had some help from Q on the tech side," Rocky said. "He showed me how to clone a drive."

"So, let me get this straight…" I said, turning back to Zander. I bit my lip and pretended to be deep in thought. "You're mad at us for not telling you, but it turns out us breaking the rules was a good thing?"

"It gives us a chance to get ahead and find leverage before he finds out what you've done," Zander said, his expression darkened as he rolled up his sleeves, "but breaking my rules is *never* a good thing."

"If your rules made sense, I wouldn't have had to break them," I spat.

"Being a Seven is about trust and loyalty." Zander rose to his feet, his lip curling. West tightened his grip on my leg. "You need to learn that when I say I'm handling it, it means I'm handling it. If we don't have trust, we have nothing. We are nothing."

"So, I have trust issues!" I threw my hands in the air. "What are you going to do about it? Kick me out?"

"You still don't understand, little one," Zander said. "You can't *leave* the Sevens. When you're in, you're in. But disobeying has consequences and you need to learn to trust us."

"Trust is something to be *earned*," I insisted.

He may have been brought up in a world where everything could be traded, but my trust could not be negotiated. Trusting someone was about more than words.

Zander's gaze lingered on my lips. "Then, let us earn it."

I rolled my eyes and tried to ignore how his probing stare set every nerve in my body on fire. "You say that like it's easy..."

It's not like there's a magic pill to take to trust someone. Sure, I'd let the Seven men into my life more than anyone else in years. I'd shared my body with them. I'd learned things about each of them, but did I fully trust them? I wanted to, but a part of me was still holding back.

"It is easy." Zander pulled a blindfold out of his jacket pocket. What kind of person carried something like that around with them? Most guys carried around condoms, not softcore bondage accessories! "You want me to teach you how to trust us? Keep the blindfold on for the next thirty minutes."

"Really?" I scoffed. "You think me not being able to see will change things?"

"Humor me," Zander said.

"Fine," I relented, standing and snatching the blindfold from his hands. I never shied away from a challenge. "Who is going to tie me?"

"Let me," Rocky said, standing and gently placing the soft black fabric over my eyes. He paused. "Are you sure about this, C?"

"Just fucking tie it, Rocky," I snapped, wanting to prove myself.

He was careful and methodical so as not to catch my hair. He bound me tightly, forcing my eyes to close, and descending my world into darkness. "There."

"Our girl needs to be taught a lesson in trust," Zander purred. "Start the timer, West."

Footsteps circled me. Without my sight, all of my other senses were heightened. The heat of a figure closed in from behind, pressing their muscles against me and gently stroking my hair. Then another in front, sliding warm hands under my shirt to stroke my stomach.

"This is really how you build trust, huh? This is just an excuse to—"

Before I could say 'see me naked', lips pressed against mine hungrily. *Rocky.* I recognized his soft, but aggressive kiss. He kissed me like it would be our last, sweeping me away in the passion and fear that this moment could slip through our fingers.

"What happened to you?" Rocky murmured. His fingers ran over my hips, where the skin was tender. I suspected bruises were already blossoming from being bent over the hood of Giles's car. It didn't take him long to put two and two together. "You did this? You hurt her?"

"Do you think I'd still be standing here if I did?"

West spat in reply behind me. The Hulk had a point. "She enjoyed every minute of it."

"How do we expect to bring down our enemies when we're working against each other?" Zander snapped at them from somewhere in front of me, he sounded close by. "How can she trust us if we can't trust each other?"

Rocky mumbled a few curse words under his breath.

"We're brothers until the end," Zander said. "And Candy? She's our Seven girl."

"You all know I'm still standing here, right?" I said. "I told you already, I'm not some piece of property."

"No, you're *our* property," Zander corrected. His breath tickled my cheek as he pulled West's T-shirt over my head. "You'll see…"

Strong hands from behind helped him slide the fabric from my body, leaving me half-naked in nothing but a pair of panties.

"We'll show you how to trust us," Zander whispered in my ear. "There's just one final thing…"

He pulled my hands together behind my back and bound my wrists with silky fabric. The bind was tight enough to completely restrict my motion but still allowed my blood to flow… *just.*

"Hey," I objected, my voice a pitch higher. "This wasn't part of the deal."

"No one is going to hurt you," Rocky murmured, brushing his lips against mine.

For someone who valued control above everything, submitting was scary. It was different when it was me and Zander alone in his office. When I'd stretched out over his desk, I'd voluntarily offered myself to him to prove I wasn't afraid but submitting to all of them at once? I was vulnerable and, even though I couldn't see, it felt like a giant spotlight was shining down over my head.

"You need to let go," Zander said.

I opened my mouth to argue, but Rocky's kiss swallowed me whole. A different pair of firm hands ran down the length of my body from behind. My bound hands rested on a large bulge. *West.* Wherever we were, he'd always have my back and make me feel safe.

I was so wrapped up in our kiss; I yelped a moan of surprise as Rocky's hand slipped into my panties, while West yanked them down to expose me. Suddenly, I was glad of the blindfold as I stepped out of them like a caterpillar shedding its skin.

A second later, muscular arms scooped me up like I weighed nothing. From the smokey cologne, I knew it was Zander. He cradled my naked body and carried me to another room, where he placed me down carefully on a bed, trapping my arms under me. The luxurious satin sheets felt incredible against my bare skin.

"Look at our girl," Zander admired. "She's all fucking ours."

The sound of belts unbuckling, unzipping, and fabric falling to the carpet made me gulp. I was completely at the Seven's mercy.

The mattress dipped as bodies joined me, and the kissing began again. Someone different this time. *West.* His giant hands cupped my face, then slipped down my neck and squeezed my nipple between his thumb and finger. At the same time, another body coaxed my legs apart, spreading me wide open. Rough kisses ran up my inner thighs, nibbling and biting until I could feel hot breath against my pussy. I couldn't keep track of what was happening; all the sensations blurred into one to heighten my pleasure. I moaned as a tongue dove into my wet pool and slid up to my clit.

"She tastes so fucking good," Rocky groaned as West continued to play with my nipples and send bursts of pleasure rippling through my body.

My senses were overpowered, melting away any lingering self-consciousness I had.

"Let me taste her," Zander ordered.

Rocky pulled back momentarily, and West broke away from our kiss. Did he want to watch? A second later, two fingers ran down the length of my slit, then teased my entrance. Zander pushed in deep and slow, allowing my wetness to coat him down to the knuckles, then withdrew. I heard the small pop of his fingers leaving his mouth.

"Delicious," Zander said. I could hear the smile in his tone. If I didn't feel so overwhelmed, then I may have blushed.

Rocky replaced Zander's fingers as he returned to eat my pussy with even greater enthusiasm. His tongue plunged in and out of me, while West stroked and caressed my breasts, leaving a trail of kisses in his wake. I moaned, gyrating my hips into Rocky's face as West took my nipple into his mouth and sucked gently. That, and the rhythmic licking against my clit, felt like an inferno had ignited and I couldn't stop it. Every inch of my skin was ablaze with their touch.

Then, just as quickly, they both stopped and pulled away.

"Hey," I objected, breathless and panting. "You can't just stop like that."

"Isn't our girl so beautiful?" Zander praised; he sounded far away like he was watching from a distance. "Why don't you give her what she wants, West?"

A moment later, a heavy body rolled on top of me.

"I'll take care of you, princess," West whispered. His hands slipped under my ass and rolled us over, so I was straddling him. His cock dug into me, hard and swollen from longing. When we'd fucked outside, I hadn't felt his body against mine. Now, it's all I could fucking feel. His muscled body lay in my wake. My breasts pushed against him, our skin covered in a slick sheen of sweat. The beast may have taken from me, but it was my turn to take from him.

I arched my hips, sliding my wet pussy over him. The heat from his erection warmed my lips as his soft head pressed into my clit. I ground against him, using him for my pleasure. West growled in lust, squeezing my ass hard. Him wanting me so badly was the biggest turn on.

"What a view," Zander purred as West spread my ass wide and reminded me we weren't alone. Knowing the others were watching made me soaked and even hotter for them. "Make her feel good, West."

"Are you ready?" West asked as his cock rubbed against my entrance. For someone not keen on the idea of sharing, he was coping pretty well. Maybe that's why Zander was letting him claim me first?

"Yes," I moaned. *I mean, hell fucking yes — I'd do anything, yes!*

West guided my pussy down onto his cock. I perched above, my thighs burning as I stretched to accommodate him.

"Do you like him fucking you, little one?" Zander

asked, his words short and breathy. The sound of his hand pumping up and down his shaft made me grin. Knowing Zander was pleasuring himself made me want to give him a show to remember.

"Sit up, C," Rocky encouraged. "I want to see you."

I did as he asked, inhaling deeply, as I straddled West, and every inch of him sunk deeper. How was there enough room for him to fit? It felt like I was being impaled to my belly button.

"Put your arms out," Rocky asked in a gravelly voice. I held them out, following the sound of his voice. He took my wrists and untied my binds. "You're going to need them."

West wasn't happy with Rocky's interruption and growled. His hips bucked violently and made me fall forwards. The big man wanted my attention, but he had to be taught a lesson. Even though I was wearing a blindfold, West needed to remember that I was the one in control. I slid up his shaft, almost to the tip. He groaned, trying to pull me back down, but I resisted. I circled my hips, dancing around his head until he almost fell out, then suddenly plunged his cock in deeper and made him gasp. I enjoyed the power and how fucking crazy it made him, hoping it had the same effect on the others.

As I turned my head, a pierced dick hit me straight in the nose.

"Ouch." I laughed, then felt around in the dark for robocock.

Bingo. I took it in my hands.

"C—" Rocky began, then gasped.

"Shh," I murmured, looking up in the direction where I thought he was kneeling, hoping he could hear how thick my voice was with desire for him. For them all. "I want to taste you, Rocky."

He guided his cock to my mouth, sliding the pierced end over my lips until I opened to welcome him. The balls of his piercings slid along my tongue as I licked along his length like an ice pop. If Zander enjoyed watching West fuck me, what would he think of this? I heard a grunt from behind us. The boss approved.

"Shit," Rocky moaned as West's thrusting forced his cock further down my throat. "Your mouth feels incredible, C."

Rocky's hands grabbed my hair, pulling it into a rough ponytail, then pushed my head down his length to the rhythm of West's thrusts. The two of them were using my body, but they were working as a team to make sure I was comfortable. What could be more freaking hot?

I gagged as Rocky's Prince Albert hit my tonsils, coating him with my spit. His hips shuddered, holding me there. While the last time we had sex was gentle and loving, he was also an animal too. What guy didn't want a girl to choke on his dick?

"Have you ever been fucked in the ass before, little one?" Zander asked.

I tried to answer, but my mouth was full. I almost choked on Rocky as he yanked my head away, leaving a trail of spit dripping down my chin.

"N-n-n-no," I stammered breathlessly.

Hell, I'd basically been a virgin before coming to the club. Being fucked by two men at once was a lot to handle, but three?

"It's okay. Be a good girl and lean forward," Zander soothed. I stretched out over West, burying him, as two powerful hands spread my ass further apart. "We'll be gentle with you."

West didn't move as Zander's hot spit dripped down my ass. I expected him to stroke me, like West, but squeaked as the tip of his nose tickled me and his tongue darted out to probe my entrance, tasting me where no one else had before.

"Fuck, she likes that," West said, as the sensation sent vibrations to my pussy and made me quiver. They had overwhelmed my senses, making fireworks explode in my brain and suspending me in a state of pure ecstasy. Nearby, Rocky let out a groan as I heard him touching himself. "Don't you, Pinkie?"

I couldn't talk. Words wouldn't come out, but I arched my back in agreement, hoping spreading myself wider to give Zander a better angle would answer West's question. Zander wanted me to trust them fully. He wanted me to give myself to them, and for them to give themselves to me to fully bind our bond. If we did this together, there was no going back.

Zander paused, withdrawing his tongue to stroke me with his finger and slip it inside gently. I let out a moan as my thighs clenched around West's torso.

"See?" Zander said, pumping his finger in and out of my ass. "I knew you'd like it."

As Zander eased another finger into me, West's hand found my clit and caressed it softly. I pushed myself down onto his hand, sliding against it to increase the friction.

"Rocky?" I groaned, reaching out blindly for his cock.

It wouldn't be fair to leave him out, right? I wanted to feel him. I *needed* to feel all three of them filling me at the same time. Rocky took the hint and positioned himself to give me better access. I clutched onto his muscular thighs, feeling upwards until I found his balls, gently cupping them, and taking him into my mouth. I moaned over his shaft, making his cock twitch and a fat drop of pre-cum spill over my tongue. He was close, but I wanted this to last. I slowed down, running my tongue over every little piercing playfully.

"She's ready," Zander announced, withdrawing his fingers and squirting something cold over me. I tensed as something bigger rubbed against my ass. He sensed my hesitation, slathering what must be more lube over the two of us. The sheets would need burning after this.

"Don't worry," West murmured to reassure me. "I'll stay still."

I stayed frozen in place as Zander's cock edged his way into my ass. After the initial squeeze, he eased deeper, giving me an inch at a time. I took it slowly, fearing he was about to rip my asshole in two, but the tight pain gave way to another feeling... it felt *fucking good*. Zander grunted as he started to slide back and forth easier.

"She's so wet for us," West murmured, thrusting to match Zander's pace. "Do you like being fucked by all three of us?"

"Uh-huh," I gargled back onto Rocky's cock, making him groan.

"She was made to be our Seven girl," Zander said. "She fits us perfectly."

Could he and West feel each other inside me? They must be able to. For me, it felt like there was nothing but a thin wall separating them as their cocks slid together. Double-penetration felt fucking incredible. As well as their motions, the friction of their dicks against each other flooded my body with new sensations. As Zander pushed in further, and West's shaft rubbed against my G-Spot, Rocky plunged to the back of my throat, making my eyes water.

"That's it, baby," West encouraged. "Drench me with your pussy."

Before I even realized what was happening, Zander thrust into my ass and I tightened around them both. It was all too much. The heat, the friction, the overwhelming fullness... *fuck*. My insides felt like they were imploding as an orgasm ripped through my body. I was so stuffed, there was nowhere for the release to go, amplifying the feeling tenfold. My whole body shook, but six firm hands held me in place as they continued to rock me into oblivion. Rocky's cock muffled my screams, as Zander teased new feelings out of me I didn't think possible.

"Fuck," Rocky growled out. His hips shuddered as I sucked on him hard. He couldn't hang on any longer, spraying the back of my mouth with his salty cum. I swallowed it down, sliding my tongue over his head to make sure I got it all before releasing him.

"We're not finished with you yet, little one," Zander purred as Rocky pulled out of me and I took a gasp of air. "You're going to take until we tell you it's time to stop."

"Zander, I-I-I..." My voice trailed off and turned into moans as he and West continued to fuck me. "Fuck!"

I didn't think my body could take any more, but the two of them sliding against each other caused a new strange wave of pleasure. An intense, almost ticklish, feeling built up from my toes and fizzed through my limbs as their cocks defiled me.

I cried out as they tipped me over the edge again. I expected my orgasm to be over quickly, but it wasn't. It kept on going and going. Wearing a blindfold made no fucking difference. Bliss blinded me. I couldn't hear or think... all I could feel were them. Crashes of pleasure rippled through me, and I cried out again and again. I'd read about full-body orgasms before and thought they were bullshit, but now I knew I was wrong...

Zander's thrusts sped up as my ass latched around him. His breathing grew more shallow as his hands gripped my cheeks tight, and he blew his load.

"You feel fucking incredible," West breathed as Zander pulled out.

Now, he had me all to himself and didn't hold back. With a final push, he exploded and filled me with his warmth all over again. He put his arms around me and brought me closer. I was a shaking mess. I couldn't move, even if I wanted to. The three Seven men had ravished me.

Beep. Beep. Beep!

"What the hell is that?" West growled.

"The timer's up," Zander replied.

Holy fucking shit.

Rocky undid my blindfold to reveal West grinning underneath me like a sweaty Cheshire cat. I may not have been able to see what was happening and, if it wasn't for the cum dripping down my thighs and out of my ass, I wouldn't have believed it either.

I looked around at the enormous bed we were lying on. I'd never been inside this room before, so it must be Zander's.

"Well?" Zander asked.

I rolled off West to look at him. He was busy buttoning up his shirt, but his cock was still out on display like it was for sale in a store window. No amount of money could buy such a high level of confidence. The guy looked like a fucking Greek statue someone had graffitied over.

"Well, what?" I raised an eyebrow. "Do you want me to score your performance?"

I'd give them all a ten, not that I'd let them know that. There was always room for improvement, right?

Zander scowled. He needed to lighten up. "Have we proved to you we can be trusted now?"

I paused, considering his question. They could have done anything to me without my sight and use of my hands. "It's helped."

Zander looked down at me in disbelief. "What more can we do?"

"That," I said, grinning wickedly. "Again and again."

"She's definitely our girl." West laughed as his cock sprung back into action again. Hell, we'd fucked earlier and now again... his stamina was insane. As good as screwing him again would be, even I had limits — if I wanted to walk again tomorrow.

"Are you, Candy?" Zander asked, his cool gray eyes burning into mine. "Our girl?"

Even though I'd thought about their offer a lot, I'd not officially given them my answer. He, Rocky, and West stared at me. Waiting. Fuck knows how the three of us would work. It'd make everything more complicated, but if they were happy to give it a try, then so was I. Sure, the mind-blowing sex helped. But Zander's trust exercise had proved to me I wasn't afraid to be vulnerable around them. These were men I could trust. Men who made me feel safe.

"Yes, fine," I relented. "Whatever this weird as fuck arrangement is, I'm in."

I sat up and looked for something to cover myself with. Rocky was already waiting and handed me his shirt. West growled, he preferred me to wear his clothes, but I was teaching him how to share.

"Even though I'm in, I'm sleeping in my own bed tonight, okay?" I declared, getting up shakily to my feet. There's no way my vagina could cope with any more action tonight. She needed time to recover with a hot water bottle and binge-worthy Netflix series. "I'll see you all in the morning."

Their eyes watched me leave.

I may be their girl, but the Seven men? They were all fucking mine.

NINETEEN

After being railed by three guys in the early hours, I planned to stay in bed until lunchtime. I needed time to recover and wrap my head around what happened. Not just how incredible the sex was, because it was out of this freaking world, but how *right* it had felt. I'd questioned how being in a relationship with all three of them would work. Now, I couldn't imagine being with one over another. There was no other way; the Seven guys were a package deal.

My thoughts were rudely interrupted by Vixen bursting into my bedroom like a runaway train hurtling down the freaking alps. "Get up."

"What's wrong?" I sat up and checked the clock. It was almost noon. Why the hell was she up so early? I expected her to be confined to bed and nursing her hangover. Had I accidentally used her shower without asking? Or worse, had she overheard our sexcapades last night and wanted me out of her closet for good?

"Get the fuck out of bed. Now!" Vixen screeched.

She looked like she'd snorted ten lines of cocaine from the way her eyes were wide, like saucers.

This was bad.

Really fucking bad.

Even with a gun held to her head, I'd never seen Vixen so rattled. A crazy banshee had possessed her body.

Something was wrong.

"What is it?" I asked.

"It's West," she said, her voice breaking. My mind ran through the possibilities; each of them worse than the last, but none as bad as the words that came out of her mouth next. "He's been shot."

I had to be with him. I threw my comforter to the floor and jolted upright as a spike of adrenaline surged through me. My body went into autopilot as my limbs moved of their own accord. I slipped my feet into the nearest set of sneakers. "Where is he?"

Rocky's shirt hung lifeless and limp around my thighs, but there was no time to change. We needed to get him. *Fast.*

"He's on his way to the hospital," Vixen said. A tear slipped down her cheek, but she sniffed, refusing to break down. She knew she had to get her shit together. West's life was on the fucking line. "We can meet the ambulance there. Zander and Red are already on their way."

We raced through the penthouse and down the stairs. I took two at a time, cursing my legs for not being able to move any faster. Why did I have to get fucked by three guys the night before? My aching thighs burned in resistance, but I pushed on.

Outside the club, Vixen threw keys into my hands. Her face paled like she was going to be sick.

"Can you drive?" she asked, gesturing towards the closest car. West's prized SUV. "I... I don't think I can."

I nodded and jumped inside. My body somehow went through the motions of turning the key in the ignition while I was screaming internally. As soon as Vixen shut the car door behind her, I slammed my foot on the gas. The rubber wailed against the concrete as we hurtled away. I'd passed the hospital on my old commute, so I knew where to go.

"Who did it?" I asked. "Who shot him?"

Would West forgive me for wrecking his car if it meant we got to the hospital faster? West was usually the speed demon, but it was my turn to channel my inner racer.

"I don't know... I don't know anything..." she stammered, still in shock and clinging to her seat. "It's bad... real bad."

We needed to get to him.

Vixen continued to blather in broken sentences, but I couldn't comprehend what she was saying. All I could focus on was getting to the hospital. I wove between lanes and cut in front of people, ignoring the beeping horns following us. Memories of Crystal bleeding to death on the sidewalk flashed through my mind. A few seconds could make all the difference. Did they get to him in time?

"Blood everywhere... ambulance..." Vixen kept talking, but my thoughts were a complete scramble.

Please don't let him die.

I kept repeating it over and over like a mantra.

If there was a God, perhaps they would listen? Not

that my prayers did any good for Crystal. Willpower wasn't enough to start a heart beating again.

Please don't let him die.

None of this made any sense. Who? Why? Where? Was he shot because we stole Giles's car? Surely even Giles wouldn't be so petty, especially when Bryce was waiting on our answer about whether he and the Sevens could join forces. Then again, Giles's last temper tantrum resulted in Cheeks being shot dead, so attacking West didn't seem like a stretch.

"There," Vixen yelled, pointing at a sign by the next turn to make sure I didn't miss it. I swung a sharp right towards the hospital, making Vixen scream.

Please don't let him die.

My bruised hips reminded me of how alive West had been a few hours before. He was the strongest of all the Seven men. My big strong Hulk. How could this have happened?

We're nearly there, West...

In some stroke of luck, we made it to the hospital without crashing. I maneuvered into the nearest parking spot. We flew out of the car, leaving the keys dangling in the ignition and the doors wide open. Someone could steal the fucking car for all I cared. A car was replaceable, but The Hulk wasn't.

We sprinted through the hospital doors. Our feet hit the ground. One after the other.

"This way." Vixen grabbed my arm and pulled me along like baggage in an airport. She seemed to know where she was going as we rushed past the sea of gowns, trolleys, and faces. Everything streamed by in a blur.

Please don't let him die.

Rocky and Zander stood at the end of the hall,

talking in hushed serious tones with a doctor wearing bloody overalls. *West's blood.* In my previous line of work, I'd never been squeamish, but my stomach turned at the sight of it. I knew a fatal amount of blood loss when I saw it.

"He's in surgery." I heard the doctor say as Vixen and I neared. "We're doing all we can... touch and go... internal bleeding... bad condition..."

Zander listened to the doctor intently, only glancing away briefly to acknowledge our presence. Rocky tried to put his arm around my shoulder, but I shook him off. The only person who could make this better was bleeding out through the wall on the operating table. A hug didn't solve anything.

"What happened?" I gasped, finally daring to take a breath and realizing my chest was heaving for air.

"He was over in Bayside Heights," Zander explained. "If a kid didn't follow a blood trail, West would have bled out at the scene. No one saw anything or who pulled the trigger."

Bayside Heights. Jacob. The car. *The fucking car.* West will have gone over there to check our deal had gone smoothly. Someone had to have followed him. Whoever used West as target practice would pay.

Stealing the car had been my stupid idea. It was my fault. I'd been so hellbent on annoying Giles that I hadn't thought about the consequences. We may not have any proof Giles was behind West's shooting, but I was ready to decapitate the bastard and mount his head on a pole if I found out he was responsible. No one would be able to stop me. Until then, there was nothing I could do but wait, and it was fucking infuriating.

"Will he be okay?" Vixen asked as her bottom lip wobbled. "How long will he be in surgery?"

"However long it takes to dig out the bullet lodged in his thigh. It hit his femoral artery," Zander replied bluntly. How could he be so fucking casual? If I wasn't imagining West staggering through empty streets alone and injured, I'd have swung for him.

A familiar face raced towards us. Mieko's wet hair was scraped back in a ponytail as if she'd jumped straight out of a shower.

"I came as soon as I could," Mieko said, pulling Vixen into her arms. "Have you heard any more news?"

"Not yet," Vixen said, falling into her embrace. "You didn't have to come here, Mimi."

"Of course, I did," Mieko said, smoothing down Vixen's hair. The look of tenderness passing between them was almost too much to bear.

"He'll be okay, C," Rocky murmured. Although, from the way he was biting his lip in concern, he didn't seem to believe his own words.

"You don't know that," I snapped. "Nobody does."

"You need to calm down, C," Rocky said in his best attempt at a comforting tone.

"Calm down? He could fucking die," I blasted, clenching my hands into fists and digging my nails into my palms. "How can you stay so fucking calm?"

He and Zander exchanged a 'she's losing her shit' look, making me want to rip their heads off. Why were they looking at me like *I* was crazy? How were they keeping it together? Images of pools of blood and broken bodies were all I could see. Even the world's strongest man wasn't immune to having an artery ripped open.

"I'll get you all some coffee," Mieko said, sensing it may be a good time to leave us alone for a few minutes. She squeezed my shoulder as she passed, but I couldn't meet her pitying eyes. I didn't want her sympathy. Sympathy didn't heal bullet holes.

Please don't die, West. Please.

Minutes stretched into hours.

I clutched the cold polystyrene cup, coffee untouched, in my hands.

Doctors moved around us in a frenzy of activity. Hospital machines beeped. Wheels ran up and down the corridors. The smell of disinfectant and cooked canned food lingered, but it couldn't disguise the scent of death lurking around every corner. Hospitals were designed to make people better, but not everyone made it out of their walls with a pulse.

Vixen and Mieko sat away from us, whispering in a corner. Rocky paced and kept trying to assure everyone that West would be fine, but his attempts to lift our spirits diminished with every second West remained in surgery. Zander's initial cool exterior was starting to break. He stared at the clock in brooding silence, only breaking off occasionally for a controlled angry outburst.

"Whoever did this will pay," Zander muttered to himself.

For once, revenge wasn't the first thing on my mind. Sure, it was a close second, but before I wished someone dead, I needed to know he would live.

Please don't let him die.

A doctor burst through the door, and we all jumped to our feet. His expression was difficult to read and somber. The face of a man who was used to being the bearer of bad news.

"How is he?" Vixen asked.

"Stable," the doctor confirmed. "He's lucky someone found him when they did. Not many people survive after losing so much blood. We need to keep monitoring his condition, but he's through the worst."

He was going to be okay.

Relief swelled inside me, flooding through my body like rain falling after a long drought. Vixen's shoulders slackened as the weight of her worry lifted, and Mieko pulled her closer into an embrace. Rocky mumbled 'I knew it' under his breath, while Zander simply nodded in acknowledgment, processing the news in his quiet way.

"When can we see him?" I pressed, having to stop myself from barging past to be at West's side. "Can we go now?"

"Not yet," the doctor said. "I'll send someone to fetch you when he's somewhere more comfortable."

Zander thanked him, but I couldn't relax. Not yet. It didn't matter what the doctor said. I had to see West with my own eyes to know he would pull through. Life had a cruel way of twisting you in the gut when you thought you were safe and through the worst.

"I need to get some air," Vixen stammered. We'd all been on an emotional rollercoaster. It'd take time to work through the shock. "And more coffee."

"I'll go with you," Mieko insisted, taking her hand and leading her away.

They may have only recently started dating, but

they'd already been through more challenges than most married couples. From burning bodies to seeing Cheeks get shot, it brought them closer together. Hopefully, like Mieko and Vixen, my guys and I would come out of this ordeal stronger.

"I'm going nowhere," I said, returning to my seat and crossing my arms stubbornly. "Not until I've seen him."

Rocky sat next to me and slipped his fingers through mine. "I'll stay with you."

I managed a small smile and squeezed his fingers back. Sometimes it takes almost losing someone to realize how much they mean to you. Not just West. All the guys, Vixen, Mieko, and Q. Maybe we were, in our own fucked up way, the real family I'd always wanted...

Rocky didn't let go of my hand until the doctor returned half an hour later.

"You can see him now," the doctor said. "But only two at a time."

"Let Candy and Vixen go first," Zander said.

The doctor took us into West's private room. I'd waited for this moment all day, but now that it had arrived, I didn't know what to do with myself. I awkwardly shuffled in after Vixen. Inside, West was hooked up to a host of beeping machines and drips hung out of his arms. He looked like he'd fallen into a deep sleep.

"Can he... hear us?" I asked the doctor as Vixen and I sat at his bedside.

"He's out cold," the doctor replied, writing notes on

a clipboard and nodding in satisfaction. "We had to give him extra tranquilizers to, um... keep him under... I'll leave you both to it."

As soon as the drugs wore off, I'm sure West would be ripping the wires out of his arms and discharging himself. It was strange. Usually, our lives were filled with constant threats and movement. It didn't feel right to stop and... just sit. Shouldn't we be doing more to make whoever did this pay?

I took West's hand. You did that in hospitals, right? He may not know I was there, but it wasn't for his sake. I needed to feel his skin, his warmth, the blood pumping through his veins, to really believe he would pull through.

"You care about him, don't you?" Vixen asked softly, taking West's other hand.

"He's a Seven," I snapped, watching West's eyes flicker underneath his lids. "Of course, I fucking care."

"That's not what I meant," Vixen said. "I mean, you *really* care about them. All of them."

I let my hair fall over my face. "I mean, I guess..."

"Look, I'm no expert and I don't even want to know what kind of arrangement you guys have going on," she continued. "But I do know I've never seen the guys like this before. There's not been another girl around since you came into the picture, and the penthouse used to be like a freaking revolving door. When you first arrived, I thought you were another fake ass bitch—"

"Are you supposed to be trying to make me feel better? Because it's not working—"

"If you'll let me finish," Vixen talked over me, sighing dramatically, then picking up where she left off.

"What I'm *trying* to say is, whatever the hell is going on, I'm glad they have you. You have our backs."

"Didn't a tattoo prove that to you already?" I muttered sarcastically. Or, maybe she'd expected a spare kidney to symbolize my loyalty…

"Having a tattoo doesn't prove you're a Seven," Vixen said. "Being a Seven is about family. No one could fake the reaction you had this morning. I know you're all in."

Mieko had seen past Vixen's bullshit when I thought there was nothing more to her than being a snarky slave driver. She hid a sensitive side underneath her badass bitch persona, and her words meant a lot. Vixen knew who I was. She knew about all the mistakes I'd made, the horrible things I'd done, but it didn't matter. She accepted me, anyway. They all did. I had spent years fending for myself but, with them, I didn't have to be alone anymore. Finally, I belonged.

"Since when are you going soft?" I asked, quickly wiping my eyes before she could see and never let me live it down. I wasn't used to this type of affection. West being shot had turned me into a pile of mush. "Mieko must be getting to you."

She scowled, but her eyes lit up at the mention of Mieko's name. After the worst day, it was a small glimmer of sunshine amongst the darkness.

"I've never met someone like her before," Vixen admitted. "She's…"

"Too nice for you?" I scoffed, helping her out. "If you hurt her, you'll have me to deal with."

"If I hurt her, I'd want you to," she said earnestly then bit her lip. "I've never really… felt… like this about someone before."

"Have you told her how you feel?"

"Have you told *them* how you feel?" she rebutted and raised an eyebrow. "What do you think?"

For people like us who tried their darndest not to show vulnerability, prying off your toenails would be easier than admitting you had emotions.

"Well, don't wait too long to tell her," I said, dismissing her question and stroking the back of West's hand. "Not everyone would be able to put up with your bitch ass."

"Says the psycho who has all three of the Seven guys on a fucking leash."

"I'll need more than a leash to keep them in check," I mumbled. If getting shot is what happened when I wasn't around, I didn't want to let any of them out of my sight again. West stirred in his sleep; he looked so... helpless. "He *will* be okay, right?"

"He's strong," she said fiercely. "He'll pull through, and he has you now. He won't want to leave you in the hands of Zander and Rocky for long."

She had a point there...

We'd been in the hospital for eight hours, but I had no intention of leaving.

"You need to eat," Mieko urged. She'd been looking after everyone all day and refused to leave Vixen's side. "Come with me and Vix to the cafeteria?"

"I'm not hungry," I snapped, then my stomach rumbled to give me away. "I mean, I wouldn't hate it if you brought me a sandwich."

She hid her smile, then nodded curtly. "Of course."

The two of them hurried away, leaving me alone in the corridor. The doctors had insisted we give West time to rest, but I was already itching to be back at his side. As soon as Zander found out West was out of surgery, he and Rocky returned to Lapland to try to work out who was responsible for West's attack. Although, you didn't need to be Scooby Doo to work out that fucking mystery...

Before the guys left, Zander insisted on enlisting two henchmen to guard West's room and keep an eye on me. As if I needed a babysitter. Not that Zander listened. He ignored my arguments about not needing extra protection, and the men stood outside West's door like a pair of oversized angry thumbs. I made a mental note to ask West whether shaving their heads was part of their job description when he recovered.

My head snapped up from my lap as the click-clack of heels grew closer.

What the fuck was she doing here?

Penelope swished towards me in a fog of Chanel Number 5 with a Birkin on her arm and a lavish bouquet in hand. She had some nerve showing her face after what her new boyfriend had done. West didn't need fucking flowers.

I gritted my teeth and stood up, waving aside the two henchmen who tried to make a human wall between us. I could protect myself better than either of those jerks could.

"What do you want?" I spat, squaring my shoulders.

"I brought flowers," she chirped. She shot me a perfect white dazzling smile, which was too straight and shiny to be trusted. "They're from the whole Briarly family."

"Were you saving these to put on his grave?" I snarled, snatching them from her and throwing them straight in a trash can. For all I knew, they'd be laced with poison. They'd already tried to kill him once – what was stopping them from trying again?

"Can I go in and see him?" Penelope asked, craning her neck to get a look through the blinds.

"Over my dead body," I growled. "He's still breathing, and we'd like to keep it that way."

Penelope looked me up and down like she was considering whether she could make a dash around me. I may be a foot shorter than her, but I was a thousand times deadlier. "I didn't realize you were his guard dog."

I stood my ground, planting my hands on my hips. "I'm not a bitch you want to mess with today, Penelope. I suggest you leave unless you want to be lying in the next fucking hospital bed."

"Fine, but before I leave, there is one more thing," Penelope said, narrowing her eyes. If she thought playing the high school mean girl act would turn me into an insecure wreck, she was freaking delusional. "I'm also here to deliver a message. For you."

"I'm not fucking interested in anything you have to say."

"I think you'll be interested in this," she said. Penelope took a step closer, almost gassing me with the amount of perfume she'd layered on. "Someone told me something was taken from the mansion last night... and I'm not talking about a set of wheels."

The evidence from my time in the Romano mansion. Rocky cloning Bryce's hard drive. *They knew.*

"Oh, really?" I looked down to check my chipped

nails. Speaking to her was more boring than watching cleaning commercials on repeat. "Maybe the mansion should consider improving its security?"

"You think you're so clever, don't you?" Penelope hissed. When she was angry, her whole face contorted and twisted, making her resemble a gremlin over a Victoria's Secret model. "But the Briarlys don't take kindly to things being taken from them."

"So, you've come here to threaten me?" I laughed. Puh-lease. If they wanted to intimidate us, they shouldn't have sent Barbie to do it. "Isn't coming to gloat over what your new boyfriend did to West enough?"

"Giles didn't do this!" Penelope gasped as her eyes widened. "He wouldn't."

"If you think that, you don't know him or Bryce at all," I said. I considered telling her about how Giles blew Cheeks's brains out over the Christmas table and ruined a perfectly good pecan pie, but decided against it. She'd learn who he was the hard way. "You should get out while you still can."

Giles may be a spineless coward who didn't mind shooting a defenseless man, but Bryce was pure walking evil. If someone stole from him, he wouldn't hesitate to do whatever it took to get revenge. Including shooting West.

"You want me out the way so you can keep West all to yourself," Penelope said. "You're threatened by me."

I resisted the urge to laugh. The Sevens were facing many threats, but Penelope? She was nothing more than a stupid bitch who believed the world revolved around her and that every man would drop at her feet. Looks could only carry a person so far.

"I thought you were here to deliver a message?" I reminded her, taking a step forward and making her flinch. "Why don't you spit it out before Vixen comes back and rips your fucking tongue out?"

She winced at the mention of Vixen's name and said, "Bryce wants to meet with you tonight to discuss his proposition. Alone."

"Why me?" I asked, cocking my head to the side. There had to be an ulterior motive. "Zander is the boss. His word is final."

"For some reason, Bryce thinks you may be able to influence him," she said, then couldn't resist adding, "although... I can't see the appeal myself."

I grinned smugly. "West can."

Her face turned to stone. "If you don't come tonight, Bryce said there will be consequences."

Where had I heard that line before? Like father, like son.

"Did you think blackmail would work?" I threw my head back and laughed, then stopped suddenly. "I'm not going anywhere."

"Has West ever told you about what happened when we were at school together?" Penelope changed the subject. "How a student was hospitalized after a 'nasty fall'?"

The bitch just didn't quit. Her attempts at scaring me hadn't worked, so she wanted to use West's past to get me to do what she wanted. West told me about how Bryce had paid off the school, and his classmates, to cover up what happened after he'd lost control in a fight. Who would believe her all these years later? Why would anyone care now?

"I know you received a sizable amount of money to keep your mouth shut," I said. "Remember?"

"Not everything is about money." Her eyes darted towards the door of West's room. She gave off seriously obsessed stalker vibes. This was about more than getting me to meet with Bryce. It'd become personal. She couldn't hide how much she wanted West back, and if she couldn't have him? She didn't want anyone else to. "The boy West hurt came from a powerful family. I'm sure they'd like to know how an out of control scholarship kid cracked their son's skull and how his rich friend's daddy covered it up. The guy was in a coma for two years. He never recovered. Brain damage for life. It'd have been easier if he was dead."

West hadn't told me any specific details about what happened the first time he lost control, but I knew he agonized over it and regretted his actions every day. Penelope may be calling my bluff, but I didn't want West to have to wake up and relive his biggest mistake again.

"You wouldn't fucking dare," I snarled, wanting to grab her by the hair and smash her face into the wall until she needed reconstructive surgery.

"Do you want to take the risk?" She leaned in to slip a piece of paper into my hand with an address written on it. "Be there tonight, or else."

I heard Vixen before I saw her. "What is *she* doing here?"

I crushed the paper into a ball as Vixen stomped towards us like an angry rhino ready to trample whoever stood in her path.

"I was in the area," Penelope replied, flicking her glossy hair over her shoulder. "I wanted to see how he was doing."

"Or finish what my bastard cousin started," Vixen cut in, her spit sprayed over Penelope's perfectly made up face.

Mieko caught Vixen's arm to hold her back. "Not here," Mieko whispered, trying to calm her down. She was the only thing standing between Vixen and Penelope's expensive weave.

"Why not? We're in the best possible place," Vixen replied. Her body trembled, torn between following her instincts and not wanting to disappoint Mieko. "They won't have far to move her when I'm finished."

Penelope cackled, sensing she was on borrowed time. "Don't worry, I'm leaving."

Penelope sauntered away, catching my eye as she passed.

"What else did she say?" Vixen questioned.

I shrugged, gesturing at the discarded flowers. "Same old bullshit..."

No one else had to know the real reason Penelope came by. Loyalty and trust were what the Sevens valued most, but which did they value more? Was keeping a secret from them worth it to protect West?

TWENTY

"I told you, we'll let you know if anything changes," I said for the tenth time, finally breathing a sigh of relief as Vixen relented and agreed to go back to Lapland. After sitting in the hospital all day, Penelope's visit, and the food not being up to her standards, Vixen's sulky mood was driving me insane.

"I would not wanna be Mieko right now," Rocky muttered under his breath.

"She has the patience of a saint," I agreed.

Rocky had been glued to my side since he'd returned from wherever he and Zander disappeared to earlier. His lips were firmly sealed about what the two of them had been up to and discovered in the hours since they'd left the hospital. I would have forced him to tell me if I hadn't been keeping a secret of my own. This made us even.

"Let's hope Mieko's patience holds out long enough for Vixen to track down a cheeseburger," he said.

I snickered as a gentle knock on the door of West's room broke up our chat. Although Zander hadn't returned to visit, he'd pulled some strings from a distance. He arranged for West to be moved to a larger room with greater visitor privileges. As well as that, he'd gained remote access to the CCTV stream for West's room and the adjoining corridor. Thankfully, Penelope showed up before Zander started spying on our asses.

West's bed was already surrounded by cards, enough grapes to feed an army, and other pointless shit people sent when you were sick. People always give more gifts when you scare the living shit out of them.

A nurse stepped inside. Her cheeks reddened as her words came out in short nervous bursts. "Only one of you can stay for the night. Well, one and the... erm... guards outside."

I spotted one of our henchmen peering through the door as her blush deepened. It seemed even nurses weren't immune from the allure of a bad boy. Who knew a goon could have attracted her attention? West's nurse was in her mid-forties and a real sweetheart. I wanted to tell her to run while she had the chance, but if she was tough enough to deliver injections then who knows? She may be down for dealing with the grisly shit they did daily.

"I'll stay," I said definitively. Well, maybe not for the *whole* night...

The shred of paper Penelope gave me was burning a hole in my panties. What harm would it do to talk to Bryce, anyway? Staying with West for the night would grant me the perfect opportunity. There was no chance in hell I'd be capable of slipping in and out with Rocky around, and Zander's cameras would only be able to follow me so far.

Rocky frowned, wrestling with contradicting

thoughts. "I don't like the thought of you being here on your own."

"I can take care of myself," I reminded him. Had he forgotten I'd murdered Raphael Jacobson and Giovanni Romano? "Security is right outside, remember? It's not like I'll be left alone."

Zander's strict instructions meant West would not be left unprotected for a second. If someone came back to finish what they started, then they'd be ready and waiting.

"I still don't like it," Rocky huffed.

"I'm not made of glass," I snapped. "I don't need you watching over my shoulder all the fucking time."

"Someone tried to kill West today," Rocky said. As if I needed a reminder. "Is it so bad that I want to look out for you? I want to make sure you're safe."

"You want me to start trusting you, don't you? Wasn't that the whole point of last night?" I reminded him. "You need to stop treating me like someone who needs saving. I need you to trust me, Rocky."

Did I feel bad for manipulating him? Sure, a little... but it was for the greater good. I was acting in the Seven's best interests and, if I could put a stop to Penelope airing West's past and find out what Bryce wanted, it'd be worth it. After all, my stupidity was the reason why West ended up in the hospital and that guilt was on me.

Penelope may be stupid enough to believe the Briarlys had nothing to do with West's shooting, but I knew better. It couldn't be a coincidence it happened the day after I'd recruited Rocky to steal evidence from Bryce and persuaded West to help steal Giles's car. If we hadn't taken the damn car, West would never have been in Bayside Heights. I owed it to him to fix things.

"If it's so dangerous here, don't you think Zander would be hanging around?" I asked to emphasize my point. "I'll be fine, okay?"

"Alright!" Rocky sighed and raised his hands in defeat. "But it doesn't mean I like it."

The nurse popped her head around the door again and tapped her watch. "It's time to go."

"Call me later," Rocky said gruffly, planting a kiss on my forehead.

"Sure," I promised. Well, if I wasn't neck-deep in Briarly drama...

I watched Rocky disappear from view. With the others gone, the beeping of machines seemed to get louder. Each beep was a welcome confirmation that West's heart was still breathing. I took West's hand in mine and stroked the rough skin on his palms.

"I'm sorry," I murmured. My recklessness had gotten us into this mess, so I had to get us out. "But I'm gonna fix this."

I wouldn't let Penelope punish West for his past mistakes. He'd already suffered enough. If meeting Bryce would prevent his secrets from being unearthed, I'd do whatever needed to be done for my Hulk.

Getting out of the hospital undetected was simple. All I had to do was slink to the bathroom at the same time one of the henchmen went to take a leak and the swooning nurse batted her eyelashes at the other. Zander seriously needed to review his security detail. If it wasn't for knowing someone would be monitoring through the cameras, I wouldn't have dared to leave West unattended.

After memorizing the address and flushing the evidence, all I had to do was shimmy out of the window and hop into the nearest cab. Vixen had taken West's car back to Lapland, and a quick flash of my seven tattoo would be enough to scare any driver in Port Valentine to take me anywhere without cash. I would already be on my way to the meet-up location before anyone noticed I was missing.

I may not know where I was heading, or what Bryce wanted to talk about, but I knew I was heading straight into the lion's den... and my instincts told me it wouldn't be pretty.

"Are you sure we're in the right place?" the cab driver asked nervously. We'd driven twenty minutes out of Port Valentine, and he looked like he wanted to speed away as quickly as possible.

I didn't blame him. Places like this were perfect for nefarious business dealings. We'd pulled up outside a disused factory in the middle of nowhere. There were no other signs of civilization for miles, so no risk of members of the public strolling by. No one would hear you scream this far out. Was coming here alone really a good idea?

"Yep, this is it," I said, mustering my confidence and climbing out. "Thanks for the ride."

I made my way toward the well-maintained iron gates bordering the property. A sign whoever owned it wanted to keep people out... or in. Thankfully, I didn't need to pick any locks. They were open, and I stepped straight through.

SLASHER HEART

I headed into the central courtyard area. Orange flickering lights mounted on crumbling walls cast an ominous atmosphere. As I got closer, two figures came into view: men with guns guarding an entrance to the old building.

Bingo.

If Bryce thought two gorillas on steroids would frighten me, he was mistaken. If anything, they should be afraid to be out here with someone like me.

"Are you lost, little girl?" A figure called over, repositioning his gun to draw attention to it. Puh-lease, him showing off his weapon was as welcome as an unsolicited dick pic. "This isn't somewhere you should be wandering around at night."

"Bad things can happen to pretty girls with faces like yours," his colleague cooed. Stupid fuck. Didn't he know some monsters had pink hair and cute nails that could squeeze his balls until they popped? "Why don't you tell us your name?"

"Cut the bullshit," I snapped unfalteringly. Their faces fell. "You know exactly who I am. Bryce is expecting me. Are you going to open the door, or do you want me to tell him you've been keeping his guest waiting?"

"Watch your step," one snarled, moving to let me pass and following close behind.

"I don't need a fucking escort," I spat, swirling around to face him as his gun dug into my back. "And if your gun touches me again, I'll make sure it's the last thing you ever do, asshole."

His face screwed up into a snarl, but he took a step back as I entered the building into a vast windowless room. The steel walls, cold temperature, and rusty hooks hanging from the ceiling indicated it may have once been a meat production facility. Although, if Bryce owned it, I'd guess animals weren't the only creatures slaughtered here.

A red chesterfield sofa looked out of place in the center of the sterile surroundings, like a throne in the middle of a walk-in freezer. Bryce and Giles lounged across it with drinks in hand. As well as the guards who'd followed me inside, four men were positioned in each corner of the room, watching from the shadows. Should I be flattered that Bryce decided this level of security was necessary?

My eyes sought out the escape routes. Aside from the door I'd come through, the only other exit was a second door at the opposite end, which led deeper into the complex.

"You came." Bryce stood to greet me. His voice echoed around the space. "I knew you would."

"You say that like I had a choice," I said sarcastically, putting my hands on my hips. "Why don't you spare me the fucking formalities and tell me why you brought me here?"

"I'm an English man," Giles piped up. How could I forget when I constantly fantasized about smothering him with a Union Jack flag? "We still believe in good manners and old-fashioned Briarly hospitality."

"Yeah, just like you believe in shooting an innocent man and leaving him to die," I said, throwing him a withering look. "Your psycho stalker girlfriend wasn't happy that you almost killed the man she's obsessed with."

"You bitch—" Giles began, rising to his feet.

Bryce coughed to intervene, making Giles sit straight back down again.

"That's right," I mocked. "Sit down like a good boy, and let the adults talk."

Giles's face flushed in anger, but Bryce raised his hand to stop him from retaliating and motioned for a guard to advance. I stood straighter, ready to act. Instead of attacking, the guard pulled a chair from the darkness. The legs grating across the blood-stained concrete made the hairs on the back of my neck stand on end.

"Why don't you join us for a drink, Candy?" Bryce offered. "You are our guest."

"I'm not thirsty."

Well, not for drinks, anyway... but I wouldn't say no to cutting Giles open.

"Suit yourself, but take a seat," Bryce said, motioning towards the chair that his guard had set down opposite them. "It'll be much more comfortable."

I'd rather sit on a cactus, but I wanted to get our meeting over with. Bryce thrived on drama, and I didn't want to give him the satisfaction of getting another rise out of me.

"Gladly," I snarled, sitting down and surveying the room with interest. "Nice place you have here. But it's not quite the manor you're used to."

Bryce ignored my comment and clicked his fingers for his men to bring him a martini. "Are you sure we can't tempt you?"

"Positive."

Bryce shook his glass, swirling the liquid around the sides, then took a long sip. I balled my hands into small fists in my lap. He was testing my fucking patience.

After a long pause, Bryce cleared his throat. "Well, Candy... it seems you took something that belonged to us. I am willing to overlook your lapse in judgment if an agreement can be made. I'm looking for a new partnership to support our new endeavors."

Bryce's cordial demeanor contradicted the brutal edge of his stare. A cut-throat merciless psychopath lay beneath Bryce's smooth businessman exterior. His eyes may be the same color as Zander's, but they couldn't be more different.

When I looked into Zander's eyes, I saw a fire burning. Zander may be fucked up, but he cared about those he loved in his twisted possessive way. He'd shown me his softer side when he talked about his mother and how far he'd gone to protect Vixen. Zander was capable of feeling. Why else would he have sacrificed his inheritance for a half-sister he'd never met? Bryce was the opposite. There was nothing but emptiness in his rotten core. Bryce had killed the only woman he'd truly loved because he didn't want her to be with someone else. He was more deadly than I'd first given him credit for.

"Do you really think the Sevens would work with you, after everything you've done?" I sneered, narrowing my eyes and wishing my stare was enough to disintegrate him into nothingness. "Zander may be considering your proposal, but I think we all know what he's going to say. If you think I'd be able to convince him otherwise, then you don't know your son at all. Zander would never partner with you. Ever."

Bryce threw back his head and laughed.

"I didn't realize I'd said a fucking joke," I hissed.

This only spurred him on further. Giles joined in, clutching his stomach, and they laughed maniacally like they were riding the high of a mushroom trip. What was going on?

Bryce's laughter slowed. "Oh, Candy," he said, shaking his head in pity. "I wasn't talking about Zander."

Behind him, the second door creaked open, and a shadowy figure stepped out.

"Hello, Kitten." Hiram's voice sent a shiver racing down my spine. "I've been waiting for you."

Adrenaline surged through my limbs as I jumped to my feet. My heart pounded in my throat like a tennis ball trying to force its way out of my mouth. I'd kill every motherfucker in a mile radius and hang their cocks to the overhead hooks if that's what it took to get away.

One of Bryce's men dove forward to contain me. I dodged his lunge, then swung a punch and made contact with his nose. It snapped under my knuckles. He staggered backward as another advanced to take his place. I took him out just as quickly. I drove my knee into his balls and delivered an uppercut to his chin to knock him out cold. A stream of them kept coming. Too many of them.

I thrashed around, but they descended like a swarm of angry bees. Hands grabbed my arms, forcing them behind my back to hold me in place. My chest heaved from the exertion as I looked up to face him.

Hiram.

Footsteps reverberated off the steel walls as he swaggered over with the arrogance of a celebrity on a red carpet. He arched an eyebrow in amusement. "Are you ready to put your claws away, Kitten?"

I gritted my teeth, trying to keep my shit together. "Tell them to put me the fuck down."

Bryce looked at Hiram for approval, who nodded in agreement. He knew I wouldn't be stupid enough to continue fighting outnumbered. As talented as I was in combat, I couldn't tire myself out too soon. I needed to bide my time until it counted. In the meantime, I'd have to use my brain.

"Retreat," Bryce ordered his men. They let me go and doubled back like obedient robots.

I readjusted my clothes, wiping my bloody hands on my shirt, and smoothing down my hair.

"What is this?" I demanded. "An ambush?"

"Why don't you sit down, so we can continue our conversation?" Bryce suggested. The sadistic bastard was enjoying every second.

I took a seat — not because I wanted to comply with Bryce, but because I needed to reassess the situation. There were ten guards, not including the two lying unconscious, along with Giles, Bryce, and Hiram. I had two escape routes, both blocked by Bryce's men, with no way of knowing how many reinforcements were hiding elsewhere in the building. Hiram's eyes burned into me from where he stood next to Bryce, knowing what I was thinking.

Shit.

"When I discovered the photographs of you at the Romano mansion, we conducted some research of our own," Bryce said, gesturing with his arms as he talked like he was performing a magic trick. "Zander would never have agreed to work with me, but inviting you to the manor bought me more time to find who would be interested in a real partnership... for a price. After learning what you stole from me, I knew I had to act."

Hiram smiled. He circled my chair, then stopped. His leather-gloved hand reached out to stroke my cheek. I shrunk away from his touch but knew better than to break his wrist. "You didn't think I'd let you leave me forever, did you, Kitty?"

"Fuck you," I spat. "I'm not going anywhere."

"You're coming back home with me," Hiram said. He smiled, which made Giles recoil like he'd seen a ghost. "Or your *fiancé* won't be the only one of your new playmates in the hospital."

"You shot him," I murmured, more to myself than to anyone in particular. History had repeated itself all over again. First, Crystal... then, West. Where would it end?

"Did you think I'd waste *my* time killing him? You know how much I love treasure hunts. If I killed him, his body parts would be strewn so far over the country he'd never be found. " Hiram shook his head like ending West's life was beneath him, making me hate him more than ever. He turned to address the Briarlys, who cowered under his furious stare. "Unfortunately, I didn't realize I was doing business with *amateurs*."

"I had assurance that he was dead," Giles stuttered, turning an uneasy shade of green and confirming my suspicions about his involvement. If he wasn't wearing black trousers, we'd see stains spreading through the fabric.

In Port Valentine, Giles sat on his plush lily pad, like a slimy toad, picking off easy targets like flies. Next to Hiram, everyone could see Giles for the coward he really was. Hiram swam in the darkest depths of the ocean. He was a Great White that could tear you apart before you saw it coming... if you were lucky.

"Let's hope your men are better with business than they are at killing, Briarly," Hiram sneered. His disapproval was clear. "You'd better pray your new development makes the profit you claim it will because my men never miss."

"It will," Giles stammered. "Investing in Bayside Heights will triple your money. It'll be all profit."

The Briarly fortune must be drying up if they were looking for external investors, and even Bryce looked nervous at Giles's sales pitch. Was he having doubts over the success of Giles's new venture when Hiram's threat hung over their heads like a guillotine? The bastard only had himself to blame. Bryce was already heading straight to hell, but making a deal with Hiram would get him there much faster.

"Plus, you have the girl," Giles continued, almost pleading. His desperation and desire to impress only made him look more pathetic. "We brought her here like you asked."

My whole body shook as rage tore through me. If my stare could fire lasers, I'd have burned holes straight through his empty skull. "You wanted me to come here tonight, so you could get a fucking investment?"

Before he could respond, an explosion of gunshots firing outside caused the guards to disperse and Giles to drop to the floor in fear like the little bitch he is.

"It seems we have company," Bryce said wryly, looking down at Giles's trembling body in disapproval.

Hiram shrugged like an annoying mosquito was

buzzing around his head. Gunshots were simply a nuisance.

Seconds later, the door flew open. Zander stepped inside like a sexy tattooed knight in a suit. He kicked a corpse out of his way like a piece of trash. Rocky followed close behind him, looking around with wild eyes like an animal unleashed. His gaze sought me out immediately, and relief flickered over his face to see I was okay, but something else lurked behind his brown eyes... *hurt*. I'd tricked him into leaving me alone at the hospital. I'd betrayed his trust.

"Excuse us," Zander snarled, narrowing his eyes at his father. "I see we're late to the party."

The guards didn't know what to do. They stood hesitantly, pointing their guns at the intruders and awaiting Bryce's instructions. Zander and Rocky may have killed two of their colleagues, but Zander was also a Briarly.

"Zander." Bryce stood, motioning for his men to lower their weapons. He drew himself up to full height like a parent getting ready to scold a young child. "To what do we owe this pleasure?"

"I heard you were trying to *sell* a member of the Sevens," Zander confronted him as he and Rocky made their way toward us. Zander wasn't a little kid Bryce could bully anymore. He was taller, stronger, and more imposing than his father.

"Not *sell*," Bryce corrected, "we are here to make a *delivery*."

"And what about the money from the Bayside Heights development?" I cut in, blowing up his argument. "It sure sounds like selling to me."

"The Sevens don't belong to you, father," Zander

spat, ignoring my input. He hadn't looked in my direction since they'd burst in. "It's not your deal to make."

I tried to read Zander's expression, but there was nothing but emptiness behind his chiseled jaw. How did they know where to find me? I'd been careful to cover my tracks: flushing the note, leaving my phone behind, hitching a cab...

"You're too late, Zander," Bryce said. "You have to learn that not everything goes your way. Candy came here tonight willingly."

Hiram's hand rested on my chair possessively. He may be content surveying the unfolding altercation between the Briarlys, but he wanted to make sure everyone knew I belonged to him.

"Her coming here isn't a fucking agreement to be traded. Candy is one of us," Rocky snarled. The veins in his neck throbbed in fury as he glared at Hiram. "She's not going anywhere."

If Zander and Rocky stood in Hiram's way, he wouldn't hesitate to kill them. They may have come to save me, but their valiant rescue was nothing but a fucking suicide mission!

"The deal's already been made," Giles rebutted, then smirked. Thinking he was on the winning side had made him miraculously rediscover his vocal cords. "We have a contract."

Zander narrowed his eyes. "You're wrong—"

"Zander, don't," I interrupted, aware of Hiram's looming presence breathing down my neck. I don't know what the hell he was going to come out with next, but I knew Hiram better than anyone. Resisting his wishes meant death. West would already be dead if Giles's idiot henchman had done their jobs right. I couldn't let them die because of me. Not here. Not like this. "I'll go with him."

"Shut the fuck up, Candy," Zander growled, finally looking at me for the first time. His gaze darkened. "You don't know what you're talking about."

"Yes, I do," I insisted. My voice sounded stronger than I felt as I implored him and Rocky with pleading eyes. Couldn't they see why I was doing this? It was for the Sevens. For them. To keep them safe. "I'll go with him, but I have one condition."

"I said, sh—"

"Let her speak," Hiram roared, cutting Zander off. Everyone else in the room was irrelevant to him. He didn't care about making money from Giles's development in Port Valentine. The whole thing was a ploy to get him what he wanted... me. Hiram's voice softened, as he turned his attention back to what I was saying. "I'm intrigued. Go on, Kitten. I'm listening."

I took a deep breath to brace myself for what I knew I had to do.

"I'll return to Blackthorne Towers and void our contract *if* the Bayside Heights development doesn't go ahead."

Even though I'd be leaving my new family, I wanted to be damn sure that Bryce and Giles wouldn't profit from it.

"No! That's fucking insane, C!" Rocky shouted, reliving his worst nightmares all over again. We'd been here before. He looked at Zander in desperation. "You can't stand by and let this happen, Zander. Are you even hearing what she's saying?"

"Perfectly," Zander said in a short clipped tone.

Surely, he could see I was protecting them? "Candy has chosen where her loyalty lies."

Relief flooded through me. Zander understood. He knew why I had to do this. He knew I'd chosen where my loyalty lies. With him. With the Sevens.

It had been inevitable that Hiram would find me. He was an obsessive collector of people, and I was his prized possession. It didn't matter how far I ran, he would never be far away. As long as he lived, danger would stalk me. With me gone and the Briarly empire floundering, maybe the Sevens would be safe? Maybe they could even take down Zander's father for good like they'd always wanted. Zander must know it was the only way.

During my time with the Sevens, they'd taught me how to trust again. They'd seen past my bullshit to the real me. I'd let them into my life, my body... and my heart. They'd shown me how it felt to be part of something. How life wasn't for living alone. The Sevens gave me a fucking family, and now? I had to prove my loyalty to them, even if it meant having to lose them forever...

When Crystal died, I vowed never to let another innocent life be lost because of me. Returning to Blackthorne Towers would be hell, but it would be easier to live with than the knowledge everyone I'd ever cared about had, or would, die at Hiram's hands. The only solace I had was knowing my departure would have a lasting impact — at least the kids at Bayside Heights could keep their homes, and I'd be wiping the smug smirk from Giles's face. I may be signing myself up for a life filled with hatred and ruin, but those kids didn't need to have the same fate. Maybe there was still hope for them...

"Done," Hiram said, stroking my cheek. Zander's gray eyes blackened like the sky before a storm. I'm not sure what angered him more: Hiram agreeing to my deal or him touching me. "Consider it a homecoming gift."

"But we had a deal," Giles burst out like a petulant child whose toys had been taken away as Bryce pursed his lips, seething under the surface. "You can't back out of it now!"

"Actually..." Zander stepped forward and held out his hand. A slow smile spread over his face. The smile of a twisted psychopath who'd murder a whole family while they slept. "*We* had a deal."

Hiram shook it. "It's been a pleasure doing business with you."

Wait, what?

I blinked, making sure I wasn't imagining Hiram and Zander shaking hands and conversing like old friends who'd won a game of fucking baseball. I pinched my arm to wake myself from whatever nightmare I'd fallen into, but the image didn't go away.

The walls closed in around me, suffocating me in my disbelief. I wanted to be sick. I wanted to scream. I wanted to stand up and claw Zander's eyes out... but I couldn't move. Everything I thought I knew came crashing down around me.

"You did this?" Rocky's voice shook in horror as he began to comprehend what was happening, turning to his boss in disbelief. "Zander?"

Zander arriving unannounced was no fucking accident. He'd known where I was going all along. He'd planned this. Hiram had told him.

"I make the rules, Red," Zander snarled, then

addressed Bryce. "You see, father. I am the one who controls the Sevens, and the money Hiram promised you? It's all mine. It always was."

"But... the development..." Giles mumbled, his mouth opening and closing in disbelief.

"The development was never going to happen," Zander sneered, then laughed. Goosebumps spread over my arms. How hadn't I seen it before? I knew he was ruthless, but I'd thought he had another side to him. A caring side. Was everything a lie? "Hiram and I came to an understanding. The development was just a little fun on my part. Hiram agreed to play along. I wanted to get your hopes up, then crush them. Think of it as a warm-up for what I'm going to do to the rest of your dying empire. Your hold on Port Valentine will be over."

Bryce's lip curled as he wrestled with what to say next. He hadn't seen this coming. Zander smiled like all of his birthdays had come at once. Who was this person? Where was the guy who'd talked to me about his mom? Where was the guy who said I was unlike any girl he'd ever met? Where was the man who said they'd do anything to protect me?

All these months, he'd been busy brainwashing me. Making me think I was safe... making me think *he* could be trusted. When, all along, he'd been plotting how to make the most out of me. All he'd ever wanted was to make his father pay. I was nothing more than a vessel for his fucking revenge.

I'd thought being a Seven meant something. Why did he keep me around for so long? Did he enjoy fucking me while knowing what he was planning? Did knowing he was going to ruin my life make him hard, while I cried out his name, and thought I'd finally found someone worth fighting for? I used to think Hiram was the worst person to walk the earth, but Zander had proved me wrong.

"You're a fucking traitor!" I screamed, finding my voice again. I leaped out of the chair, but Hiram wrapped his arms around me, holding me tightly until I couldn't move. "What happened to loyalty being everything?"

"Some opportunities are too good to miss," Zander replied with an impassive shrug. "We all know who you are. Don't pretend you wouldn't have done the same."

"Never," I shrieked, battling with Hiram to be free of his grasp, but not going anywhere.

Zander looked at me in disgust. I recognized his expression. It's how he used to regard Bella and other women he'd grown tired of. Was that all I was to him? A hole to fuck until the time was right?

"Oh, Kitten..." Hiram purred in my ear. "Don't tell me you didn't suspect something like this happening? Did you really think he cared about you? I tried to warn you."

How didn't I see this coming? Zander broke my guard down. He'd pushed past all my resistance until I let him in. The blindfold trust exercise was probably another way for him to throw me off the scent of what was about to happen. I'd been a naïve fucking idiot to have believed anything he said. I'd thought Rocky's betrayal was bad when I was a teenager, but this? It was worse. So much worse. At least Rocky felt he had no choice. He'd handed me over to Hiram because he thought he was saving my life, but Zander? He knew exactly what he was doing.

"No hard feelings, Kitten?" Zander said, having the fucking nerve to smile.

I roared as fury erupted from me in a burst. I'd chosen to go with Hiram to save their lives, but now? All I wanted was to wring Zander's inked neck. He'd used me. Entrapped me. Lied to me. Violated my trust. His hatred for screwing over his father had come at the expense of subjecting me to a life of hell, but he wanted no hard fucking feelings?

"Come on, Kitty. You were happy to make a deal yourself, remember? What difference does it make?" Hiram said, stroking my arm. "I'll still honor your proposal and make sure a development on Bayside Heights never happens if it makes you feel better."

"That was before I knew you had no intention of ever investing in Bayside Heights," I shrieked. My stare burned into Zander, as I pointed my finger, wishing I was close enough to blind him. "*You* were playing me this whole time. You were playing all of us. Me, Bryce, and Giles... like you always do."

"My poor Kitty," Hiram whispered. "It looks like you got out of practice during our time apart."

"This isn't happening. You're not taking her, Hiram. Not again," Rocky snarled. He'd been watching our confrontation in stunned silence, but he'd heard enough. He pulled a gun from his waistband and aimed it at Hiram's head. Without hesitation, he squeezed the trigger. Then, nothing... a small click. This isn't what he'd expected to happen. His brow furrowed as he checked the chamber, then realization dawned on him. Rocky turned on Zander, his face contorted in vicious fury. "You took out the fucking bullets?"

You couldn't fake a reaction like Rocky's. He hadn't

known what Zander was planning, but what about the others? West? Vixen? I'd like to think Zander had been working alone, but how could I be sure?

"Let her go, Red," Zander commanded. "I'm your boss. You do as I say."

"No!" Rocky yelled. "Candy's not going anywhere. She belongs here. With us... with *me*."

"I'm getting rather tired of you getting in my way," Hiram drawled, clicking his tongue in impatience. "If I remember correctly, you were happy to give her to me before."

Hiram knew how to get into people's heads. He could find your most shameful secret and force you to confront your demons. Rocky's jaw clenched. He knew what mistakes he'd made and would stop at nothing to make sure they didn't happen again. He'd tried to kill Hiram, but it wasn't enough… Zander had made sure of that.

"We're better off without her, Red." Zander's words tore through me like a knife, cutting straight down into my core and ripping me in two. "She was never a Seven."

"If you want to take her, you'll have to kill me first," Rocky growled, his eyes met mine. I saw the boy I used to love. The person who would do anything to protect me. "I'm not leaving you, C. I *fucking* love you."

His words made my heart sing, but they were also fucking stupid. Without bullets, his gun was about as useful as a water pistol. How did he expect this to end?

Hiram pulled a gun out of his jacket and sighed, pointing the barrel straight at Rocky. "If that's the way it has to be..."

Whatever lie I had been living in Lapland, at least

some of it had been real. Rocky hadn't turned against me, and that was enough for me to hold onto... which is why I had to do this.

Before Hiram could squeeze the trigger, I snatched the gun from him. I took the cool metal into my hands and fired once. The surprise on Rocky's face made my heart ache, but it was the only way. The only way he'd let me go. I had to do it. He left me with no choice.

The bullet flew through the air in slow motion. It headed straight for Rocky's shoulder as I'd intended, but he was moving...

Shit, he was fucking moving!

I hadn't meant to... I didn't mean...

My body shook from the release as Rocky's wide eyes met mine for a split second. They were filled with shock, hurt… betrayal. It's a look that would be burned into my memory forever. He staggered on his feet, looking down at his chest in confusion, then dropped to the concrete.

"No!" Zander yelled, diving to his knees and ripping off his jacket to stem the bleeding as Hiram hooted with laughter.

The Briarlys stayed frozen in place and watched the scene unfold. Both of them were too terrified to move. Neither of them wanted to be on the receiving end of another of my bullets.

"Welcome back, Kitty," Hiram said, putting his hand firmly on my arm to steer me away. I could hear the smile in his voice. "Let's go home."

I allowed Hiram to guide me. I couldn't think rationally. A jumble of thoughts raced through my head, and my ears were still ringing from the bang of the gunshot. A shot I'd fired to save the only man who'd ever loved me, but that had torn through his chest and broken his heart in the process.

"Before we go, why don't we leave a parting gift behind?" Hiram suggested. He brutally yanked the ruby ring off of my finger, almost breaking it, to sever my connection to the Sevens. "You won't be needing this anymore."

The sparkling jewel hit the floor and was instantly lost in the red pool spilling from under Rocky's body.

Zander's hands were covered… the blood… there was so much of it…

I'd shot Rocky to save his life, but as his blood continued to flow, I realized I may have killed him.

DID YOU ENJOY SLASHER HEART?

Sign up to Holly Bloom's newsletter to receive a Lapland Underground series prequel novella for free!

This novella is exclusive to newsletter subscribers only.

You'll also be first to hear about new book releases, author updates, bonus content, and more…

Sign up to the Bloomies Club newsletter to get your FREE book today by visiting:

www.hollybloomauthor.com

"Kitten"

A Lapland Underground Prequel Blurb:

My heart is still beating, but does that really make me one of the lucky ones? Nothing in Blackthorne Towers is left to chance. My captor is keeping me alive for a reason...

Obeying his orders will keep me alive, but what is the price I'll have to pay for my life?

When you're surrounded by monsters for long enough, there's only so long you can resist the pull to the darkness... especially if I can get my vengeance.

AUTHOR NOTES

Before I go, I'd like to spend a moment getting emotional…

Much love to my long-suffering husband who cooks 99% of the time to give me the time to write. You're the best… and a damn good chef!

A huge thank you to my wonderful friend and beta reader, Brianna. Your constant support and encouragement has undoubtably made this book better. Finally, a special thanks to Brittany Caraballo for naming the Seven Sins casino - what a babe!

Finally, thanks to YOU, for reading this book and for giving this indie author a chance. Words cannot express how grateful I am for your support.

Thank you, thank you, thank you!

ABOUT THE AUTHOR

Holly Bloom has a degree in English Literature, but don't let that fool you... she would pick a steamy romance over a Shakespeare play any day!

Holly writes contemporary romance - the dark, gritty and twisty kind. She loves creating badass babe characters, who aren't afraid to speak their minds, and writing about the men who can handle them - often, there is more than one! Why choose, right?

When she isn't working on her next project, Holly spends an unhealthy amount of time watching true crime and roaming around the woods near her home in the UK.

As well as gooey chocolate brownies, Holly's favourite thing in the world is hearing from her readers - her characters may bite, but she doesn't! Promise!

Find out more about Holly Bloom's books at: www.hollybloomauthor.com

Printed in Great Britain
by Amazon